AT HARMONY CHURCH

*The Chronicle of an Unlikely
United States Army*

William Stuart Gould, M.D.

PublishAmerica
Baltimore

First printing

All characters appearing in this work are fictitious. Any resemblance to real
persons, living or dead, is purely coincidental.

At the specific preference of the author, PublishAmerica allowed this work to
remain exactly as the author intended, verbatim, without editorial input.

ISBN: 1-4241-6075-8
PUBLISHED BY PUBLISHAMERICA, LLLP
www.publishamerica.com
Baltimore

Printed in the United States of America

Marlene,

Thank you for the light. I cherish you and it.

AT
HARMONY
CHURCH

The Chronicle of an Unlikely
United States Army

PREFACE

The night my orders arrived in early 1968, I sought one avenue after another to escape the assignment. Begging for the appointment to be commuted, I besieged friends, and friends of friends, anyone who knew anyone, to intervene on my behalf. I petitioned the Pentagon not to commute my orders for the more pleasant, and, from what I'd heard, safer alternative: a combat assignment in Viet Nam. I moaned to my wife that the reputation of The United States Army Ranger School was so hideous, graduates would not share what they had undergone. Even dropouts blanched at the word Ranger.

Over the past two generations, while swilling countless beers and laughing through my commando tales, friends have asked many times what it would take to get a man back to Ranger School, to try it again. "Come on Willy, there's got to be something on earth worth it. What if they gave you wealth, happiness, and perpetual good health? Wouldn't you give Ranger School another shot? Come on."

For nearly forty years the fleeting thought of even setting foot on the military bases that hosted those unsettling days triggered a recurring dream, actually a nightmare, in which the dread of taking a step back into Ranger School left me sweating, heart pounding, my next days lacking repose.

That reaction lasted until a few months before my sixtieth birthday, when I looked up one morning and realized I was no longer a young man; I understood that day that I wasn't building a career any longer, but putting the finishing touches on one. Studying my life critically, I nodded peacefully to myself that, all in all, even with the inevitable ups and downs of life, the years since Ranger School and Viet Nam had been fulfilling and positive, and that perhaps the lessons I'd learned during those two unpleasant interludes, by now but blips on the radarscope, had, in fact, been instrumental in my success.

And if that was so, might I tell others? Might I recount to the people of the nation I love, a country once again cleaving over a tragic war, that military training is not about the waste of two or three years of a person's life, but that it is a journey along which young people develop skills of leadership and teamwork, where they garner a sense of personal pride, and enter a potentially fertile field in which they may cultivate the notion of honor and dignity, all crucial life skills no university or job could ever dream of offering.

And so I awoke that day nearing my sixtieth, and decided that going back to Ranger School to redo the initial phase, while implausible and impossible, was to be the next step in my life. I had kept myself in excellent physical condition, another priceless lesson of my military experience, particularly of Ranger School, and felt, knowing what I know now, I could meet the demands of simply tagging along at Harmony Church for three weeks. Little did I realize, as hard as I had sought to avoid being sent to Ranger School nearly forty years before, I would fight infinitely harder to be allowed to return.

This time I petitioned old friends, the lieutenants, captains, majors, and colonels with whom I had served four decades before, many of whom had risen to the level of general. Though still friends, they were, first and last, pragmatists. No matter how many thousands of dollars I personally spent on medical and psychiatric studies to attest to my physical and psychological ability to keep up with the young troops for three weeks, the answer from the Pentagon came back each time with a denial.

Eventually, one of the generals wrote, "Frankly, Bill, they're scared you're gonna drop dead."

Nearing my sixty-second year, it was time to accept that the two years of effort were also just a blip on the radarscope. But then my daughter, a graduate of the United States Naval Academy, and a marine officer who had served in the Gulf twice, told me that one of her naval heroes had uttered, "If there isn't a way, make one."

And so I made a way. But that is another story. First, I want to tell you about Harmony Church.

William S. Gould, M.D.
Index, Washington
2006

CHAPTER I

Harmony Church

The United State Military Academy
West Point, New York
Early 1968

The minister pronounced, "You may kiss the bride," and saber-bearer Second Lieutenant J.W. Weathersby snapped to attention. On command, he and the other bearers brought their blades into salute, raising an arch of tooled silver over the path of the newlyweds. As the only non-West Point graduate the groom had invited to join the complement of saber-bearers, J.W. inconspicuously scrutinized the lieutenant to his left and mirrored that Pointer's practiced movements, for the arch was an ancient military ritual. J.W. smiled knowingly, loathe to share with his seven compatriots that he had never before touched a real sword.

The sabers arched upward to form a canopy of gleaming blades over the bride and groom, and J.W. closed his eyes, duping himself into believing that, despite the repeated rejections for a congressional appointment to the United States Military Academy, he had finally realized his dream of becoming a West Pointer. In his reverie, he closed his eyes, permitting his sword to droop ever so slightly, allowing the tip of his long knife to pierce the bride's lace headpiece, hurling her crown and veil with a snap to the polished mahogany floor.

J.W.'s eyes opened to the contorted stares of the attending nobility, and to the gasps of their ladies. Even the groom's eyes rolled upwards. But through the haze of the goblets of Piper-Heidiesk J.W. had enjoyed at the prenuptial festivities, he was not even sure it was his saber that had launched the lace, and he ignored the *faux pas*, maintaining his ramrod straight posture. By the time the guests were seated at the reception, glasses of champagne overflowing, J.W. was not positive the incident of the denuded bride had ever really happened.

After several additional sparkling tumblers of bubbly, he wobbled into a marble-lined men's room. He was instantly awed by the eight-foot-high, beveled glass windows that overlooked West Point's manicured courtyards and parade grounds. Having never toiled on those fields, he stared wistfully through the crystal panes of leaded glass, dazzled by the cut edges prisming the cold winter sunlight into brilliant primary colors. He was mesmerized by the Gothic structures in which the Grants, MacArthurs, and Eisenhowers had sweat blood during their four years in the Corps.

For a moment he was angrily jealous of the groom and his classmates, but the ethanol reexerted its dominion, stirring J.W. Weathersby's insides with a pride and happiness more profound than he had ever before experienced. He was bearing the uniform of the United States Army, chosen by his country to defend his family and his nation against the maniacal threat of world communism. He was twenty-two, soon to be a combat hero in Viet Nam, and positive he would survive the war to rise to the highest levels in the military. And if he perished in the struggle, so be it. He would die with honor.

A senior officer took a position at the next urinal. Out of the corner of his eye, J.W. noticed three embroidered stars on the man's gold epaulettes shining as brightly as the brass fittings on the porcelain sinks. Without opening his fly, the man turned his head toward J.W. and nonchalantly mentioned, "Major, you know, those green epaulettes on your shoulders and the gold piping on your dress blues, well, Major, to be frank, they clash. No combat ribbons on your jacket. You have to be the only field grade officer in the army who's managed to avoid Viet Nam. How'd you do it?"

"Actually, sir, I'm on orders to the 11th Cav. Colonel George S. Patton commanding, sir."

The general's face relaxed for a moment. "I'll be darned. I served under Patton's father in the African desert. Where you stationed now?"

"I'm a platoon leader with the groom at the 6th Cav at Fort Meade, sir. It's a new unit, sir. Got some growing pains."

"Does it, Major?" The general's face tightened, and his eyes widened. His bushy eyebrows peaked. "I was unaware that military police majors are filling armor lieutenants' slots these days. Guess the war has changed a lot of things."

"Well, to be honest, sir, you see, sir, I *am* armor, not military police. I left my epaulettes in Baltimore, well actually back at Fort Meade on the dining room table, sir. I discovered my oversight an hour before the wedding this morning, sir, and had to borrow…"

"You're not a major?"

"No, sir. I'm a lieutenant. But I had no choice, sir. I had to borrow the epaulettes, sir. You see, sir, I was staying at my mother's house last night in the Bronx, sir, and when I discovered I had forgotten the brass for my uniform, she recommended I call the nearest military installation this morning, and that was right here, sir, the Military Academy, sir. I asked the post operator for a lieutenant, sir, but she put me through to a major, sir, Major Norton Bettigole. He's the commander of the military police detachment here, and he lent me the epaulettes, sir, because…"

"Lieutenant."

"It's not his fault, sir. It all made good logistical sense, and…"

"At ease, Lieutenant. You mean to tell me that you took it upon yourself to create a new military uniform? The part I don't like is the color, Lieutenant. You're an armor officer. There's a matter of pride when you represent one of the combat arms. You've got gold piping on your uniform; armor branch. But that green on your shoulders; military police branch! What is that? A cop in a tank?"

The general turned away from Weathersby and stared through the

13

windows onto the Academy grounds on which he had sweat blood some thirty years before. He finally turned back to J.W., took a deep breath, and sighed. "So, let's put this together. You took it upon yourself to introduce a new uniform at a West Point wedding, promote yourself by three ranks, and nearly decapitate the bride. And all in less than an hour."

J.W. found himself braced, chin sucked in, the way he imagined cadets spent "beast barracks," that first dreadful summer at the Academy. He chose a midpoint on the general's tunic as the focus of his stare, but through the haze of the champagne, he observed that one of the star-encrusted, eagle-head buttons had been sewn on upside down. That brought a smile to J.W.'s face, and an olive drab notebook from the general's breast pocket, into which the senior officer inscribed J.W.'s name, real rank, and serial number.

"What's he going to do," J.W. whispered to himself, "send me to Viet Nam?" That made J.W. chuckle as well, until a terrifying thought crossed his mind. "Sir," J.W. asked, his voice wavering, "are you going to make me go to Viet Nam with the 6th Cav?"

The general's eyebrows again billowed, and as he strode through the oak door he muttered, "No, I am not."

J.W. was still standing at attention in front of the urinal when the door to the latrine swung again. He assumed it was for round two, but another officer entered, a rear admiral this time, who stared at J.W. before availing himself of the facilities.

* * *

Nearing midnight, three days after the wedding, a telegram arrived at the Weathersbys' quarters. PRIORITY, FROM THE DEPARTMENT OF THE ARMY was stamped in red on the envelope. J.W.'s wife, Krista, prayed it was a communication forgiving her husband's impetuous decision to volunteer for Viet Nam. In a sense it was.

ORDERS ASSIGNING YOU 11TH ARMORED CAV-ALRY REGIMENT IN VIET NAM HEREBY RE-SCINDED STOP REPORT WITHIN TWENTY FOUR

HOURS TO UNITED STATES ARMY RANGER
SCHOOL FORT BENNING GEORGIA CLASS 68-B
STOP IF TRNG NOT COMPLETED YOU WILL
REPORT IMMEDIATELY TO IST INFANTRY DIVI-
SION VIETNAM STOP

Krista read the telegram twice, then asked, "J.W., what does the First *Infantry* Division have to do with anything? You're armor branch. I thought your orders were for the 11th Cav. You're armor. How can they change that to infantry?"

J.W. numbly shrugged, then grunted, "I don't know."

Krista went on. "I keep hearing from the wives about all those infantry platoon leaders getting hurt. And all those infantry officers do is walk in the rice paddies. At least in the Cav, you ride in a tank. Isn't that right, Sweetheart? Can't you get this changed?"

Army Headquarters at the Pentagon was staffed in the wee hours by a duty officer who snapped, "Lieutenant, phone back in the morning at a more appropriate time." The phone dropped in a loud crack. At 0700 hours, the next duty officer, a colonel, speculated that sudden changes in itinerary were usually precipitated by special requests. Despite J.W.'s adamant protest that he hadn't requested anything but a transfer out of the 6th Cav., and that he would offer his first-born son to avoid Ranger School, the colonel remained steadfast.

"Are you aware, Lieutenant, of the value of Ranger training in terms of one's career? Only one percent of the officer corps is chosen to attend the commando school. That's a rarified atmosphere. Ever noticed who wears the Ranger Tab? Just every ranking officer in this man's army. Your file says you're a Distinguished Military Graduate from Penn State, a pilot; looks like you're regular army. You must've been thinking of a military career at some time. What changed your mind?"

"Nothing, sir. I just want to go to Viet Nam and do my duty, sir."

"That's admirable, Lieutenant, but no changes allowed. I know you've heard all about Ranger School, but look at it this way: Georgia's a tropical paradise. Lot warmer down there than up here in the north. Anyway, is anything in this world as bad as they say it is?"

"I guess not, sir."

There was a long pause and then a smirking laugh. "Lieutenant, I hate to tell you this; Ranger School's worse."

"Sir, is there any way I can sign up for the short course?"

"What are you talking about? I've never heard of a short course."

"Sir, that's where you jump off a footlocker and eat a worm."

"Sorry, Charlie, they're waiting for you down there at Harmony Church. Sounds like the training might do you some good. And, you might want to finish the course. I hear the First Infantry Division's running low on platoon leaders out there in the rice paddies. Attrition—eighty to ninety percent."

"Sir, if I graduate from Ranger School, do I still have to go to the First Division?"

"Nope. 11th Cav'll be waitin' for ya with open arms. See, Lieutenant, you might want to keep your mouth shut and play the game."

* * *

Late that afternoon, dressed for the deep South in his summer-weight, short-sleeved khaki uniform, J.W. shivered uncontrollably as he paced the shoulder of a dusty, frozen, Georgia highway. As the Columbus Airport taxi driver unloaded J.W.'s suitcases from the rusting trunk of the '54 Chevy, Weathersby grumbled, "How long this gonna take, sir?"

The cabby answered in a slow drawl, "Well, that's up to you, soldier. Be a lot faster if y'all give me a hand changing this here tire. When we git the wheel fixed, then y'all give the Chivy a push. Hep me git it outta this here ditch. And where in the hell you headed in such a dang hurry?"

"Ranger School."

The driver stood up, shook his head, then reached into the cab to turn off the meter. An hour-and-a-half later the Chevy pinged through the gates of Fort Benning, coming to rest under an enormous poster imprinted with the black silhouette of an infantryman, arm raised high above his head, and the motto FOLLOW ME painted in titanic, light blue letters. A spit-shined guard examined J.W.'s papers, then saluted smartly as the car drove off. "Enjoy that one. May be the last salute y'all be gittin' for a while, soldier," the cabby offered, pokerfaced.

They rolled past clean, new, white barracks, a monstrous PX, theaters, the post gymnasium, and troops lounging at restaurants and playing basketball on outdoor courts. J.W. noticed a sign for the bachelor officer quarters a hundred yards before they approached the red brick structure. He slid toward the door of the cab, readying himself to be dropped off, avoiding the rearview mirror in his embarrassment for having overreacted, for having carped at the driver, for having groveled at the feet of the Pentagon colonel. But the cabby didn't pull over, and they drove several more miles through the Infantry School, coming finally to a sign:

LEAVING MAIN POST—ROUGH ROAD AHEAD

The cab bumped along pockmarked military roads for several miles until they passed a tumble-down frame building with a decaying steeple. The cabby mumbled, "Harmony Church; be there presently." The Chevy coasted into a rustic area dotted with pre-World War II barracks, coming to a stop in front of a small, windowless, wooden shack bare of all decoration, save for the freshly-painted replica of the orange and black Ranger Tab. J.W. got out of the cab, and facing the door, noticed a circular patch of washed out crimson-black paint at eye level on the rough wood directly under the tab. He turned to ask the cabby what that meant, but the driver had already pulled J.W.'s bags from the trunk and was driving off.

A scowling staff sergeant appeared from behind the shack, glanced at J.W.'s nametag, and ordered, "Get your butt into Bravo Barracks." J.W., taken aback by the sergeant's tone, glared irritably at the man, expecting a salute, but the man humphed and bristled away, striding up to another lost soul, bellowing in his ears, "You, Delta Barracks."

A thin, moth-eaten, khaki blanket, a two-inch thick tattered GI mattress, and a neat pile of papers lay on the springs of each bed in the unheated barracks. J.W. dropped his suitcases in front of the rack with "Weathersby" stenciled in still-wet white paint, then sat upon the wire springs and read through the life insurance, next of kin, and medical questionnaires. The last card in the heap had but one question: "How far can you swim?"

Shavetail lieutenants filtered in, found their names, and started on their stacks of forms. They nodded to each other nervously, but remained quietly on their own beds until dusk, when the staff sergeant marched into the barracks and ordered the anxious assemblage to fall in at the stark wooden shack J.W. had noticed during his first moments at the camp. Outside the barracks were a dozen cadres, officers and enlisted men, all under cover of black berets bearing fiery orange and jet-black Ranger Tabs.

At precisely 1800 hours, with J.W. and his 159 colleagues at rigid attention in an unbent queue, stretching, it seemed, halfway back to main post, the first of his colleagues knocked on the rough-hewn wooden door of the hovel until enjoined to enter by a muffled, angry voice from within. Each soldier remained inside behind closed doors for seconds, then flew out with an expression of terror, the likes of which J.W. had seen only when looking in the mirror before showing his father his high school report cards.

One by one, each of the cadets made his way to the shack. At nineteen-thirty hours, it was J.W.'s turn at the unpainted door. His eyes fixed on the mysterious crimson-black central circle. The staff sergeant screamed in his ear, "Knock hard, Ranger. You want them to hear you in there, don't you?"

J.W. struck the door with his fist, though his first efforts apparently fell short of Harmony Church standards, for by the time he was allowed entrance, his hands had been beaten raw, bubbles of burgundy oozing from his knuckles, spurts of it added to the red-black circle on the door, his life's fluid jumbled with that of countless previous generations of Rangers.

A single, bare, forty-watt bulb swinging ever so slightly at eye level illuminated the inside of the shack. J.W. came to attention with his nose an inch from the bulb, the light so glaring, he could make out only the shadow of a human form seated below it. J.W. squinted, and through that attenuated brightness, was able to discern the reflection of captain's bars marred by the tiny pits of age and untold encounters with the Brasso rag. J.W. craned his neck forward for a better view.

A voice boomed, "Ranger, what the hell do you think you are looking at?"

J.W. shouted, "Nothing, sir!" When there was no word further from the seated figure, J.W. continued, "Lieutenant Weathersby reporting as directed, sir!"

"So you're Weathersby. We've been alerted you were joining the class." The figure rose and stared at J.W., who could now make out a pockmarked, pasty-complexioned face. J.W. glanced down to the captain's nametag; VOCK was embroidered above the right pocket. The captain sat back down behind the tiny, olive drab field desk. On the wall behind him was a water-stained portrait of Lynden Baines Johnson.

Captain Vock lifted a pile of papers from the desk. J.W. waited to be complimented for having arrived in Georgia in so timely a manner, but Vock shuffled through J.W.'s papers, yawning. "The big football hero. Mister tough guy. Betcha the girls like that." He perused a few more forms, then snapped, "You are not a lieutenant anymore. You are a Ranger. You got that straight?"

"Yes, sir."

"Dismis... Wait a minute." Vock had come to the last sheet in the pile, the "How-far-can-you-swim?" question. "Says here Ranger Weathersby can swim, what is this...'FOREVER'? Read this for me First Sergeant Cowsen. Is that what it says? Maybe I should get glasses."

J.W., though still braced at attention, shifted his eyes imperceptibly to the right. He discerned another soul, a tall enlisted man with master sergeant's stripes on a Class A uniform. The senior sergeant took a step out of the shadows, and J.W. saw the black man's pleasant face, crisp uniform, and shoulder patch from the First Infantry Division. J.W.'s eyes focused on the rows of combat decorations, several of World War II vintage, some from Korea, and a few from Viet Nam. Though he did not know what most signified, the two ribbons at the top gave him pause, and J.W. braced more rigidly. Every soldier recognized the Silver Star and the Distinguished Service Cross, the second and third highest medals for heroism, below only the Medal of Honor. And he'd never seen even one of these on an enlisted man's chest, to say nothing of two. J.W.'s spine straightened even harder.

Sergeant Cowsen peeked over Captain Vock's shoulder and concurred. "Yes, sir, that's what it says. Man says he can swim forever."

"Nah, couldn't be. Nothing can swim forever, can it Sergeant Cowsen?"

Cowsen shrugged, "No sir, nothin' ceptin' a fish or somethin', sir."

J.W. allowed silently that there had really had been no reason to antagonize these gentlemen so soon after arriving, but it was, he laughed to himself, water under the bridge.

"That's pretty Goddamn funny, Ranger, isn't it? We'll see how many laughs you get at the pool tomorrow. Dismissed!"

As each of the cadets ran from the shack, they were directed into another hut where a grinning corporal ordered them into a folding chair, and then to sit at rigid attention. "Remove your hat and sit still," the soldier decreed as he swiped a clipper over their heads. And in eleven seconds, the depilated, embryonic commandos were back out in the night, guided, not tranquilly, toward the supply shack.

* * *

It was bitterly cold at 3:00 A.M. the next morning as J.W. and his bedraggled barrackmates marched past Harmony Church along the bombed out road that had delivered them to the Ranger school twelve hours earlier. J.W. paired up informally with a thin troop whose skewed nametag read FRICKER. The two bitched incessantly, about the cold, their fatigue, their hunger, their boots and socks, even about old girlfriends, until they ran out of breath an hour-and-a-half later, having been ordered to double-time back to main post, where they ran past the BOQ, the PX, and finally the basketball courts. Then they were right-turn marched onto Morrison Avenue, where they were forced to sprint for several blocks and then come to a sudden halt, accordioning into each other, in front of the Officer's Club.

J.W. nodded to his new friend, "Finally, some breakfast. I'm starved."

Fricker smiled back and whispered, "Breakfast at the O-club. I'm going to have oatmeal and English muffins."

Though several troops to J.W.'s flanks nodded approval and several smiled, there came from the rank directly behind them an angrily whispered, "Oatmeal, my ass."

Surreptitiously, J.W. turned, meeting the sullen eyes of a diminutive black man with a pencil-thin mustache. When J.W. looked harder, the soldier lifted his head arrogantly. J.W. let his eyes drop to the soldier's nametag. BRANCH was embroidered in neat letters.

As the company of sweat-drenched, shivering Rangers was ordered into the carpeted lobby of the Officer's Club, Fricker whispered again, "Told ya!"

But they were ordered to jog past the ballroom and the dining room and through the men's dressing room, exiting via the polished mahogany verandah doors to the ice-covered swimming pool. First Sergeant Cowsen counted off the first ten men and told them to stand at attention flanking the stairs to the high diving board. He then ordered the second ten men to jump in and use their rifle butts to breach the glacial crust on the pool.

Several of the troops laughed nervously, hoping Cowsen was simply making an attempt to be amusing, but one of the other sergeants burst from within the club, ran forward like a linebacker, and shouldered two of the men onto the ice, through which they plunged immediately. When they surfaced gasping, Cowsen and the other cadres carped at the freezing aquanauts to use their rifle butts to flail about until the ice was pulverized to their standards.

With the Officer's Club pool a functional ice slurry, Cowsen mounted the high diving board to address Class 68-B. From a dozen feet above the one-hundred-and-sixty men he shouted, "Each of you will leap from this here board in full combat gear. You will hold your weapon above your head, tread water for ten minutes, swim to the edge, and climb out. If you drop your piece when you hit the water, you will dive for it, get out of the pool, return to this here diving board and repeat the whole cotton-pickin' drill until you get it right."

J.W., who had worked his way inconspicuously to the middle of the queue without comment from Cowsen, chided himself for having laid awake all night fearing reprisal for his aquatic braggadocio. He turned to Fricker and joked and bitched until his turn on the high board, then leapt proudly into the ice water, holding tight to his rifle. J.W. swam manfully for the requisite ten minutes and then dog paddled to the edge of the pool, but as he was about to pull himself out, Captain Vock appeared from inside a heated cabana, leaned over the edge of the pool and ordered, "Stay in the water *forever*, Ranger." With a look of scorn that chilled J.W.'s bones more than the frigid water, Vock turned and strode back to the cabana.

J.W. scissor-kicked until the last man passed the swimming test, and then until First Sergeant Cowsen was satisfied that the dripping mass of Rangers braced at attention had fixed their stares unwaveringly upon Weathersby. Captain Vock emerged again from the heated bathhouse and addressed the company. "Rangers, we are going to be here for a long time…a very long time. The reason I say that is because forever is a long time. Ranger Weathersby can swim forever. He said so. And we're going to wait here until he does. Now, Rangers, we know that Ranger Weathersby can swim forever. Do you know how we know that?" Without waiting for an answer, he went on, "Well, I'll tell you how we know. Because Rangers don't lie." Vock called over his shoulder as he and Cowsen walked back toward the heated cabana. "Keep swimming, Ranger."

It was hard for J.W. not to notice the conspicuous lack of charity in the faces of his associates. He drew himself underwater, feigning total collapse, seeking pity, and perhaps a colleague's rescue, but when he resurfaced alive, the disappointed stares of the others had only deepened. He tread water for another minute, then swam to the edge and lifted himself out of the pool, steeling himself for the order to return to the three-meter board, or worse, to the front of the line that was being reformed to have the entire company scale the tower for another assault on the pool. As the first man furiously took a step forward to mount the high board, Captain Vock stepped from the cabana and bellowed, "Where are you going Ranger? Fall in."

Entropy in reverse, a shattered teacup reforming, 160 men coalesced instantaneously into four perfectly rectangular platoons of water-logged, head-shaven, shivering, famished, nation's finest fighting men. J.W. turned his eyes upon the troops to his sides, seeking to ensure that he had melded back into the nameless, faceless masses, but the man on his left sneered, and the one on the right whispered "Pussy! What the hell you starin' at?" J.W. looked harder to his right. It was the little black man named Branch.

Before J.W. could explain that his words had been misunderstood by the cadres the night before, that he had only meant to tell them he was a strong swimmer, having learned at an exclusive summer camp in the Catskills Mountains in rural New York State, the company of Rangers was marching back through the club, dripping on the carpet, past the ballroom, past the dining room, back out onto Morrison Avenue, and finally along the freezing road toward the Ranger School at Harmony Church.

J.W. raised his hand and asked, "First Sergeant Cowsen, how far is it back to Harmony Church."

Cowsen answered, "Same as what it took to get here." And with his answer, the first sergeant shook his head irritably, hissed under his breath, and then hollered the Rangers into a double-time that lasted for the next hour. With their boots squishing in rhythm to Cowsen's cadence, he ran them at a sprint for a few minutes, then relented and allowed them to jog the flats and speed-walk up the hills. When they passed the decrepit remains of Harmony Church, J.W. grasped that it would not be long before they would be back home, and he sighed with relief, a peculiar warmth filling his frozen chest.

* * *

Five minutes later, a sliver of the mess hall appeared over the horizon, and Fricker grinned excitedly, "This time I *am* going to have oatmeal. Toast, too."

But when half the building was finally visible, Cowsen turned the formation, still at the double-time, to the south onto a dirt path away from camp headquarters. The company continued for another mile cross-country, coming ultimately to a lone set of rotting bleachers deep within the tundra of Fort Benning, Georgia.

After the order to halt, Sergeant Cowsen positioned himself at the front of his dripping, steaming, troops. "Rangers, any of you don't like heights?" A dozen hands shot up, J.W.'s the highest. "Good." Cowsen remarked casually, "You Rangers take a seat up there in the balcony."

J.W. tried to hide behind one of the other Ranger cadets, but Cowsen spied him and pointed toward the highest row. "Up there Swim-Forever, top row. Move your butt."

J.W. took a seat in the upper gallery of the bleachers, shivering as he looked down through the rickety floorboards into what he perceived as a two-hundred-foot-deep, craggy ravine directly under the rotting planks. In his backless seat at the top of the bleachers, he shifted forward and to his left seeking human contact, coming to rest shoulder to shoulder with the small black man, Branch, who had seated himself there originally in order to get away from J.W. Though Weathersby was soothed by the touch of another being, Branch slid away grunting disgustedly, "Pussy."

Cowsen grunted, "Top row, what's going on up there?"

"Nothing, First Sergeant," Branch answered.

But Branch continued sliding away from J.W., and when he reached the end of the plank, Cowsen shook his head and yelled again, "Where you goin' Ranger Branch? Let's get nice and cozy up there."

Cowsen approached the lectern, standing at attention to deliver his welcoming speech. Though the sun had barely risen, the shafts of moonlight glistening off the toes of his spit shined jump boots burnished his silhouette as if footlights were playing upon it.

"Rangers," he began, his voice as torpidly penetrating as a Southern Baptist minister's, "you are embarking on a journey many of you won't finish. But welcome anyway. Rangers, our school was founded by General William O. Darby. He was a commando leader during World War II. I had the privilege of serving with this exceptional man. The name Ranger was chosen in memory and honor of our Revolutionary War commandos. Those men displayed individual courage, initiative, determination, ruggedness, fighting ability, and achievement.

"Rangers, if you don't want to be here, if you don't want to develop those traits, just say so. If you utter the words, 'I quit,' you will be sent away immediately. Some of you who leave will be assigned to combat units in Viet Nam. You who go will find that duty easier than being here.

On the other hand, finishing this school is a life insurance policy, 'cause all of you are goin' to Viet Nam sooner or later." His voice rose. "But, if you don't want to be here, we don't want you. You must make that decision by yourself. The question you must ask yourself every minute, every second of the next months of your lives is, how much are you willing to pay for that insurance policy?

Now Rangers, there is a Ranger Creed. It talks about the fact that every one of you volunteered for this training; that as a Ranger your country expects more of you. It says that you will never fail your comrades; that you shoulder more than your share of the task. Surrender is not a word, Rangers, and you will never leave a fallen comrade to allow him to fall into the hands of the enemy. A Ranger fights on to the objective, no matter the obstacles, even if you are the lone survivor. Gentlemen, this assignment is not for the weak or faint-hearted.

"Rangers, the secret of remaining here is simple. We will tell you frequently. It is just two little words: 'Drive On.' When you can't go another step, we will tell you to 'Drive On.' When you are in so much pain you want to quit and die, we will tell you to 'Drive On.' When you are so thirsty your tongue is too thick to draw back into your head, we will tell you to 'Drive On.' Sometimes we will scream the two little words at you. Sometimes we will whisper them. "Now, Rangers, the only equipment you will need to survive in this here Ranger School is one ear so you can hear the words, 'Drive On. Drive On!'"

Cowsen's sublime expression hardened. "Rangers, some of you are going to be strong leaders in the United States Army. I like strong leaders, 'cause I saw with my own eyes what happens when the weak are given the mission to lead men in combat. I seen it in three wars, gentlemen, but the worst was in Viet Nam when I served in the First Infantry Division."

Cowsen paused, the muscles of his face tightening. "We had a lot of Ranger dropouts in that unit. Now, I don't give a hoot that they didn't want to pay for the insurance of doin' this here program, and I don't give a hoot that they got themselves blown away. But I do care that they got my men hurt. I don't want any more weak officers leading my men. Never again, gentlemen."

For a moment he stared into the dawn sky, his face hardening as the

25

gathering rays of sun raised the temperature of Harmony Church one or two precious degrees. J.W. had forgotten his angst, hypnotized by the First Sergeant's intensity, and by the fact that he had served in the First Infantry Division in Viet Nam, where J.W. was headed if he failed to complete the course.

Then Sergeant Cowsen dropped his eyes from the heavens, drew a deep breath, and went on quietly. "Rangers, we got a lot to cover over the next eight weeks, got no time to waste. When we eat in the mess hall, you will be given forty-five seconds to sit and finish your meal. You notice I say 'sit.' That is because a doctor once told me you should always sit down when you eat, and doctors know what they're talking about, because they're doctors. Rangers, forty-five seconds is plenty of time to eat if you choose your food carefully and correctly.

"O.K. Rangers, I've given you a lot to digest. Go ahead and take a break, but think about what I said. Stand on your seats. Smoke 'em if you got 'em."

The top row rose carefully and extracted packs of plastic-wrapped cigarettes from web belt pouches that should have held first aid kits. J.W.'s smokes were, however, so wet from his extended swim, he wadded them into a ball and flipped the wad above his shoulder and over the back of the bleachers into the canyon. Before the lump of water-logged cancer sticks hit bottom, though, Cowsen was charging up the bleachers, coming to rest so close to Weathersby's lips, J.W. tasted the master sergeant's breath. Cowsen whispered, "Ranger, this ain't the Bronx where you came up. That ain't no garbage pit. Now get down there and police up that mess you made." Cowsen turned, shook his head in disgust, and retreated down to his podium.

J.W. prepared to descend into the ravine, first bumming a cigarette from Branch, who grudgingly handed him a Chesterfield, the first J.W. would ever smoke. When J.W. asked for a light, Branch snarled, "Shit, man, you need a kick in the chest to get started?" Branch shook his head, and with an irritated flip of the thumb propelled the matches toward J.W., who casually lifted a single hand to catch them. But J.W.'s fingers were so cold, the matches fluttered off his fingertips into the ravine, joining his saturated smokes.

From the podium, a dozen feet below, Cowsen added, "You can bring them up too, Ranger. And if you don't hurry up, I'm gonna have the cadres hang you from that there rope stretchin' over the pit. That's a special rope, a hangin' rope, Ranger. Now get your butt in high gear, causin' your fellow Rangers is goin' be in the push-up position until you get your work done. And they gonna be the ones to hang y'all from that there rope if'n you keep wastin' their time."

J.W. crawled down the bleachers, bumping into wet, freezing, angry colleagues on the way, fellow Rangers dropping slowly onto their hands and toes to await his return. He struggled to ignore their heated comments. At the bottom of the stands, he peered into the chasm, at its nearly vertical walls, hesitating a second too long, for Cowsen was by his side instantly, grumbling so vociferously, the boom of his voice impelled J.W. into the cavern. J.W., after allowing his feet to catch up with him at the bottom, picked at a few items, but when he uncovered a snakeskin and a rock-hard rat carcass, he shot out of the gorge with neither the smokes nor the matches.

Cowsen stood by the lectern, his back to the troops and to J.W. as the embryonic commando crested the lip of the ravine. One of the Rangers, a tiny slip of a man, watched through thick glasses at Weathersby's record-setting egress from the pit. J.W. passed the man as he tried to sneak up into the bleachers, but Cowsen, still facing away, bellowed, "Weathersby, come here." The tiny Ranger surreptitiously slipped J.W. a pack of cigarettes.

J.W. presented himself to Cowsen. "Sergeant, Ranger Weathersby reporting. Mission accomplished, First Sergeant. Here are the cigarettes that fell out of my hand."

Cowsen crumpled the smokes, walked to the edge of the abyss and threw them in. He pointed to the top row, and J.W. returned unsteadily to the balcony. Cowsen marched to the bottom row and confronted the small man. "Smith, get your slim butt into that pit and get the smokes that slipped out of my hand. And when you're done, go back and retrieve the trash Ranger Weathersby forgot."

"Yes, First Sergeant."

As Cowsen returned to the lectern and began to speak, J.W. plopped down next to Branch, who growled in a whisper, "Hey man, you're bad luck. Go sit somewhere else."

Cowsen stopped lecturing and stared up into the balcony, his eyes widening in mock surprise. He raved, "Rangers, I didn't say you two could talk. Branch, Weathersby, both of you, assume the position and gimme fifty up there in the cheap seats. And while you're at, add one at the end for the Rangers of old."

Head to head, the pair began batting out the first of the nearly half-million push-ups Class 68-B would execute during its tenure in Dixie. At push-up number thirty-five, J.W. looked up contritely at Branch, but all he saw of his colleague was the thick stain around Branch's hat band, the lipid remnant of long-forgotten Rangers who had donned that very same unwashed cap over the millennia. J.W. laughed quietly, "Your lid needs an oil change, my man."

Branch was silent, but several of the Rangers in the balcony snickered, a humorous interlude that cost them several fifty-one-repetition sets of calisthenics. That culled snorting laughter from the troops in the loge seats, though it was not until Smith crept out of the ravine with an impressive array of debris—a slice of toast, a condom carried precariously at the end of a stick, and a huge night crawler—that Cowsen ordered the loge boys to knock out fifty-one as well. Not placated with Smith's pickings, for it did not harbor the original pack of wadded cigarettes, Cowsen sent the entire company, minus the balcony, into the prone position while Smith descended yet again into the valley. When he finally crawled up over the lip, Cowsen shouted, "O.K., Rangers, breakfast. Fall in."

Cowsen let the company relax into an easy march, smiling contentedly, J.W. believed, at the quality of their pre-dawn performance, but after two hundred meters the cadence mutated into the double-time, Cowsen, sprinting to the head of the column, calling incessantly for the next hour:

Some day—my son—will be—like me
He'll run—all day—he'll jump—for his pay.
RANGER!
RANGER!

RANGER!
RANGER!
RANGER!

"I can't hear you, Rangers."

At first, J.W. was comfortable with the cadence he'd learned in airborne school, but the midnight runs there had been far shorter, and it was not long before he and the other better-fed cadets became reluctant to comply with Cowsen's urgings. After his legs seized in muscular breakdown, J.W. became nearly recalcitrant to the first sergeant's demands to speed up, and several of his exhausted cohorts, as if suffering from an airborne poison, dropped to the ground like so many sacks of sand, refusing to go on. These men, it came to pass, were the fortunate sons, a cluster of the pudgy soon to be loaded aboard a trailing quarter-ton truck and drummed out of the course. The remainder of the formation continued at the double time, eyes to the front, threatened with expulsion if they let their gaze fall back upon the pikers.

* * *

The company halted at a drab wooden structure back at Harmony Church. J.W. tried to whisper to Branch that maybe they were finally going to eat, but J.W.'s voice cracked in its hoarseness, and Cowsen ordered both of them into the prone position for fifty-one more push-ups. J.W. concentrated on the red mud inches from his eyes, pretending not to hear Branch's hissed threats of bodily harm. He could not, however, ignore the scent of bacon, toast, and home fries slithering along the soupy ground, taunting him. As J.W. screamed, "And one for the Rangers of old," during his fifty-first push-up, he jerked his legs under him, and snapped back up to attention, searching for Cowsen, but the first sergeant was gone, replaced by the grumpy staff sergeant from the night before.

The lesser non-com stepped to the front of the company. "Rangers, welcome to the best meal in Harmony Church. We sincerely hope you will enjoy the repast we have spent hours slaving to prepare for our new guests. The price of admission is a mere fifteen pull-ups on the bar you see to your front. That's the introductory price. By noon, it's goin' up. Now gents, this bar, like the door of that there command shack, has serviced eons of Rangers. You will treat it with respect and add one pull-up at the end for the Rangers of old. Are there any questions?"

A hand was raised, and a hesitant voice called from deep within Second Platoon. "Lieutenant Fricker, sir."

The staff sergeant smiled broadly and cupped his hand behind his ear. "Did you hear something, Rangers?" He winked, grinned warmly, and dashed into ranks, coming to rest a sixteenth of an inch from Fricker's lips. "You see these stripes, Ranger? I work for a living. You don't call me 'sir,' you call me by my first name."

"But I don't know your first name."

"It's 'Sergeant,' you idiot. Do you understand? And you are not a lieutenant any more. You are a Ranger! Do you understand, Ranger, Ranger, Ranger, Ranger?"

"Yes, Sergeant."

"Now," the staff sergeant continued, his voice calmed to a near whisper, "what was your question?"

"I have a bad shoulder, Sergeant. I can't do pull-ups. I have a note from the Main Post dispensary. It's right here in my pocket."

Fricker presented the soaked paper to the staff sergeant, who nodded and commiserated, "Oh, I'm sorry. I had one of those once." The staff sergeant walked out of ranks. "Ranger Fricker, front and center."

Fricker took a martial step forward out of ranks, snapped to the left, marched to the end of his rank, took a hard right and approached the staff sergeant, saluting and assuming the position of attention as he came to rest.

"Good Ranger, that was very impressive marching. Now do that again and come to attention in front of and below the push-up bar. The rest of you gimme' fifty, and one for the Rangers, while Ranger Fricker here warms up the bar."

Fricker raised his hand to protest, but the sergeant shook his head and then nodded toward the bar. Fricker sighed and mounted the apparatus, though on pull-up number six, he let go, staggered for a few feet, then collapsed onto the ground, coming to rest in the T-U position. "I can't do any more," he whimpered. The staff sergeant dropped to his knees, placed the doctor's note back in Fricker's breast pocket, then brought his lips to Fricker's ears and shrieked, "Drive on, Ranger! Drive on, damn it."

Tears formed in Fricker's eyes. That brought a simpering smile to the staff sergeant's face, and a whoop to his lips. "Drive on!"

Fricker choked back his sobs, rose to his feet, then turned and took a step away from the bar and the sergeant. J.W. thought Fricker was going to run away, but Fricker hesitated before turning, and that delay brought the staff sergeant's lips back to Fricker's lips. The sergeant hissed, "Get your sorry ass up there, Ranger."

At this point, Ranger Fricker dropped to his knees and fell back to the red clay earth of southern Georgia. A veil of silence descended over Ranger Class 68-B, and then over all of Harmony Church, Georgia. The clattering of dishes, pots, and eating utensils within the mess hall ceased as well. Even Cowsen was voiceless as he peered through the screened door. The world was holding its breath, waiting for Ranger Fricker to decide if he would do a pull-up or be sent willy-nilly to die in a rice paddy half-a-world away.

The others had stopped their push-ups to watch, but a cadre screamed from behind, "That wimp's gonna cost the rest of you Rangers twenty-five more, and twenty-five for every thirty seconds he stays off that bar. You hear that, Ranger Fricker?"

Fricker rose to his knees like a boxer desperately trying to clear his head before the ten count, but his shoulders drooped in resignation, the tears now dripping off his cheeks. He managed to come to his feet, staggering and crying. But Fricker was an officer in the United States Army, a member of the one percent chosen for the Ranger School, and that didn't come cheap, everyone knew. And so did Fricker, for his jaw tightened, suddenly looking to all the world as if he was just gaining space, creating room to build up momentum to lunge back at the enemy pull-up bar. Smiles crossed the faces of the Ranger cadets, and a sense of pride and acceptance of the ways of the Ranger School suddenly built in the men of the ranks, but instead of reversing course and reapproaching the bar, Fricker took another step away from it, and then another, and he started to run toward the barracks. He had taken maybe ten steps when a voice rose from the push-up position at the back of third platoon, an angry growl that roared, "Drive on, Ranger. Goddamnit, drive on!" Several more voices percolated from the ground, urging Fricker to reconsider.

The staff sergeant yelled, twenty-one seconds, twenty-two…"

By twenty-five, the entire company was grunting, "Drive on!"

At twenty-seven seconds, Fricker turned back to the bar. At twenty-nine he began his leap, but it was not until thirty-and-a-half seconds that his fingers finally touched it, and the staff sergeant relaxed in a broad grin, addressing the company of sweating Rangers. "Now, Rangers, there's a lesson to be learned here. That Ranger was late. That's gonna cost you all another twenty-five and one. Remember, Rangers are always on time."

Fricker restarted the count from number seven, but the staff sergeant reset the meter to one. Fricker faded on number six again, but managed to hold on. The staff sergeant studied the dangling corpse with intense interest for a moment, then screamed, "Nobody move, including you, Ranger Fricker." He ran into the mess hall, came out with a chair, stood on it, placed his lips next to Fricker's ear, and urged, not inaudibly, "Drive on, Ranger!" Fricker bawled, but sweat through numbers seven to fifteen, and then screamed in pain, as if anyone was listening, as he belted out one more for the Rangers of old. When he dropped to the ground and crawled into the mess hall, the staff sergeant was on his chair again with the next victim, Ranger Fricker's life altering experience no more momentous in the greater scheme of things than a chin-up or two.

The bar was hot by the time J.W. stepped up. As smooth as chromed steel, subtle concavities had formed at the point where the hands of thousands of Rangers had done millions of pull-ups. J.W. was afforded the chair treatment as well, and when he dropped after number sixteen, twisting his ankle, Cowsen rushed out of the mess hall to greet him.

"Just let me take your arm, First Sergeant. I really think I screwed myself up."

"That happened a long time 'fore you got here, Ranger." Cowsen pointed toward the serving line. "Your cryin' just cost you fifteen seconds. Get your butt on line."

* * *

Inside, the food was flying as if a southern tornado was sweeping through the mess hall. Chow was served up by a squad of privates who carelessly slapped ladles of wet eggs, grease-saturated bacon, and waterlogged mashed potatoes onto the Rangers' metal trays, much of it flying onto the sweat-soaked uniforms of the famished. J.W. grunted impatiently as a large, blubbery troop to his front, Morelotto, stopped in his tracks to pick runny eggs from the front of his fatigues and push them into his mouth. Turning to J.W., he snipped sarcastically, "Hors d'oeuvres. How delicious."

The cooks, though laboring behind raw-wood barriers which hid their faces from the Ranger cadets, had no trouble hearing what their guests had to say about the cuisine. When Morelotto stuck his tray forward at the next station for mashed potatoes, the thump of the spoon striking his plate was so loud, even the seated Rangers looked up. Morelotto's tray dropped and clanged on the floor.

Cowsen was on him in a trice, explaining, "Ranger, we don't waste food here. I already told you how important food is. What about that don't you understand? Now police up this mess and go to the start of the line and try again. Clock's a tickin'."

Cowsen turned to J.W., staring at him as if bewildered. "What are you waiting for, Ranger? You're wasting precious time. Now you're down to twenty-five seconds to eat your chow. MOVE IT!"

J.W. ran to an open seat, threw down his tray, and was about to start jamming food into his mouth, but was distracted by a chaotic slurping to his left. Branch, face buried in a metal tray, was inhaling mashed potatoes. It turned J.W.'s stomach, and instead of eating, he tried to open a container of milk, but in his panic, fought with the wrong side. Cowsen laughed, "Ten seconds, Ranger, nine, eight..."

J.W., cured suddenly of his gastrointestinal uneasiness, dropped his face into his tray and sucked in the pool of translucent mashed potatoes, then slid a strip of bacon between his lip and upper teeth, grabbed a tiny packet of granulated sugar and stuffed it, along with the container of milk, into his fatigue pocket just as the final bell rang.

The staff sergeant, who had barged into the mess hall to help control the exodus of Rangers, locked his attention on the bulge in J.W.'s pocket and slammed it with his fist. As milk dribbled into his boot, J.W. ran through the door under the big clock that read 6:55 A.M.

* * *

Outside, the company crept into formation, soon cruising at the double-time back onto the freezing prairie. J.W. tried to guess where they were being sent, and he asked Branch, "Now where we going? I can't do this much longer." When Branch did not answer, and when the man to J.W.'s right ignored him as well, Weathersby's attention shifted to the burning in his legs and his lungs. He began to slow down, and twisted his head to see if any cadres were watching from behind, though all he saw was a gaggle of the less stalwart lying on the frozen earth, and then the meat wagon quarter-ton truck materializing out of the of the dark mist toward them. As the stragglers were pulled into the bed of the open-air ambulance, J.W. turned to Fricker and hissed, "I can't take this shit any more. I'm going on the truck. Coming with me?"

Fricker nodded, and they both slowed to a trot, and then to a walk, the penultimate statement of resignation. But as J.W.'s and Fricker's legs finally ceased all movement aside from post-mortem twitching, the truck suddenly broke ranks, the bed already over-full, and sped past them, headed back toward Harmony Church, its cargo to be fed breakfast's leftovers, discharged from the school, and sent to trudge the paddies as silage for the infantry machine.

As the ambulance disappeared into the haze, J.W. cursed himself for having failed to fail. A moment later, though, the first real rays of sun broke over the hills of Georgia, and J.W., fortified by the radiance, hobbled weakly back into ranks. Fricker started to run as well, but when J.W. glanced around for his pal, there was a stranger at his side. Fricker had made it only as far as the tail end of last platoon. J.W. then studied the men to his flanks. It was the first time he had seen the unshaven, beaten faces of his compatriots in the light. He smiled to himself at the wispy mustache above Branch's lip.

* * *

At the bleachers, Cowsen ordered, "Face the man by your right side. He is now your Ranger buddy."

Most of the troops accepted that closest neighbor, comfortably pairing off, shaking hands and introducing themselves to the men on whom their survival over the next eight-plus weeks would depend. For J.W., that would have been Branch, had Branch not turned and darted away. So J.W. shrugged and laughed defensively, casually drifting toward Fricker, but Fricker was already standing shoulder to shoulder with Morelotto. J.W. searched in several directions, but it was only when he turned to his rear that he spied a man without a buddy, the little troop with thick glasses who had slipped him the pack of smokes in the pre-dawn hours. The tiny man's face brightened. He stuck out his hand. "Ivan Smith, Johnstown, Pee Ayy. Deer huntin's my favorite thing in the world. What's your game? Water sports?"

J.W. began to clarify why they had made him swim for so long, but Cowsen snapped, "SEATS!" and Smith nodded to J.W., motioning toward the bleachers. "No, Rangers," Cowsen ordered with a bellow, "SEATS! HERE!"

With Class 68-B rooted at seated attention on the polar ground, Cowsen commenced the second piece of his reception opus. "Gentlemen," he began, "and I use the term loosely, welcome to the obstacle course. This is Phase Two of the selection process. You will finish the sequence in eighteen minutes. That means three times around. There is a nice surprise at the end of the third lap for those of you who get that far.

"And, Rangers, you must cross the finish line *with* your Ranger buddy. Gentlemen, your Ranger buddy is the key to completing this here school. General Darby believed in the 'Me and My Pal' concept of survival. You will march together, sleep together, do guard duty together, train together, and eat together, assuming you characters can find some food. Now back on your feet and get in file for the **obstacle course**."

Smith meandered as slowly as he could toward the starting line, tugging at the back of Weathersby's wet fatigue jacket to slow him down.

"Conserve energy," Smith whispered. "Let the others burn themselves out."

Branch and his buddy, an olive-skinned, high-cheekboned man with the patina of shaved off, but still jet-black hair, fell in behind them. Branch cautioned the dark man just loudly enough for J.W. to hear, "If that asshole gets in your way, kick his butt. He ain't gonna make it anyway. Too fat. Goddamn loser."

Weathersby ignored the commentary until Branch became impatient and pushed his way past him. Frustrated, J.W. swung his elbow angrily, striking Branch in the shoulder.

Branch lashed a fist out wildly. J.W. sprang for Branch, hissing, "Loser, huh? I'll kick your...ass!"

The two nearly came together, but Smith pulled J.W. to the ground, and the high-cheekboned man wrenched at Branch. The small black man glared at J.W., then seethed, "You were gonna say nigger, weren't you, weren't you, honkey?"

"Fuck you, man. I never used that word in my life. Just stay away from me."

Smith jumped in angrily, admonishing, "Hey, jerkoffs, you're not enemies, they are," pointing to Cowsen and the staff sergeant. "Shake hands, Goddamnit."

The two grumbled and growled like little dogs for a few seconds, then slapped hands, barely touching fingers. Branch and his buddy acquiesced and took their original spots behind J.W. and Smith, neither team uttering another word to the other.

As the first two soldiers in line commenced round one of the obstacle course, Cowsen shouted, "We lost ten men at the swimming test this morning. Twenty more along the road. We're down to one-thirty. By this time tomorrow, Rangers, we'll be missing some more." Cowsen then disinterestedly continued recording names and starting times as each pair of Rangers stepped up to the line, barely glancing at the bedraggled men until Smith and J.W. appeared. Cowsen cocked his head and remarked under his breath, "Lord have mercy. You still here, Bad Weather?"

J.W. sucked in a deep breath to explain, but Cowsen pushed the button on the stopwatch and hissed, "That's fifteen seconds you already done frittered away, Wet Weather."

A hundred yards through the red Georgia slop, J.W. and Smith came to the "gallows," a set of thick, wet, hemp ropes hanging from stout wooden cross arms. The two leapt forward, grabbed ropes, and oscillated most of the way across a three-foot deep pool of crimson-orange mud. But, as in pregnancy, most of the way was not far enough, and looking down into the pool of freezing mud, the two swung back, kicking wildly, seeking to gather sufficient momentum to avoid the mammoth puddle. Cowsen shook his head in disbelief that these college boys were unaware that the rope had been engineered by the cadres of old to insure that, twist and pump as one might, even the most Tarzanic of Rangers would land many feet short of the edge of the sty. Branch screamed irritably from behind, "Stop swinging. Let go! Goddamnit!"

But Weathersby and Smith ignored Branch's entreaty and swung once again, though in futility, conceding finally to the laws of physics, dropping resignedly into the mire, their bodies eventually resurfacing enshrouded in the viscous, scarlet, near-frozen mud of Georgia. A lane grader in pressed fatigues stepped back away from them as they exited the bog. He yammered at them, "Move on Rangers. Time's running out."

Smith and J.W. skidded to the next hurdle, an eight-foot, vertical, wooden wall coated with a thick glaze of viscous red clay over which they slowly scraped. Branch waited below, cursing and spitting, then flew over the wall in a single try and caught up with J.W. and Smith at the third station, a parallel set of two-foot diameter, stainless steel culverts buried several feet under the mud. J.W. and Smith dropped into the openings, finding it nearly impossible to grip the ridges and pull forward, though J.W. sought to negotiate the lubricated tubes by flailing his arms and legs. That, however, only served to lacerate his knees until they bled through his fatigues. Unable to move, he became hysterical in the enclosed, darkened tube and scratched wildly, but that got him nowhere—he simply could not pull himself through. J.W. ceased his flailing, accepting that he was going to die in a pipe, or if someone took pity on him and pulled him out, he would die in the jungle in a God forsaken land half-way around the world. The latter seemed preferable.

Smith, however, emerged from his cylinder, looked around for his new Ranger buddy, and instantly dove into J.W.'s and dragged him out. They stood face to face, crusted with dirt and sand. While Smith laughed, J.W. babbled incoherently.

Smith's rapture, though, was short-lived. A cadre called to them, "Hey tube worms, you just pissed away a minute."

Smith grabbed J.W.'s fatigue jacket and pulled him at a sprint to the oval cinder track and the quarter-mile run that marked the completion of round one. Branch and his buddy took advantage of Smith's burden to gallop past, arriving at Cowsen's station long before the stragglers. The first sergeant stood in front of a growing cluster of mud-soaked troops, those who had refused to crawl through the tube, those unwilling to bestir the effort to scale the muddy wall, and one man who was so disoriented, he ran the quarter mile in the wrong direction.

Other cadres screamed students' names as they passed Cowsen, who silently checked them off the master list, speaking to no one until J.W. and his buddy crossed the line. Then Cowsen smiled, "You two got less than eleven minutes left for two more circuits. So, take a rest, gentlemen. Y'all ain't got the time to make it. Simple as that."

J.W. breathed a sigh of relief—defeat with honor he nodded to himself. But Smith looked quickly into Cowsen's eyes and swore, "Hell no! We got more minutes than that!"

Without waiting for a reply from Cowsen, Smith dragged J.W. back to the gallows for round two, a circuit they finished with four minutes to go. Passing Cowsen on the fly, the old sergeant laughed aloud, "I told ya. You two is done. Pack your bags, duds."

But at the gallows on the third trip, with the cadres conspicuously absent, J.W. and Smith followed Branch and his buddy, both of whom ignored the ropes, slogging through the soup on foot. The four of them then ran around the wall and the tubes, not bothering to squander time even glancing at them. At the final problem, the quarter-mile track, J.W. searched quickly for the prying eyes of a cadre, and seeing not one of the evil spirits, grabbed Smith by the sleeve and cut across the track.

Cowsen had abandoned the starting line for a position at his podium by the bleachers. As the other Rangers struggled around the track for the final lap, a third cadre appeared and waved them away, and a fourth emerged from the frozen mist gesturing them into a file across the chasm from the back of the bleachers. J.W. and Smith arrived at the tail end of the line three seconds before their eighteen minutes expired.

"It's a game of inches and seconds. Don't forget that," Smith breathed in relief. "We're home free. They can't hurt us now."

* * *

Over the deep abyss hung the frayed horizontal climbing rope, the hangin' rope Cowsen had threatened to use on J.W. an hour before. It was the only path back to the bleachers. The staff sergeant, the one who had greeted the Rangers the night before, the very same man who had convinced Fricker of the capacity of any Ranger to execute 16 pull-ups, and had probably deafened Fricker in his right ear permanently doing so, now stood, clipboard in hand, at the far precipice of the gorge. He was perched on the top seats of the bleachers, where Weathersby and his pal Branch had idled away the pre-dawn festivities.

"Gentlemen," the staff sergeant bellowed across, "The obstacle course is not yet complete. There is a single task yet to execute. Rangers, you will monkey climb across this obstacle. My end of this horizontal rope, as you can see, is anchored to a twelve-inch granite ledge many feet below me. There is sufficient room to stand there—*if* you are careful. And a Ranger is always careful. Once on the ledge, you will face the vertical rock wall and climb up the last twenty-five feet to where I am standing. You will use the cargo net you see suspended from the top of the back of the bleachers. You will complete the task in two minutes. You will then climb down the bleachers and report to First Sergeant Cowsen. He will be thrilled and delighted to see you, those of you who make it. And you will make it if you climb like hell and always maintain three points of contact: two hands and a foot, two feet and a hand. That is a golden rule, Rangers. I will say it again. When you climb in Ranger School, when you climb anything in Ranger School, whether that is a horizontal rope over a cavern, like you see before you, or a vertical cargo net that you see below me, you will *always* maintain three points of contact. We hate it when Rangers fall into the valley. Lotta paperwork. Now, first man, begin."

With that declaration, the staff sergeant grabbed the edge of his clipboard and hurled it across the gorge. It flew like a boomerang, curving left and right, up and down until arriving at the queue of Rangers waiting to mount the rope. Though most of the troops saw the rocket coming and ducked, Fricker, no doubt praying for a bowl of hot buttered oatmeal at lunch, was staring up at the dawn sky when the missile caught him in the back of his head. The clunk was audible, so loud in fact, that Sergeant Cowsen charged up the bleachers and shook his head sadly as he stared across at Fricker's rumpled form writhing on the ground. Cowsen breathed deeply, and then hollered forlornly, "Rangers, you must always pay attention." With that pearl of wisdom, he spun around and ran back down to his podium.

The staff sergeant screamed, "Move it!" but when the first pair of Rangers on line hesitated, the sergeant launched himself off the top of the bleachers, down the cargo net, onto the rope and across the ravine in less than eight seconds. The Rangers were relieved that Fricker's wound was going to be addressed, but the staff sergeant simply pushed the first man onto the rope, waited until the quaking troop was halfway across, then jumped back on the rope himself and pumped his legs up and down until the single strand of thin rope oscillated like the Bridge of San Louis Rey.

By this point, Fricker was back on his feet with his first aid dressing pushed against the spurting gash in his head. Morelotto, Fricker's Ranger buddy, apparently not a candidate for a profession in the surgical arts, had witnessed the gush of blood, gagged, and was now occupying Fricker's spot on the ground.

The swarm of Rangers, sensing a far from copasetic end to the obstacle course, milled about, though each step took them farther from the rope, a swarm of flies slowly buzzing away from danger. J.W. grabbed Smith by the shoulder and gasped weakly. "Man, I can't deal with this. I'm afraid of heights. I'm not going across."

"I don't like 'em either, but we can do it. I learned how when I had to go down mountains to get deer we bagged in the Alleghenies. Watch me,"

Smith demanded. "It's a piece of cake. Just don't look down, man. Always look up. Watch me."

Smith pulled J.W. by the sleeve to the edge of the ravine. When J.W. looked down into the cavern, Smith screamed, "Watch me, I said!" Smith spit onto the ground haughtily, then dove onto the sagging rope, his eyes glued to the heavens. At first, his slight body vibrated parallel to the earth, arms and legs wrapped tightly on the prickly nylon as he began the downswing of the climb. He slithered down easily, and at the bottom of the sag in the rope, he craned his neck all the way back as if in a seizure, and before even seeing J.W. drooling with fear, staring into the void, he snapped, "Ranger, I told you to look at me!" J.W. raised his eyes out of the cavern, and as Smith pulled himself along the upswing toward the ledge, he called out to Weathersby. "Hey man, it's fun. Don't worry. Pretend you're going after that eight-point buck you just bagged. Follow me!"

J.W. was about to grasp the rope, but he hesitated for an instant, and Branch and his buddy jumped ahead of him. When Branch stared into the chasm, however, he hesitated just long enough for another pair of Rangers to step up, the front one shoving Branch out of the way. Branch shoved back. The three were soon engaged in animated jostling, but it was just so much Brownian motion, with no one actually sucking it up and dropping onto the rope.

The staff sergeant on the far end was apoplectic. He charged up the cargo net attached to the back of the bleachers and shrieked, "Rangers, get on the Goddamn rope, now!"

Smith hollered up, "Hey Sergeant, gimme a minute before anyone else gets on, huh—just a minute." By the time the staff sergeant's ire had built to the boiling point, really just a few tenths of a second, Smith had pulled himself onto the tiny ledge. He shrieked, "Driiiiiiiiiiiiive on, Ranger," and with a proud laugh sprang onto the cargo net, a man possessed. He yelled back to J.W., "Come on Ranger. Nothing to it. Just don't look down."

M-14 rifle strapped across his back on a leather bootlace, a "Ranger sling," Smith crawled vertically, hand over hand on the thick hemp of the net. Ten feet from the summit, with the staff sergeant standing on the balcony of the bleachers throwing small rocks onto Smith's helmet, Smith stopped to suck in a deep breath before the final assault.

The staff sergeant smirked down and called to him, "Too late for your sorry ass!"

Smith lifted his left hand off the net, raised a perfect bird, and while aiming it at the staff sergeant's face, took a mighty step upward. With his middle finger still wagging, Smith pulled his right hand off the net to grasp at the next rung. With that deed, Ivan Smith of Johnstown, Pennsylvania, became the first Ranger of Class 68-B to violate the golden rule, the three-points of contact commandment.

His spare body peeled slowly backwards away from the net. For a long moment, it appeared as though he was suspended horizontally, perpendicular to the side of the mountain, as if back on the gorge-crossing rope, but gravity exerted its fist, and Smith's body was drawn toward the valley floor, miles below, J.W. was sure. At first slowly, with arms flapping desperately, Smith grasped wildly at the net for a chance to undo his critical mistake. But soon the acceleration of 32 feet per second per second, certainly a number he had learned by heart as a mechanical engineer at Pitt, declared itself, and he sailed more and more quickly downward, the process it seemed an hour.

The men on the far bank stood motionlessly, observing in utter silence the olive drab projectile accelerating toward the valley floor. And they remained stock-still as Smith, through a miracle J.W., to this day, has never come to understand, bounced to rest on the meager foot-wide ledge thirty feet below, his journey ending with a thud and a loud crack, as if a green bough had snapped. When the recoil and shuddering was over, all that stirred was a splintered piece of polished mahogany rifle butt that dangled by the bootlace into the valley, swinging like a metronome in cadence with Smith's moaning.

No one moved or spoke until J.W. Weathersby broke the silence, crying out, "That's my Ranger buddy!" His shoved his way forward, closing his eyes as he dropped onto the rope, keeping them shut tightly while slithering across, arms and legs flailing on the rough hawser. He pulled himself onto the insubstantial ledge, barely able to kneel as he took his first look at the flickerless, ashen face that drooled blood from eyes, nose, and ears. J.W. froze, transfixed not by the trauma he was witnessing, but by the shattered rifle butt, and the acknowledgment that, dead or alive, Smith would soon have to answer for the destruction of his army weapon, a blunder that often ended an officer's career. J.W.'s chest gripped even more uncomfortably as he considered Sergeant Cowsen's dictum about the responsibility shared by Ranger buddies, precarious liability, he mumbled to himself, recalling the pre-law class he had endured at Penn State. That warning still ringing in his ears, J.W. wondered if his future was also dangling by a shoestring over a bottomless pit.

Smith's eyes fluttered. He raised his head slightly and pointed tremulously toward the tiny GI-issue first aid pouch on his web belt. "Man, you gotta stop the bleeding," he pleaded. When J.W. reached for his own bandages, Smith whispered, "No, mine first. Save yours," but when J.W opened Smith's pouch, it was empty of both first aid bandages or cigarettes, the latter having been sacrificed hours before into the bottom of the pit over which Smith now faced his own mortality.

His Ranger buddy of sixteen minutes lay dying, and J.W. made the brave decision that Smith's life was worth breaking a cardinal rule. He went for his own first aid pouch. It was empty. The first aid packet that had begun Ranger School in his pouch had been tossed along a country road hours before in a feeble effort to lighten his load by an ounce or two. The smokes that had taken its place were also on the floor of the ravine, and J.W. looked away from Smith to search for them with his eyes. He saw both crumpled packets far below on the earth beside the snakeskin and the hard carcass of the dead rat. He removed his own tee shirt to tamponade the now spurting vessels of Smith's face and scalp, but the man's breathing became shallow, and his eyes again closed weakly.

From atop the bleachers, the staff sergeant glowered and bellowed, "Move your asses, Rangers! Tell that son of a bitch to get off his butt and climb."

He was joking, of course, J.W. sought to convince himself, but when the staff sergeant screamed louder, "Get off your ass, Ranger!" Weathersby's middle finger snapped to attention, mimicking the aplomb with which his fallen comrade had saluted the staff sergeant just seconds, and a lifetime, before.

J.W. accompanied his bird with a snapped, "He's hurt. He can't move. I think he's dying. Get a Goddamn doctor."

The staff sergeant straightened his spine, grinned, and addressed his audience, bellowing to the column of besilenced soldiers, men barely out of their teens, one-hundred-and-thirty of them paused in frozen bewilderment on the other side of the ravine. "That'll show you duds that Rangers don't bounce!"

J.W. stayed beside Smith despite the staff sergeant's not subtle instructions to mount the cargo net and get on with the training. Noting the lack of J.W.'s obedience, and the looks of confusion on the men across the gorge, the sergeant launched into an increasingly vociferous tirade demanding Weathersby abandon his vigil and mount the net. But J.W. didn't, and after half-an-hour, a stretcher was lowered, and two captains edged toward J.W. and Smith, both officers anchored to the mountain by heavy ropes. One captain ordered softly, "We'll take it from here, Ranger. Go on up and join your company."

J.W. mounted the net, grinding through each step, griping the bristled netting with three very sure points of contact, deciding to stay alive long enough to summit the obstacle and then quit. At the balcony, he touched the seat he had warmed so many hours before, stopping for an instant to contemplate just how to tell the staff sergeant and Cowsen he'd had enough.

But the next thing he felt wasn't the sweetness of knowing it was over; no it was a kick in the ass from the impatient man behind him, a jolt that sent him over the top seats of the bleachers, arms flailing, down to the lectern, where he reported to Cowsen that he had completed the obstacle course.

* * *

Smith was gone and J.W. was sure that he, too, was history. He stood at attention with what was left of his platoon, singled out as the focus of the staff sergeant's glare, waiting for the clap on the shoulder pulling him from formation. He played in his mind how he would feel as the cold orders came to fall in alongside the losers, and he wondered if the lasting misery of the incident would be relief or shame. Without much rumination, he knew it would be the pangs of remorse.

But as the last of the washouts was called by name and instructed to mount the deuce-and-a-half truck for the ride back to Harmony Church, J.W. realized incredulously, and with some disappointment, that he had made another cut. As the bedraggled company marched, toward where he and his mates had no idea, what overwhelmed him more than the loss of Smith, more than the sight of Smith's broken body, was that eighteen hours before, both of them had been at home, warm, and comfortable.

* * *

The hand did not fall that morning, his first as a commando conscript, and he dragged along during the forced march back to Harmony Church, a thrash that terminated outside the mess hall. The company remained at attention for an hour, batting out sporadic cycles of push-ups for infractions ranging from unpressed, muddy uniforms to dirty fingernails. The mission for that period turned out to be a wait, yet again, for the list of those who had made the cut, though Ranger lists, J.W. discovered, were not catalogued in the usual fashion. Yes, there was a typed catalog of names posted on the command shack door, and he plodded over with resignation to search for "Weathersby" amongst those who had failed. But the names were in haphazard order, badly misspelled, and only a few capitalized. The list was so long, by the time he found a name that might have been his, the cadres had commenced a summons to fall in, and Cowsen screamed, "Bronx Boy, what is your problem? Get your sorry 'beeehind' into formation."

The men whose names were clearly on the list were shrieked into a mini-formation, their last as Rangers, and marched off in defeat, heads down, hearts lost in self-disgust. J.W. watched, his head only a degree or two higher than his departing colleagues, as the tossed-out contingent converged on the mess hall. Yet, as he watched them, he noticed their spirits seemed salvaged, several even cheered as they entered the drab structure, for a cold brunch of mashed potatoes and bacon left over from the pre-dawn meal lay spread as a banquet before them.

Branch laughed sardonically, "Man, every one of them duds ate too much this morning. Loaded their bellies with so much lead, they couldn't move. Now they're payin' for their moment of pleasure. Ain't that life?"

Fricker, who had wrapped his head in a tee shirt to stifle the bleeding from the staff sergeant's clipboard, held a different view, suggesting, "No, man, they're the smart ones. Bein' rewarded twice. Got to eat this morning—gettin' to go home now."

Branch snapped, "If you hate it so much, why the hell don't you just shut up and quit?"

Though Fricker pretended not to hear, J.W. glanced quickly at Fricker's eyes and saw the red returning. With that, he punched Fricker in the arm good-naturedly and cackled, "Don't listen to 'im. That chip on my man Ranger Branch's shoulder over there; it'll bury 'im. Wait and see. He ain't goin' anywhere. Too much baggage."

Branch stood and took a step toward J.W., but the little man's Ranger buddy, the dark man with the chiseled cheek bones, half-stood and wordlessly stretched an arm out to stop him. Branch spit on the ground and hissed, "You watch your ass, white boy. It's gonna happen, and just when you ain't lookin'."

* * *

For the first hours of the afternoon, following a meal that had been promised, but in the end not extended, Ranger Class 68-B was enrolled in the Pugil 101 course. Armed with padded sticks, they were encouraged to practice the art of beating the living crap out of each other within the confines of a sumo ring. Though there weren't enough of the archaic leather football helmets to go around, Cowsen insisted J.W. don one. "You scare me, Ranger," he muttered. "A little more brain damage, and y'all gonna believe y'all can fly forever."

Despite Cowsen's reassuring words, J.W. fretted all afternoon that it would not be long before his presence was challenged, that Cowsen would soon discover the gaff of not having included his name on the list of washouts. The first sergeant would dismiss him publicly, requesting from the balance of the Rangers a moment of prayer for the enlisted men of the First Infantry Division who would soon find themselves under the leadership of Lieutenant J.W. Weathersby, Ranger drop out. By mid-afternoon, however, after hours of verbal torture from Cowsen and the staff sergeant, Fricker began to taunt J.W. as well, "Hey, pal. I got some bad news for you. Looks like you're gonna be a Ranger."

J.W., moved by the notion of acceptance, became desperate to suffer through more so they would allow him to suffer through more. He fought his way down to the last man in the pugil pit, his final opponent none other than Branch, who must have believed the rumor that the prize for winning was an extra thirty seconds at the evening meal.

When they faced each other in the final round, Branch growled like a pissed off mama brown bear, and then proceeded to pummel J.W., who finally lay on the ground on his back, the blistering, freezing, Georgia sun vibrating in circles in his battered brain. Branch, meanwhile, danced disdainfully in the winner's circle until a hornet, uninterested in the dictum that hornets don't fly during winter, stung him on the arm, launching him into a dance of mock agony, chin strap undone, looking more a black Knute Rockne than a Ranger hero. But rather than an award for having prevailed in the ring, his only compensation for his hard-won success was a distended welt on his arm, the gift of a toxic Vespidae, and an order to ignore the pain, fall in, and start marching.

J.W. straggled behind the remaining troops who, as he had come to expect, had been ordered to move at the double-time, bayonets fixed, grunting toward the next torment. Along the road, one of the Rangers tripped on an old C-ration can, fell forward, and stabbed the troop in front of him in the ankle with his bayonette. J.W. stopped to help, again trying to stifle the bleeding of one of his comrades, but seeing the staff sergeant bristling in from who-knows-where, ran off to rejoin the main contingent. In the distance, he heard the staff sergeant shouting over Cowsen's cadence, "Get off your lazy ass, Ranger. Drive on, Ranger! Drive on, damn it, your ankle's four feet from your heart!"

After the bayonet course, the company double-timed back to the mess hall for pull-ups and forty-five seconds of mashed potatoes, cold bacon, and warm milk. Following the after-meal pull-ups, they moved at the double-time to a new set of bleachers. Fricker had developed a technique for carrying his bad shoulder close to his chest so that he waddled while he ran; the troop who had been stabbed in the ankle dragged his leg behind him like Frankenstein, and Branch's arm had swelled to twice its usual size, forcing him to hold it above his head. Cowsen kept asking, "Ranger Branch, do you have a question or a comment?" After an hour, Branch's face swelled as well, and Cowsen halted his troops and walked up to Branch. "Ranger, you need to get those lips under control."

At the bleachers, the cadres spoke for two hours, delivering an articulate critique of their students' first day of training. The staff sergeant was the last to deliver his message. "You Rangers who think this is some kinda vacation ain't gonna be here long. I'm here to tell ya', this ain't no holiday."

* * *

At 10:00 P.M., the company force-marched back to Harmony Church. Most of the troops dropped on the nearest rack in what was left of their filthy, shredded uniforms, though a few undressed and washed their faces. One or two even brushed their teeth. Some of the men talked for a while before closing their eyes, and Branch and Kenyon, the only other black Ranger cadet, spoke in whispers, laughing quietly. "Man, I came up in Spanish Harlem," Branch divulged. "I don't know shit about 'dem woods out there, my man."

Kenyon laughed, "Man, I'm city too. Philly, but I figure I know about jungles, man. Can't be that different. Urban concentration camps, man. You hear what I'm sayin'?"

J.W. sat up in his rack and called quietly to Branch and Kenyon, "Hey, man, I came up in the city too, the Bronx. I don't know nothing 'bout the forest either. I know 'bout the city though: never stare at no one. I never look down when I'm on the street, always straight ahead, hands out of my pockets, not hiding a weapon."

Kenyon nodded politely, then whispered, "I can dig it."

But Branch did not answer. Muttering grouchily, he left his rack to go outside for a smoke.

In seconds, loud snoring and the rustling of beaten men resonated with the bootsteps of First Sergeant Cowsen, who had ambled into the barracks. Those who were awake jumped off their beds and snapped to attention, but he told them softly, "Get back into your racks, gentlemen." He went to the side of J.W.'s bunk and ordered, "Ranger, report to the command shack. Captain Vock wants to see you."

And so the series of mistakes that had kept J.W. Weathersby in Ranger School had finally been uncovered. He pulled out his last clean uniform from his footlocker and his second pair of boots, still gleaming from the daily spit shine back at Fort Meade, Maryland. He checked his gig line for the straight arrangement of his fatigue shirt hem, the edge of his brass belt buckle, and the fly on his fatigue bottoms. No use in antagonizing the cadres anymore than he already had.

Weathersby knocked so hard on the wooden door of the command shack, the superficial scabs on his knuckles rubbed off, and though he could feel the blood oozing from his hand, it was too dark to appreciate the life fluid that he had just added to the burgundy patch. Vock sat at his field desk. "Do you have to make so much damn noise when you knock, Ranger?" Before J.W. could answer, Vock went on. "That was very brave of you today, Ranger. Wasn't it?"

"What is that, sir?"

"That little episode with Ranger Smith."

"Just doing my job, sir. Sticking by my Ranger buddy."

"Well, the commandant thought it was hot shit. Don't you?"

"No, sir."

"You dodged the bullet this time, Ranger, but I promise you, one more episode and you will pay. You were awarded minus twenty-five points by me," he pointed animatedly at his own chest, "for disobeying a direct order from the staff sergeant, but the commandant gave it back to you, and then gave you twenty-five more for some unknown reason. But screw up again, Ranger, and your ass'll be on a Flying Tigers Airways tub to Viet Nam so fast, the blood on your knuckles won't have had time to clot. Am I understood?" Before J.W. could scream a yes, sir, Vock spit out, "And God help us when you're put in command of an infantry platoon." The captain dropped his head and started writing in J.W.'s personnel file. When J.W. did not move, Vock blurted without looking up, "Dismissed."

As J.W. lay in his rack, he turned the day over in his mind, the thousand snares barely eluded, the relief over having survived, and the disappointment and fear of having done so. But it was the discussion with Vock that kept him from drifting off to sleep. He guessed from the captain's words that he had somehow made the cut, and that was good and bad, but his gut soured as he contemplated how his presence could already have been made known to the commandant. He also thought of Vock's welcoming words, that he had been alerted J.W. was joining the class. But then J.W. relaxed, and reassured himself that was what Vock told everyone. Of course it was.

He looked up and saw Branch tossing about in bed and called softly, "Hey, man, did they tell you last night they knew you were coming?"

"What the hell you talkin' about? Go to sleep, fool."

* * *

As fast as the barracks lights were extinguished, they snapped back on. J.W. and Branch were in adjoining bunks, lying on the bare, rusted, metal springs, too tired to have unfolded the thin GI mattresses. The soldier who had been stabbed in the ankle was on the bunk above J.W., the puncture wound wrapped in his mattress, but the blood had soaked through, and a few drops had plopped down and spattered on J.W.'s face during the night. When the barracks lights flashed on, J.W. rubbed his eyes and noticed the blood, but he was unconcerned, believing it to have come from his own battered knuckles.

A voice screamed from another upper bunk, "Hey, turn off the Goddamn light or I'll kick your ass into the next fuckin' time zone." But the lights stayed on; it was Cowsen standing there with one hand on the switch and the other holding a thin stack of white envelopes.

"Good morning, gentlemen. Off your butts, on your feet, fall in." Most of the men tore for the door, but Cowsen screamed, "No, in front of your bunks!" Those who had taken the time to get out of their fatigues were in their drawers, all except Fricker, who had slept in the buff. He still had toothpaste on his chin.

Cowsen walked the center of the room and barked, "The new

company mailman," flipping the envelopes at Fricker, who had taken a position at rigid attention in the middle of the barracks in all his glory. Stripping the rubber band from the bundle, Fricker called out names.

"Bearchild!" Branch's Ranger buddy, his dark cheekbones towering, stepped forward, nodded, and accepted an envelope.

"Branch!"

"Yo!"

"Weathersby!"

"Yo!"

Branch ogled Weathersby's envelope, laughing contemptuously at the scribbled, secret messages and the extra upside-down stamps Krista had placed on the letter to insure it got there post-haste. J.W. sneered back, folded the envelope, and shoved it into a pocket. He headed for the latrine, seeking peace to read his missive, but Cowsen had slipped outside the barracks and bellowed, "Fall in. You got three minutes. You will be freshly shaven and presentable. You are soldiers, and more important, a few of you will be Rangers some day—maybe."

J.W.'s fellows ran past him into the latrine, splashing water on their faces at a row of communal sinks; the others, who could not squeeze in, dashed from the john dry-shaving. By the time J.W. ran back to his footlocker for a razor, and then back to the sinks, he could not help but notice that he was the final soul left in the latrine. He sprinted back into the barracks. It, too, was empty. Unshaven, only half-dressed, he ran frantically to the window and peeped through a streak in the frost-covered glass. A tight formation of his comrades stood weaving in the freezing, early morning mist.

"Welcome to Day Two of Ranger School. Rangers, ten hut. Left face. Some of you will still be here tonight. Some will not. At the double-time, forward march." For J.W. Weathersby, that moment of hesitation, that six-tenths of a second had cast a die. He realized he was done, that the game of inches and seconds Smith had described had hanged him; he was through. He just couldn't believe it had happened that fast.

The heavy leather boots of his compatriots pounded off into the distance, Cowsen bellowing cadence. J.W., hiding under the window, rose and peered out again as the company jogged away from Harmony

Church, sparkling crystals of frozen mist on the stubble of what was left of their hair. As the beat faded, J.W. nervously retreated into the latrine and placed himself on the center throne. His only refuge was the letter from Krista, which he read and reread, and for a few seconds, he was blanketed in pleasure, oblivious to the sufferings of Branch, Bearchild, Fricker, and the Ranger with the bloody ankle. His tranquility was, however, short-lived, as guilt soon roiled in his chest as he poured over Krista's declaration that he was a fine and noble man, a brave soldier. Within seconds, shame wormed its way into J.W.'s heart, and he snuck back into the barracks proper, pacing, struggling to think of a way to undo the felony that had begun innocently, but grown so quickly critical.

J.W. sighed heavily when the answer came. He redressed in his last clean uniform, donned the spit shined boots, and walked, head hung low, toward the door. He would do what the honor code at West Point demanded: report to the command shack and face his punishment. As he walked toward the door of the barracks, he came to the unopened mail scattered on the floor. On the top was a letter upon which the writing was a scrawl, the scratchings of a soul who suffered a terrible tremor, or had barely learned the alphabet. Nonetheless, J.W. smiled as he made out the letters of the return address: Bessie Branch, 127th Street, New York City. J.W. thought for a moment about 127th Street, realizing it was deep within the belly of Harlem. He asked aloud with a smile, "Branch has a mother?"

He gathered the envelopes and placed them in a neat pile by the door, then walked out into night, deep in thought. Nearing the mess hall, his trance was nettled by the thump of distant combat boots closing on Harmony Church. For a moment he was confused, not understanding how the company could already be back, but he remembered that on some mornings, rumor had it, they would just run loops around Harmony Church for as long as it took to weed out a few more of the less sturdy. His remorse faded as a plan to sneak back into Ranger School washed over him.

He stole through the icy fog, the black mist shrouding him as he loitered in the shadows behind the mess hall. The lead elements of the company soon filtered into base camp. He was as still as a tree. When the main body shuffled past, he waited twenty seconds, then loped into the mass of those drifting on the edge of expulsion, imitating the beaten gait of the stragglers. Though expecting an iron hand to snatch him and toss him aboard the meat wagon, nary a cadres nor Ranger detected the Rosie Ruiz of Ranger School.

The only crack in J.W.'s scheme came when the letter from Krista flipped out of his pocket. He stopped to pick it off the ground, but out of the corner of his eye he saw Cowsen antagonizing the meandering few bringing up the rear, and Weathersby made a hasty decision not to retrieve it. As J.W. turned a last time, he saw Cowsen pick the letter up, stare at it for a second, then stash it into his pocket.

Cowsen hounded the dwindling company for a few hundred meters, then halted them in front of the mess hall, announcing that due to inflation, the price of admission had risen to twenty pull-ups, and breakfast number two had been reduced to thirty seconds. Ranger Gillette, another small man with thick, rimless glasses attached to his head with an elastic band, raised his hand and was recognized by the first sergeant.

"Sergeant Cowsen, excuse me, but that calculates to an inflation rate of thirty-three percent on the pull-ups and sort of like a crash on the stock market of fifty percent for food consumption time. Doesn't the military budget for the Ranger contingent?"

"Ranger Branch," Cowsen asked quietly, "what did he say?" Branch looked up from his stupor and was about to ask the sergeant to repeat the question, but Cowsen barked," All right, pull-ups and breakfast."

Twenty minutes later they sat in the bleachers, though half the seats that just yesterday were occupied by beaten men were now empty stretches of rotting planks. The uniforms of the surviving beaten, aside, that is, from J.W.'s, were thick with fresh, red, Georgia clay from the spin through the obstacle course on the morning jaunt he'd missed. Branch and Weathersby were again perched in the penthouse overhanging the ravine, the soggy pack of smokes still maintaining its vigil on the valley floor. Cowsen stood at the podium, a hardness having transfigured the boyish, handsome face. J.W. muttered, "Now what?"

"Rangers," Sergeant Cowsen said flatly, "Martin Luther King is dead. He was shot by a madman, a bigot. Rangers, there is bigotry in America, and there is fire in America. Atlanta is burning. Washington is burning. But there is no bigotry in Ranger School, Rangers, and there will be no fire here, 'ceptin that one burning in your gut. You will drive on and become Rangers no matter what madness happens in America, no matter what price you have to pay. You are the chosen, the lucky ones. ON YOUR FEET! FALL IN!"

* * *

The announcement saddened J.W., for he had grown up in New York City, and a black woman had worked in his house as a maid, and for much of his childhood served as a surrogate mother. For years, J.W. inferred that by watching his bed and meals being made by Posie, and by being yelled at by her when he picked on his little brothers, that he knew what it meant to be black. He looked with sympathy toward Branch, but J.W. had to turn away quickly when Branch glared back at him with frozen, onyx eyes, and then spit furiously on the red earth.

Cowsen spent some seconds surveying the faces of his two black Ranger cadets, Branch and Kenyon. When they looked away from him, he quickly ordered the company to attention, and then into a forced march. He screamed cadence for the entire pilgrimage, much of it in Branch's ear, but the little man had fixed his gaze on a distant obstacle course, silently enduring the first sergeant until a tear rolled down the nascent Ranger's cheek.

Cowsen eventually tired of his torment and trotted off to antagonize Kenyon. J.W. took the absence of Cowsen's authority to pull alongside Branch and console, "I'm sorry, man," but Branch stared forward as if he hadn't heard.

* * *

At the edge of an empty, ice-covered expanse, they were ordered to halt under a mammoth tree from which was suspended a wooden sign engraved with the burnt letters "Victory Lake." Behind the last rank of Rangers was another set of bleachers and a wooden shanty not unlike the command shack at Harmony Church. On the shore of what seemed to J.W. a vast frozen body of water—perhaps they had double-timed all the way to the Atlantic or the Great Lakes—stood a fifty-foot-telephone pole. Thirty feet into the iced-over ocean was another pole, the two masts connected by an eight-inch-wide board stretching from top to top. Halfway along the plank, in the middle of absolutely nowhere, sat an arrangement of wooden steps, three up, three down. Fricker pointed to a third pole, fifty feet farther into the water and shivered, "Shit, that thing's a hundred feet high."

Cowsen cleared his throat. "Seventy-five feet. Rangers, you are at Victory Lake. You have made it this far; consider it a victory. You are the lucky ones. You will climb the first pole, start walking, and negotiate the horizontal plank, never touching it with your hands, NEVER touching it with your hands. Can you see the cable going from the second pole to the third, the one way out there, Ranger Fricker? You will monkey climb that cable just like you did at the ravine. When you get to the little Ranger Tab hanging at the far end, you will slowly and carefully let your legs unwrap from the cable and ask permission to touch the tab, and then ask permission to drop into the lake, screaming the word 'Ranger' as you fall the seventy-five feet."

Fricker raised his good hand. "What about the ice, Sergeant Cowsen?"

"Ranger Fricker, do not be concerned with the ice. As you know, we are interested primarily in your welfare."

With that answer, Cowsen and his confederates disappeared into the little hut behind the bleachers, and within a millisecond of their departure, an explosion of nuclear proportions shook southern Georgia, slamming the entire company of erstwhile Rangers to the ground and into a crawling mass of olive drab. A funnel of ice lifted off the surface of Victory Lake and showered over a two-hundred meter circle, though most of it, along with a thousand gallons of frigid water, rained down upon the ranks of troops. As they shooed chunks of ice from their soaked, tattered uniforms, Cowsen, accompanied by his cadres, emerged unscathed from the hut and herded the disoriented Rangers into a file at the base of the lakeside pole.

The first Rangers climbed vertically up that pole with gusto and bravado toward the horizontal plank fifty feet above the surface of the lake, but when confronted with the narrow level board and the midstream, tilted staircase, they slowed and tiptoed with trepidation toward the cable anchored at the far end.

There, the commando novices began a monkey climb on a sagging stretch of freezing, ice-coated wire no bigger around than a pinky finger, first down hill along the droop, which was easy, but then up slope toward the Ranger Tab, which wasn't. As the initial warriors reached the orange and black insignia, several, pleased indeed with their triumph, allowed their legs to undrape from the wire too quickly, the extra weight hurtling them sideways seventy-five feet into the already re-crystallizing water. The sideways slam into the ice-thickened soup of Victory Lake moved even the staff sergeant, who, after cursing aloud each time a Ranger fell, rowed out in a dinghy and dragged the floundering troop to shore.

J.W. slid back a few spaces to the rear of the line as everyone's attention fixed on Branch. The little man moved rapidly up the pole and crept as far as the steps, but he touched one inadvertently, and Cowsen bellowed at him so hard, Branch lost his balance and fell into the shallow water. He lay there for a moment, and one of the cadres started in after him, but Branch struggled out of the water on his own and hobbled back to the pole, reclaiming his rightful position in the greater scheme of things by pushing the next Ranger out of his way. He was back on the plank in seconds, blood dripping from his left ear. He ran up the stairs this time, stopping on the top step to spit arrogantly into the water, the glob landing not far from Sergeant Cowsen, then sprinted to the end of the pole, monkey climbed up to the tab, which he slapped with disdain, and screamed, "Ranger Branch is dropping."

Without waiting for permission, he sailed gracefully, a sepia dart, into the water. It was an eternity before he surfaced, and the staff sergeant crossly piloted the rescue rowboat toward the last place the world had laid eyes on Ranger Branch. Branch, however, bubbled up and swam awkwardly to shore, crawling to a seat in the bleachers, leaning back peacefully, lighting up one of his Chesterfields.

Each time J.W.'s turn neared, he stole to the rear of the line, but Cowsen, who had never taken his eyes off the steps, yelled, "Ranger Weathersby, get your sorry butt on that pole. You're next!"

A single nail fastened each rotting wooden rung into the pole, allowing them to rotate easily. One had to grasp at the rung above with both hands and do a pull-up to keep from sliding back to earth. Scared to look down, J.W. fixed his eyes, ala the forgotten Smith, directly ahead, on the black droplets of congealed creosote clinging to the pole, imagining them to be the petrified tears of past generations of Rangers. The first few feet of the plank were easy, but the board narrowed quickly and the miniature staircase vibrated in concord with the twitching of his legs. The steps were canted to the left, but more meaningfully, glazed with an icy sheen, and his hand brushed each step lightly.

Cowsen was silent until J.W. had traversed the steps and crept along the plank to the end, sweating in abject fear in the freezing Georgia air. As he was about to drop onto the cable and begin the climb toward the Ranger Tab, Cowsen shouted up to him, "Not so fast, 'Swim Forever'. Back along the board and over the steps. Let's try it in reverse this time."

J.W. followed the order, conscious of the amplified shaking in his legs as he navigated the steps backwards. Again he touched them lightly for moral support, though Cowsen was silent, and J.W., assuming the first sergeant wasn't paying attention, crept to the end of the plank, reached for the cable, and swung out, wrapping his quivering legs around the down sloping wire before being given permission to do so. Cowsen bellowed, "Back down Ranger, and try the whole thing over again."

By the third time through the exercise, J.W. became bored with the plank, and when Cowsen allowed him to swing onto the wire, he was surprised at how much easier it was to hold on than he'd imagined. But that was the downhill arch of the cable, and as the parabola swung into the up stroke, his arms began to burn as if there were sizzling bayonets pressing heavily against his triceps. His fatigue pants had unbloused, and the soaked hem froze in the winter gusts. Benumbed at one end, burning at the other, J.W. considered his options. Clearly, he could go no farther on the wire, and he could certainly not drop into the lake from that height; but he could, he suddenly realized, crawl back down the cable, mount the plank, easily walk backwards across the steps, spit like Branch, climb down the rungs, and scream, "I QUIT THIS SHIT!"

WILLIAM STUART GOULD, M.D.

He would lose only face. That was not a big deal he convinced himself, for no one was paying attention anyway. He was destined to wind up in Viet Nam no matter what he did, be it in eight weeks, eight days, or eight hours; it no longer mattered. Sooner or later, he would face the music for his foolish, impetuous decision to enter R.O.T.C., and the compounding of that mistake by imploring the Pentagon to allow him to volunteer for duty in a war in which he had suddenly lost interest. But, off he would go; anything was better than this. He would distinguish himself in combat, and then laugh at the fools who survived Ranger School and wound up in Viet Nam anyway. He would earn his decorations in combat, not at the hands of a paper tiger corps of stateside enemy Ranger cadres.

Seconds passed and his fingers blistered with the pressure of the metal cable. His right hand loosened for a rest, and then the left, for just a breather, and in an instant he couldn't help but notice that he was hurtling toward the drink, head first. He cursed himself for having learned so few of the commandments of his two days of training, particularly the one about three points of contact. J.W. opened his mouth to explain what had happened as the staff sergeant screamed up, "No one gave you permission to drop, Ranger," but a blast of freezing water filled J.W.'s throat and drove into the pit of his stomach. His chest locked in a clench, as if a bear trap had snapped shut on him. The brutal pressure soon expelled, in a submerged cough, his last trace of air, and also squeezed an acidic squirt of gritty water from his innards into his mouth. Helplessly, he gulped another mouthful of water to dilute the putrid taste.

As he threw his arms toward the surface in a last effort to clear a path to air, J.W.'s hand hit a piece of wayward ice, opening the lacerations on his raw knuckles. An ooze of dark purple leaked from the water-shriveled skin.

* * *

In an hour, the ninety or so remaining Rangers shivered in the bleachers. A few of them tried to light smokes, but no matter how many layers of plastic had protected their cigarettes and matches, aside from

Branch's, all were too wet to light. Other men wrapped dripping arms around themselves to trap what little heat they were generating; still others, impervious to the looks of the cadres, huddled together silently, letting their bodies touch.

Cowsen called to the staff sergeant. "Sergeant Hartack! Front and center. Talk to these sorry Rangers."

Hartack took the podium. Spit-shined, starched, and dry, he complained, "Rangers, you did not do well. These exercises are for your benefit. But some of you did not follow our instructions. Some of you did not touch the Ranger Tab. Some of you dove headfirst into Victory Lake. That is NOT a victory. You cannot expect to complete the training if you are not willing to play the game. And if you don't play the game, you can't expect a ride back to Harmony Church."

He raised his arm and waved away a pod of chubby, dry GI's lounging by the lake shore, cattle truck drivers who, with the snap of Hartack's wrist, flipped their half-smoked cigarettes into the lake, climbed into the cabs of green trucks, and fired the massive diesel engines to life. To a man, the Rangers inhaled deep breaths of the pearl-white clouds of stinking effluvium, wonderful exhaust, which aroused dreams of lounging on the wooden truck beds for the multi-mile holiday back to Harmony Church. Some of the Rangers who had been asleep during Hartack's critique drifted unconsciously toward the vehicles, but they were rousted from their insensibility by Hartack's scream. "HALT! You didn't earn the right to sit on your lazy maggot asses. Rangers, fall in."

As the Rangers coalesced into a shivering rectangular formation, the trucks pulled out with empty cargo beds, save for the morning's washouts. The massive rigs left behind a huge cock's comb of red Georgia dust hanging in the frigid air. Cowsen waited for the cloud to waft over and stick to the dripping fatigues of those who had endured. He took his place in front of the column. As the dust consolidated on the uniforms, he laughed, "You Rangers look like fried chicken. On the double time, forward march."

* * *

It took less time to move through the mess line that evening; fewer Rangers—now eighty-two. It would have been eighty-three, but for Kenyon, who had told his Ranger buddy just that morning he'd never make it, "Cause I'm black and there *is* prejudice in the army. No nigger mess hall cook gonna ever wear the Ranger Tab."

According to rumor, the cadres had begun tormenting Kenyon on the obstacle course that day. Maybe it was because Kenyon was huge, and the cadres loved to pick on the big guys, for as a class of men, the cadres suffered desperately from a deep-seated illness: SSS, the Small Shit Syndrome. Kenyon also looked strong, like Sonny Liston, and the cadres must have thought because he was black, enlisted, and big, he was in shape. For two years he had worked as a cook at Harmony Church, until he tired of being chided by the cadres and went to Vock, insisting he be allowed to enter The School, for real.

Though the staff, cooks, drivers, and clerks assigned to Harmony Church wore black berets, it was without the Ranger tab. As enlisted men, there was little chance they would be chosen to enter the actual training, though in the annals of the school it had come to pass, though rarely. Those of the workers who graduated had been elevated to Ranger legends, their names spoken in reverence by the older cadres, examples for the present sorry lot of cadets. Perhaps Kenyon had dreamed of wearing the real beret someday, perhaps that is what he dwelled upon while slapping loose, lumpy mashed potatoes onto the mess kits of the chosen for those two years. Maybe he had dreamed of finishing Ranger School, muddling through Viet Nam, and returning to the ghetto wearing the Tab. He would stand forever above the rest and escape the depression of the unemployed, those burning away their time guzzling cheap talking wine, rapping in front of some decaying bar in West Philly.

Perhaps Kenyon would have escaped the entrails of Philadelphia and become somebody, if he had lived beyond the trek back to Harmony Church from Victory Lake that morning. Kenyon, however, after a few miles, began to walk a serpentine course, drifting from the main column, tripping on pebbles, babbling in a daze to the Rangers who defied the staff sergeant and tried to carry him. Yet Staff Sergeant Hartack wouldn't give up, as if the saga of Ranger Smith had been for naught. He poked at Kenyon with a stick, screaming, "Move your ass, fat Ranger. Drive on, Ranger. Look at your sorry ass, Ranger. You ain't even sweatin'."

Then Kenyon fell on the road, and Hartack kicked him in the belly. When Kenyon closed his eyes, the staff sergeant kicked him harder and harder, yelling, "The taxpayers ain't about to pay no twenty-five thousand dollars to send a dud to Ranger School. Get off your fat fuckin' ass, Ranger. Drive on, Goddamn it." According to the stragglers, that was when Kenyon crawled into a drainage ditch and stopped moving.

"You can't die from getting kicked, can you?" J.W. questioned Fricker incredulously during the afternoon forced march.

Fricker waited until the double-time was over to gasp to J.W., "I heard he was killed right there on the side of the road." Fricker paused to catch his breath, then reflected, "Kenyon's lucky. He's out of the crap. At least he's resting."

"That's illogical." Gillette interjected. "You think you need to die to get out of Ranger School? All you have to do is say, 'I quit.' You don't have to be so dramatic."

Fricker considered Gillette's wisdom, then mumbled, "All I know in the world is that now there's near a hundred lucky guys, and a handful of chumps with fifty-four-and-a-half days and a wake-up to go. You tell me who's better off."

* * *

Staff Sergeant Hartack wasn't at the pull-up bar that night, and though Cowsen M.C.'d the preprandial activities, he was unusually subdued in his demand that the Rangers execute twenty-six pull-ups before chow. The staff sergeant wasn't in the mess hall either, and the Rangers nodded knowingly, albeit surreptitiously, aware the cadres had suffered a powerful lesson, one that would insure them a humane passage. Class 68-B would be carried on the coattails of Kenyon's demise.

Though the spuds were wetter than usual, and the cooks slammed them onto the trays so hard much of the meal splattered onto the uniforms of the silent Rangers, bitching about the rations was more hushed than usual. J.W. guzzled milk, but it was warm and even more bitter than it had been that morning.

Evening formation commenced with pull-ups, and then a solemn-faced Cowsen marched the company south toward the bleachers for a night jungle navigation problem. As they broke into the double-time, Branch's face twisted and his lips closed even tighter than when he had heard about Martin Luther King. He mumbled to himself for a mile or two, speeding up toward Cowsen, then dropping back, grumbling more and more vociferously to himself, until he broke ranks and charged along the side of the company to Cowsen's side.

"First Sergeant," Branch thundered breathlessly, "Kenyon was lynched 'cause he was a nigger. What are you going to do about that, First Sergeant?"

Cowsen accelerated the pace, the rhythm of his barking slowly eroding from a cadence into a monody. He ran faster, as if trying to escape, but Branch pursued, shadowing Cowsen, who stared fixedly into the glacial Georgia darkness. For another mile he tolerated Branch's shadow until Branch again demanded, "What are you going to do about it, First Sergeant?" Cowsen snapped his head to the right and stopped short.

As the company passed the two black men, Cowsen shrieked, "I told you. There ain't no bigotry in Ranger School. Now either get your butt back into formation, or get out of this school. You think you're gettin' special treatment 'cause you're a black boy?"

Cowsen pivoted into the night, running not with his troops, but from them, disappearing into the gloom. Branch remained by the side of the road, glaring contemptuously as the leaderless company of cadets passed in perfect obedience. He finally loped slowly toward the column, but suddenly spun north and followed Cowsen's path into the darkness back toward Harmony Church.

Captain Vock met the company at the bleachers. He stood nearly at attention, silently waiting, as deep, grumbling, angry voices approached the bleacher clearing. J.W. turned his ear toward the sounds, and as he squinted to hear, his eyes caught the glint of cigarette-pack plastic at the bottom of the ravine.

When the voices suddenly stopped, Branch appeared from beyond the shadow of the bleachers. As he climbed to the top row, Cowsen and the staff sergeant emerged together, though their heads were turned slightly away from each other. Cowsen stepped to his podium. Vock slid back into the night.

"Rangers, welcome to the map course. You and your buddy will be issued a set of compass directions and distances to various checkpoints. At each checkpoint, there is a prize: instructions to the next checkpoint. At the last station you will find directions back to Harmony Church. The faster you complete the course, the sooner you will be in your rack. Questions?"

J.W. raised his hand and asked, "Is this some sort of scavenger hunt, like when we were kids?"

"I don't know. I was never a kid, but I'll scavenger your butt, Ranger, if you don't close your wise-mouth behind."

The staff sergeant ordered, "Ranger Weathersby, you tag with Branch and his buddy until someone else drops out or dies."

Branch heard the order, muttered to himself, then set out in a sprint toward Bearchild, who spun toward the tree-line silently, sniffed, took a compass reading, and melted into the forest. Branch hurriedly ducked in behind him, and Hartack snapped at J.W., "You're already lost, Ranger. Get your ass moving."

J.W. kept up for a couple of miles, but his eyes slowly became choked with what he believed were giant cobwebs. He brushed them away, though still his eyes refused to stay open. Each time Bearchild stopped to take a compass reading, J.W.'s head dropped and he drifted off into an uneasy sleep. It was hard to know if he was awake or just dreaming when he heard Branch ask Bearchild, "Hey, man, where'd you learn to track like that.

"On the res."

Those were the first words J.W. had heard, and amongst the only he would ever hear, from Bearchild, one of the few Native American officers in the army. In fact, as J.W. thought about it, though there had been a number of American Indian enlisted men who had returned from Viet Nam and had been shoved into the 6th Cav to await discharge, he realized he had never heard of an Indian officer. He peered at Bearchild in the meager moonlight and saw the resemblance to the Native American soldiers who had served under him at Fort Meade, yet there was something very different in his piercing black eyes. J.W. remembered that the Caucasian troops used to like to call the Indians soldiers "Chief," but he knew he would never utter those words to Bearchild.

The three walked on, Bearchild staring at the ground, then studying the trees, picking off twigs, tasting them, sniffing the air, occasionally grunting quietly when he was pleased with what he had unearthed. Branch, however was of a contrary temperament about the forest. He jabbered endlessly as the fatigue pressed in, first bitching about the cold, then, with a few hills behind them, about the heat. After two hours of listening to Bearchild smelling the air and Branch grousing, J.W. finally asked Bearchild, "What the hell are you sniffing?"

"Smellin' for urine."

Branch mocked, "Yeah, like you can tell the difference between animal and human piss. Right! You're just wasting calories, my man. Let's just get this shit over with and catch some Z's. I ain't here for no nature walk, Bro."

"Man, I wanna head back, too," J.W. moaned, his team pride dulled by exhaustion. "Maybe smell for the urine from Harmony Church. Find us a way back right now. We'll tell 'em we ran the course in record time, or some such bullshit like that. I don't care any more. I wanna go home."

Apparently, Bearchild didn't care either, for he nodded, took a compass reading, and set off on a straight northerly tack back toward Harmony Church. For twenty minutes the three busted brush like mad men possessed, but when they encountered a thick patch of razor brambles that stopped them dead, J.W. was astounded to see these two tough men of color no more able to move through the barrier than he. They struggled with the prickers, the hunger, and the pressing fatigue as did he, the blood from the increasing number of gashes on their arms and faces glistening in the bare moonlight just as red and glistening as his.

It suddenly dawned upon him that though the three were children from disparate lives, that night there was no option—they would bleed and freeze together, and their legs would burn with the same pain, under the same night sky. For however long that night lasted, they were three souls denied a simple fate. For an instant J.W. smiled, grasping the notion that the brainless army had created a trivial miracle, the no nonsense melding of three incongruent civilizations. It was a deed seldom encountered in the real world. He beamed with pride, with the same contentment he had enjoyed so long ago that moment at West Point in the men's room, five days before.

After another mile of tearing through the frozen brush, however, they came upon an even more deeply wooded area, laced with the hoots, screeches, and the hisses of sullen and dangerous forest creatures. J.W. muttered, "I don't like this shit at all."

Branch snapped, "Calm down, Bronx boy. That shit's bein' piped in by the cadres. It's like forest Musac. You hear what I'm sayin'?" But the waver in Branch's voice belied an uncertainty, for in all his years of ghetto survival, for all the years of gunfire, screams, and sirens, Branch had never beheld so portentous a cacophony.

The shrieks, growls, and yelps even caught Bearchild's attention. In the mist-filtered moonlight, J.W. saw Bearchild's pupils dilate cavernously as he warned, "Stay awake."

At midnight, J.W. celebrated the beginning of a new day by pausing to take a leak against a huge, old-growth oak, though keeping the crunch of his compatriots' boots in the crosshairs of his consciousness. The next recollection, however, was not of their boots, but of a moist, warm feeling on his leg and then the piercing silence of the woods. As the moon was engulfed by a black cloud, darkness the likes of which he had never dreamed descended upon the forest. Only his ears saw. J.W. sought to follow Branch and Bearchild by targeting the snapping twigs in the distance, but after a few minutes, even that thread of reassurance unraveled; the crunching ceased and only the animal din remained.

He sat for a moment on a rotting log to rest, recalling the myriad speeches he had slept through in those first painful hours at Harmony Church. He knew Cowsen wouldn't have sent Rangers into the mouth of the lion without the wherewithal to survive, but all he could remember was the primary rule for that night's exercise: "Rangers, you do not speak on a mission. That means absolute silence unless you are spoken to by one of the cadres."

"Screw 'em." J.W. hissed, then took a deep breath and shouted in a whisper, "Where the hell are you guys?" The deadfall rustled, and he moved forward quietly, relieved to hear the heavy breathing of Bearchild delivering another of his urologic diagnoses. But as he stumbled into a tiny clearing, all movement ceased, and he caught the sudden flash of luminous eyes the size of silver dollars reflecting the fleeting moonlight. Though he did not remember Branch or Bearchild having green eyes, he moved forward cursing, "Will you guys slow down, Goddamnit?" There was no answer, not even the cluck of Branch's brash tongue.

When the moon appeared again, J.W. saw more of the head that held the emerald eyes, and as the clouds parted further, the entire body of a great buck deer became visible. Catching J.W.'s scent, the beast's nostrils flared and it moved slowly forward. A foot from J.W., it shivered violently, then backed into the timber, its hindquarters, however, whacking into a spiked trunk of deadfall. With that abrupt poke in the ass, the monster screeched, sprang forward, and reared on his hind legs, slicing at the freezing air with razor hooves. It then shot frontward, head down, as if a mad bull, the rack aimed at J.W.'s chest. No matador, Weathersby dropped to the earth, scrambling as he had in the mud-filled tube at the obstacle course. This time, however, his fingers dug so fiercely into the earth, he found himself propelled to a defensive position behind another great oak. The buck followed, banging at the massive wood trunk with its horns. J.W. spoke aloud tremulously to no one, "Damn, that thing can see at night."

J.W. remained perfectly still as the buck's thick, musty scent burned his nostrils. Though nearly disabled by fear, he also felt a rush in his chest, a sense of mortal adventure, an enervation soldiers returning from Viet Nam had told him they missed stateside. This was combat. Now he understood. J.W. was, for the first time in his life, facing a formidable enemy that could end his life in a trice. In his childhood, he would have tried to reason with, or better, bullshit those tougher and bigger than he, but at that moment, he understood that he would fight or die. It was a fear and an exhilaration he would feel only once again in his life, just months later on a very dark moment in his life in Viet Nam.

He grabbed his M-14 and raised the weapon into the air by the barrel, the muscles of his arms tensing as hard as steel, as he prepared to smash the skull of his enemy.

"O.K., Goddamnit. You wanna fight?" J.W. roared as he peeked around the tree to aim. The buck froze at the sight of the tremulous olive drab form, then turned and wandered slowly into the blackness. Paralyzed, J.W. waited until the buck fully retreated, then propped himself against the oak and pulled a pack of cigarettes from his first aid pouch. With the flare of the match, however, the stag reappeared, leapt into the air, and slammed into the tree against which J.W. leaned. A piece of the creature's antler speared the moss-covered trunk and snapped off with so loud a crack, J.W. thought a rifle had been fired. The animal kicked and screamed, then backed and charged again, but as the maddened beast hit the tree a second time, it dropped to the ground in pain.

J.W. sprinted through the forest, deeper and deeper, ears cocked for any living form of life, even a Ranger. He heard the groan of a distant vehicle and headed west toward it, but when the rumble came again from the east, he realized he had been enticed not by a car, but by thunder. Finally he slowed his retreat, sat and enjoyed a cigarette sans company of a forest tyrant, and let himself fall off into a restless sleep for a few seconds. He awoke to the sting of a pest on his arm, and took to his feet, walking for, he was sure, hours, backtracking, forwardtracking, pacing for a time in circles, until happening upon a macadam highway, the centerline of which served as a guide as he marched away from the lightning-charged western sky.

He went on for another hour, reviewing his life, musing morosely of friends in graduate school and those working for salaries, buddies building families, safe, warm, unafraid of their tomorrows, or of their next months. He thought sadly about the years of study he had put into his engineering, a degree that would be worthless in five years when he was released from the army. He was learning to do push-ups, to face Bambi's father in mortal combat, and he feared that would be all he knew when he got out.

He cursed himself for being drawn into the army's web of promises at Penn State that day in the early 60's when the R.O.T.C. commanding officer addressed the freshman class in Wagner Building 212. Painting images of the Berlin Wall and the Cuban Missile Crisis to keep his teen-aged audience awake, the gray-haired colonel intoned, "Gentlemen, America, the country that has given us so much, for which we will fight and die, is in trouble. There is a ground war brewing in Asia," he warned. "Mark my words. It is inevitable. Everyone is going. Do any of you want to go as privates toting an M-1?" The colonel surveyed the room quickly but regardfully, and continued before any of the children in his audience had a chance to consider his query.

"Hell no, you don't! I'm here to tell you, you want to go as officers."

J.W.'s hand shot up. "Sir, how do I get to go as a pilot?"

"Good question, very good. Meet me after class, and I'll tell you, son," the colonel offered warmly. And within an hour, J.W. had signed away nine years of his life, three more in R.O.T.C., a year in flight school, two as a ground-pounder lieutenant, and three more tacked on for the privilege of having been selected a Distinguished Military Graduate.

While the army had kept the colonel's covenant until J.W. graduated from flight school, he hadn't seen the inside of a cockpit since. Armored cavalry units, riot control units bridling hippies at the Pentagon, airborne units shuffling through Fort Bragg before dawn, and now Ranger School, each assignment further and further from the years of work he had burned away learning to fly; each year and each task another notch on the long list of disenchantments.

* * *

What he believed were hours and miles passed on the highway, each laced with loud curses for having relinquished his best years, for not having quit earlier that day. "There's nothing keeping you here," he yelled louder with each hill. "I've seen dozens of good men, a lot better than me, get kicked out over the past two days. Not a single one of them's been beaten. There ain't no record in heaven of what happens in this bullshit school. And even if there is, I got a whole career to earn redemption. Man, I quit this shit."

When lights flashed in the distance, he started toward them, but they soon disappeared, and he realized he had no sense of where on earth he trod. He took a breather and sat by the highway, uttering a firm oath to resign the moment he set foot back in Harmony Church. He lit his final cigarette in the darkness, seeking one more time to consider his future; but his mind was clouded in exhaustion, and he saw nothing but gloominess. His head dropped and in seconds, he saw nothing at all.

* * *

"Hey, soldier, you O.K.?"

He heard the sounds, but thought it a dream, and rolled onto his other side to carry on in his delicious sleep. But the voice boomed again, and J.W. opened his eyes to the glare of stationary headlights. The voice thundered again, "I said, are you O.K.?"

J.W. shook his head violently into consciousness, answering, "Yes, sir. I'm O.K. Just need directions back to Harmony Church. I must have dozed off."

"Get into the car. I'll give you a lift before you get run over. You're lying in the middle of the road."

"I can't do that."

"You have to get out of the road, soldier."

"No, I mean I can't get in your car."

"Why not?"

"It's cheating to accept a ride."

J.W. painfully came to his feet and stumbled along the highway, but the civilian drove slowly alongside him, and after a few yards spoke kindly, "What are you talking about? Hop in son, before you get run over."

The timbre of the words, though spoken soberly, were more a command than a choice, and almost by reflex, J.W. opened the door. "What the hell. I'm done with the training."

The civilian turned the car around. "You were headed the wrong way, soldier. Hey, are you one of those…" he paused and spoke with admiration, "Rangers? That why you're going back to Harmony Church?"

"Yeah, I'm a Ranger."

"Why you so far from your unit this close to dawn? I thought you guys were supposed to have buddies. Don't tell me we left him back there."

"My Ranger buddy? No, he's dead, I think."

"Dead?"

J.W. recounted the field compass problem and how he'd become separated from his temporary buddies, and then he spoke of Smith and Kenyon, and how he would resign in another hour and be on his way to Viet Nam. While J.W. expected the driver to be shocked and moved, all the man asked was, "How long has this hell been going on?"

J.W. thought for a moment. "I'm working on finishing day two, sir."

"Whew! Sounds awful." He was silent for a while, then asked, "You mean to tell me a man has to work that hard to get a Ranger Tab? Why? Army doesn't give a damn about you, does it?"

"Look, sir, I'm tired and I'm hungry. Do you mind if I just rest for a little while?"

"Sounds like you've been through a lot. You made it past the cuts. You've proven yourself. It's time to go into combat and show 'em what you've learned. Sure, take a rest."

J.W. sat silently, hypnotized by the colors of the Oldsmobile Ninety-Eight logo on the glove box. He nodded off in the warmth of the leather seats and the mellow, green glow of the dash lights.

"Say, Ranger, figure your men are going to get tired and pissed off in Viet Nam in a few days?"

J.W. sat up. "Yes, sir. I'm sure they will, but that's combat. Viet Nam means something. It counts."

J.W. lowered his head greedily and soon dropped off back to sleep, tranquil for the rest of the trip. He was shaken awake at the base of a hill near Harmony Church and toddled out of the car. The civilian pointed the way back to the command shack. "Up there, soldier. That's the Ranger School. No one'll see ya. You'll be able to slip in and resign, no sweat. It's right up there Ranger, you can you see it, I know you can. And

I don't blame you. I can't figure why the army does these sorts of things. What's wrong with them?"

J.W. was about to agree, but the civilian's words piqued him, and he took a step toward the command shack. But then he heard his mother chastising, "You say thank you. Do you understand me? Always say thank you."

So J.W. turned back to acknowledge the man's kindness, to thank him for the lift that had hauled him off the centerline of the Georgia highway, but the power window snapped shut before he could speak. In an instant, the car rolled off toward main post.

* * *

Cowsen was lounging in a lawn chair by the command shack, peacefully whittling on a green stick as J.W. crested the hillock. Staff Sergeant Hartack was on his back, snoring, on a nearby bench, and J.W. quickly shifted away toward Sergeant Cowsen to demand an audience with Captain Vock. With wobbly legs, he reached the First Sergeant and took a deep breath to utter his final words of Ranger School. Cowsen sat forward and stared at J.W., shaking his head in disbelief. He asked, "You the first back? Good lord. Where's your Ranger buddies, Bad Weather? You screw 'em up, leave 'em out there to die or something?"

J.W. was about to answer, but the squish of muddy boots echoing up from the base of the hill distracted him, and soon strings of returning Rangers interrupted the bucolic silence. Cowsen rose to his feet and gathered up his clipboard, ignoring J.W., who cursed under his breath for having missed another opportunity to escape. He mumbled angrily to himself, no problem. I'll do it right after breakfast. I still got a few more minutes left in me. Then he sputtered aloud, pointing to the wood line. "No, Sergeant Cowsen, they're O.K. Both of 'em are on the way. I got a little excited and ran the last mile or two. I couldn't wait to see you again."

Cowsen's lips twisted skeptically, but pockets of bedraggled Rangers kept climbing the hill and, as if drawn by a radar beam, descended upon the first sergeant. With the night coming alive, he pushed his chaise lounge into the command shack, and went to work crossing names off his list, dozens and dozens of them, eighty and some Rangers all converging at the same moment, strangely as if it had all been designed to end that way.

With the inventory of his charges relatively complete, and the staff sergeant dispatched to round up the stragglers, the inevitable ten-percent, Cowsen walked to the door of the command shack, folded his knife away, held the stick he had been whittling to the moon, nodded in satisfaction, stretched deliciously, and screamed, "Fall in! Rangers, you are going to be split into platoons."

With that dictum, a new sergeant materialized out of the darkness and ordered troops into squads and fire teams. J.W. was shoved into a slot flanking Branch and Bearchild. Branch's face twisted in agony and he whispered, "I thought you was dead, honkey." But J.W. grinned, letting Branch suffer, not willing to share his secret.

Cowsen announced, "Rangers, your vacation is about to come to an abrupt end. The core members of the class have been chosen."

"The elite," Fricker whispered

"Let's see how elite you feel in a few days," Cowsen hissed. "The rigorous training is about to commence. Gentlemen," he continued, "we are about to set off on our first challenge of Ranger School: a tactical problem—a real combat mission. This is why y'all volunteered for this training, to learn how to fight. Your enemy, or aggressors as we will call them, for this problem are Green Berets. They're the army's best, because in order to become a Green Beret, you need to graduate from Ranger School. We've lost a lot of men so far. There'll be more. Drive on, Rangers. Your training starts now. See you at the bleachers."

"What about breakfast?" J.W. grumbled as the command to march at the double-time was barked. When no one answered, he understood that there was to be no meal, and that his carefully designed plan must change; he would have to stop in the middle of the run to utter the magic words and end his two days of madness. Yes, he nodded roughly, reassuring himself, he would not permit himself another hour of the cruelty. After all, he'd uttered that oath to the kind civilian in the Oldsmobile. How could he ignore that pledge?

Yet, though desperately tired and hungry, J.W. Weathersby could not understand why he maintained his place in formation, being pushed harder and harder each mile, his only prospect for peace to wait for the exact moment to fall to the earth and whimper his words of resignation. That plotting allowed him to savor the notion that his brief stopover in Georgia was nearly over, that he, himself, was finally in control of his destiny. J.W.'s last run would be the most peaceful of his military sojourn, a voyage that would go on for many, many more years.

* * *

At the bleachers, he took his balcony position, but this time he sat up straight, his mind gathering steam, slowly rising to a screaming pitch. After a few moments of rest on his butt, J.W. finally obeyed the voice and sprang to his feet, surging forward, pulled by a power outside himself, propelled by a deep need to face Cowsen *mano a mano*. As he hurtled down the planks of the bleachers, he envisioned himself committing the first brazen act of his life, executing a rite of passage, the wrenching of control of his own life, the transcending of an obstacle in order to move on; he was achieving manhood before an audience of children. He was about to become his own master; from that moment on he would no longer play the weak-willed crybaby of his former life.

With each step down though, J.W. also felt a fragment smaller, surrounded by a deepening blackness. As his mind shot forward to Viet Nam, the adventure of the coming year began to leak from his heart, the lure of jungle combat losing its luster as he approached Cowsen's lectern. But it was not the ugly scenes of war that confused and frightened him; it was the here and now, the tunnel that was closing in around him, the black walls, the deep abyss. He stopped for a moment at the bottom of the bleachers to clear his head, but the darkness only deepened.

He turned and looked back at the Rangers in the bleachers, at those the civilian in the Oldsmobile had believed were qualified to be there. J.W. thought for a moment that he had been one of them, once, that he had proven himself, but then the truth roiled into his heart, and he knew he had only obliquely earned the right to have traveled to Georgia. He would go to Viet Nam as penance for his mistakes, but so be it. He wanted no more of the army, of their advanced training, for he was not a military man, he was, well, he was something else.

He turned about and took another step toward Cowsen. As he closed upon the first sergeant, Cowsen ceased lecturing and bristled into rigid attention. He stared at J.W., but there was no malice in his dark eyes, just an expectant, accepting quietness. Not a twitch issued from the bleachers.

Suddenly, a fragment of the darkness lightened and J.W. saw the image of his wife, and then heard the timbre of his parents' voices droning through the haze of his fatigue. As he wavered, he felt an invisible hand on his shoulder, as if he were now being controlled by a new force, one silent and conflicting. It wasn't a voice that tugged at him this time; it was a hand jabbing and prodding him, a fist stronger than his misery.

He found himself marching back toward the bleachers, and then settling in the front row between a few cadres and a Ranger. He stared into the dark sky, unaware of his shaking limbs or the heat that radiated from his face. He waited for an order to return to the high seats, but he was ignored, the incident a distant memory. Once or twice during the next hour his eyes met Cowsen's.

* * *

When the Ranger cadets moved out the next morning, it was in platoons, each with a separate mission. Branch, Bearchild, Fricker, Weathersby, and Morelotto, the Second Fire Team of the Second Squad, along with the other shaven heads of the Second Platoon, were ordered to attack aggressors entrenched on the banks of the Upatoi River, miles from the bleachers of Harmony Church.

"Expect heavy resistance from the enemy," Cowsen warned. "If captured, you will provide nothing other than your name, your rank, of which you Rangers have none, your serial number, and your date of birth." Cowsen went on to advise, "The security of the nation is riding on your shoulders. This is a serious mission. Intelligence reports indicate actual enemy troops, communists, lurking in the woods. You are to be the first soldiers to challenge them." The Rangers whispered amongst themselves that much had occurred in the United States over the past two-and-a-half days.

Cowsen walked up to Fricker and tapped him on the shoulder with the green stick he had been whittling. "You are the first victim of the course, Ranger, the first student platoon leader. Plan an attack." Cowsen handed him a manila envelope stuffed with military papers stamped, TOP SECRET. Fricker shuffled through the stack, put the loose sheets on a big rock, then stared uncertainly at Cowsen. "Hey, wait a minute. That's twenty-five kilometers from here!"

Just as Cowsen turned away, a dawn breeze sent Fricker chasing the classified documents over and under the bleachers and into the gulch. Cowsen leaned against a tree, picking his teeth with a weed. "Better get your butt on a stick, Ranger," Cowsen prodded. "The more ground you cover during daylight, Ranger, the less chance you got of getting late and lost. You got three 'sees' to do before sundown."

Fricker, having rescued much of the paper, but not all of it, a detail that would undoubtedly resurface, called over to Cowsen casually, "O.K., Sarge, I give up, what's a 'see'?"

Cowsen turned and walked farther away, so Fricker went to the staff sergeant and asked, but Hartack glared back. "Ask First Sergeant Cowsen, Ranger. He's the boss. He's the one that knows everything."

Then Fricker went to J.W. and asked, "Hey, man, what's a 'see'?"

"I don't know. Maybe they can't spell, and it means kilometers, like 'Ks'."

Branch tried not to bother listening to the neophytes, but when he couldn't stand another second of the chatter, jumped to his feet and snarled at Fricker, "A guy climbs a tree, picks a point as far as he can see, and that's one 'see', man. Is that so damn hard to understand? Now move your ass. I'm hungry."

Fricker shoved the papers he'd been able to salvage into his rucksack, raised his arm in a fist, screamed, "Follow me," and headed for the wood line. Second Platoon had begun Ranger School, yet again.

For hours they followed dutifully behind Fricker, busting and hacking through the brambles and thickets of southern Georgia, an army meandering without a battle plan, thirty of the country's elite searching for the Upatoi River, a geographic aspect that Morelotto sneered several times existed only in the minds of the sadists running the school. At the edge of another great forest, Fricker scratched his head and asked J.W. for a position report.

"Fricker, to be honest, man, I'm not much use when it comes to a map and compass. I'm left handed. We can't spell or tell directions."

"Then how come you were the first one back from the compass course last night? Look, if you don't want to help, just say so."

"No, man, it's not that. See, last night, I ahhh…"

"Well, then gimme a hand." Fricker shoved the map at J.W., whose index finger wavered for a moment then settled on an open area.

"But it's a WAG, man, a wild-ass guess." J.W. mumbled. "Looks big enough though to bivouac and chow down. That's the most important mission you got, Fricker. You gotta care for your men. We need to eat. An army travels on its stomach. Tell Sergeant Cowsen that's where you want to feed us."

Fricker nodded and searched furiously for the orders specifying a rendezvous point with the mess personnel. "Look harder, man," J.W. suggested. Cowsen drifted over and told Fricker he must have lost that information in the wind, and demanded that Fricker show him on the map where they were. Fricker couldn't remember where J.W. had pointed, so he closed his eyes and pointed to a dot on Cowsen's map.

"Ranger, are you sure that's where we are?"

"Yeah, that's the place, Sarge."

"Ranger, I'm going to cut your tongue out of your cotton pickin' head if you call me 'Sarge' or use the word 'yeah' one more time. You got that Ranger? Now get your slim butt goin'."

"Yeah, ah yes, but what about dinner?"

"Yes, what?" Cowsen boiled.

"Yes, Sergeant. Can I ask about dinner?"

"Yes, you may ask," Cowsen answered softly, as he walked off to the back of the column, ignoring Fricker's pleas for a menu.

Fricker finally raised his fist and yelled, "Follow me," again, and headed into the forest. They trod for hours, though every few minutes another troop approached and whined, "When we gonna to stop and eat?

It's been more than a day." After nearly eight hours of harassment from his fellows, Fricker snapped at each entreaty, "I don't wanna hear it. Just drive on, Ranger."

As darkness closed in on Second Platoon, Cowsen touched Fricker on the shoulder with the stick. "You're dead, Ranger. Snake bit." Cowsen then turned and beknighted another of the troops, LaVoy, by snapping him on the head with his now whittled-thin bough. LaVoy, however, unaware that he was to be chosen the next leader, had taken the break in the mission to fall asleep on the wet earth. When Cowsen took the disheveled packet of documents from Fricker and dropped it on LaVoy's head, he stirred, but his eyes remained shut.

"Hey, Sleeping Beauty, where are we?" Cowsen yelled. "How many men do you have? How many enemy are waitin' for you? When are you going to feed your troops, Ranger? You don't know, do ya, Ranger? The rest of you better keep awake; better know where you are at all times. You never know when LaVoy here's gonna die."

Though LaVoy roused a bit, he didn't look up, and Cowsen threatened, "I'm going to whup you upside the head if y'all don't get alert in a hurry." LaVoy's eyes actually opened, but he just lay there, dazed, until Fricker crouched by LaVoy and shook him. LaVoy looked up long enough to accept the envelope of orders, but as soon as Cowsen departed to roust the other dreamers, he nodded off again. Branch, however, took over for First Sergeant Cowsen, arriving to spur the mission forward, believing the sooner LaVoy issued orders, the sooner they would eat. His contribution consisted of kicking LaVoy in the ribs so hard, J.W. winced as he heard the breath blow out of the man's chest.

The blow caught LaVoy's attention, and he sat up long enough to create a plan, though his men were dismayed to learn that, while a meal was in the offing, as outlined on the sheet of paper Cowsen had surreptitiously slipped deep into the pile, the marching orders on top revealed they had to walk eight miles to get it. An eternity, they growled, little realizing how they would come to yearn in a few weeks for a jaunt of only eight miles to find something to eat. After several hours, Fricker appeared at the head of the column to complain that he was dying of hunger and wanted a bowl of oatmeal, but LaVoy, without turning toward him, spat, "Shove your stomach up your ass, Ranger."

* * *

As the shafts of sunlight disappeared from the woods, Class 68-B was exposed to the second dictum of commando longevity in the forest: remain five meters behind the troop to your front. Any closer cost a whack across the face with a tree limb, one that was silent coming, but slapped so resonantly, it extracted a round of snorting laughter from the cadres. If the Ranger was sufficiently star-crossed to have collided with a pricker bush, and said flora struck the cadet's eye, there was the usual smack, the reflex laughter, and invariably, an added period of banging, crashing, cursing, and finally silence as the blinded troop acquired the aptitude to see with his ears. For an hour, the wounded soldier was compelled to listen for the footsteps of the Ranger to his front, stop when he stopped, and start again when that Ranger's feet ground forward. Most importantly, the Ranger with the bleeding eyes had to steel himself to swim out of the freezing ponds and water holes into which he stumbled as if drawn magnetically.

A Ranger who found it problematic to acquiesce to the unwritten or unscreamed rules, like never complaining about the bleeding and the blindness, was soon descended upon by cadres, swarms of cadres, packs of wild dogs, goading and gnawing until that Ranger screamed at the top of his lungs, "I quit this shit!" Then the cadres dispersed, smiling in gentle serenity, quietly retreating to summon the rescue helicopter to carry the quitter away from the fold. But more importantly, the vessel that took the not-up-to-snuff cadet back to Harmony Church also brought hot coffee for the instructors. For the next hours, while waiting for the chopper, both the cadres and Rangers spoke in hushed tones of the soon-to-be-departed.

* * *

By 4:00 A.M. the next morning, solaced only by dreams of someday boarding an airplane for Viet Nam and being allowed to sleep for the twenty-six hour journey, J.W. followed Branch's crunching footsteps through the pitch darkness. Branch trod on groaning a mantra for hours, an entreaty to a God with whom J.W. was not familiar. "Sylvester," he moaned, "where are you? I need you, Sylvester. Tell me you haven't abandoned me, Sylvester."

During a stop in the march, when platoon leader LaVoy realized he had piloted his men up the wrong mountain, J.W. crawled to Branch and whispered respectfully, "Is Sylvester a God in your church?"

"Yeah, he's a God. Man, you *are* a damn fool," Branch snorted as the column began to track back down the hill.

J.W. shrugged his shoulders, turned to Fricker and sighed, "*Now* what did I say?" But Fricker would not answer, for the air was so frigid it burned his throat, and he determined that he could not suck in sufficient wind to both live and talk. J.W.'s social anxiety was short lived as the cold bore through him. Though he couldn't move fast enough to stay warm, he was being driven just hard enough to sweat a patina of mist that froze on his clothes.

Near the Upatoi River, Fricker, while walking a step to the side and behind Platoon Leader LaVoy petitioning for food, hit a soft spot in the humus and collapsed five feet into a frozen stream, causing a crust of ice to shoot rearward, ripping through the holes in the torn crotch seam of J.W.'s fatigue pants. Fearing he had been shot in the genitals, J.W. grabbed himself and screamed, "Sergeant Cowsen, help!"

Cowsen arrived at the accident scene shaking his head, "What the hell is it now, Ranger?" But J.W. had since discovered the shards in his pants were icicles, not shrapnel from a mortar round. He proffered an apology to Cowsen, who had already walked off to occupy himself fishing Fricker out of the brook. That chore went on until Cowsen had to abandon Fricker in order to silence the platoon's point men, two Rangers who had crashed back through the deadfall to the main body, yelling at the top of their lungs they had spotted the enemy just over the next ridge.

Excitedly, the two reported a large group of lounging aggressors, some of whom were asleep, though none of whom had been posted as security. LaVoy rubbed his hands excitedly, then called for his men to quiet down and prepare for the attack. Fully awake, LaVoy ordered Second Platoon to drop packs in an open field to allow them to move faster and with greater stealth. He gathered his men in tighter for a final briefing and an attack rehearsal, during which he had his charges move in slow motion, as if in a practice football play. The men feigned firing their rifles, which forced them to utter pop-pop sounds and pretend to overtake and bayonette the imagined enemy. After running through the dummy drill several times, until all the men were grunting like machine guns, he moved to the front of the platoon, pumped his rifle into the air, and took off toward the objective.

At first, they busted brush slowly, carefully, protecting their arms from the thickets of brambles, but LaVoy, quaking in anticipation, prodded his men to move faster, tantalizing them with the coming thrill of battle. At the crest of the next hillock, his scouts pointed out the clearing in which they had spied the aggressors. LaVoy's eyes shrank into focused slits. Fist repeatedly piercing the air upward, he shouted, "Follow me!"

In the pitch dark of the moonless night, he dove forward, gathering speed, down the final hill, screaming obscenities at his men, instilling in them such fervor, Morelotto and Fricker actually followed at a sprint. When J.W. spotted Cowsen watching, he joined the fight at a trot, though Branch and Bearchild had taken it upon themselves to protect the rear, walking disinterestedly down toward the ensuing battle.

When the lead elements of Second Platoon spotted the clearing and their enemy in the spare moonlight, they began firing their rifles. With the racket of thirty rifles and machine guns throbbing through the forest, even Branch, Bearchild, and the rest of the stragglers were suddenly aroused. The platoon streamed through the undergrowth, M-14's pointed forward at the ready, soon firing all their blanks, laughing, truly happy, the last time many of them ever would be.

They were greeted at the clearing by the shadows of enemy troops rushing about in disarray. The hostiles had been surprised beyond LaVoy's wildest dreams, and he ran through the enemy camp screaming at his underlings to fan out and subdue those attempting to escape. While many of the conquered plopped down on the earth, their arms lifted in surrender, a new problem emerged, for LaVoy had failed to include in his attack briefing counsel in the appropriate stewardship of prisoners.

Fricker looked to J.W. for guidance, yelling, "We supposed to hit them in the head with our guns?"

J.W. did not answer, for he was enjoying the battle zone of running soldiers and sitting soldiers, enlisted aggressors and officer Rangers, two populations with very different pasts and far different futures. Though dressed identically, he believed it was easy to discern his platoon from the opposition, and as one of the aggressors ran tauntingly in front of him, he whacked him so hard in the mid-section with a football forearm, the man puked. Second Platoon had fostered a level of bedlam the banks of the Upatoi had never before witnessed, and J.W. stopped to drink in the pandemonium, to watch and listen, to enjoy the grunt of retching and rolls of belly laughter.

Just about the time J.W. had laughed himself into dizziness, however, a fuming voice screamed, "Cease fire, assholes!"

The tenor of that utterance had the mark of a Ranger instructor, and it brought a dramatic silence to the war zone. A parting cloud exposed the moon, making it easier for the two sides to glower at each other. In the murky blue light it became obvious to the combatants how similar they really were; identical faces, identical shaven heads, identical, red-mud-stained uniforms, identical oil stained hats. The aggressors were armed with M-14s attached to their pistol belts with bootlaces, just like the Rangers. It was hard for J.W. to believe the army dressed and treated the teachers' helpers as badly as they did Rangers. "No," he shook his head and yelled to Fricker, "Something's wrong here."

"Assholes," the staff sergeant thundered. "Those aren't aggressors! You attacked the your own Third Platoon, you fuckin' idiots! Do not move."

Cowsen walked quietly to the center of the clearing then snapped, "Fall in." He paced, his hand rubbing his chin. "Rangers, your field intelligence was lacking, not so much in quantity, as in quality. There is a lesson to be learned here, Rangers." He paced a bit farther, then looked back at the young men who waited in great anticipation for the pearl of wisdom, that distillation of a twenty-five-year career as a combat infantryman in three different wars, the single concept that would one day save them and their men. "What the heck you looking at,

WILLIAM STUART GOULD, M.D.

Rangers?" he clucked. "You'll do it again, and then do it again until you get it right."

The cadres dove into the puddle of troops, ordering them into squads and then platoons, but as the Rangers drifted about in the winter night searching for the faces they had known for but two days, clouds again enshrouded the moon, and the staff sergeant screamed, "I don't want no cluster fuck, Rangers. You're going to be very sorry if you don't form up quick like. Do you hear me, Rangers?"

The class came to attention where they stood, brand new squads and platoons taking form in the pre-dawn minutes of the Fort Benning outback. Second Platoon, now with several hesitant, but silent, Third Platooners interspersed, was marched back up the hill toward the clearing in which their heavy gear had been dropped. Though LaVoy was absolutely sure he had led them to the right spot, the equipment, every stick of it, had disappeared.

LaVoy walked to the center of the clearing and sat on the ground shaking his head sadly. Cowsen stood above him and spoke softly, "Ranger, you got a lot on your plate. You need to find your equipment, redeploy into attack posture, overrun the enemy, try the real one this time, and then sweep past the objective and mop up straggler aggressors. And maybe," he smiled, taking a tuna sandwich out of his rucksack, "you should consider chowing your men down." Cowsen started to walk away, but called over his shoulder, "And you'll do it all before 'oh-five-hundred'." And that's less than three minutes from now, Ranger."

For a time LaVoy seemed frozen to the earth by the weight of his world, but he eventually jumped up and called out, "Rangers, I have chosen first to attack. We must accept that our gear is gone forever. For the hours we would spend tripping over deadfall searching for it, we could be done with our mission, and on our way to breakfast."

Fricker raised his hand. "My mess kit's in my rucksack. What am I supposed to eat out of, my hat?"

LaVoy turned and set out grouchily down the hill for the new objective. Cowsen caught up with him, banged him on the head with a small log and asked, "Are you going to brief your men before the attack, Ranger?"

LaVoy called the troops together halfway down the hill for a new pre-battle conference. He ordered them into attack formation, and then insisted upon a rehearsal or two, and held them there until the "pop-pops" were issued with sufficient enthusiasm. Then he started with the arm pumping again and took off down the hill. Fricker and J.W., however, had become engrossed in a conversation, chattering about the dream of a canteen cup of gritty GI coffee, its bitterness sweetened with a few grains of the stolen sugar J.W. still carried. Fricker fantasized aloud, describing his image of lounging against a tree, hands cupped around a hot, dull, GI-issue aluminum canteen mug of java. Occupied by the illusion of a cup of coffee, the two ambled all the way down the hill and were oblivious to having stumbled into Third Platoon's staging area where they were captured and gagged.

Minutes later, the two platoons met again at the bottom of the hill. Prisoners were exchanged, new orders issued, and the business of commando school revived. LaVoy, despite arming himself with a fresh plan, took another wrong turn, and the end of the hour found them even further from the river than when they had started. The new platoon leader, Gillette, made a quick map assessment, laughed derisively at LaVoy's ineptitude, then drove the platoon back up the hill into the clearing where LaVoy had stopped to brief them.

"Seats, gentlemen," Gillette ordered with delight, and his men collapsed on the frost-laced forest floor. Bearchild's face became peculiarly sedate, and when Branch looked at him inquisitively, Bearchild whispered, "I'm pretending it's a pow wow."

"Gentlemen, my name is Ranger Gillette. I am your platoon leader. I am going to brief you on the plan I have devised to capture our objective." Branch's eyes rolled up in his head as he whispered, "Who gives a rip about a plan? I need something to eat. I could be sleeping, and this jerk off's worried about an objective."

Morelotto had the courtesy to raise his hand. "Hey, Ranger, are we gonna chow down or not? I'm hungry as hell."

"Fellow Rangers," Gillette began, "We have a mission to accomplish. The status of your appetite is secondary. With the help of God, half of the Second Platoon will ford the river, spot the enemy from the far bank, signal the troops on this side, and we will then strike in a double-pronged attack. Those remaining on the far bank will clean up the enemy and capture prisoners as they run from us. Gentlemen, if this is done properly, they will be taken by complete surprise."

LaVoy raised his hand. "Are you outta your mind? That river's like ice. Let the enemy swim in it. Let them freeze their peckers off. That'll slow 'em down."

"The enemy will never expect Rangers to work that hard," Gillette suggested condescendingly. "Are any of you aware of Vo Nguyen Giap?"

Without raising his hand this time, Morelotto offered, "Man, I don't give a shit about no Jap. I need some food and some rest."

Bearchild raised his hand. "North Vietnamese general. Defeated the French at Dien Bien Phu in 1954."

"Precisely," Gillette smiled approvingly at Bearchild. "That's what I'm trying to tell you. He motivated his men to lug cannon up the impassable mountains of central Viet Nam. The French never dreamed humans had the will to fight so undyingly for independence.

"Independence, gentlemen, had not meant much to the French during World War Two." His hand waved in a grand professorial arch over the stump upon which he had piled the worn mission orders. His eyes were now focused on the heavens, enjoying a lecturer's bliss. "Yes, a few of the French became partisans, indeed, but most of the Frogs pandered to their Nazi masters. On the other hand, the entire North Vietnamese army was willing to die to get those armaments into position, to drag cannon up those hills no matter how badly it hurt, no matter how many men would die doing so. Are we the French, Rangers, or the Vietnamese?"

Morelotto, who had fallen asleep, tipped over onto Fricker, who fell over onto the legs of the staff sergeant, who lost his balance and stumbled forward, though Cowsen caught him and broke his fall.

"Ranger Gillette, get this Goddamn patrol on the road. Now!" the staff sergeant ordered, brushing off his forest-mulch-stained fatigues. When the men began to move, Cowsen ambled up to Gillette and asked, "Ranger, where'd you learn all that?"

Gillette offered brusquely, "Harvard College, First Sergeant."

"They lettin' any old black sergeants in there, Ranger?"

* * *

On the trail to the Upatoi River, a circle of malcontents met during a three-minute hiatus in the march. Morelotto spoke first, grunting that they should waste as much time as possible in order to delay the crossing until dawn, to allow the sun to warm the river. "Fuck Gillette," he sneered, "I hate them Harvard assholes."

Branch laughed, "Sylvester ain't gonna be warming the river none. He'll warm the air, not the water. And man, is it worth a tenth of a BTU to screw one of your own? You white people really are somethin'."

Morelotto ignored Branch and turned to Bearchild for support, but Bearchild had drifted off toward Gillette. When Morelotto queried J.W. with his eyes, seeking support for his mutinous strategy, J.W. walked silently toward the main body of the platoon, leaving Morelotto straggling far behind.

In astrophysical terms, Morelotto's ploy to delay the progress of the mission was for naught, for while he succeeded in dawdling sufficiently to effect a tardy arrival at the river, the shafts of winter sunlight were little warmer than those of the setting moon. Wet or dry, the bodies of Morelotto and his companions would undulate in the cold that day, and for many to follow, Sylvester rarely acceding to Branch's endless supplications.

* * *

Clean-shaven and in pressed fatigues, Cowsen met the platoon by the river, as chipper as if he had consumed a country breakfast of pancakes, bacon and scrambled eggs, a side of hash browns, and slices of buttered white toast, and had then driven back to the jungle for a fresh day at the office. He surveyed the lot of young commissioned officers milling about the banks of the Upatoi, hunting with his eyes until happening upon a target of opportunity, J.W. Weathersby. "Get your butt over here," he snapped. "You're the one who can swim forever, right? Take off your fatigues, Ranger."

"Sergeant Cowsen, right here, sir?"

"Don't call me sir! Yes, right here."

"I didn't think you cared," J.W. chortled, but when Cowsen's eyes hardened, he unbuttoned his ragged fatigue jacket.

Cowsen snapped, "You, Ranger, are christened the company swimmer. You are designated to forge water obstacles from this dawn forward till doomsday. Like I said, take off all your clothes." Cowsen's eyes opened, black, wide, searching until he nodded in satisfaction and walked behind the gnarled trunk of an ancient great oak. The Ranger who had carried the fifty pounds of climbing rope for the last twenty-four hours lay on the ground, asleep. Cowsen could see through wood.

The master sergeant hovered for the first few of the fifty-one push-ups, then, becoming bored, pulled from the pocket of his crisply starched uniform a tiny reel of fishing line. He handed one end of the thin nylon thread to J.W. "You will swim this line across the river, Ranger. If you make it, Ranger Branch will tie this here three-quarter inch hemp rope to the nylon, and you will pull the whole dog gone thing across so the rest of your troops can ford safely."

Cowsen's eyes dropped to J.W.'s drawers and socks. "Ranger, I thought I told you to strip. Give your clothes to Branch here. He's gonna wrap 'em in your poncho and ensure that all your gear gets across nice and dry. Aren't you, Ranger Branch?"

Off to the side, the staff sergeant squatted disinterestedly at the Upatoi's edge, filling his canteen cup with bits of crusted ice and then water, to make coffee J.W. imagined, but as J.W. hesitated to spring from the bank into the river, planning to suffer the cold inch by inch at a tiptoe, the staff sergeant became impatient and tossed the ice water at his back. J.W. shot forward and was instantly paralyzed by the cold, unable to make his arms tread against the freezing, brown current.

Cowsen watched J.W. drift downstream, then yelled, "Better start swimmin', Ranger. Y'all be floatin' into The Walter F. George Reservoir if'n y'all don't get them arms a'churnin'. Pretend yo arms is yo mouth."

For a few seconds, J.W. swam like his departed Ranger buddy had climbed the cargo net, a man possessed, but soon his arms tired in the frigid river, and he began to float downstream again. He pictured Smith moribund on the ledge and realized it was now his turn. He wondered if he, too, would be forgotten so quickly. But Cowsen screamed again, and J.W. kicked with a mighty effort that propelled him toward the far bank. Soon, there was frozen mud under his feet, and he crawled up onto the deadfall breathing as heavily as if he had carried those rotting logs across that tributary of the Upatoi on his back. With Cowsen's bellowing from the far shore, J.W. reached down to his ankle to untie the nylon fish line. But it was gone, loosened, he guessed, by his mad flailing.

Cowsen yelled from the near bank, "Turn around Ranger. Get the line back."

J.W. obeyed, crawling dejectedly into the water, but in an instant, his arms turned back to lead, and, blinded by the blistering cold sun just rising in the east, he began a slow drift down river again, no longer caring.

Cowsen, however, had other plans, and he threw several rocks at J.W., though the only one to hit home, did so in his head, and, as was SOP for Ranger School, it was the biggest one Cowsen had hurled. Whether it was the pain, or the sound of the crack, J.W. could not determine, but he found himself suddenly awake, struggling upstream toward the ripple on the surface of the water created by the nylon line. As he relaxed momentarily before reaching out to grab it, he noticed a small dark patch in the roiling waters near his hand. The patch was, interestingly, attached to a pair of fangs nestled in a field of white, behind which spiraled a squirming tube of greenish-brown. It took a moment, but within his frozen brain a few neurons remained sufficiently warm to fire, and J.W. screamed "SNAKE!" as if yelling, "PASS!" as he had on defense at Penn State, expecting help, a teammate, someone, anyone, to react. Though he tread water, begging with his eyes, no rescue party was dispatched. In fact, no one on the bank budged.

Cowsen called over the rush of the nearby rapids, "Drive on, Ranger. Swim upstream and get the doggone line back. Don't pay that cottonmouth no heed. He'll be movin' on shortly."

And indeed, the current of the Upatoi carried the snake past J.W.'s face, the serpent's white jaws opening and closing rhythmically in tune with the violent slapping of Weathersby's hands.

Sweat mixed with the foul river water as J.W. struggled up the far bank again, still in the buff, pulling the waterlogged hemp across the frigid waters. Despite his best effort to stretch the rope, it reached just to the trunk of a rotted tree, only inches from the waterline. Though he shouted several requests to the first sergeant urging the playing out a bit more rope, there was no answer, and he ran out of breath and patience, and settled on tying the hemp to the rotten tree trunk. His numb hands created a complicated knot, one whose name escaped him, for he had slept through that lesson the day before. He had also slept through the practical where some of the Rangers had actually learned to actually tie the knots, and he was surprised when the rope held Branch, who was first to monkey climb across the Upatoi. The small muscular man moved with the same power he had on the wire at Victory Lake, and over the gulch at the obstacle course. Bone-dry, he handed J.W. a basketball-sized, sort-of poncho-wrapped packet of dripping, river-scum-coated fatigues, drawers, socks, and boots. There were large gaps in the seams of the parcel where Branch had afforded the packaging less care than he might have.

Fricker, Bearchild, Gillette, and even LaVoy, crossed without incident as J.W. husbanded the rope, tightening it, repositioning it, taking care and some pride in having been an integral part of the crossing. When the last man, Morelotto, plunged onto the rope, his two hundred and thirty pounds strained the wet hemp until the anchor stump cleaved from the bank, dropping the primitive bridge into the drink. Nonetheless, Morelotto held fast to the line, twisting in the muddy current of the Upatoi, a harpooned, olive drab whale. While aiming a gurgling string of Mediterranean epithets at J.W., he swallowed gallons of river water, and it was some time before, at Cowsen's urging, Morelotto turned his attention away from retribution and back to the struggle for land.

Cowsen was resting against a tree, picking his teeth with a weed as Morelotto pulled himself ashore on the near bank. "Do it again Ranger until you get it right. And this time, you take the rope across."

Despite Morelotto's inflammatory expression, and J.W.'s penchant for self-blame, Fricker reassured him that none of them had taken courses in college about frozen tropical rivers or cottonmouths. "It's not your fault the tree trunk was rotten and the rope didn't stretch to one of those good trees. Don't worry about it, man."

"That's right," J.W. answered, encouraged by the words of his colleague. "He can kiss my ass. I didn't ask to be in Ranger School in the first place."

But when Morelotto finally reached the far bank, he whispered threateningly to J.W., "I'll get your ass, chump," and J.W. set off on a fifteen-minute apology, ending with a promise to never let it happen again.

* * *

The two squads Gillette had ordered to form the pincer movement across the river shuffled into attack position and waited for the other two squads of Second Platoon on the other bank to initiate the battle. The vise began to close on the enemy. When the two halves of Second Platoon struck within seconds of each other, the Green Beret aggressors dropped to the ground in perfunctory fashion, leaning against trees, drinking coffee out of thermoses and smoking dry, fresh cigarettes.

Gillette strutted about the battle zone, jabbing his fist forward, grinding his jaw, "Damn that was perfect! Man, that was good."

When he jigged past Cowsen, the first sergeant kissed him across the back of the head with the magic stick. "Ranger, you're dead. Choked to death on a silver spoon." He then snapped the wand on the bald spot of an older Ranger dozing under a bush. He growled to the new platoon leader, "Choose a rallying point. Designate a spot on the map where those who survive the attack rendezvous, regroup, and care for their wounded. Then plan the next mission." Cowsen warned as well, "The rallying point you choose Ranger, it better be one the enemy can't find in a thousand years. I'm giving you fair warning."

The new platoon leader studied the map and the instructions for half-an-hour, wrote formal commands, then announced he had found a perfect site, one even the Green Berets could never find. He carefully laid plans for his men to eat and then rest at the rallying point, a promise that brought cheers, and a grand whoop of delight when he declared, "Gentlemen, our rallying point is only one kilometer from here. That's less than a mile as the crow flies!"

It took an hour to find the clearing, and when they arrived, it was piled six-feet-high with their lost battle gear from two leaders ago. As Second Platoon dug through the heap, Fricker noticed that Cowsen was not at the clearing, and Gillette opined, "A serendipitous absence." The new student leader, however, had not devised a plan to continue the attack after he brought them to the clearing, and in the absence of orders and, peculiarly, of cadres, he stood to the front of his platoon, confused and silent.

Morelotto called out from the ranks, "Hey, man, I say we go administrative."

The entire platoon grunted its approval and, without waiting for ratification from their leader, dropped in mass mutiny onto the ground. By the velvety feel of the twigs, J.W. could tell they were near water. When the crunching of soldiers collapsing on the deadfall ceased, and all the men were comfortably curled in the fetal position, J.W. heard the burble of a nearby stream, and the churn of the Upatoi's rapids in the distance, sounds that dampened the pain of the penetrating cold. Soon, he sensed a peculiar glow in not having to move. Though J.W. noticed his feet lying in a puddle of freezing slime, he was so comfortable, he chose not to lift his legs out of the pool of nearly frozen ooze, even when the water wicked slowly into his army issue, leak proof boots, up into his socks, and finally into the hem of what was left of his fatigues. While he could see the osmosis with his eyes, he could only imagine the pain of the icy water on his skin, each sheet a degree colder than the last, for his feet had hours before become insensate.

Fifteen miles had passed since sunset, but J.W. was oblivious to how those hours had passed. Forgetting that he was on the ground, his only memory was of the incessant crack of twigs and the thousand boughs of cedar and pine that had cuffed his face getting there. When he heard the rustling of undergrowth becoming louder, an uncomfortable twinge shot through his chest, and he panicked that it might be time to resume the death march, but it was only Branch skimming about the clearing, gathering dry stalks and bits of grass.

Branch dumped his pickings alongside chunks of hefty wood, then dropped to his knees, struck several matches before one lit, and started a tiny fire with the blades of grass. He husbanded the flickering yellow flame like a starving man worshipping a granule of food, reverently adding another shred of grass here and one there, blowing gently on the candle-sized fire. Tenderly, he took the thinnest twigs, little more than grass themselves, and added them one by one to the tiny pile. The tinder began to glow cool red at first, then a warmer orange. Branch looked up confidently, a smile of triumph and excitement gracing his pleasant features. He seemed not to notice the flame degenerating a shade or two deeper, back into the red hues, cooling.

Bearchild observed the darkening embers. He hovered behind Branch as the fire nearly died, then dropped to his knees and pushed Branch out of the way, blowing gently on the remaining sparks, bringing a glint of orange to the surface. Bearchild slowly added slightly larger twigs until a tiny yellow flame struggled out of the embers. He rubbed a few strands of wet grass on a dry patch of his fatigues, then added them one by one until the flame brightened. Branch tried to drop a few larger pieces on the barely glowing venture, but Bearchild sidled around on his knees, blocking his Ranger buddy. Bearchild blew harder, carefully situating a few more tufts of grass and moss on the coals. The yellow brightened.

Branch's eyes glazed over, a man possessed by an insatiable desire to be warm, to touch the flames, to burn himself. He pushed his way around Bearchild and placed larger twigs on the fire, but one by one, Bearchild picked them off with his callused fingers, replacing them with shafts of grass only a micron larger than the last. As the flame built, the smoke dissipated, and Branch's face relaxed as milli-BTUs radiated from the birthday-candle flame. Bearchild added more grass, each blade a fraction larger than the last. He picked through his stock of kindling and chose, with some deliberation, a twig so thin a toothpick would have gloated over its own great girth. With this, his inferno rivaled the flame of a fuel-starved Zippo lighter.

With the diligence of a symphonic conductor, Bearchild chose for his next movement only subtly larger and barely more impressive kindling, twigs as hefty as chopsticks. Still, he had not uttered a word. No one had. Instead of speaking, the soldiers gathered in silent prayer, waiting expectantly for a Rose Bud Sioux Indian to deliver them.

As the twigs collapsed into red embers, some of the troops sighed, but Bearchild was not dissuaded. With eyes focused more intensely, and a jaw strongly set, he deposited smaller twigs gently on the coals, gently blowing life into them. They ignited brightly. Bearchild cautiously added sticks, then thin boughs, and in a few minutes small logs, and finally a tree trunk. Delicious minutes later, the air seared with a heat so fierce, Branch backed off several feet. Bearchild, however, held his ground, the pilot in command of a great engine.

When he was sure the fire would sustain itself, he jumped up and ran into the forest, howling incantations, ripping rotten trees widely from the ground, though when he returned to the clearing, each new log was placed onto the blaze with great decorum, as if he were placing a tiny baby into its mother's arms. When the timbers caught, Bearchild sought more, soon flinging onto the fire wet wood and dry wood samples of every natural fuel in the Georgia timberland. He worked as if the sun had exploded, leaving only hours on the clock for all of mankind, as if it were his charge to warm the entire nation and save every freezing American from the curse of cold. When he finally stepped back, the forest glowed as if an entire house had been set ablaze.

Within thirty seconds of Bearchild's triumph, however, the woodland rumbled and Cowsen emerged from the tree line, walking slowly, a cold-blooded snake slithering toward a comfortable, hot rock. "Rangers!" he called out, "no order was given to start a fire." The few cadets not inert from their pleasure crawled closer to the inferno. "Every man will deploy their entrenching tool and bury that excuse of a fire. Ranger Branch, did you light that thing? You Rangers are going to learn this ain't no picnic. This ain't college no more. This is the real thing, Rangers. Do it. Now!"

Second Platoon shoveled slowly, scraping peat and kindling off the forest floor and sprinkling it into the blaze. Cowsen observed the effort for a few seconds, then snatched Branch's shovel and excavated through the soft forest detritus into the layer of Georgia red clay, heaving lumps of dripping earth upon the blaze. In half a minute it was all over, and as the last ember expired, the platoon of Rangers began to shiver all over again.

Cowsen stood with arms folded across his uniform, warm, free of river water, comfortable. J.W. mimicked him and noticed the front of his own fatigue jacket had dried in the heat, a reminder of the ecstasy he had so briefly tasted. He resolved to preserve that feeling of dry warmth, no matter what the cost. And with that personal declaration began Day Three, or was it Day Four of Ranger School?

* * *

Cowsen drove them through the forest, double-timing the clearings, power walking amongst the heaving timber. It was not long before the strain boosted J.W.'s body temperature back into the low one hundreds, and the front of his fatigues again dripped with sweat. In fifteen minutes, his uniform was soaked, though the hems of his pants and fatigue jacket were frozen solid with rime ice.

At noon, Cowsen drew the magic stick from his pack, and despite the mad rush of Rangers dispersing into the periphery of the clearing, a fruitless effort at avoiding the curse of leadership, he easily caught up with the next sufferer. He snapped the newly-anointed platoon leader on the head with the flimsy baton, handed him a set of orders, and then disappeared into the forest. The latest student chief called a formation. "Relax, gentlemen, Sergeant Cowsen assures me we have breakfast to look forward to. A man can endure just about anything with a hot meal simmering at the other end. Hang in there a little longer, and this whole thing'll be over. It says so in the orders. Our next objective is the mess hall at Harmony Church."

He thrust the manila envelope into the air to shouts of "drive on" and "hot damn,"—victory. With the howl of hope, Second Platoon dashed toward base camp for the beginning of what was rumored to be the end of the breaking down process and the commencement of the rebuilding. J.W. had heard meals would be nutritious and plentiful; Rangers were from that point to be treated like the elite soldiers they had been selected to become. There was finally something to live for. J.W. sprinted near the head of the pack.

At the barracks, LaVoy, lips curled down, was sent to knock on the blackened, wooden door of the command shack. J.W. saw him as the rest of the company was driven at the double-time toward the pull-up bar. Soon, there were more crestfallen troops standing before the shack, and after a brief breakfast of leftover greasy bacon, watery, lumpy mashed potatoes, and warm milk, they fell into a company formation riddled with not a few gaps. The Rangers who remained instinctively closed ranks to make up for the missing mass of the defeated, a schema of military orthodontia in which every cleft was swiftly filled.

After classes all day in the sweating bleachers, and with the sun setting behind the ruins of Harmony Church, those who had survived the first tactical mission moved on the double toward the mess hall, the staff sergeant calling cadence, grinning through clenched, smoke-stained teeth. When they sailed past the pull-up bar, most smiled at the promise of dining without the calisthenics, but they sailed past the front doors of the mess hall as well, past the back doors, and back into the fields.

Straw men had been erected for the class's second visit to the bayonet course, victims at which J.W. lunged viciously, driving the foot-long blade poking from the business end of his M-14 into their cellulose guts. With each stab, he bridled more furiously in contempt for the platoon leaders who had failed their missions and cost him food and sleep. That the most bungling of them were gone was no consolation; it only deepened the rage. His fellows joined him in tearing violently at the mannequins, spitting on them, cursing them, so incensed that all they left behind was shredded fodder and the echoes of violent anger.

When they finally force-marched back to Harmony Church, the staff sergeant croaked, "Rangers, the ante has been upped: twenty-five and one to be granted entrance to the hallowed hall of mess. We don't want to see any of you gettin' fat."

A new sergeant stood guard over the messline. "Formation in five minutes," he importuned as J.W. picked from the smorgasbord of cold eggs, cold bacon, cold buttered Wonder Bread toast, warm melon balls, and tepid milk. J.W. piled his dented metal tray with the offerings, imbibing in the bacon before putting his meal down across from several devout troops, Gillette at the center, who had bowed their heads in a silent prayer of thanks. J.W. managed to gobble several heaping forkfuls of mucousy eggs before the worshipers looked up. His fingers moved with skill back to the collection of greasy bacon strips, several of which flew into his open mouth, as if by magnetic force.

As the oily pork slid past J.W.'s pharynx, his esophagus spasmed, a semiconductor, incapable of swallowing, but not of urping up thick, bitter jets of acid, reminiscent of that which had filled his throat during the fall into Victory Lake. Branch looked up, searching for the source of choking, but when he discovered it was just J.W. Weathersby writhing, he went on packing his face.

Slowly, the abject pain in his gut evened, the sensation of a fifty-pound slab of granite taking its place. He could not consider another mouthful, and he left his seat early. Dumping the balance of his meal into the garbage barrel, he burped up more acid as the congealed cuisine rolled off his tray. Perhaps he should have been a bit more furtive in his strategy to exit the mess hall before he wretched up dinner, for, as the last lump of mashed potato plopped into the tub, the mess sergeant bristled over to demand an explanation. "You know how many hours of toil it took to prepare what you just discarded, Ranger? Ranger, what the hell's wrong witch you? Throwing away food! Throwing away food? Why, in few days Ranger, you'll trade a piece of ass for half a peanut butter and jelly sandwich. You mark my words."

J.W. tried to respond, but the cramps doubled him over. Cowsen, attracted by the commotion at the garbage pail, gaped into the barrel, tightened his lips, conferred with the mess sergeant, and sighed. "Ranger, there are countless hungry folk in this world. You don't care, do you?" His voice rose. "Ranger, I told you a long time ago, this ain't the Bronx. In Ranger School, you ain't no spoiled rich kid no more. Get your food out of that can, put it back on your tray and eat it."

J.W. glared into Cowsen's eyes. "No, First sergeant, I won't. That's it. I'm not eating out of garbage cans. This time you pushed too far."

"You'll eat, or your butt'll be next to LaVoy and them on the bus. Take your pick."

J.W. stood his ground. He could not help but hear the utter silence in the mess hall, and he realized he was again at the epicenter of the tumult. This time, though, he would not lose face, enough was enough, and as he fixed his eyes even deeper into Cowsen's, the choice became clear.

With his front teeth, he scraped from his tongue the yellow-green scum that had been incubating there for days. He blended it with bits of half-chewed scrambled eggs, bacon, and the stomach slime that continued to drool up his gullet. Then he balled the slop-mix into a wad and aimed for Cowsen's lips, smiling, imagining the blend dripping from his first sergeant's chin. But as the slime congealed just behind his teeth, he also imagined the thud of Cowsen's fist against his mouth.

Seconds passed and so did the atomic standoff, for Weathersby fell back into his old mode, the life of obedience. His shoulders dropped in defeat just before he leaned forward, dipped into the can, pawed at the swill, squeezed a handful past his lips, and mixed it with the ball of debris in his mouth. With his submission, he allowed himself to start back into the position of attention, though, despite his best purpose, he gagged in Cowsen's face. Both the first and mess sergeants, acutely aware of the possibility of an oncoming projectile, as if, perhaps they had suffered this scenario once or twice before, lurched backwards, but J.W. retched nonetheless, and the two non coms were shocked at the speed with which the salvo flew out of his mouth.

Perhaps what saved his career, and life, was that, just before the orb flew, he twisted his neck furiously to avoid Cowsen's released fist. And so the clump arched like a Pershing missile and landed, by happenstance, back in the garbage can. J.W. unfolded, drooling slop, and arrived at a full position of attention. With bits of food flying from his mouth, he hollered, "Yes, First Sergeant. Won't happen again, First Sergeant."

J.W. dashed out of the mess hall, but broke into a stealthy, tiptoeing attempt to avoid being discovered when he noticed the staff sergeant discussing with Fricker the value of pull-ups in the rehabilitation of the human shoulder. J.W. made it as far as the command shack before Hartack called out, "Back here, Ranger. Execute twenty and one on general principles, and then eleven more for a failed escape attempt."

Half-way through, Hartack demanded, "What you smilin' at, Ranger? You like them or somethin'?"

"Actually Sergeant, it stretches my stomach. Makes me feel better. Kinda like an after dinner mint."

* * *

As the sun set, Cowsen gathered the company. "Rangers, this is a significant night. We will be spending it at the machine gun range. You will learn more about the M-60 machine gun," he said calmly, "than you ever knew there was to know."

The troops, however, were not calm. A hum of excitement spun through the ranks as the desperately tired reflected upon the prospect of being taught to use a .30 caliber machine gun. "Hey, man, I can't wait, finally some fun," J.W. hummed to no one in particular.

"I'm ready for a rest. An easy night." Fricker smiled.

But Cowsen, though he was dozens of yards away, snapped, "You think so, Ranger?" The only easy night in Ranger School is the night after the last night of Ranger School. If you ever get there."

And all J.W. would learn that cold evening was how to carry the nearly twenty-pound weapon on the run. At the machine gun range, he and his select group of munitions bearers turned their cargo over to a gallery of cadres sergeants, angry NCOs, more than one of whose faces sported long, deep, facial scars. Though these men had shaved only hours before, they had stubbles it would have taken J.W. three days to breed.

One of the machine gun sergeants grinned with nicotine-stained, gold and silver-capped teeth as he placed the weapons with loving care onto tri-pod mounts. Only the tips of the guns protruded beyond horizontal steel pipes welded both above and below the barrels. Those tubes were there to insure the muzzles, and the bullets spewing from them, could not rise above, or drop below, a safe path.

Fricker whispered to J.W. nervously, "Shit, they look like pirates," then raised his hand. "First Sergeant, why do those bottom pipes have a "V" shape in them?"

"Must be the gun's name is Victor."

"All of 'em have the same name?"

"That's enough questions," a gruff voice declared from inside the first cage. "Welcome to the machine gun range, gentlemen. I am Sergeant Poliak. You will crawl the machine gun course flat on your bellies. The rounds will pass eighteen inches above the ground, directly over you.

These here pipes here," he tapped the downward bent, "V-shaped" metal under the muzzles with a swagger stick, "are here for your safety. Do not be concerned. If you have lost the weight you should have, you will not be in danger."

J.W. measured the depth of his various bodily structures with his hands, finding the most prominent area to be his hips and butt, nigh sixteen inches front to back he estimated. Then he spread two inches between his thumb and index finger, added it to the space he had gauged with his hands, and raised his hand. Poliak ignored J.W., but called out to Morelotto, "Your fat ass is mine, son of a big shot."

The other sergeants laughed hysterically, the cue for the Rangers to be sent, one by one, crawling onto the course. A cacophony of sharp explosions and the staccato of dazzling starbursts from the muzzles of six weapons greeted the first of the scrambling cadets, four of whom jumped up and ran back, refusing to go on. J.W. and Fricker, and dozens of other Rangers screamed, "Ceasefire, ceasefire!" over and over, but the blare of the guns drowned their pleas. With a break in the firing, the whole class stood, tensed, fists clenched, while the resigning Rangers ran back willy-nilly toward the starting line. They were all incredulous that the pirate gunners hadn't stopped their mad firing when the Rangers, those that had given notice with their feet, bolted from the course. J.W. assured himself that even Cowsen would not tolerate the brigand gunners' refusal to cease fire in the face of men jumping up in mortal fear, but when he looked over at the first sergeant, Cowsen was shaking his head cheerlessly. When, somehow, the men who had declined to go further in the course made it back to the starting line uninjured, Cowsen met them, his fists clasped. He carped at the first troop, "What's wrong with you, Ranger?"

"There were bullets hitting the ground directly in front of my face. They weren't eighteen inches off the ground, First Sergeant. I'm not going to be murdered here."

"Yeah," the other man added.

Cowsen shook his head again sadly. "That was only the dry run. They were using blanks. The real bullets haven't even started yet. Get back out there, and just for that, the rest of you Rangers, drop and gimme twenty-five and one for the Rangers. And you'll do them again and again until these few fearless Rangers finish their business."

For unclear reasons, the four cadets obeyed, and somehow made it around the course unscathed. With this evidence in mind, though J.W. did not understand it, he slumped onto the ground at the starting line and took his turn. He soon came to freshly created hillocks of red mud, which rendered it impossible to stay within eighteen inches of the ground. "Speed bumps," Poliak laughed. "Slither on your back Rangers, and keep your heads turned to the side—that might save your nose." When Weathersby did so, he noticed Cowsen throwing little stones in front of the Rangers faces.

The real bullets started halfway through the second dry run. The report of the genuine munitions was greatly louder than the blanks, and some of the troops jumped up precious inches in fright, startled by the incessant, rapid boom of the weapons. More shocking was the air-splitting crack as the supersonic rounds flew inches over their ears.

Trembling as his turn neared, J.W. commanded himself to cull the nerves of steel required of a hero in training. "Drive on, Ranger," he hissed to himself. "Start crawling. Move out!" His fingers moved forward, but the rest of him did not. He lay shivering as the thick, blue smoke and the acrid scent of the red phosphorous from the tracer rounds condensed into a reeking soup over his head. When the gas slowly sank toward earth, it enveloped him, the scent of cordite sparking an unfamiliar excitement. The odor stirred the memory of childhood war games, of bunkers fashioned from cardboard refrigerator boxes; of sticks for guns, and of the tossing of firecrackers at the enemy. But mostly, the smell evoked the time, in a mock battle in his pre-teen years, he culled the valor to jump out of his cardboard barricade in the face of withering enemy firecrackers and run toward the invaders from Jerome Avenue. He fought his way along the hot tar of his home street, Morris Avenue, to save his fellows, crawling up to the enemy's cardboard box, into which he hurled a cherry bomb. When the battle was over, J.W. was the Morris Avenue hero for an hour, an episode that still burned in his heart.

Suddenly overwhelmed by the power of the olfactory memory, he was filled with a thrilling surge of bravado. J.W. began the course in a cautious

WILLIAM STUART GOULD, M.D.

slither, but was soon sprinting on his belly, sweating, smiling, cursing easily as he passed the next Ranger on the course, and then the next. As the stream of searing lead cracked overhead, J.W. fought with himself to keep from thrusting a hand into the air to touch it, to see if it was real. Instead, he flipped up a small rock, then a second and a third, until one was pulverized by a .30 caliber round, blasting dust into his eyes and mouth. He saw poorly after that, forced to feel his way along the circular path, which eventually deposited him directly in front of the guns.

Despite his partial blindness, he could make out through the blue clouds of cordite Sergeant Poliak's silhouette firing from behind the blistering white muzzle blast. The barrel of Poliak's weapon glowed red, and J.W. stared, waiting for it to droop from the heat and send the trajectory of the bullets two precious inches lower. As for the sergeant, his eyes were wide, his lips pursed; madly, he banged the barrel of his machine gun against the bottom pipe so hard, sparks skittered out. In his burning zeal to lower the barrel a few more sixteenths of an inch at the tip, he had visibly deepened the "V" in the safety bar.

Several more guns were suddenly manned, and so began a mad minute of detonations that shook the ground. Then, suddenly, without warning, as fast as it had started, the firing ceased. Poliak exited his cage and laughed, "Those of you who deferred on the first opportunity to experience the course are given one last opportunity for redemption."

The troops who agreed to reinstate themselves did the course twice with live fire, and once after that with blanks, "for the Rangers." And when the firing ceased for good, the young men of Second Platoon took steps to the right to plug the empty spaces in formation left by those who had declined the final invitation, then filed past the cages to gather the machine guns for the march back to Harmony Church. Innocent of the ways of modern combat, J.W. grabbed the barrel thrust at him by Poliak. The still-glowing metal melted the fat in J.W.'s palm, and the gun slipped through his grasp, clunking noisily to the ground. It was not until push-up number twelve that the stink of burned flesh began to turn his stomach. He dipped his hand in a puddle of wet clay every few minutes during the march back toward Harmony Church.

In the morning, he presented a silver-dollar-sized blister to the staff sergeant and asked to be taken to sick call or at least have his hand dipped in scotch, his mother's treatment of choice for childhood burns. Hartack patted his own pockets and smirked at J.W., "Sorry, fresh out of Johnny Walker." The sergeant bent forward and unsheathed a hunting knife from his boot so quickly J.W. did not have time to pull his hand away. Hartack lunged forward and unroofed the blister in a fluid stroke. Then, smiling as if satisfied with his surgical prowess, the staff sergeant loped off, leaving the wound oozing a translucent, straw-colored, Knox gelatin-like substance. J.W. calmly removed his ragged tee-shirt, bound his hand, found the trunk of a great oak to sit beneath, and lit a cigarette.

Through the curls of smoke, J.W. thought about the gaps in formation, the ghosts of troops, those riding deuce-and-a-halves back to Main Post. He wondered which of those men would die in Viet Nam first, and if the Rangers would speak those names in whispers over the coming months. Had LaVoy learned anything? Would he again dive into withering fire as he had on his first patrol in Ranger School; would he run in front of his men to martyr himself in the pursuit of so-called honor? Would his name be inscribed on a dusty plaque in a city park somewhere in Iowa or Nevada, and would he, like most tragedies, be forgotten in four days? J.W. would come to wonder by the end of his first week at the funny farm if he would even remember the name LaVoy on Day Eight.

Though he shook his head grieving for the lost, his next thought was that while the washouts would be in Viet Nam within a week, on the other hand, they would also be eating as much as they wished, and reading mail from home, and drinking beer at the officers' club each evening. Despite J.W.'s antipathy for every hour of Ranger School, for every second of the so-called training, he admitted it had become a delaying tactic, and he spent a lot of time trying to determine who was really better off.

* * *

Soon on the march, Cowsen announced, "Rangers, the nucleus has been chosen. You are the elite who will rise to the surface and carry the torch." J.W. felt better, believing those who had been through the final test of courage were certain of graduating, and more importantly, of having paid the price for the life insurance. From that point forward, they would be treated as humanely as the rumors had promised. It was with that sense of relief that he and his fellows slopped through the obstacle course one last time for the day. On the double-time back to Harmony Church after midnight, however, Cowsen prodded them, "Gentlemen, close in those gaps, and do it on the double." It was not long before J.W. heard the rumor that two more Rangers had dropped out at the gallows.

At the barracks, they were released to sleep. It was 2:30 A.M. Most collapsed directly onto the metal springs, using the furled, two-inch-thick army mattresses as pillows. Fricker bitched that the blankets had disappeared and wanted to find the staff sergeant to complain, but Branch shook his head. "You outta' your Gotdamn mind, Ranger? Shut up and go to sleep."

A few troops shaved quickly, donned old fatigues on which the mud had dried, then covered up against the cold using as blankets the muddy, wet uniforms they had just stripped off. They fell asleep as soon as they touched the metal springs, dreaming repeatedly, as did J.W., of machine gun fire and of traipsing through hour after black hour of crunching twigs, snapping twigs on the dry hills, then velvety, soft twigs in the valleys near streams. Fricker jumped up several times lamenting that all he could hear was the crush of deadfall and then the slosh of creeks and rivers. "Every time I put my foot in the water, it freezes right there. Man, I can't move. Pull me out. Pull me out!"

J.W. ignored Fricker's raving and finally dozed off. But he, too, suffered a hallucination, witnessing himself outside his body, the last thread of his fatigue pants rotting away before his eyes. Underwear that chafed the first couple of days had been abandoned, and there was nothing left between his manhood and the seventeen-degree Georgia outback. His business hung out in the breeze like a limp, moth-eaten windsock at an abandoned landing strip. J.W. was exposed to the world, and while it should have bothered him very much, he could not muster the energy, even in his dream, to care.

* * *

Long before the sun crested the eastern sky, J.W. woke fitfully from the fifty-first repeat of the nightmare. He shook his head wildly. He was incredulous and smiled inwardly. "Oh my God! I believed it. It all seemed so real."

Suddenly, he thought it was true, that he was at home at Fort Meade. Krista was asleep at his side. There had been no Ranger School, no Georgia, just a dream sculpted by the orders to commando school that sat on his bed table. His relief was muted, however, by the mental image of those orders, and he waited a moment before opening his eyes, savoring the seconds left in bed, lying next to Krista, nuzzling her warmly, realizing it was to be his last time in bed with her. Nonetheless, he smiled to himself at his foolishness for having suffered so in a nightmare—nothing, not even Ranger School, could be that dreadful.

He allowed his eyes to open slowly. For a moment it was simply mild confusion that rattled his head. The befuddlement, however, deteriorated into mild agitation as he began to wonder if Krista was, in fact, next to him at all. Then he came awake sufficiently to believe she was there, and he clutched at his mildewed mattress, holding her tightly. But his consciousness sharpened, and in short order he began to understand that Krista never smelled bad, no matter what, and that he wasn't holding anyone or anything at all. With that insight, a terror blanketed him as he realized the warmth stroking him was actually his quasi-Ranger buddy Branch, and that they were trudging alongside each other, shoulder to shoulder, crossing a frozen clearing in the winter forest.

At first, J.W. reassured himself this was just a part of the awful fantasy, the sick dream that had taken his night, the last act of the melodrama. He could not conceive, though, of how he could know Branch if he hadn't yet met him. Then it all became clear. "Ah, that's it," he whispered to himself. "I've been sent home from Ranger School. I'm a dropout. And so what? At least I'm warm." But the next sensation was a feeling of dread, for he knew he would be on a plane for Viet Nam in days, assigned to die at the hands of the First Infantry Division as an infantry officer; cheap platoon leader fodder.

He again turned to hold Krista, looking to her for succor, but when his arms spread before him he grasped only at a thin, cold emptiness. Snowflakes burned his face, and he rubbed the melted crystals away with frozen hands; then opened his eyes again, discovering not a bedroom, but the vision of an olive drab mass lying at the base of a tree and a staff sergeant standing above the glob bellowing, "Ranger Morelotto, I'm going to count to three, and if you're not off your fat ass, you're going to carry me for the rest of this mission."

Slowly, J.W.'s knotted consciousness uncoiled. There was no choice but to accept that he wasn't at home with his wife, and that even having returned to the barracks the night before was an illusion. He perused the crop of new bruises and lacerations on his face, arms, and the family jewels, and accepted they were the badge of a twenty-kilometer mission through which he had apparently slept—on his feet. He massaged his eyes for another try at orienting himself, but there was only a patch of dark land in the distance toward which Cowsen and the staff sergeant broke ranks to run. Thank God it was just the bleachers.

Piled in front of Cowsen's lectern, in a two-foot heap, were cans of olive drab C-rations: vitamin-laced Crackers and Cheese; vitamin-laced, soggy, Fruit Cocktail; vitamin-laced, powder-dry, silver-dollar-sized discs of vitamin-laced, bitter, dry dark Chocolate; and a dozen main course selections fabricated of the permutations to which the army had subjected beef and pork. J.W.'s true nightmare from basic training, however, was the Fruit Cake, an unsavory desiccated dessert of barely baked, vitamin-laced, lard-laced flour, poured tightly into tins only slightly larger and harder to open than tuna fish cans. To its credit, Fruit Cake was packed with "fruit", though, on closer inspection that turned out to be sugarized, crystallized bits of orange peel, cherries, stems, and, to his dental officer's delight, an occasional pit as well. It, too, was flavored with the FDA-times-one-hundred minimum daily requirement of vitamin powder, which imparted to it all the appeal of the ABDEC vitamin drops his parents had dripped down his craw as a child. The "cake" moiety of this offering was a greasy, yet, somehow still sub-Saharan dry, light brown, carbohydrate preparation. J.W. considered kneeling in prayer to beg for any alternative to the canned cake.

He stood to Branch's left, eavesdropping on a conversation in which Branch confided to Bearchild that he loved the tins of Ham and Limas so much, he had made many one-sided trades over the years to procure them. I got no regrets," he smiled to Bearchild. "Yeah, they got vitamins, but they remind me of the ham hocks and peas my mama made when I was a kid. That's the best food on earth, my man. Ever tried 'em?" Bearchild shook his head no. "I'm sorry," Branch said sadly. "You really missed out growing up, man."

J.W. was confused. He thought back to the discarded C-Ration cans he had kicked around back in the ravine that first morning, and how all had been licked clean by his Ranger ancestors, all, that is, except the Ham and Limas. He had tried them in the past, and no matter how hungry he was, he had invariably, after the first spoonful, spit out the remains, and then flung the can so hard it nearly reached the next time zone. Nonetheless, as he tucked Branch's admission away, J.W. laughed at the notion that Ham and Limas could ever bring anyone anything but cramps and gas.

The company waited impatiently for the moment Cowsen turned them loose on the pile of Cs, but first there came first another lecture on knot tying, and then a treatise on foot care and the importance of changing socks in the field. When Cowsen finally delivered the command to approach the aggregation of cans, he warned, "You will do it in an orderly fashion, one-by-one. You are soldiers, not savages. Secure only the C-ration closest to you. Do not pick through the pile, Rangers."

Be that as it may, Class 68-B sprinted to the collection en mass, digging voraciously for favorites. Though complete anarchy ruled, Cowsen waited patiently until each man appeared satisfied, then invited the gathering of smiling, flushed cadets to fall in. The plasma of olive drab instantly formed three neat, abbreviated platoons. Cowsen went on, "Gentlemen, turn to the man on your left. Trade your can with him. No, Ranger Branch, not to the man on your right, to the man on your left."

Branch hesitated, staring longingly at the black print on the top of his can, then subconsciously bit his lower lip and handed his tin to J.W., who was shocked at the speed and ease with which he had managed to take control of Branch's soul. J.W. cradled the tin of Franks and Beans he had drawn, excited over his grand fortune. Hot dogs were J.W.'s ambrosia.

Even cold and impure, they were enormously more edible than the crunchy, gritty, overgrown, yellow beans and lard-laced ham of Branch's dreams. J.W. traded cans with a smile and then, licking his lips, walked off. Branch followed, holding the Franks and Beans behind his back. "O.K., man. Two cigarettes and the tube steak for the Ham and Limas. And I'm not goin' any higher."

"Four smokes, and half your chocolate," J.W. countered.

Branch humphed. "Honkey always think he can stick it to the black man, don't he? No deal."

Branch slowly spread his thighs apart and began to put the can of beans in his crotch to warm it, but J.W. grabbed his arm and sputtered, "O.K., two smokes and a little bite of the chocolate. Deal?"

Though Branch scowled, a deal was struck in the frigid dawn of south Georgia, and they sat anxiously awaiting the provision of tiny P-38 can openers to begin the feast. When none were proffered, Fricker went to the first sergeant and asked, "How we supposed to open these?"

Cowsen answered, "Not time to eat yet, Ranger. We'll tell you when. Got a class to do first." He pointed to the bleachers and the company sulkingly took their customary seats.

Chalkboards and props were set in front of the bleachers. On the center table were several Claymore mines, anti-personnel devices the size and shape of a thin bible, but curved like a crescent moon. Inside the weapon were sheets of C-4 plastique, a deadly explosive impregnated with hundreds of miniature steel ball bearings. The mine was designed to explode to the convex, the outer-rounded side of the crescent, and shower an enemy over a wide area with the metal pellets. Imprinted on the outside surface in bas-relief was the alert, THIS SIDE TOWARD ENEMY. That admonition was actually a warning intended to remind commanders that, as opposed to machine guns, Claymores were to be handled only by troops with an IQ of sixty-five or better, and those who were able to read English.

One of the main uses for the Claymore was to protect small groups of soldiers who had been sent out of base camps to act as listening posts, early warning patrols for the main body of soldiers. The listening post troops set the Claymore mines in front of them, then ran an electrical wire back to where they had dug in. When they heard the enemy closing in, the soldiers flipped off the safety on their end of the wire, pushed hard on the crank of the detonator, and the mine went off instantly, propelling supersonic steel balls over a wide arch.

In Viet Nam, however, the entreaty about which side faced in and which out was sadly lost on the young Vietnamese soldiers who had been armed with donated U.S. ordinance. The Saigon troops often mistranslated those instructions, but each time the mistake occurred, no one lived to warn his compatriots that a modicum of English was required to survive on the battlefield when using American munitions. Vietnamese listening posts were usually so far away from the main contingent of soldiers, the bodies of victims who had placed them incorrectly were not discovered until the next morning. For years it was assumed that the mines had been set out correctly, but that enemy Viet Cong sappers had infiltrated stealthily, crawled up to the mines, turned them around, then jumped up and down and made a ruckus. The South Vietnamese soldiers, joyful in their weaponry superiority, confidently flipped the switches and willy-nilly blew themselves to their final reward. At least that is what the South Vietnamese commanders told the families of the dead. It was not for years that a sticker was finally placed on the Claymores written in Vietnamese.

J.W. was a past master with the Claymores, having learned several tricks one could perform with the mines from the combat veteran troops in his first duty station at the 6th Cav in Maryland. Most of the men in the platoon he commanded at the 6th were Viet Nam returnees who had spirited ordinance and materiel home from the Nam: starlight scopes, pistols, even AK-47 enemy assault rifles, shipping them through the mails over many months, piece by piece, to avoid detection. One of J.W.'s problem children at the Cav, Private Morris Schlamowitz, had eschewed the mails and simply carted two Claymores home in his luggage. His plan was to scoop out globs of the C-4 explosive inside the mine for barracks pranks, like heating the boots of the soldiers who teased him mercilessly. He was, however, soon relieved of his booty by the very troops against whom he sought revenge. These men found it an enjoyable pastime to flush fiercely burning lumps of C-4 down the 6th Cav barracks toilets.

They blamed the ensuing deep-thud explosion, and its attendant flood, on Schlamowitz, who was repeatedly punished with barracks arrest and toilet cleaning duties for weeks at a time.

J.W. looked about the area around the bleachers. None of the cadres were present, it seemed, so some of the men had used their bayonets to pry open their C-ration cans and were festively, without screaming reprisal, consuming their first meal in days. Anxious to capitalize on his prior Claymore training, J.W. pilfered one of the mines from the display table and carried it under his fatigue jacket to a corner behind the bleachers. He pried off the back with his bayonet, scooped out a golf ball-sized mass of the putty-like C-4, resnapped the cover into position, and gave the mine to Fricker, warning, "Hey, man, put this sucker back on the table before the cadres miss it. Then I got a surprise for you."

Fricker was nervous and backed away quickly when J.W. touched a match and brought it toward the glob of C-4. "Calm down, man. This shit only explodes when it's detonated with a blasting cap. But it burns like a mother if you touch it with a match. Watch this." Fricker came back cautiously, and he and J.W. heated their meals over the white-glowing plastique until the olive drab paint on the outside of their cans vaporized. J.W. invited a few of the others to heat their meals, and when they were done, the empties were tossed into the ravine. Branch was the last to finish, investing extensive time and care into extracting the final film of "pot liquor" from his Ham and Limas, until he sliced his tongue on the can edge and threw the tin angrily into the gulch.

Fricker shook his head, "Man, that thing was so clean, you could'a put it back on the shelf right now, refill it, hand it to Class 68-8." Branch had wrapped his fatigue jacket around the wound in his mouth and answered only with his eyes.

* * *

The demolitions class that followed dinner introduced the art of blowing bridges with plastique explosive molded into the bottom of champagne bottles, and of setting road mines using detonating switches made from an old flashlight battery, twigs, and the aluminum-covered paper at the top of cigarette packs. But J.W.'s favorite seminar taught the destruction of a car by wrapping plain old adhesive tape around the spoon of a hand grenade and then pulling the pin. "Gentlemen," Sergeant Poliak, the machine gun maven, grinned, "drop that puppy into the gas tank of someone you care for, and after a couple of hours, the gasoline dissolves the tape, the spoon flips off, the grenade is activated, and four point six seconds later, the car explodes in flames. The most beautiful part of it is you, the saboteur, are miles from your deed. Rangers, you can't beat that with a stick!"

They listened excitedly through that discourse, for they had been promised an opportunity to actually blow the mines and try the tricks they had been taught. But before the lab practical, they had to sleep through several more lectures, the last a treatise on toilet protocol in the woods. Cowsen, who had been sitting in the grandstands in rapt attention, emerged from the bleachers and began handing out the various weapons, presenting J.W. with the very Claymore from which he and Fricker had made the withdrawal.

"First Sergeant, I kinda wanted the champagne bottle with the C-4 in it, if that's O.K."

Cowsen smiled, took the Claymore out of J.W.'s left hand and slapped it into J.W.'s right more forcefully, ordering, "Stop flapping your lips or I'll glue them to the outside of this device. Now set the mine out there and get behind the bunker. I'll tell you when to blow it, Ranger."

J.W. positioned the device, struggling to remember which end suffered the deficit of C-4. Balancing it on the tip of his index finger, he surmised it was on the left, and aimed the apparatus far to the right, then ran the wire back to the musty, mossy, Second World War bunker in which he and his compatriots would hide during the blast. As he jumped behind the barricade, his boot accidentally and lightly brushed the crumbling concrete, knocking off a large chunk off the wall, which collapsed on Cowsen's spit-shined boot. The gaff cost him several dozen push-ups during which he occupied his mind by picturing the diseased Claymore blasting backwards and killing him. That thought slowed his calisthenics to a delaying snail's pace until Cowsen kicked his arms out from under him. With J.W. suddenly lying in the prone position in the bunker, Cowsen snapped, "Do it, Ranger!" And J.W. sucked in a deep breath, squeezed his eyes shut, and cranked the switch.

The mine ruptured with a blistering crack, not the thud of the other munitions. It flipped hard right and broke in half. One piece spun into the gulch like a fluttering maple seed, inciting a cheer of appreciation from his compatriots; the other fragment arced over the bunkers, landing on Cowsen's lectern. J.W. had guessed wrong.

"What artistry," Gillette complimented.

Cowsen, however, grunted in disgust, "Your time's a comin', Ranger. The rope's gittin' shorter and shorter."

They sat in class for several more hours, reawakened with pauses for push-ups each time a critical mass of Rangers' heads bobbed. At midnight, they were given a break, but Sergeant Poliak ordered, "No lights. No matches or flashlights."

Fricker raised his hand and asked, "How you supposed to smoke?"

Poliak did not answer. Instead, he began the next lecture explaining, "Rangers, it requires at least twenty minutes of pitch black to hone your night vision. Do not stare directly at what you want see at night. Look at a point twenty degrees to the side of target. That allows the light to fall on the optic nerve, the most sensitive part of the retina."

Gillette raised his hand. "What is it, Ranger?"

"Sergeant, it is the fovea of the eye, not the optic nerve, that is receptive to weak light."

While Gillette was finishing his push-ups, J.W. tried the stratagem of looking to the side, and was amazed at how well it worked. He raised his hand. "Sergeant Poliak, thank you. That's the first useful bit of information I got out of this school."

Sergeant Poliak did not wait for J.W. to finish his push-ups before he communicated via a handheld PRC-25 radio-transmitter with a counterpart several miles deeper in the woods. Poliak ordered into the microphone, "Start display number one."

In the distance, a tiny flicker of yellow appeared; an instant later it became bright white, faded, reappeared, faded again, flashed, then disappeared. "Rangers, was there ample time for a sniper to aim his weapon and fire at least once at the distant light?"

When most nodded, Poliak went on. "What did you see, Rangers?"
After a long pause, Bearchild called out from the balcony, "A match."
"Gentlemen, that is exactly right. Three soldiers lit cigarettes. Anyone heard the expression, 'three on a match is bad luck?'"

The next demonstration was an auditory cue, the clanking of metal far in the distance and the barely perceptible sound of grinding earth. Again, only Bearchild was sufficiently awake to answer. "Tailgate. Deuce-and-a-half off-loading infantry."

"How do you know it's infantry, Ranger?"

Bearchild thought for a moment. "One truck, ten men crunching gravel, one squad. Who else is crazy enough to walk at night."

The class turned toward him to stare, including J.W. who had barely heard the sound of the clanking metal. Bearchild held a sheet of paper rolled into a cone to his ear as if an eighty-year-old listening to his wife.

Poliak droned on until the rain began, as it did late each night, the showers a signal to the cadres to move the company further into the forest away from shelter. They halted at another set of decrepit bleachers, taking seats in the drizzle. Poliak pointed to the northern sky. It glowed in green-blue horizontal streaks, an eerie, monochromatic rainbow. The show went on for miles, fading finally into the blackness.

"The aurora borealis," J.W. called out.

"Nope, not even close." Poliak sighed and shook his head sadly.

"High tension electric lines," proffered Gillette, and Poliak nodded in surprised respect until Gillette added, "ionizing the atmosphere. The field surrounding the flow of electrons of that potential..."

"Shut up, Ranger."

The company was sent marching in a quest for Gillette's lights, perceiving a static hum long before reaching the wires. Coming closer, they could make out droplets of rain roiling about the cables, glowing in foot-diameter shimmers of turquoise, more a disco than a soaking forest night. The waves of static electricity made J.W. very tense at first, then overtly jittery as they came closer to the high tension power lines, leaving him with a chest as tight as if he had guzzled too much of the coffee he had not had in nearly a week.

The company was dismissed to barracks at three A.M. J.W. asked

Branch if they were really indoors, or if it was just another dream. Branch stared at him irritably, but dropped onto his bedsprings and fell asleep before offering up a snotty homily.

J.W. tossed for a long time seeking warmth, thinking about food, and crying over the threat of going on. He wondered if his dad had suffered through the half-decade in the Pacific war. During those endless, sleepless years without a break in combat, had he ever thought of quitting? "Pop, how did you do it? How do you still do it? I'm what, five days into your routine, and I'm sinking fast."

* * *

By six A.M., they had finished the second loop of the obstacle course. While less threatening than the first morning, it was certainly no cleaner. Mess hall life, however, had degenerated. Gillette mumbled, "It's an increasingly inverse, no, no, perverse, relationship between the number of pull-ups and the quality of the chow."

Gillette asked Cowsen, when told the calisthenics requirement had inflated to thirty, "First Sergeant, are a viscous mashed potatoes the entirety of the army's culinary offering?"

Cowsen stared at him for a moment and answered cautiously, "That is correct, Ranger."

To be fair, though, there was the odd packet of sugar to be spirited out of the cadres' section of the mess hall by sufficiently intrepid Rangers. And there were also containers of milk, though the latter lay untouched after Gillette lectured, "It doesn't require a degree in physiology to deduce that it's the protein, the casein from the milk, that curdles in the stomach. That's what causes the stitch in your side during the after-dinner run. I'm not touching any dairy product for the rest of this course."

* * *

J.W. guessed he'd already shed fifteen pounds when he saw himself in the mirror on the sixth morning. At first, he didn't recognize the gaunt, bruised face as he started to shave, but each stroke of his razor matched

112

that of the apparition staring back at him from the mirror, so he guessed he really was looking at himself.

After toiletries and thirty seconds in the mess hall, the company returned to Victory Lake, this time the south shore, to execute the "Slide for Life." There, erected along the shore, was a seventy-five foot high telephone pole capped with a flimsy, three-foot-square wooden platform. A slack, rusting, metal cable fell in a parabola from the terrace to a short telephone pole staked three hundred feet into the lake.

"Rangers, each of you will be issued a pulley welded to a handlebar. These are delicate devices, just like you. Treat them with respect, as you have been treated by the cadres. You will climb to the top of the pole and place the pulley over the cable, grab the handlebars, and on command, you will jump off the platform. You will be able to hang onto the handlebars because you have trained over the past week in the art of hanging on to metal bars and ropes. You will slide down the cable, reaching sixty or seventy miles per hour, and maybe eighty by the time you smash into the far pole. You will notice that surrounding the far pole are a few truck tires. They are old, gentlemen. They might not stop you. Our suggestion to avoid death is to kip, that is, bring your legs up parallel to the water, and drop into the lake before the end of the run. Land on your butt and skim to a stop before the pole. But that's just a suggestion.

"There is a challenge here, Rangers. The sooner you let go, the farther you drop; the longer you hold on, the faster you hit the water and the closer you get to the pole."

Fricker's hand flew up. "First Sergeant Cowsen, what is your opinion?"

"Ask Ranger Gillette. Gentlemen, I draw your attention to the sheet of ice on the surface of Victory Lake."

In the deep recesses of J.W.'s mind there was an image of this very scene, though it wasn't until the cadres disappeared that he understood. But by the time he, along with several of the more or less alert Rangers dove for the bleachers, the explosion had already heaved an ice-laden tidal wave of freezing water onto the company. A round of derisive laughter came from the cadres as they exited their lean-to.

Poliak stationed himself at the base of the pole, handing each Ranger

113

the handlebar device welded to the pulley. He called Morelotto front and center to climb first. "You dodged the bullet last night, Ranger, but your daddy ain't gettin' you outta' this one. Get your fat ass up there."

One of the higher wooden rungs split under Morelotto's mass, and he fell a few feet, but caught himself, reached the platform, and then stood wavering in the wind until the cadre on duty on the platform placed the pulley over the wire for him and kicked him in the ass. Morelotto slid for less than a second, tried to kip, but his legs were far too plump, and in a panic, let go of the handlebars almost immediately. He fell, bellowing for help as he tumbled toward the lake. Staff Sergeant Hartack heatedly rowed out to rescue him, but as the big man tried to climb into the rowboat, he almost capsized it, allowing gallons of the frozen water to roil in and soak Hartack's boots. The staff sergeant was so livid, he refused to allow Morelotto into the boat, and made him hang onto the stern to be towed in like a whale carcass.

Fricker was next up. He asked for hammer and nails to fix the rung Morelotto had broken, but the sergeant just jammed a pulley into his hands.

J.W. was summoned. He complained, "Sergeant Poliak, the weld bead on my pulley is cracked. That's dangerous."

Poliak angrily mumbled, "Of course, Ranger. Safety first." Poliak snatched the pulley from him, handed it to the Ranger behind J.W., then searched his cache of pulleys, chose another, held it up to the light, and presented it to J.W.

Fricker, who had not yet started up, began to examine his own device. He took a breath to speak, but J.W. cut him off, complaining, "Hey, Sergeant Poliak, this one's cracked worse than the first one."

Poliak did not answer. He pointed an index finger at Fricker and then up the pole. When Fricker had ascended four rungs, Poliak pointed at J.W. "Get goin', Ranger. Let's see if you can *slide* forever."

At the broken crossbar on the way up to the platform, Fricker lost hold of his pulley, which clunked onto J.W.'s head and tumbled to the ground. Fricker started down, but, reticent to touch J.W.'s bleeding scalp, couldn't get his legs over J.W.'s head. Contorting to pass J.W., Fricker caught his leg on a nail and ripped his skin, sending both bleeding men into a moaning retreat down the pole.

Poliak yelled up, "Weatherman, Frigger, both of you halt! Weatherman, hand Frigger your pulley. Frigger, take Weatherman's pulley and get your ass up the pole!"

Fricker called down, "Begging your pardon Sergeant, but I want my old one back," and continued toward terra firma.

On the ground, the cadre took J.W.'s handlebar, gave it to the Ranger behind him, handed Fricker one from the box, then gave J.W. back his original bar. When J.W.'s mouth opened, the sergeant growled, "Drive on, Ranger."

J.W. climbed mumbling. On the platform, the sergeant grabbed him by the back of the pants. The gesture reassured J.W. as the two swayed in the winter breeze seventy-five feet above the lake. The sergeant snatched the pulley from J.W., swung it over the metal cable, then ordered, "Stand on the edge, grab the bar. Now fall forward." As J.W.'s hands touched the handlebars, the sergeant let go of his pants and shoved him. The last thing J.W. felt was a kick in the butt.

At first, the fall reminded J.W. of airborne school, the wind hitting his face harder and harder as the seconds flew by, but the snap he had come to cherish in jump school, the moment the life-maintaining canopy burst open and caught the air, was tardy. As he approached sixty miles per hour, still waiting for the canopy to deploy, his body weathervaned into the wind, but backwards, and he kicked and twisted madly, trying to spin forward. Cowsen yelled, "Drop Ranger." But J.W., in his terror, did not hear the command and was still squirming when Poliak joined Cowsen, screaming, "Drop Ranger!" Still, J.W. held fast to his pulley. It was not until Cowsen, Poliak, Fricker, Gillette, the staff sergeant, and Branch shrieked, "DROP RANGER! NOW!!" that his hands opened.

So began the eternity before he came to rest. Touchdown commenced with an impact on the ice-soup water absorbed by his neck and back. He skimmed like a skipping stone, still backwards, over the glazed portion of the lake, eventually tumbling onto the heavier ice where, in contradiction of Newtonian physics, he gathered speed instead of slowing. J.W. turned to look behind him, which really was in front of him if you considered the direction in which he was fluttering. He couldn't help but notice that he was continuing to skid on a trajectory aimed directly at the anchor pole, leading J.W. to believe that was where the trip, and his stay at the Ranger School, would terminate. He grabbed at the first safety tire, but his arm jerked painfully and he had to let go.

At the second tire, instead of using his arms, he jammed his foot into the hole. When the tire came to the end of its fifty-foot hemp tether, J.W.'s back wrenched, sending an electrical charge zinging into his right leg. Nonetheless, the rope held, and propelled him into a sweeping arch, a demonstration of angular acceleration worthy of a high school physics experiment. The rope, taut with J.W.'s momentum, whipped him around the pole back toward the defrosted portion of Victory Lake. He timed the removal of his foot from the tire to allow his body to be slung back into the water, where a weak sidestroke and the waves he had created carried him toward shore.

He dragged himself to the water's edge, yelled to the cadres that he had really hurt his back, crawled onto the sand, and waited for the pain to wither. Hartack glanced over from the rescue boat and lit a cigarette, but noting Branch was next up on the slide, tossed the smoke overboard and rowed out in preparation to where the great bulk of the Rangers had landed.

J.W., still writhing in the frozen sand, rolled onto his side to watch Branch make his drop, but lost him in the sun. In a few seconds, Branch dog paddled to shore and, after nearly tripping over J.W.'s hulk, hauled the moaning Weathersby to the bleachers as though dragging a fallen soldier from the beach at Normandy. Branch dropped him in front of the stands and observed, "Hey man, you're covered with dirt," then climbed to the top bench and sat back to light a cigarette.

The longer he lay on the ground, the tighter J.W.'s back spasmed, and while the others milled about to keep warm, J.W. was relegated to generate heat by shivering harder. When not a single cadre commanded J.W. to get off his lazy butt and join the main contingent of Rangers for the voyage back to Harmony Church, he considered remaining there on the ice-hardened sandy beach for the rest of his life. But as the cold burned more deeply into his chest, he thought better of dying on that spot, and dragged himself to his feet. He ran scrunched forward, limping in concert with the pain radiating into his leg, the peculiar numbness along the outside of his calf scaring him until he confided nervously to Fricker, "Man, I think I had a stroke." Halfway through the endless run back to Harmony Church, however, J.W. realized the lack of feeling in his leg was a godsend; for had he been able to feel the burning pain, he would have collapsed in a ditch along the dirt road, and gladly let the staff sergeant kick him into brothership with Kenyon.

* * *

The lecture that afternoon examined the art of hand-to-hand combat. Sergeant Poliak directed the company to close their eyes and imagine they were on a great, barren desert with nothing but fine sand for a thousand miles.

"Rangers, you come upon a sentry that you must neutralize. You cannot make a sound. You have no weapon but your toilet kit and your hands. What do you do? Well, I'll tell you what you do. You put a bar of soap in a long army wool sock, swing it hard, and pop that son of a bitch in the head with it. Rangers, this is a hell of a bludgeon."

Fricker, who had been nodding off, awakened, suddenly alive with interest in the subject of exotic weaponry. He began to raise his hand, but Branch pulled it down and warned, "No." Fricker, however, sat erectly in the bleachers as Sergeant Poliak produced from a burlap bag a quiver of piano wire cut in two-foot lengths: thick, bass note strands and thin, silvery alto wire.

"Technique number two, Rangers, entails attaching a small stick to each end of a piece of tactically useful piano wire. Shoot, you can just wrap it around your hands if you don't have a stick. Now listen carefully. You sneak up behind the unsuspecting sentry, slip the wire around his neck, cross your hands rapidly and firmly over each other, and, *voilà*, the enemy's head falls off. It's as simple as that."

Fricker looked to his left. Branch was asleep. His hand went up, waving wildly until the instructor recognized his burning question. "Hey Sergeant, where do you get piano wire in the desert?"

"You're not in the desert anymore. Close your eyes and imagine you're in Carnegie Hall, ASSHOLE!" He calmed quickly and added. "Now,

117

please give me twenty-five and one for the Rangers for Ranger Fricker's failure to correctly assess his tactical location." When only Fricker assumed the position, the sergeant screamed, "All of you!"

With the task accomplished, Poliak asked, "Who wants to volunteer to try the next technique on Ranger Frigger?" Those who hadn't fallen back to sleep raised their hands greedily, and J.W., though considering it, thought back to his father's admonition, "Never volunteer."

That stemmed from somewhere in the Pacific, when one of J.W.'s father's sergeants asked if anyone in formation knew about music. The elder Weathersby had raised his hand, as did the man next to him. The two spent the steaming, tropical afternoon struggling with a grand piano, hoisting it to the second-floor of the officers' club.

Since J.W.'s hand was the only one that did not shoot up in petition to harm Fricker, Sergeant Poliak surveyed the audience, ordered Fricker front and center and told J.W. to join him. Fricker faced the class while Staff Sergeant Hartack had J.W. skulk up from behind and throw his forearm across the front of Fricker's neck, then pull it powerfully with his other hand.

Sergeant Hartack, who had been standing quietly on the side of the bleachers sipping hot coffee, snapped "Harder, Ranger," at J.W., and then, "Harder I said!" until Fricker's face took on a peculiar blue cast and his hands and arms vibrated in a violent tremor. Poliak commanded, "That's enough, Ranger," and Fricker was released to hobble like a drunken sailor back to the bleachers and drop noisily onto the planks next to Branch.

Branch, awakened abruptly, grumbled, "Quit movin' around, man. I'm tryin' to pay attention."

Convinced by the terrified expression on Fricker's face, few of the Rangers felt the need to test the maneuver on each other. Nevertheless, Poliak insisted, "Each Ranger, you will perfect the stranglehold on the troop to your front until you get it right."

Though being violently suffocated was terrifying and painful, and left the Rangers quietly anxious and not in the frame of mind for further instruction, it was not to be the end of the lesson. The company still had to polish their skills in the art and science of the scrotal grip, the eye stab, and the cardiac death punch. The troops, however, performed each maneuver with less and less gusto until Hartack screamed, "You Rangers are going to do push-ups until one of you gets hurt from these skills."

J.W.'s mind, addled from the stranglehold Morelotto had put on him, drifted for seconds at a time during the push-ups to the fantasy of a ten-minute nap, and once even, fleetingly, to the co-ed's breasts he'd caressed at Penn State on his first night as a freshman. His thoughts, however, always returned to the image of a peanut butter and jelly sandwich.

* * *

Though it had been a painful, frightening night, the concepts of warfare J.W. thought had gone in one ear and out the other were not lost on him. He had been able to store away in his memory bank one particular tutorial, the stranglehold, a technique he would not extract for some time, not until he found himself the terrified, unwilling guest of the Viet Cong a year later in Viet Nam.

* * *

As the sun crept below the hills west of the bleachers, class was adjourned and the Rangers sailed into formation for the march home. Split into platoons, the men of the three units eagerly stretched in preparation for the trot along the couple of miles of pockmarked roads back home to Harmony Church. J.W. smiled to himself knowingly, for by cleaving the company, the cadres could speed the return of their troops to the mess hall. Surely also on the minds of First Sergeant Cowsen and his lot were the flakes of snow that had begun drift onto the heads of their charges. Not dressed for winter storms, the Rangers would certainly be quickly tramped back to the barracks to don proper attire.

The Rangers moved with an uncommon willingness until Cowsen ordered the three units to disperse separately into the woods. In seconds, a cloak of gray dread tumbled down over the cadets. That shroud turned to abject black when Cowsen tapped a Ranger with the whittled stick. J.W., the instant he witnessed the beknighting, began to quiver, sick with

WILLIAM STUART GOULD, M.D.

revulsion that another mission would intercede before they were allowed back to Harmony Church to eat. Perhaps, he prayed, the mission would simply be to deliver the starving troops to the base camp, but the new student leader was handed a thick manila envelope, and Cowsen ordered several Rangers to the new leader's side to assign duties.

J.W., nearly numb with fear and cold, dropped into a squat in a thicket, out of the deepening snow, to sleep for the precious minutes the new commander squandered orienting himself. After a few seconds, however, J.W. believed he was again dreaming, for the vicious cold was blunted by a thick, rich, humid warmth radiating from the earth. When the column began to move again, he realized he had made a major discovery, that by hunkering within the heavy stands of hickory and oak, one could harvest the forest's entropy, the dark energy of warmth saved from the day's sun that was given back, though sparingly, to its nocturnal creatures.

The company moved so slowly, it was easy for the troops at the rear to fall into trudging sleep, marching on in body only. Though the soldiers generated as much noise as did the winter thunderstorms that rolled in the distance, it wasn't long before Morelotto drifted off from the main body, forcing the platoon to a halt. The new leader grudgingly called Morelotto's buddy aside. "We gotta' find him, or we don't get credit for the mission. Sergeant Cowsen told me that if you whistle like the whip-poor-will, and keep doing it, lost troops'll get the idea and find their way back. He says it works."

Indeed, the power of the Ranger Bird's song revealed itself as Morelotto stumbled back to the fold, dripping from head to toe, saturated with pond scum in various stages of freezing. "Hey, it did work," Morelotto's buddy sneered caustically, and from that night forward, the call of the Ranger Bird became the official forest signal of Class 67-8.

But the budding guerrillas were as yet unschooled in the pitfalls of resorting to remedies so easily applied, particularly ones circulated by the cadres. And soon, as every class before them had eventually discovered, when the real whip-poor-will cried, Ranger dreamers floated off from the main body by reflex, and often remained missing for whole nights and days.

* * *

Hours passed that night with J.W. so deeply comatose, he remembered nothing of the trek except the hunger and cold. He had again been dreaming of home, of warmth, of forgiveness for the transgression that had brought him there, a wickedness he must have perpetrated, but where and when he could no longer remember. Now and again, the dream of being home filled him with cheer, but not enough to ease the throbbing in every muscle and joint on the endless trek across the forlorn hills of the Georgia backwoods.

Sometime after midnight, when the column halted, he accordioned into Bearchild, slipped, and fell backwards onto the frozen earth. His back snapped, and an electric pain flashed again into his legs as it had at Victory Lake. He tried to regain his feet, but could not, and finally collapsed, conceding there was no way to go on, and no way to stop the agonizing numbness in his leg. He rolled about, seeking a position that did not hurt, and in those gyrations, his frigid, nearly numb fingers came to rest on a slick, gelatinous substance coating the ground. J.W.'s hands swept across the nauseating wad. Perhaps he was touching the carcass of an animal planted there by the cadres, another of their ploys to frighten a Ranger into screaming "I quit this shit!"

He brought a bit of the goo to his nose and accepted grudgingly the mass was not edible. In fact, the scent was so rank, J.W.'s hands retracted to his side in violent reflex, fear and disgust peaking along with the pain in his back. He rolled off the creature's remains, sliding on the viscousness of it, then sprang to his feet and groaned in a bloodcurdling whisper, "It's a dead body, man! I think it's human."

Bearchild calmly snapped on his flashlight, shining it at J.W.'s feet. All that glowed in the weak illumination was a flattened carton, a gigantic cardboard box with "REFRIGERATOR" stamped on it, rotting in the winter moisture. J.W. took a deep breath, squatted and touched it again, now smiling bravely, accepting that he had been the victim of a tactile mirage. Though he wondered for an instant how it had found its way to that spot on earth, a different train of thought sparked suddenly in his brain, and he lifted the box out of the snow. Though mildewed pieces broke away, he discovered solid patches toward the center, and he folded those tightly into a packet the size of a grocery bag, one he soon hallucinated was filled with bacon and eggs and bread and cookies and coffee. In the seconds before the platoon moved on, he finalized his decision to take the cardboard, despite its weight, with him, and lashed it to his rucksack, marching on, a man reborn, driven by machinations of Ranger-think that transformed putrefied paper into a trinket of salvation.

As he trudged forward, it became clear to him what had happened as he slipped in the snow: his foot had struck a genie's urn, and the cardboard was actually a bestowal from that spirit, a gift laced with the power to provide warmth and somehow, food. For several hours, this notion deepened, and he drove on through the forest with assurance, relishing the sweet vision of the pleasure he would soon savor.

That moment came at four A.M. when Cowsen's magic stick waved, inaugurating a new leader. The respite allowed J.W. time to unfold the gummy cardboard and hack it into soggy sheets with his bayonet, pieces to line the ground, a foundation, and pieces to serve as a blanket, and finally a slice to function as a roof over his head. Bearchild watched longingly until J.W. handed him a slice. Bearchild nodded subtly.

The two placed their ponchos on the freezing loam, then unfurled a rasher of cardboard on the rubber sheet. They dropped onto the compressed paper pulling the second sheet of cardboard over their bodies. Finally, they flipped the rest of the other half of their ponchos over them, and, wrapped in separate cocoons, slowly drifted off, escaping reality, sealed away from even the slightest invasion of the frigid air. When word filtered back, seven minutes later, to prepare to move out for the next sector of the forest, J.W. awoke dripping with sweat. Yet, despite that disappointment, for a brief moment, the first in many days, all was right with his world: J.W. Weathersby was fat and delicious. Though his fatigues were already icing up from the sweat he'd generated in his hovel, his tattered pants encrusted in a layer of frost as thick as that on a Piper Cub's wings plying the Alaskan peaks, he whispered to Bearchild, "What else could a man want?"

As the march resumed, however, the nirvana J.W. had relished quickly vaporized as the hunger, fatigue, and arctic cold reproclaimed themselves, reminding him that pleasure in this universe was ephemeral at best. Bearchild's fatigues were frozen solid with sweat-ice, but his expression did not change, and he toted his slice of salvation for hours, finally handing it back to J.W. with a mumbled, "Give it to Branch."

The next time their boots stopped shuffling, J.W. presented one cardboard sliver to Branch and the other to Fricker, both of whom dropped to the earth to create nests. But the platoon pushed off immediately for an assault, leaving no time for the two Rangers to crawl into their shelters, nor, sadly to pack them up. In the fog of battle, both Fricker and Branch had thus relinquished their gifts back to the forest, as all grants of nature in Ranger School would eventually be returned. At dawn, when they confessed the loss to J.W., he ran back along the trail, but found not a shred of the genie's benefaction.

J.W. yelled at Fricker, "Where the hell are your priorities, man? It'll be a cold damn day before I give you anything again."

Fricker thought a long time before he responded. "Yeah, well maybe somebody from 68-8'll find 'em. It just goes on, man, the circle of the cosmos."

"Cosmos, my red rosy ass," J.W. raged.

* * *

As the sun's cold rays peaked over the hills, the company converged on Harmony Church for two circuits through the obstacle course. Since pride in appearance had become an extravagance long forgotten, no effort was expended to avoid the mud. Breakfast was fast, but Gillette mused, "Adequate. There's enough calories to cover the energy expenditure. And don't forget, our stomachs have atrophied to the size of walnuts, like the brains of Tyrannosaurus Rex."

"Like the brains of the cadres," Morelotto added more loudly than he had intended, bringing upon the company fifty plus one.

After a few inhalations of mashed potatoes and greasy toast, Fricker left the mess hall complaining, "Man, I feel bloated, like all of a sudden, I'm fat."

Branch shook his head. "Ninety seconds ago, you were bitching about days in the field without food, eighty miles on forced march. Now you're complaining about bein' fat? Ranger, your head is screwed on wrong. Just shut up and enjoy it."

Cowsen, having overheard the conversation, obliged Fricker and announced, "Rangers, Ranger Fricker here's feelin' fat. Rangers are lean and hard, not fat. So we will move at the double-time back to the bleachers where we have a special lecture. This will be your last formal class in Ranger School, Rangers." The cheer that rose was, however, expensive: fifty plus one, and halfway through the run out into the tundra, yet another fifty plus one for the lack of respect Ranger Fricker had conveyed with his counter-anorexic babble.

"Rangers, this instruction is for you. It is priceless. You should be screaming for more."

At the bleachers, First Sergeant Cowsen introduced the speaker, a captain in Class A uniform, tie perfectly wound, low quarter shoes as bright as patent leather. He stood proudly and announced, "This morning, we will discuss the menace of Communism. When we are done, you will understand more about this peril than you ever knew there was to learn."

"Gentlemen, I just stepped off the plane from Viet Nam. You are getting the latest information available, as up to date as President Johnson's. You have been gathered here to become enlightened, to understand why you must learn to hate the Communists. I cannot begin to tell you about the atrocities the Viet Cong have committed against our soldiers, to say nothing of what terror they have unleashed on their own people."

The troops listened in rapt attention, waiting to be told of the honor with which the American soldiers had served, and then the inventory of horrors perpetrated by the Viet Cong. But as the captain spoke of the "insanity of Communism," and "the need to stop these madmen," Branch leaned over to Bearchild and whispered, "Hey man, I know that combat patch on his arm. This dude's a political advisor, some kind'a information officer. Betcha he never left Saigon. Fuckin' armchair commando."

As the captain preached passionately, and his young audience hung on every word, Branch rolled his eyes in boredom and turned back to Bearchild. "That Bronze Star he's got doesn't even have a "V Device" for valor. All that thing is a medal for showing up in Viet Nam and not gettin' caught in a whorehouse. He ain't no hero. Man, that's just the officer's good conduct medal. Everybody gets one. This guy don't know diddly shit 'bout combat."

As Branch's disgust deepened, some of the troops behind him "shushed" the little man, and for a few minutes he was silent, but every time the lecturer bristled with contempt for the Vietnamese Communists, Branch howled in a whisper, "Cut the shit, man."

Exactly one hour after he began, the captain, the skin of his shaven head furrowing in disgust, raised his voice and declared, "These Communists would have you believe their system is better, fairer. I'm here to tell you it isn't. It is a system of slavery, and we all know it!"

The captain nodded to Cowsen, and there was a bit of applause from the cadres who realized those were his final words. The Rangers, however, were silent, waiting patiently for the punch line, for the truth this man had witnessed, for the poison he had seen the people of Viet Nam suffer at the hands of a political system so cruel, every Ranger there was willing to die to crush it. Cowsen picked himself up smartly from his seat in the bleachers and ordered the company into ranks. There was a flourish to his commands, as if now there was a reason to drive on, as if they were the privileged few with whom the secret had been shared.

J.W. fell into formation and shook his head, asking Fricker, "What did that dude say? I must a missed it."

Marching again, Cowsen assured them, "Rangers, things are for real from now on."

* * *

For days on end, they slogged through the frosted mud. J.W. woke occasionally from his walking sleep, hunger always his first thought, food and the never-ending steps weaving incessantly through his consciousness. At dawn each morning, with Sylvester cresting the eastern hills, there remained only the memory of constant movement, and J.W.

sought to record that which he could remember, sneaking off behind a tree to write in a notebook his images of the past night. Staff Sergeant Hartack, however, caught him one early dawn and snatched the book away, burning the paper to heat water for his own coffee.

Alone with his thoughts for days and nights on end, there were hours when all J.W. heard were dark, reverberant voices calling him, screaming at him. The dissonant chant thundered in his ears as he marched and climbed and crawled the thickets and hills; unintelligible voices, the violent timbre of their rumble terrifying him. He cupped his ears against the shrieking, then tried ear plugs of the scraps of olive drab wool he'd torn with his teeth from his socks. Some nights he tried to sing in a violent bravado above them, but still the voices quavered unceasingly.

* * *

There were occasional breaks in the marching, and on one slog after nearly three weeks of training, J.W. and Fricker rested against a tree at four in the morning, smoking, wondering why the company had been allowed to rest. Though the woods were crawling with cadres, J.W. took the opportunity to recount to Fricker the story he had heard the night before. It was a sordid tale passed down from class to class.

"Didn't you hear it? Word is Captain Vock's mother's a nut case," J.W. related with sarcastic laughter. "She's been in like a dozen loony bins, and still she comes around here when she's out on parole to yell at him."

Fricker smiled and asked, "You mean out here in the woods?"

"I don't know if she comes in the woods, man, but she's supposed to have been in Harmony Church. That's what I heard, and then, get this shit, she…" but J.W. stopped, hearing rustling behind him, sensing the presence of cadres. He turned to his rear, and behind the tree, not eight feet away was a gaggle of instructors standing silently in the darkness. J.W. could not be sure, but one of them looked like Vock. J.W. tried to convince himself that he had been so quiet that no one could have heard him, and he asked Fricker, "Man, I was whispering, wasn't I?"

"I don't know. I heard you pretty good. What did his mother do, anyway?"

J.W. was about to continue when First Sergeant Cowsen commanded the company of reposing cadets to their feet and into a crude wooden shelter deep in the Benning woods. Once inside, Sergeant Poliak spoke. "Rangers, prepare for chemical warfare." Without giving them a chance to pull from their rucksacks gasmasks that should have been hanging on their web belts, he shouted, "GAS!" flipping half-a-dozen hissing CS teargas grenades onto the floor. A crystalline vapor spewed belligerently from the little bombs, the musty air of the tiny cabin quickly saturated with the caustic CS. The chemical burned the chafed skin of J.W.'s neck, where he had been commanded to dry-shave for the past days as punishment for having yelled back at the awful voices that had continued to order him to drive on.

With equipment scattering all over the floor of the hut, most Rangers found their gas masks and managed to get them on, in a fashion. The hastily donned protectors leaked, but the screaming of the cadres to come to attention was such that each Ranger had to accept the fit, and they stood in ranks, masks askew, coughing, their eyes dripping.

Several cadres, Captain Vock among them, in well-fitting masks, positioned themselves in front of individual Rangers and ordered, "Mask off," then kept that cadet at attention until a sufficient number of questions had been answered to insure the Ranger had sucked in liters of the acrid teargas. As each Ranger began to list to the side, primed to collapse, the cadre questioning him ordered, "Get out of here, Ranger."

Vock chose J.W. and hovered far longer than any of the cadres had made the others wait. By the time Vock asked his first question, J.W.'s eyes had swollen to a point that he could not focus. He was, however, able to appreciate Vock's furious stare. The full inquisition did not begin until J.W. had nearly exhausted the last deep breath he'd saved before peeling off his mask.

"What school did you go to, Ranger?"

"Penn State, sir!" J.W. screamed, dissipating the last of his precious savings on the absurd question. Trembling, now without any air, he gave in and sucked a tiny wisp of poisoned gas. It burned so fiercely, his throat gagged shut. J.W., however, was not concerned, because it was at that point the other Rangers had been allowed to escape. He leaned weakly to the side as he had seen his compatriots do as they feigned total disintegration and turned to face the door, readying himself for the escape. But Captain Vock was unmoved.

"I never heard of that place, Ranger."

"No sir? Great school, sir," J.W. sputtered, his eyeballs burning as if they had been soaked in Fels Naphtha soap.

"You one of those fraternity boys? Wasting your time drinking and carousing like a dog in heat?"

"Yes, sir. I mean no, sir."

"What the hell are you, Ranger?" he demanded.

"I'm a proud Nittany Lion, sir. N-I-double T, A-N-Y, sir." With the last letter, J.W. dropped to his knees, searching the dirt floor for a pocket of uncontaminated air, but it was worse the lower he went, CS having been designed to sink into crevices and pool into bunkers, not to rise and evaporate.

Vock ordered, "On your feet, dud," but the gas had crippled J.W. and he crawled in circles, the searing flood of tears pouring from his eyes forming little puddles of mud in the dirt. Vock screamed furiously, "Get your sorry ass out of my sight," and J.W. lunged for where he had last remembered the door.

"It's gone. Bastards moved it," he cursed, crawling on his knees. Blind and suffocating, he bashed his arms and head furiously against the rotting planks of a wall until the wood splintered. He crawled through the hole he had beaten in the wall of the gas chamber, exiting into the midnight air, diving head first into a freezing stream. Despite the bath, for hours afterwards, the staff sergeant ordered him to stop coughing, and several days passed before J.W.'s eyes lost their deep crimson cast. "The red badge of courage," Gillette laughed.

* * *

There was still an occasional whiff of tear gas wafting out of the folds of his filthy rucksack when Class 68-B dragged into Harmony Church at the end of the three weeks. They stood in a loose, unchaperoned formation. The student leader looked about for cadres, for guidance, but Harmony Church was apparently devoid of all cadres.

J.W. became bored and left ranks for the barracks latrine to spend the serendipitous interlude on the throne, a peaceful yet exciting prospect, after weeks of squatting over pricker bushes. He had luckily not been privy to the pustular bullae of poison ivy, oak, and sumac that had claimed several of the recently departed, victims of commando crotch.

J.W. entered the latrine with a jaunty step. The same five, backless, shiny, white, porcelain toilets stood exposed like fresh, perfectly spaced, military gravestones at Arlington Cemetery. A body jumped from the middle crapper and bellowed in J.W.'s face, "What the fuck are you doing in here, Ranger? Get your sorry ass out into formation."

"Yes, Sergeant Hartack."

Hartack pulled up his fatigue pants and bristled out into the main barracks, buttoning his fly and screaming for the troops who had followed J.W. into the billets to fall into formation. Vock appeared from inside the command shack and made his way down the ranks, curiously quiet as he turned the corner to inspect Second Squad. J.W. had not seen him since the gas chamber, and there was gossip that Vock had taken emergency leave to have his mother committed to a lunatic asylum in San Francisco.

That didn't surprise J.W., who had finally learned the truth about Vock's mother. He had just finished the story to Fricker a day before, that the real legend was that Vock's mother had, years before, traveled by bus to the Virginia Military Institute where her son, "Verner Vock," as he was known after a stint as a court martial judge, was a tactical officer. She had purportedly planted herself outside his office and bemoaned that he had abandoned her, finally removing her blouse to obtain his attention. According to legend, Vock hated his mother, abhorred the concept of marriage, and despised married Ranger cadets. At least that was what J.W. had heard.

Vock stopped in front of Bearchild and glanced fleetingly at his uniform, checking it up and down. J.W. sensed, though, that he had stared for a second too long at the man's crotch. Vock said nothing. Instead, he shifted his gaze slowly up into Bearchild's black, sparkling eyes, then moved on without a word. J.W. could see him out of the corner of his eye, heading slowly toward him, marking time, toying with his prey. J.W. tried to cover his wedding ring, but Vock looked only into his face. The captain lowered his voice and whispered, "Ranger, when this formation is dismissed, I would like a private word with you. Report to the tac shack."

"Yes, sir!" J.W. answered, relieved at the gentleness of the request, sensing the meeting was to make up for past misunderstandings.

When J.W. sprinted to the operations shed as the formation dissolved, the others ran to the barracks to shower and leave for town. The first three weeks were over. The Benning Phase was at an end, and though the mountains were next, a six-hour pass was first, and J.W. rushed to see Vock to get it over with. He knocked on the black-stained door and was invited in without any bloodletting. Vock sat at the meager desk and ordered calmly, "Sit, Ranger."

Without expression, Vock stood and walked stiffly around the flimsy, olive green, folding table toward J.W. His pasty white skin was marred with a dozen shaving nicks. Though Vock's eyes were as cold blue as a malamute's, J.W. did see in them the sparkle of intelligence that had carried Vock through his years at VMI. J.W. looked away from the expressionless face, but sensed Vock's lips relaxing as if to form a smile. He turned back to face his commanding officer just as Vock's right hand started to rise. J.W. was about to thrust his own hand out to shake Vock's, but before J.W. could lift his arm, Vock slapped him, then grabbed what stubble of hair the butcher barber had left three weeks before. Vock pulled J.W.'s head back, then punched his mouth.

With utter disgust Vock hissed, "You are the sorriest sack of shit I've ever had in this school. You've been a fuck-up your whole life. We know all about you. I will personally ensure that you never graduate from this school. You will never, never, wear a Ranger Tab. Get out of my sight."

J.W.'s mind fogged from the punch and he started to weep, but, true to his New York roots, lunged reflexively toward Vock, screaming, "I'll kill you, mother fucker, with my bare fuckin' hands, and then I'll bite out your mother fuckin' blue eyes!"

Vock jumped back and laughed. "Try it, dud. If I don't snap your neck or blind you for life, you'll spend the next fifty years in a military prison gettin' butt fucked. Now, get the fuck outta here…GET OUT!"

As the warning soaked in, J.W.'s head dropped and he managed to wobble from of the shack toward the barracks, trying to hide his face from the others who were in civvies, heading toward the road that lead to main post. With each step, J.W. accepted more deeply what he had been promised as a child, that he would someday reckon for his crimes. He would not avoid retribution for the embarrassment and shame he had brought upon his family, for all the mistakes, the poor behavior, the trouble at school, in sports, and even in the Boy Scouts. He remembered clearly his mother swearing his perverse behavior would elicit payment in the end, but it was not until that moment that he finally believed her manifesto of fire and brimstone, that he was, in his core, loathsome.

In the past, though punished for shooting his brother in the ear with a BB gun, setting fire to the neighbor's lawn with a cherry bomb, the awful grades throughout his schooling, and then trumpeting a ram's horn out his dormitory window at Penn State and the subsequent riot he fomented, he had, in the past, convinced himself that her words were false, for he had always been able to talk himself out of trouble. He had heard of real sins, far worse than he had ever committed, of Nazi war criminals who were never punished, monsters who lived in peace, forgotten, all over the world. It had convinced him in his heart that with the passage of time, all trouble passed, that nothing lasted forever.

But as he staggered toward the barracks, he began to respect his mother's wisdom, and decided that perhaps Vock had been designated by fate to even the score. As his jaw began to throb, he closed his eyes and applied gentle pressure to the mandible, easing the pain as he walked. That helped until he tripped and fell into a mammoth pothole, causing a blast of lancing pain to course through his head as he lay furiously motionless, waiting for the agony to ebb.

By the time he dragged himself to the barracks, the sun was setting and he forced himself to stand straighter as he watched the last of his compatriots in civvies, cackling as they walked jauntily toward main camp. The last to pass him was Branch, who flew out of the door in black pants, a black Banlon, and pink shoes, sprinting down the gravel road to join the others.

Only Bearchild was in the barracks, in his drawers, supine on his bunk, staring up at the World War I raw-pine rafters that had reddened over the years, pockets of their petrified amber sap collected in droplets along the lower edge. J.W. worried the ancient roof was leaking, then wondered how many GIs had rested on those bunks staring at those same beads of orange, waiting for one to fall. How many were still alive? How many had survived both World Wars and Korea? How many Rangers had already died in Viet Nam? He tried not to think about how many were going to.

"Hey, Bearchild, how come you're not going to town?"

Bearchild grunted, "I've got better things to do with my time than get drunk," then picked up *The Two Vietnams* and started to read. J.W. dropped onto his own bunk and fell asleep.

* * *

In what seemed minutes, J.W.'s rest was disturbed by the alcoholic cursing of his cohorts. According to the comments flying about, each of them had been gouged for their steaks in Columbus, and repulsed by the snotty women, from the waitresses to innocent customers, all of whom had ignored their propositions and shaved heads. Branch walked by J.W.'s rack and stared at his face. "What the hell happened to you?"

"Nuthin," J.W. grunted without moving his jaw.

Branch's once gleaming pink patent leather shoes were now clay-red with dust swirls, and his black Banlon a deep henna. J.W. rolled on his side, facing away from the returning troops, wrapped again in the peculiar distant depression he had known for so many years, fearful everyone knew of his trouble and had spent the evening laughing at him. He was sure they would continue their diatribe against him once they saw proof of his shame. The troops, however, ignored J.W. Weathersby and dove onto their racks without taking off their civvies or brushing their teeth. Nothing had changed, even after four hours in civilization.

Lights dimmed, and J.W. fell into his usual nightmare. It went on for what he thought was a full night, but in fact, seconds after he'd fallen off, he was jolted awake by the door banging open and the lights flashing on. Cowsen stood in the middle of the floor. In a curiously quiet, human tone, he spoke. "Get your butts out of the sack and pack duffels for the trip to Dahlonega."

Fricker asked, "Please, First Sergeant, could we wait till morning?"

Cowsen grunted, "Ranger, by sunrise you'll be halfway there."

* * *

Cowsen directed the Rangers of Second Platoon to pack all their cold weather gear for the Mountain Phase. That struck Morelotto as a bit odd, and he grumbled indelicately after the first sergeant had apparently left to pester Third Platoon, "Man, that's the same shit I been lugging around for the past three weeks, and I still froze my ass off. He's full of shit."

Cowsen, however, was still standing beside the barracks door and Fricker tried to signal Morelotto, but Morelotto, head buried in his foot locker, was flinging mud-red-stained, olive drab clothing over his shoulder, cursing louder as he contemplated the coming misery. Fricker finally yelled, "Hey, Sergeant Cowsen, are the mountains colder than Harmony Church?"

Cowsen stepped back inside. "Rangers, it's only gonna get worse, and you ain't gonna have me to protect your sorry behinds. Look here," he added, stepping up to Fricker, "Dahlonega's hundreds of miles north. There's lots a snow in them mountains. They's thousands a feet higher than where y'all's standing. Y'all been to college. Y'all tell me if it's gonna be colder."

Only minutes passed before Second Platoon fell into formation, dragging stuffed duffel bags. Morelotto was still carping, "Why do I have to hump this useless crap?"

At the mess hall, the staff sergeant urged happily, "Morelotto, why don't you shorten the trip to the embarkation point by sprinting. You carry Fricker's stuff too. He's got a bad shoulder."

The company was sent waddling under fifty-pound duffel bags. During the run, J.W.'s helmet popped off and bounced forward, tripping Morelotto, who was so incensed, he dropped both his bags, grabbed

J.W.'s helmet, and flung it by its canvas chinstrap, ripping the strap rivet out of the metal. J.W. retrieved the helmet angrily, pushed the strap back into place, then bit the grommet with his teeth to reseat it, but only succeeded in chipping an incisor.

At the truck point, they stood shivering and waiting, eighty men, the victorious final half, hopping up and down against the bitter cold. Fricker suggested that perhaps they were going to walk to Dahlonega. That brought scoffing laughter and Gillette's comment, "A little comic relief is good for morale."

An hour passed, and there were neither trucks nor laughter when Fricker warned again through chattering teeth, "Accept it. Anything's possible. They're gonna make us walk."

When Fricker spotted a cadre his hand rose, but Branch and Bearchild grabbed his arms and held them by his side. J.W. agreed, silently, that it was better to contemplate the agony of a walk to Dahlonega than actually take the first step. Though he had learned in Psych 101 at Penn State that the human mind was incapable of distinguishing between reality and a belief deeply held, after three weeks of Ranger School, J.W. knew that was wrong. He would have waited there for one month thinking about walking, fretting about walking, rather than take the first step.

Another half-an-hour passed, and four empty cattle trucks bumped and bucked up to what was left of Class 68-B. Morelotto grunted, "Those are the same Goddamn trucks that'a been parked behind the mess hall since yesterday afternoon."

Fricker, when he was sure Branch and Bearchild were not looking, raised his hand and asked, "First Sergeant, why couldn't we have waited in the trucks. At least we could a been warm for a while."

After the fifty-first push-up, the warmed troops gratefully flung their gear aboard and crawled onto the vehicles, pawing for seats on the wooden sideboards. Bearchild, last over the tailgate, saw there were insufficient places, and settled onto the truck bed, arranging several of the duffel bags into a queen-sized mattress. He took *Idylls of the King* from his pocket and, by the beam of his flashlight, escaped into the pages. The rest of the Rangers drew closer to each other to capture what heat they could.

The suspension of the cattle trucks had been engineered, Gillette suggested, by the same designers who forged the M-60 A-1 E-1 tank, a design that insured the comfort of field artillery pieces, not troops. The ride into the Smokys, to the Ranger Mountain Training Camp in Dahlonega, northern Georgia, degenerated into a drill of seeking to remain upright, Rangers burning more calories in the trucks than at the pull-up bar. With every chuckhole, Branch's compact body launched a foot or so above the unpadded benches, snapping back onto the wooden seat when the miracle of gravity reasserted itself. J.W. levitated only a few inches, but his jaw rattled in agony with each landing.

After a few miles, Bearchild propped his dying flashlight against the tailgate and read happily until they struck a Manhattan-class pothole. Though his torch flipped out the back and J.W. yelled for the driver to pull over, Bearchild had already rolled on his side, covered himself with his cold rubber poncho and gone to sleep. The truck rattled on into the night.

* * *

When J.W. awoke, the air had become colder and harsher. He watched the stars from the open-bed truck, laughing that the canvas tops were stowed only when it was bitterly cold, raining, or snowing, and tonight, in the frigid winter, the tarps were somewhere, but certainly not over the passengers. After several hours, the trucks began a gentle climb, and as the driver downshifted, the Rangers crowded closer for warmth, as with each lower gear, the temperature slid another few degrees south. In the bare light from the truck behind, the troops on the opposite bench appeared huddled masses, and J.W. whispered to Gillette, "They look like my grandmother and her family when they sailed from Poland to Ellis Island in 1911."

"The only difference," Gillette mumbled, "is that your grandma was cleaner, better fed, and less diseased."

The grade soon became so steep the trucks were forced to use low-low to keep the load moving up toward Dahlonega. In that gear, every twitch of the driver's foot jammed J.W. against the wooden side rails. Part of Bearchild's mattress flew over the tailgate, but he caught the duffel bag and dragged it back aboard. J.W. tried to light a smoke, but his hand was numb, and he could not make his fingers pinch the match to strike it.

Approaching Dahlonega, as the sun rose above Rocky Mount, J.W. was awakened by a lurch to the left and then a thud. The deuce-and-a half jolted to a halt, and J.W. thought he heard the engine growl, though when it snarled again, he realized it was an animal noise, not the demise of the diesel. There followed a vicious gurgling, a weaker growl, and then the silence of the mountain dawn. J.W. peeked out. A black, amorphous mass lay like a big, dark, furry rock under the left front wheel of the cattle truck. As J.W. watched in astonishment, a tortured head popped out of the glob, twitched a time or two, then fell back to the macadam.

The truck rolled in reverse a few feet, allowing the massive lump to unfold. Fricker leaned over the rails and gasped. "It's a bear!" The thud reminded J.W. of the time his mother had run over the neighbor's collie, though this thump was far more sonorous, as Laddie Boy hadn't weighed four hundred pounds.

The staff sergeant ordered several Rangers, including J.W., to dismount and surround the creature until the Fish and Game man arrived. While they waited, J.W. played the accident over in his mind, trying to understand why the bear had been struck on the left shoulder of the highway when the truck had been traveling in the right lane.

He asked the driver, "Hey, Private, tell me how you managed to hit that thing. It was in the left lane and we were on the right. How could that have happened?"

The driver glared at J.W. and snapped, "Ranger, mind your own fuckin' business."

When the Fish and Game warden arrived, J.W. and his cohorts were ordered to move the carcass off the highway. Though the creature was motionless, J.W. remembered from third grade at P.S. 86 in the Bronx that wounded animals could not be trusted, so he just pretended to help. He watched bugs flit in and out of the bear's moth-eaten coat, and observed the deceased's yellow teeth, thick with tartar, just like his. The odor was hideous, and J.W. gagged, then turned away, facing into the mountains, beholding for the first time the magnificence of the Smokys.

A light mist hung above the craggy hills, summits capped with a delicate snow so white they glowed in the bare dawn like mid-day. The highest peak, Yona Mountain, was distantly monumental, and seemed the most remote point on earth, a challenge not even Rangers would be forced to conquer.

C

Mountain Guerillɑ

Once parked at the Ranger mountain camp twelve miles north and east of the town of Dahlonega, they were marched to primitive little wooden shelters, just huts really, but sturdily built of rough-hewn lumber that had weathered decades in the rain forest. The floors were fashioned of thick pine, worn smooth by Ranger forefathers, black dirt from their boots ground into the wide gaps between the boards. It had hardened over the years, chinking out the piercing cold.

J.W. inspected the facilities of the squad bay with a critical eye. The bedsprings were coated with a flaking layer of dull rust, and the constant moisture had also fostered a cottony patina of mildew on the paper-thin mattresses. Yet the scent of his single-celled companions blended with the surroundings, and J.W. allowed it was really quite beautiful in its own way. Though drizzle fell outside, and they would soon be cold and wet, the permanence of the camp and the ruggedness of J.W.'s new home made him feel safe and, somehow, comfortable.

He went to the back door to examine the latrine. It was, however, not as inviting as the sleeping quarters. Judging by the odor drifting from the cobweb-covered pits, they had also been there for the millennia. A

of pungent, off-white, lime sat officiously by each
that his predecessors had been worked so hard, they
rgy to scoop into the pits a few ounces of the lime that
eetened Dahlonega's ambiance.

ed to his bunk, quietly enjoying the few moments of peace,
the rain beat on the shake roof. He savored the dryness and
of his bed, and pulled from his duffel bag a book Bearchild had
m, *The Agony and the Ecstasy*. He couldn't wait to cover himself with
poncho and read, but after just a few sentences, he was asleep.

* * *

It was only moments before his dreams ended to the boot steps of a
mountain phase cadre, another staff sergeant, who marched into the hut
and shrieked, "Fall in." J.W., standing in front of his rack, looked out
through despairing eyes into a lean, stoic, perfect, Nordic face that
ordered, "Pack for the first real tactical problem of Ranger School."

After the blond hair and blue eyes, J.W. noticed the nametag,
GEHRING, embroidered in thick black over the sergeant's breast
pocket. Weathersby, still in his near coma from three weeks of no sleep,
fantasized that it was 1943, and that he was a POW in Germany, but when
he stared harder at the name, he realized the spelling was different, and
anyway, when J.W. looked down at his own red-stained, shredded
fatigues, he wondered what Hitler's second in command could want with
the likes of J.W. anyway. The sergeant paced in circles for a few seconds,
evaluating the new crop of subjects with a discerning eye, then passed
through the door without comment. The Rangers were back on their beds
in a flash, though Gehring turned and shouted, as if he was delivering the
most significant part of his message, "And no Goddamn candy, or any of
that kind of crap in the Mountain Phase. Got it?"

With that, Gehring left for the next hut, and a minute later J.W. heard
from that squad's billets, "And no Goddamn candy, or any of that kind of
crap in the Mountain Phase. Got it?"

In formation minutes later, Class 68-B dropped their fatigue pants and
touched their toes, languishing in that position while the first student

platoon leader was called aside and instructed in the art and science of the butt check for contraband. He was left with the message, "Blessed is the Ranger who discovers a candy bar hidden deep within his comrade. There's extra points for each Almond Joy you extract, Ranger."

There was, in fact, no way to sneak candy past the despots of Dahlonega. Claiming to be past masters in the detection and punishment of smugglers, they bragged, "Rangers, we've seen and crushed every trick you can think up to beat the system. Don't even try. It's gonna cost you if you do."

True to their braggadocio, one by one the cadres discovered hiding places J.W. would never have imagined. Fricker, who had come up with the worthy ploy of hiding a Hershey Bar in the hatband of his fatigue cap, was discovered when a cadre came up to him from behind and smacked him upside the head. The chocolate, which had melted, dripped out, mixing with the grease in his hat. The one survivor of the cadres' scrutiny was Bearchild, who held a Mars Bar in each hand during the purge.

Sergeant Poliak, chairman of the machine gun pirates, one of the few carryovers from Harmony Church, ordered Fricker, "First you eat the paper, and then the foil wrapper, and when you're done with that, suck on the hat brim until the last smudge of brown is gone. Ranger, when you're done, the only thing left on that hat is going to be the grease stain that was issued with it."

Poliak was curiously silent, making no threats of push-ups, or even of curtailed meals as Fricker made smooching sounds on the cap, slowly slurping the body oil enhanced chocolate into his mouth. Poliak's only words as he spluttered to the front of formation were, "Least you had the balls to try, Ranger."

* * *

The company marched along worn, meandering paths, past a frozen brook, coming finally to the Quonset huts of the mountaineering school. Waiting inside on the floor for the class in dress right dress heaps were piles of sinister hardware, chunks of black and silver metal, and robin's egg blue, yellow, and burgundy coils of nylon climbing rope. Bearchild eyed the collection and nodded knowingly. So did Gillette.

Sergeant Gehring took the podium. "Rangers, welcome to the mountains. When you depart, you will have the basic skills of mountaineering. That's for sure. But more important than the hundreds of miles in front of you, Rangers, is that you will have learned what it means to never stop, no matter the mountain in front of your eyes. This isn't the Benning Phase anymore, you know. This isn't good food and a warm bed. This is the training you were sent to Ranger School to master. This is the real thing. This is where you will learn to 'drive on.'"

With those two simple, single-syllable words, J.W.'s heart popped by reflex out of his chest into his throat, and then into his mouth. Then his bowels tightened, and though there was nothing inside of him to lose, he searched with his eyes desperately for a latrine.

"Gentlemen, anything is possible if you just do it. You already know that, I hope. It's the 'just doing it' that we're going to teach you here. We tolerate no excuses. Every time you hear the words 'drive on', you will do just that. DO IT! You will drive on and on and on…"

J.W. stood and looked harder for the john, the chances of averting a terrible accident slimming with each "on" Gehring howled.

Gehring snapped, "Sit down Ranger. You got ants in your pants or somethin'? Gentlemen," he went on, "you see before you the tools of your trade." He held up each item and called out in a crisp, military voice, "Swiss seat—D-ring—belt—rope—piton—crampon," though all J.W. could think about was finding a crouton.

Sergeant Gehring pointed to J.W. "Hey, Gunga Din, you like bein' on your feet so much, get your ass over here." He stared at J.W.'s nametag. "Hey, you're the one who said he could climb forever, right?"

"No, that was 'swim,'" Fricker volunteered from within the olive drab mass of dozing troops.

"Who cares, Ranger?" Gehring handed J.W. a fifty-foot, thirty-pound, nylon climbing rope. "Put this around your neck and stand in the corner, Ranger. You wait there until instructed to move. And you Ranger," he called to Fricker, "you hump the bag of rugs for your trouble."

J.W. walked to the ordered position, commenting through gritted teeth under his breath, "Yellow rope. Clashes with my red-mud-stained fatigues." Branch nodded in solemn agreement, and J.W. felt, for the first time, the support of a friend, one who might even take a turn carrying the line.

But Branch quickly added, "Yeah, but it matches your personality."

The rope's sharp nylon bristles dug through the raw skin on J.W.'s neck until blood seeped into the collar of his fatigue jacket. He did not want to sacrifice the other side of his neck and risk the possibility the rope would touch his swollen jaw, but when the blood dried and stuck to the material, he had no choice. The rope did chafe his cheek, which soon swelled. Gehring looked over and queried, "You got the measles or somethin', Ranger?"

Gillette mused, "I think you mean the mumps, Sergeant." Regardless about which virus Staff Sergeant Gehring had commented, the first of many thousands of push-ups to be executed in the mountains were performed that very minute.

With their arms heavy with the blood of exercise, the company, loaded as if Sherpa bearers headed for an Everest base camp, marched to a set of rotting bleachers where they were enlightened for six minutes on the strict technique they would employ to climb mountains, then ordered to bleachers at the base of a thirty-foot high wall of black-painted wooden planks that had been erected at the bottom of a hill. A Ranger tab in orange was emblazoned across the face of the mass of lumber. At the top of the structure sat a wooden ledge upon which a squad of instructors awaited their prey.

After brief introductory remarks about how to climb a mountain and then rappel down, The company of Rangers climbed the embankment to the top of the wooden wall where Gehring snorted to J.W., "Ranger, take the eight-foot piece of rope we issued you, and tie a Swiss seat around your waist and your butt." Without waiting for a retort, he went on. "Don't know how, huh? Watch me closely. I'm only gonna show you one time."

Though J.W. had tried to follow the sergeant's deft fingers weaving and looping as he tied a demonstration mountain climbing seat around his waist and butt, J.W.'s fatigue bubbled to the surface during the lecture, and in the five seconds his eye lids drooped, he missed the essence of the lesson. Gehring then handed the slip of rope back to J.W. and snapped, "Tie it!"

When J.W. failed to get the Swiss seat right on his third try, Gehring tied it for him, mumbling angrily the whole time, cautious not to allow his fingers touch anywhere along the anterior or posterior of J.W.'s pelvis, and at the same time insuring the audience of cadres and students noticed his prudence. Then he snapped two D-rings onto the climbing harness, placed a loop of nylon rope through the rings, ordered J.W. to stand at the edge of the platform and prepare for his first rappel of the Mountain Phase."

"I don't know how to repel, Sergeant." J.W. moaned nervously.

"We just gave you a full class! What is wrong with you? One more time. Turn with your butt toward the valley, feet halfway over the ledge, and lower yourself backwards until suspended parallel to the ground. Then walk down a few steps. When you get that right, if you do, push off a little and try to move a little faster. And when you get to the ground, yell, 'off repel!' Now is that so hard? And open your eyes, Ranger. Your supposed to be looking for the enemy."

J.W. slowly lowered himself backwards, praying as the rope became increasingly taut that the thin nylon cord would support him. He was surprised seconds later when it actually did.

"You're doing good. Keep going until you're parallel to the ground, Ranger," Gehring called down with enthusiasm, but J.W. asked himself how he was supposed to know where he was with his eyes so tightly locked. Gehring, seeing his student faltering, and understanding that mere screams were not going to get J.W. Weathersby to open his eyes, bent forward and snapped the rope so hard, J.W.'s feet slipped upward until he found himself head down. That opened his eyes. He hung there a while until Gehring ordered him to play out bits of rope, which he did miserly, but wriggle as he might trying to right himself, he remained head down. When Gehring yelled a final time, threatening to cut the rope with a knife if he didn't twist and get moving, J.W. released the line a bit too quickly, and was soon sliding toward the earth still in a head-down posture. He gathered speed, the air whistling by his ears as in airborne school, though it soon dawned upon him that this wasn't a two thousand foot aircraft drop, just thirty feet, which would go by very quickly at that velocity.

He opened his eyes wider, the pupils expanding to the size of saucers as he saw the ground moving up toward him at warp speed. With his chest clenched in abject fear, he exerted a death grip on the rope, drawing himself to a stop at the last second with a force that would have halted an armored personnel carrier. With the sudden stop, he rotated into the foot down position just twenty-four inches from the ground. When he let go of the rope the final time, he fell with a peaceful thud to the frozen earth. Having survived the not-so-rocky landing, he jumped up, screamed "off repel," unhooked, ran to the bleachers, crawled into a little ball, and smoked three cigarettes.

* * *

When the entire class had been afforded the opportunity to maim themselves, they were marched to a set of bleachers at the base of a sheer rock wall. J.W. remained awake for this class. After an exposition on the use of hand holds, Gehring commanded, "Ranger Weathersby, use your hands and the toes of your boots to scale it. Stop at the forty-foot level."

Fricker's hand shot up. "Sergeant. Excuse me. I don't understand. I didn't know you had to use your hands to climb a mountain. I always thought the next higher guy pulled you up by a rope or something."

Branch bent forward into the push-up position as Gehring sighed, "You must be Ranger Fricker? And, what the hell are you doing down there, Ranger?" he snapped at Branch. "Lookin' for money? Well, while you're down there, knock out ten and one."

"Yes, Sergeant," Fricker answered proudly.

"You wanna do 'em, too?"

"No Sergeant. I'm was just saying that I'm Ranger Fricker."

"O.K., everyone on your feet. You, too, money man," Gehring ordered. "Start climbing. I want all of you to stop on that wide granite ledge up there."

The ledge about which Gehring crowed was three feet, if that, of a rock out-cropping, just wide enough for the platoon to squat in a huddled formation for Climbing 101 B, the Golden Rule of Climbing. "Rangers, you must maintain three points of contact at all times. I don't know if they taught you that at Benning, but I'm teaching it to you now."

J.W. turned to Branch and whispered, "What was his name, Smith or Jones? I wonder if he made it?" Branch shrugged.

Gehring roared that the class was to climb higher, to the next level, where they were reminded about the beauty of the three points of contact. Though J.W. sought to pay rapt attention, his concentration was broken when hair-raising screams bombarded from the crest of the sheer granite wall. Three cadres stood on the precipice, another hundred feet higher, howling at the Rangers, jumping about like protective mountain gorillas until Sergeant Gehring pumped his hand in the air, a signal launching the triad into a headlong, headfirst dive off the peak. Though attached to ropes, the cables remained slack, for the flying Dutchmen sprinted down the face of the cliff, bodies parallel to the ground, approaching mother earth seemingly faster than gravity could pull them. For the entire plunge they whooped, "Drive On! Drive On! Drive On! Drive On! Drive On!" until, within a few meters of crashing into the Rangers, the climbers violently threw their brake hands behind them and touched down softly next to the embryonic commandos. J.W. did not see them stop. He was busy searching for a latrine.

Gehring smiled. "Rangers, if there had been a dozen fresh eggs on this ledge, those Green Beret's wouldn't have crushed them. And because of that, there is no way to crack eggs here in the Mountain Phase. You won't be getting good fresh food like you did in Harmony Church. You won't need it. You are obviously carrying around enough fat to survive in these mountains for several months if you get lost or miss a ledge."

Fricker raised a tremulous hand. "What happens if you do you miss?"

"Ranger," Gehring nodded in respect to the reasonable question, "if you miss the ledge, your rappel will terminate in the woods, fifteen hundred feet below. But no one ever falls in Ranger school."

Several of the troops turned gingerly to peep into the valley, though J.W. remained in a squat, his stare fixed on the rock wall two inches in front of his eyes, a sight far less unsettling than peering into the distant basin.

Fricker whispered, "What the hell is this fascination these guys have with altitude? They must be frustrated pilots or something."

J.W. shook his head nervously and hunkered more tenaciously against the rock wall, his eyes tightly shut, thankful for the feel of the cold granite against his body and the small measure of sanity it afforded.

Gehring turned toward J.W., noticed the sublime expression, and ordered, "Ranger step forward, away from the wall." The decree sent J.W. into a deeper hunker, and despite the freezing rivulets of spring water that soaked into his fatigue jacket, J.W. leaned with more pressure against the rust-tinted, sandy layers of the granite. Pushing Rangers out of his way, the sergeant strode along the narrow out cropping until he stood directly over J.W.

"Ranger," he growled, "gimme fifty, NOW, and with your Goddamn head over the side of this mountain!"

J.W. considered the usual option of standing and screaming, "I quit this shit," but realized the sergeant had said "fifty," and not "fifty and one," and that made J.W. happy. Yet rather than standing and walking to the edge like a man, he crawled on all fours, willing to endure the laughter and ridicule of his peers as a small price for the relative security of proximity to the mother earth. At the precipice, shame overwhelmed him, and he took a deep breath, shooting a glance into the valley. It was indeed beautiful, awesomely so, he nodded to himself grudgingly, and he sought to maintain that admiration of the terrestrial sphere alive in his heart.

If he fell, he laughed to himself, the last thing he would ever hear in this life would be a dozen cadres angrily ordering him to stop falling and finish his punishment like a Ranger. The notion that the cadres could yell all they wished and he didn't have to obey gave him great succor, until Branch waddled over to J.W. and whispered, "It was Smith."

J.W. then considered the maelstrom in which he would find himself if he was killed. He pictured gaggles of livid cadres, taking breaks, drinking coffee from thermoses, then going back, cursing him, busting the nearly impenetrable web of leathery-leafed rhododendron to reclaim his body.

He wondered, though, if they would be so inclined to search, or perhaps simply wait until a lost Ranger in 1974, 1981, or 2006 discovered his remains.

J.W. commenced the push-ups with strict attention to form, counting aloud in military cadence, holding his back perfectly straight, dropping his chest to touch the sharp granite ledge, then employing an explosive return to the arms-extended position. His professionalism would impress Gehring, and the sergeant would soon grow bored and turn away. As long as J.W. could be heard, he was safe, and when, predictably, Gehring looked away to pester his other serfs, J.W. switched reflexively into the surrogate Ranger push-up sequence; ones characterized with arms straight, but head bobbing in rhythm with the count. Each dip was accompanied by a more anguished, exhausted groan, as if flexing and extending the neck was as agonizing as a true push-up.

"Twenty-threeeeee, twenty-fourrrrrr," J.W. surprised and impressed himself with the authentic strain in his voice. He kept his head rotated to the right, watching the sergeant, ready to execute the genuine article if Gehring glanced back. A Ranger never gave up the element of deception. At push-up number thirty, however, the air changed. It wasn't Gehring; he was still badgering the others to use their fingers to climb the rock wall. No, it was something else, something suddenly incongruous in J.W.'s world, a disquieting static not unlike that surrounding the glowing high-tension wires at Harmony Church.

He shivered as he considered his options. If he looked to his left, toward the hostile vibration, he would lose sight of the sergeant, a lapse a crafty Ranger could not consider. On the other hand, something was making him uncomfortable. He dipped his head, allowing only his eyes to strain left. They did not have to go very far before the image of widely-bloused fatigue pants tucked into spit shined jump boots burned painfully into the fundi of his wide eyes. The crease of the bayonet-like, starched fatigues moved another inch closer to his face, and in the reflection of the mirror of the toes of spit shined combat boots, J.W. recognized a truncated face that culled memories of terror and recurring nightmares—his own.

Though he hadn't needed to look further, he could not prevent his eyes from rising beyond the Brassoed belt buckle to the interloper's nametag. J.W.'s next push up was executed in perfect military fashion, devoid of pain behavior, in crisp shouted cadence, as if only the first of many to come. He sensed both fear and security all at once, then a heavy, gripping sensation in his chest, and finally a peculiar comfort which took him back to the Bronx and the day he finally confessed to stealing candy from Mr. Boyle's candy store when he was eight. In an instant, however, the feelings of serenity disintegrated into a terrible black cloud, and J. W was overwhelmed by a sense of impending doom. Whatever the pain of the push-ups, it was going to be less than he was to experience when they were over.

"You just ain't gonna change, is you, sorry Ranger?"

"No, Sergeant Cowsen. I mean yes, Sergeant Cowsen, sir."

"Don't call me sir!"

J.W. finished the thirty-fifth push-up, then paused in the arm-extended position, resting for the final assault. He took the time to contemplate his state of affairs, wondering if this was finally the big one, if Cowsen had reached the end of his rope.

"What you waitin' on, Ranger?" Cowsen asked shaking his head in disgust. "Instead of bragging about doing push-ups forever, looks like y'all gonna actually be doin' 'em forever. I just hope I live long enough to see that. Ranger Gillette, how long do I have to live to live forever?"

Gillette began, "First Sergeant, that's a function of your blood pressure, smoking, your genetic profi…"

"Shut up, Ranger."

J.W. stared into the valley a quarter of a mile below, then laughed weakly. "First Sergeant, forever is how long I'm gonna be in this man's army. And it wasn't push-ups, it was swim."

"You gonna do that, too. Now hush your mouth and quit that threatening me that you gonna be in the army forever, and just finish your exercises."

J.W. asked himself if he had the strength to dip down for one more push-up, if he had the will to go on that far. He sneered at how easy that was, one more, and how only the weak found the next minute a challenge. No, he shook his head abruptly, it wasn't the next push-up that worried him—the next one didn't hurt; the next one was no more a challenge than the last one; nor, he acknowledged, was the one after that, nor even the next ten. It wasn't even the endlessness of the push-ups, for certainly, they would come to an end. No, it was the endlessness of the dark mist that clouded his future, the promise that, after the push-ups, after Viet Nam, after graduate school, no matter what came to him, there would always be punishment, for that had been his life, and he knew it would never end. Always another fifty, and the only hope in his future was that it would be fifty and not fifty and one.

J.W. dipped for number thirty-six, considering, as he paused to rest, the political science of Ranger School, a true democracy in which every man had a choice, voting on his own future fifty-thousand times a day, with his arms and feet, with each step. His success, as that of his compatriots, boiled down to putting one foot in front of the other. Though the pain in J.W.'s arms continued to build, he remembered his football coach's adage when J.W complained of a sprained finger, "Weathersby, your hands are two feet from your heart. His heart, Weathersby, that's where a man lives."

J.W. dipped for one more.

* * *

There was sufficient time between push-ups forty-five and forty-nine for J.W. to consider the conversation he had overheard between Cowsen and a younger sergeant toward the end of the Harmony Church phase. The junior NCO was bitching about the military, vowing to finish his enlistment and quit for good. He chided Cowsen, "You're a good man, First Sergeant. Why the hell do you keep re-uppin'? You could do better than being a lifer."

Cowsen pondered for a moment, then answered quietly. "Young sergeant, when I enlisted twenty-six years ago, I spoke three words of English: 'Whoa, gee, and haw.' That's 'cause the only thing I talked to on that farm in Alabama was the family mule. My father was a cripple from an accident, and my mother died givin' birth to my baby sister.

"When I was ten, Sergeant, *I* was the sharecropper. *I* was the one raisin' the chickens and the hogs, and that stubborn-ass mule. Now I'm married. And the army gave me an education, and my kid is goin' to the Naval Academy. A Negro sergeant's son is at Annapolis! Gonna be a naval officer, Sergeant!" Cowsen had paused as his eyes clouded over. Then he continued. "Don't you tell me this is work. Shoooot, this ain't nothin' but a vacation. I got dreams Sergeant. And they is a comin' round. You do what y'all will. There ain't no better life for me than the army."

J.W. finished his fiftieth push-up, added one on his own for the Rangers, and was then awarded ten more plus one for disobeying the order to do only fifty. As he crawled back into his squat against the frigid granite, his eyes sought Cowsen, not to greet him, not to smile broadly in his face and prove he wasn't yet dead, but just to make sure he knew where Cowsen lurked. Yet the first sergeant had disappeared into the vapor, and Gehring, sensing that he was again the alpha male, barked, "Ranger Weathersby, I know you're not going to walk, so you might as well crawl front and center."

With J.W. on all fours in front of the sergeant's boots, Gehring hissed and turned to the rest of the company. "All of you, up to the top, if you don't mind. And you too," he spat at the cowering mass at his feet on the thin shelf of granite.

* * *

At the summit of the precipice lounged the same tribe of Ranger instructors who had been on belay at the wooden repelling wall. Here, however, they were scraping their boot heels, as if preparing to anchor the very earth, against rock outcroppings so trivial, it was hard to see them. Half the Rangers were assigned to sit beside these men and learn how to grind their boots into the granite and then wrap a loop of rope around their bodies. The other half of the Ranger company was ordered to drop worn swatches of throw rugs onto the sharp granite edge of the mountain. "Gentlemen," Gehring explained, "these rugs are here to protect the nylon rope from wearing through on the edge of the rock, breaking, and falling with its attached Ranger into rhododendron thickets several miles below."

J.W. thought that a caring gesture, for the cadres to be so concerned about the security of the troops, until one of the Rangers accidentally dropped a D ring off the cliff. As it tumbled halfway into the valley, Gehring became demented with rage, cursing and carrying on about the paperwork he faced to explain the loss of United States Government property.

Second Platoon, every one of them, save the man who had dropped the D ring, was dispatched into the forest to reclaim the fallen rigging, an exercise that took until dark, and another two hours to climb through the vegetation back up the mountain. Second Platoon missed dinner, but it was better, J.W. agreed, than having to be the first specimen to rappel.

When the platoon returned to the ledge, Morelotto packed his gear, expecting to be marched to the cabins, as it had been rumored they would be given full meals and four hours of sleep in the Mountain Phase, just enough to keep the Rangers alert. Troops falling off cliffs was poor publicity for the school. Maybe one or two per class could die or be maimed quietly, but a dozen would be noticed.

Gehring, however, marched up to Morelotto and shook his head in disbelief, muttering, "Are you out of your mind? Retie your Swiss seat and hook up to the rope. Now you're going to be the first Ranger of Second Platoon on rappel."

J.W. smiled and crept into the shadows toward the rear of the line, forgetting just how adept the human eye is at detecting movement at night. Gehring stopped in his tracks and smiled broadly. "Hey, Climb Forever, front and center. I changed my mind. Hook up. You're first, again. And you, Packing-Up-Your-Pack-Too-Soon-Man, assume the position and remain there until Climb Forever here completes his mission.

Gehring turned to J.W., who had tied his Swiss seat around himself backwards again, and apparently caring not a fig for the imbecile who was incapable of wrapping a rope around his crotch, gritted his teeth and ordered, "Now turn with your butt to the valley, feet halfway over the ledge, like at the Repelling Wall. Then lower yourself backwards until suspended parallel to the ground. And you better yell, 'Off repel' when you get to that ledge, if you ever get there."

J.W. spoke to Gehring with a tremulous voice. "I still don't know how to tell when you're on the ledge."

Gehring answered by reassuring J.W., "When your feet stop, that's when. Quit your worrying, Ranger. Your safety is our first concern. I told you, no one ever falls in Ranger School. Now get your butt in gear before I give you an assist."

Slowly, shiveringly, J.W. lowered himself into the rappel position, hanging backwards, parallel to a patch of earth a quarter of a mile below. Again his mind churned with calculations of terminal velocity and impact kinetic energy.

"MOVE YOUR ASS, RANGER!"

J.W. stared straight ahead at the ledge. By the flicker of the lanterns, he could see that pieces of the sergeant's precious buffer carpet had worn through, and that short prickers of nylon bristled off his rope where it rubbed heavily against the sharp, protruding granite wall. As he placed his weight on the rope, a few new filaments popped from the rope before his eyes. J.W. started down the sheer cliff backwards. Though he could see nothing, by reflex, he gnashed his eyes shut and refused to respond to Gehring, who spit, "Spring out, Ranger. Give the rope slack, Goddamnit." To encourage obedience, Gehring dropped a rock over the side of the cliff, hitting J.W. in the chest.

This time, J.W. pushed off, then immediately and brutally threw his brake hand behind his back. To his stupefaction, he came to rest, alive, unscathed, eight feet down the rock wall, though upside down, yet again. Though his jaw spasmed with the sudden stop, that pain passed in seconds as another reminder boulder landed on the soles of his boots and rolled along his legs, chest, and then wedged into the space between his upside down head and upside down helmet. He scrambled to right himself, fussed futilely with the helmet trying to dislodge the rock which was firmly entrenched and which was followed by another stone memento, and then gave a braver push with his legs and coasted ten feet with his second effort. He hung there valuing his prowess until Gehring yelled, "You're gumming up the works, Ranger. Move down, NOW!"

J.W. shoved off, spinning fifteen feet of rope through his gloves, though it dawned on him only after he was plunging that, unlike Ranger

School, the rope was not forever; it had an end, one that would arrive long before the valley floor. J.W. realized he had no idea what fifty feet on repel felt like, or if there was a signal near the end of the rope, like tissues in a box that turned pink when they were almost gone, to let him know he was "x" feet from oblivion. So he braked to a violent stop and called up to Gehring, "Sergeant, I don't know where fifty feet is."

Gehring answered, "Think back to the cargo net on the obstacle course at Benning. Pretend you're looking up to the top of the bleachers. Now stop talking and move your ass."

Yet another rock bounced off him, and he sprang off the face of the mountain, sailing downward until he became frantic with the whistling of air through his helmet and grabbed the flying nylon with his brake hand, but once again, as on the wooden repelling wall, forgot to wrap the rope around his back. The nylon burned through his thick leather climbing gloves, and J.W. soon smelled steam from the boiling of his sweat-soaked woolen glove liners. Then he sensed the pain of a throbbing hand, the skin of his palm still as new and soft as a baby's behind, barely healed from the burns at the machinegun range. By sheer brute fear, he managed to hang onto the rope and stop himself several feet short of a meager ledge. With J.W. still bobbing on the rope like a yo-yo, slipping back into the upside down configuration, Sergeant Gehring shined a flashlight on him, tossed a few prune-sized rocks at J.W.'s head, then clucked, "Why the fuck are you still on the rope? This is not a vacation, Ranger."

J.W. forced his body into the vertical position and let a span of rope tear through the D-ring. He fell eight feet onto the ledge, hitting so hard the weak grommet on his chinstrap, the one ripped free back at Harmony Church, gave way, and the steel helmet ripped off, falling, striking ledge after ledge, clanking repeatedly as it tumbled into the valley.

Disoriented, J.W. screamed, "Off rappel," then crawled along the narrow outcropping of rock toward the shadow of trees to the side of the ledge barely silhouetted in the darkness. He sat waiting for the others, for something to happen, but nothing did. When several bodies sailed past his ledge, it dawned upon him that he had finished his rappel on the wrong shelf. He groped back along the cold granite for the rope, but the cigarette he had lit to calm himself had blunted his night vision, and after a futile search, he began the climb back up through a wooded portion of the mountain toward the company. He struggled for an hour, fighting the thick, sharp underbrush and tangled deadfall, thankful his lips were kept moist by the blood that trickled into his mouth from the laceration on his ear where the roughly woven canvas chin strap of his helmet and the boulder had ripped a gash.

The sustenance bequeathed by the few hours of sleep at the end of the Benning Phase was, by this point, long squandered, and his climb back to the company became an endless burn in his thighs, and a broadening atrophy of his consciousness. Though he realized somewhere along the trek that he had misplaced his Swiss seat and the D-rings on the climb, he kept going up, and up and up, only dimly aware of his life or his destination, an ant struggling to carry the carcass of a maggot to the family nest. His mind had descended into decay, tormented with a problem far larger than itself, but without awareness of what or why. As he went on, one unquestioning foot after the other, he was unsure sure if he was the ant or the maggot.

* * *

Following the flickering lanterns, he rose above the final ledge and came upon Gehring smoking with his cadres buddies. "What in the hell you doing up here? You were supposed to rendezvous down there with the rest of the company. Get your head out of your ass, Ranger. Wait a minute. No dumb ass Ranger's gonna fool me. You never rappelled down in the first place, did you? Answer me, Ranger."

Gehring walked furiously in circles for a time, talking to himself, more apoplectic with each turn. "And where's your Swiss seat, and your D rings? You destroy government property to avoid your mission, Ranger? I want twenty-six and one for being out of uniform, no helmet, and then you're gonna do twenty and one more for lying that you already went down."

After serving his sentence, trying to remember if the twenty and one came before the next twenty-six, he borrowed a Swiss seat from Sergeant Gehring, and was sent again onto rappel. He spun rope through his gloves, aiming toward the light of cigarettes directly below and the sound of jabbering Rangers. He managed to come to rest with a jolt on a ledge just above the rest of his cohorts, and had to jump six feet to join the main body, losing another D-ring in the process. But he spat on the rock wall angrily, ignored the compounding of his troubles with the loss of a regiment's worth of military equipment, and joined the others on the double-time back to the cabins.

It was deathly silent at base camp, except for snoring from the huts. First and Third Platoons had marched back hours before and were already asleep with bellies full. Fricker asked if he could go to the mess hall and check the oven to see if the mess sergeant had left something for them, but Gehring snapped, "Oh, we got a wise ass here. Get into your rack or I'll have you cleaning the ovens."

Second Platoon stumbled to their cabins empty-handed and dropped onto bunks. J.W. dove for his bed and pulled a cold, rubber poncho over himself when Sergeant Gehring came in and marched directly to J.W.'s bedside. "You got some paperwork to do for losing your helmet and that other stuff. You don't figure I'm gonna do it for ya, do ya? Get your butt over to headquarters and sign for that material."

Reams of thin paper forms were waiting for him, each demanding descriptions of how the loss had occurred, why he had been so negligent, what steps he had taken to retrieve the lost materiel, and how the blunder could be avoided in the future. At the bottom was a note that his pay would be docked for the missing items. J.W. signed the last form and stood to leave, but Gehring called out, "CO wants to see you."

At the command shack, a light-skinned black man sat behind the olive drab field desk. Rather than the acidic expression worn by the majority of the officers he had met at Ranger school, this man's eyes were thoughtful, as if he was about to speak and then listen, and even consider a reply. J.W. relaxed for a millisecond, but when he noticed the water-stained portrait of LBJ hanging behind the officer's desk, he was jolted back into just where he was, and what was about to transpire. He tensed his arms at his side to deflect the first blow, but the man spoke quietly.

"Ranger, I'm Major Powell, the Mountain Phase commanding officer.

I got a call from Captain Vock. He says you took a swing at him, and I want to…"

J.W.'s jaw began to drop in disbelief, but it hurt too much to open. He muttered angrily through clenched teeth, "Excuse me, sir? That's bullshit. Excuse my language, sir…"

"What's bullshit?"

"The whole thing, sir. The truth is he told me to have a seat, then he slapped me in my face, then cold-cocked me in my mouth." J.W. pointed to his swollen, black and blue jaw. "This isn't from a bramble bush, sir."

"Are you calling him a liar, Ranger?"

"Yes, sir, I guess I am."

"Are you saying you never hit him back?"

"That is correct, sir. Never lifted a hand. Never threatened. Nothing."

"Huh. This is a problem, Ranger. If what you say is true, that kind of behavior went out with General Patton. You are not to conclude that the army will tolerate that type of behavior. You have a responsibility to act to maintain the standards of the officer corps."

"I know, sir. But it's a captain's word against a Ranger's. No contest. And it'll cost me my career. You don't rat on people. Anyway, I'm still alive, sir."

"Weathersby, tell you what's going to happen here. I'm a fair man. I won't make you report this, and you may have a point about making a statement with no witnesses. Look, you're starting in the mountains with a clean slate. What happens between Vock and you when you get back to Harmony Church is your business. You can make a decision then about how far you want to pursue the matter. I'm not involved. Just don't screw up here, or I'll have your ass on his doorstep before the sun comes up. Am I understood?"

"Yes, sir."

Powell scrunched up his face in a questioning expression. "You sound like you're from the City."

"Yes, sir. The Bronx."

"Huh. Me too." Powell tossed him a banana. "I heard you got back too late to eat."

* * *

There were no pull-up bars at the mess hall in Dahlonega, but as at Benning, the shack was an ancient, peeling, wooden affair, and the line for breakfast at zero-four-hundred hours snaked around the outside through deep, black puddles of freezing mud. There was more to eat in the mountains: sausages, SOS, shit-on-a-shingle—the army's piece de resistance—creamed chipped beef on toast, and pancakes, but mountain fare burned off more quickly with the thousands of feet of hills the company was to struggle up each day. Anyway, all J.W. could do was suck milk through a straw. Even the scrambled eggs were too hard for his jaw.

* * *

The initial tactical problem commenced that morning after the perfunctory visual rectal exams, with the platoons marching from the cabins into the deep, verdant hills of the Smokys. The first miles were magical, the magnificence of the winter mountains carrying them along on a wave of beauty. Even the fifty-pound packs seemed light, just part of the adventure into the clefts and warps of America's heart. For a few moments, J.W. believed they might have been the first people in history to lay eyes on some of the primitive rock formations. Then, after being trucked and marched along dirt roads for several hours, Class 68-B came to the base of its first mountain.

Gehring addressed the company. "Gentlemen, this is Yona Mountain. The foothills are behind you. So are your childhoods. You are to run to the top of that first ridge." He pointed to a crest so far up the mountain, it might have been the summit. "This is," he went on, "the first authentic tactical mission of Ranger School. We're keeping score for real. The clock starts now.

Morelotto laughed snidely, "Yeah, I've heard that shit before."

J.W. nodded in agreement, unwilling to move his mandible in comment. The troops left the road, faced the mountain, and began the climb. The slope was gradual at first, and J.W. laughed aloud, "This is a cake walk, man. Maybe all that shit at Benning was worth the agony."

Morelotto bobbed his head in agreement. But the grade quickly steepened to forty degrees, leaving J.W.'s thighs and calves burning as if wrapped in glowing sheets of furnaced metal, and his mouth opened, despite the pain, as it spewed strings of expletives. Soon his legs throbbed so, he could not feel his jaw.

A quarter of a mile up the mountain, under heavily laden packs, several troops dropped to the ground and hollered in pain; some cried that they couldn't suffer through another second of the torment. But Gehring stood over them and laughed. Then gangs of cadres, seeing Gehring, rushed to the site to mass over single prostrate Rangers like flies over latrines, buzzing "Drive on, Ranger."

The screamed commands failed, and in short order, a mélange of harsh voices of spent Rangers blended into a dissident chorus that resounded louder and more fiercely with each troop who joined in. The crescendo of anger reached a critical mass, and the beaten fell to the earth as if crushed by an epidemic, one by one, in rapid order. Several of the infected managed to crawl to their feet, but instead of going on, ran down the hill as if machine guns had been turned on them.

J.W. was drawn toward the pack of discontented, magnetized by an overwhelming urge to turn and run with them. No one could withstand that level of misery, and he saw clearly that the cadres had gone too far, that the school would soon collapse. If every Ranger quit, there could be no recrimination. Another man surrendered and ran down the hill, the virulence of the organism growing with each troop who left the mountain. J.W. lost a bit more control.

The theory in which he had begun to believe, that just one more step wasn't painful, deserted him. J.W. had nothing left, and hunkered down against a grand, old-growth cedar to gather the strength to join those leaving the school. His final failure had come about so quickly, in so few minutes, without any time to really think about it, and that surprised him. Soon his head bowed, accepting that his training was over.

As echoes of the malcontents faded, J.W. sat steeped in the silence and loneliness of the forest. While the rough, gnarled bark of the ancient cedar pinched his back, it was less painful than considering the climb either up or down, and he remained slouched, motionless for many minutes. With that respite, he marshaled sufficient vigor to open his eyes, looking up into the rocky palisades of northern Georgia, and then down into the distant glens. He stared at the remnants of forest camps built by hoards of Civilian Conservation Corps workers, the legendary CCC, during the great depression. Though he again began to hear the voices that had plagued him at Harmony Church, this time he realized that they were of the ghosts of those souls, the dispossessed who had sweat months and years of their lives away in those mountains, working only for food. He thought of them laboring in the woods, never knowing what was to come next in their lives, when it would all be over, if ever, and when they would again hold their children and regain control of their futures. He wondered how many of those men were aware they would soon die, not of starvation, but as victims of the wars in Asia or Europe to which they would be someday shipped as GI fodder.

With a bit of his strength slowly seeping back, J.W. smiled wryly. While it was hard to imagine the war into which he was soon to be delivered, in the deep hollows of his mind J.W. Weathersby knew his future was devoid of concern about sufficient food or clothing. Only for the next hours would he starve, for soon he, too, would run down the mountain screaming in terror that he quit that shit. He would soon sleep with his wife and eat at his little table in the apartment, and then, a few days later, he would sleep and eat, this time on the airliner to Viet Nam. It gave him the strength to come to his feet and face downhill.

As he took the first painful step down the mountainside, his eyes caught the CCC camp again, and a voice yelled out to him, "You really *are* a maggot, aren't you? You are a just a parasite existing on our leavings and our sweat. We saved these forests and this country for you, and then we marched off and died in the nightmare of Hitler's dreams. We didn't cry when our legs hurt. You live off the fat of the land we built."

J.W. called aloud, "Living off the fat of the land? I have to go and fight in Viet Nam. I'm doing my part. So leave me alone, Goddamnit." The violence of his screaming further drained him, and he dropped back to lean against the old cedar, his eyes again closing, lest he see his own tears.

The rejoining shriek did not surprise him. "Get off your fat ass, Ranger. Take the next Goddamn step and drive on, dick head." This time the voice was familiar, though the words were even louder than those that had tortured him in the thick timber of the forests surrounding Harmony Church. J.W. looked about for the source of torment, but the closest man was a hundred meters off, still trudging upward toward the first ridge.

Farther up the mountain, he spied Branch and Bearchild near the head of the column, and he closed his eyes again when they stopped and turned back to watch. When they saw J.W. turn and take a step down the mountain, Branch shook his head sadly and resumed his climb. J.W. sensed Branch's disgust, and started to descend in earnest. With each step down, however, the screaming in his ears pounded harder. "Drive On! Drive On! Drive On!"

He cupped his ears, but the screaming wouldn't stop, and he turned in a circle, his eyes probing the forest again. Still there was nothing near him except a tree five steps uphill. He ran to it, the barrel of his rifle in his hand, the gun held over his head to attack the cadre tormenting him as he had the stag in Harmony Church. But the other side of the tree was barren and silent. J.W. ran around the tree, convinced that, with sufficient anger and speed, he would catch up with the bastard taunting him. But no matter how fast he chased his tail, he saw no flicker of the source of the voices.

"Screw 'em," he cried, and started back down, yet the moment his first step landed, the voices began anew, and J.W.'s brain burned with more agitation than he had ever suffered. He ran back up the hill to the next tree, his rifle held higher, ready to shatter whomever had taken it upon himself to torture J.W. But there was no one at that tree either, nor at the next one, nor the one after that. There were suddenly no more voices, and he found himself, legs burning with a fire the likes of which he had never felt, crying again, but this time, unlike when he had submitted to Vock, he was now driven by a force he could not find to hate or fear.

Even in his torment, he realized that only when he was climbing were the voices quieted, and he turned up again, running uncontrollably, the pain now thrown to the background by the depth of his rage. He loped toward the ridge, passing Branch and Bearchild, searching every tree as he climbed, reaching the crest ahead of the platoon. There he stopped and turned back, looking down into the Smokys, and at the Ranger camp thousands of feet below. He sucked air violently into his burning lungs, aware of neither his legs nor his jaw, conscious only of the absence of the voices.

* * *

At the hot meal that night, J.W. dribbled soup broth behind his bottom lip and worked it back slowly along his cheek, letting gravity draw it into his throat. Some of the watery split pea soup trickled into his wind pipe, and the paroxysm of coughing that followed tortured his jaw; it was worse than if he had chewed. Branch's eyes opened wide, and he asked, "You O.K., man? You need some help?"

J.W. shook his head and tried the mashed potatoes, but couldn't open his mouth wide enough to suck in the lumps. As J.W. attempted to puree the soggy carrots, time ran out.

* * *

At the barracks, a lane grader, a former graduate of the Ranger School, briefed them on the next day's mission. J.W. noticed the man's West Point ring, and asked, "Lieutenant, do you happen to know Harold Steel? He's a good friend of mine."

"Yes, I do, Ranger. Just got married a couple of weeks ago. I think it was at West…"

The lieutenant stopped in mid-sentence to acknowledge Fricker's raised and waving hand. "Lieutenant, sir. How long we gonna be in the field before we get back here? Can we take food? How long we allowed to sleep in the mountains?"

The lieutenant answered quietly, "Ranger, make an effort to enjoy tonight. And, before you go to sleep, each of you make a field parachute by tying a piece of this nylon onto each of the four corners of your poncho, then tie the other ends to this hook I'm going to give you. Questions?"

Morelotto grumbled, "I don't think that parachute's going to hold me. I want a big one like in jump school."

There was laughter until the lieutenant urged, "Gentlemen, the sooner you get the job done, the faster you get some rack time. When you're finished, put the ponchos in the wooden box by the mess hall." He gave them half a salute, said, "Good night," and was gone.

* * *

They slept for four hours that night. By 6:00 A.M., the six-minute breakfast was a distant memory as the company moved into the hills for a five-day problem, carrying their own C-rations, one box each. Fricker griped, "That's only enough for half a meal. We're supposed to get double rations in the mountains, six boxes a day." His hand flew up.

Gehring grunted, "You ever heard of air-resupply, Ranger?"

Fricker shook his head, "Yeah, how do we know we can trust you?"

Gehring sighed, "Ranger Fricker, have we lied to you yet?"

Those who thought about Gehring's answer nodded in agreement that the cadres had not broken a single promise. J.W. relaxed, embracing the belief that Gehring had just made an inviolable covenant that they would receive sufficient food and sleep in the Mountain Phase. While it was a comforting thought, late that afternoon when the company stopped to chow down, most of the Rangers ate only a small portion of their Cs, painfully saving in their rucksacks what they had the discipline not to devour.

J.W. cut little circles out of the cardboard boxes in which the Cs were packed, creating near-satisfactory covers for the opened cans he stashed in the bottom of his rucksack to make them harder to access. But the operative word here was "near-satisfactory," for the food dribbled out when he tripped into pits or rolled down hills, and the Rangers who had copied his idea were transformed into walking menus, wearing the near-frozen stains of Ham and Limas, Pork and Beans, and Beef Stew on their packs.

By early the second day even the most disciplined Ranger's pantry was bare, the lot consumed during the sleepless night on the move. When the column stopped for eight-minute map checks, instead of eating food that hadn't been provided, they slept. At noon the next day, Fricker challenged Gehring. "I thought you promised we were going to eat."

"I only asked if you had ever heard of air-resupply. Have you, Ranger?"

"Yes."

"Well, good, then you're the first to be picked for the air-resupply patrol."

Gehring then strolled through the forest selecting snoozing Rangers, creating a detachment to trek deeper into the mountains and rendezvous with "partisans" who would supply the next week's rations. J.W., having been discovered napping under an enchanting blanket of dripping wet deadfall and moss, found himself chosen for that detail, and as Gehring threw a rock at the last sleeping man's head, a helicopter thundered into a landing zone fifty feet from the company. Without so much as a fare thee well, Gehring and the other cadres boarded; Poliak disembarked along with several fresh lane graders.

J.W. assumed the food was aboard the chopper, and he walked happily toward it until Poliak yelled over the rotor noise, "Where the hell you goin', Ranger? You're on the list for the air-resupply. Get movin'."

By dusk, after crossing several mountains, the patrol established contact with the "friendlies," but it had been a difficult day, one punctuated by several ambushes, for the next Ranger leader, Morelotto, had opted to travel along open trails and roads instead of busting brush. During one of the attacks, J.W. captured an enemy soldier, a black troop with one brown eye and one green eye. Assuming it was the responsibility of a captor to abuse POWs, J.W. tied the man's hands behind him and began an interrogation.

The perfunctory name, rank, and serial number inquiries out of the way, J.W. turned to more psychologically devastating demands. "Prisoner, what does your driver's license say in that little box marked eye color?"

The prisoner spat back, "What the fuck do you think it says?"

Sergeant Poliak, finishing a hoagie, bits of the salami, ham, and mayonnaise still on his lips and chin, heard the exchange and entered the clearing. Patiently he said, "O.K., good job, Ranger, now let him go."

J.W., sensing a peculiar lack of brutality in Poliak's voice, answered,

"No way, Sergeant. I got me a prize. I think I'll make him carry my rucksack and pistol belt."

"He ain't a slave, mullet head. I said untie him." When J.W. hesitated, Poliak threatened, "If you don't let him go, you will physically carry him on *your* Goddamn back along with your rucksack and his rucksack for the rest of the Mountain Phase. You got that, you dumb fuck? You're not here to capture prizes, Ranger. You are here to suffer."

* * *

The patrol, less its prized POW, reached the partisans at 2100 hours in the pitch darkness and rain, but in lieu of food, an apology was proffered from their leader, a GI dressed in idiotic civilian clothing resembling a French farmer. "Rangers, we are truly sorry that our cache of rations has been raided by the enemy. Everything, every burger, every bag of crisp French fries smothered in ketchup, every single onion ring, every bottle of beer, all of it, it's gone. Your orders have been amended by the supreme command." The partisan pointed to a clearing on a wilted map of the Smokys. "You are to proceed to this point to set up for an airborne drop of supplies."

J.W. and his mates dropped dejectedly to the earth, unable to stop cursing the cadres, but there was little time to weep as they were soon on a forced march for several miles to a clearing near the peak of a snowy cliff. A familiar voice called from the forest, challenging them for a password. J.W. shined his flashlight into the woods, lighting the face of the man with the multi-colored eyes. The soldier threatened, "You get that light outta my face, or I'll kick your butt from here to Thursday."

Then an older, even more familiar voice, interceded. "I'll take care of it, Sergeant."

J.W. glanced to his side. A few rays of moonlight reflected off the mountain onto the spit shined boots of the man from whom the words had come. Even in darkness, the timbre of the voice made J.W.'s shrunken stomach smaller. A fern touched him on the shoulder, and the voice snickered, "Guess what, Ranger?"

"Yes, Sergeant Cowsen, but Sergeant, I just don't understand what's going on here. I thought you were only at the Benning Phase. What happened?"

"Ranger, you don't sound happy to see me. I'm hurt. Now you're the man for this problem, the next problem too, and maybe the one after that if you don't hush up."

J.W. coordinated a march over forested hills to the drop zone over nearly impassable trails through the rhododendrons, shaping a night free of ambush, but not of the threats of his men who besieged him to take to the roads. At midnight, the detachment reached the final drop zone, a large clearing covered in a thin patina of powdery snow. A lane grader briefed him that the friendly airfield from whence their supplies would be flown was to their south, and to assume that was direction from which the drop would come. The lane grader then warned, "Ranger, you only got ten minutes left. You got a lotta' work to do."

J.W. assigned men to create a target of flashlights in the form of an arrow pointing to the center of the DZ. Others were given the mission to wave their lights when the plane first appeared, and a final contingent was chosen to track the food-loaded parachutes as they landed. J.W. warned that they would have to gather the rations and be off in minutes to avoid attack by aggressor troops, for intelligence reports described enemy marines who would be listening for the airplane motors, attack the Rangers after the drop, and strip them of their precious cargo.

Vacating the drop zone with no delay was fine with J.W., for he reasoned the sooner they were on the road, the sooner they would pilfer the supplies and take an extra, earned share for their efforts. He felt no guilt about stealing from the Rangers who had stayed back, wallowing in their time to rest. Anyone in the rear guard would have done the same.

Around 0200, hours after the appointed time, the drone of a single Otter trembled, but it was in the northern, not southern sky. J.W. raced around the clearing stumbling over sleeping men, desperately attempting to produce the mirror image of the drop zone he had squandered so much effort designing. When he had found enough of his men to form a facsimile of what his orders had specified, J.W. tapped the barrel of his rifle three times with his bayonet, and those still awake flashed their lights to the aircraft in the prearranged signal.

Saliva pooled in J.W.'s mouth, and he had a hard time using his radio as the Otter flew directly overhead, though he became hysterical when his food-tracking patrol reported there had been no drop. The pilot radioed he couldn't identify the target zone, and J.W. screamed "Asshole," into the air and aimed a faultless bird toward the departing Otter. He used his radio to call the Otter, begging for another try, braying that he, too, was an army pilot.

The plane circled for a second pass, which now came, without warning, from the south. This time, glorious black bags hurtled to the earth from the side door of the aircraft. The first quasi-parachute landed next to Bearchild, and while the payload didn't strike him, the chute caught on his shoulder, ripping off the cloth sleeve of his fatigues. Several Rangers abandoned their posts to pounce on the cardboard C-ration boxes, ignoring Bearchild's injury and the missiles splashing and pounding around them.

As Fricker was tearing one of the boxes apart, he yelled out, "Hey, it's our ponchos. They're back!"

J.W. would have ripped the top of a C-ration can off with his bare teeth had there been a single can of Cs in the care packages. Inside, instead, were bandoleers of machine gun ammo, smoke grenades, white phosphorous, "willy peter" grenades, and fake Claymore mines with no C-4 inside them to heat the Cs that hadn't been granted. There were also dozens of cans of M-1 ammo, bullets which did not fit their M-14's. Those cans, in fact all the cans, gave off deep thuds as they were summarily flung into the bushes by men seeking to avoid carting the extra weight back across the mountains.

Morelotto shoved troops out of his path as the next offering dropped from the sky, reaching the fastest falling package before it landed. But the box, which fell as if loaded with rocks, struck his hand, the nylon strings twisting his middle finger into a dislocated zigzag. Morelotto screamed in pain. The lane grader, however, apparently having witnessed chaos of this magnitude more than a few times in his career, walked over disgustedly, grabbed the crooked digit by the tip, then yanked and torqued until the joints snapped noisily back into position.

Morelotto, back in business, his arm and middle finger held

protectively above his head, dove onto the parcel, ripping savagely at the wooden crate with his good hand. "Cs!" he yelled happily, slashing at the cardboard with his bayonet, but when the thick carton was pulled apart, Morelotto paused for a moment and then, at the top of his lungs, cursed, "Shit! It's filled with rocks."

Several of the Rangers pushed their way past Morelotto, who was expressing his disappointment with rising vehemence in J.W.'s direction. He was so shrill in his discontent, it was difficult to hear the Otter passing a mile beyond the DZ. Though J.W. cupped his ear to listen, the plane did not turn back, and as the drone faded, J.W. tried in vain to raise the pilot on the radio. The Rangers drifted about the clearing ripping the last of the crates apart, finding only ammo and bags of scarlet earth that had apparently been flown up from Benning, lest they forget Harmony Church. When it was clear there was no food, case after case of bullets and rocks arched into the forest to be stored there, the Rangers calculated, forever.

As the last of the supply drop was hurled with great violence into the brush, a heavy night shadow meandered into the drop zone, and Fricker, behind a contorted face, blurted, "Sergeant Cowsen, nice to see you, Sergeant."

"Gentlemen," Cowsen declared placidly, "you will retrieve the ammunition from the area in which you have stockpiled it. We expect you to transport every piece of ordinance back to your unit. You must not lose a single round. Your lives depend upon finding each of the thirty-six cans that you've cached. Your leader here, Ranger Weathersby's tenure in this school depends upon your searching abilities."

J.W. peered at them anxiously as the men turned slowly toward the bushes. Cowsen shook his head and laughed, "And the rest of you will go through the school twice until you find that stuff. Now get your butts a movin'."

A dozen grumbling men dug OD cans of ammunition out of the shrubs, then presented seventeen of the metal containers to the lane grader who was warming coffee over a can of Sterno. He did not count the cans. He did not even look up, but sent the patrol back into the forest *en mass*, where it took until four A.M. to find the last can, the one that had slipped into an old Ranger latrine.

J.W. divided the freight amongst the troops, Bearchild stepping up first, smiling and nodding in appreciation as J.W. handed him a share. No one noticed when Bearchild drifted off into the woods and emptied most of his load in the mud, replacing it with dry twigs and leaves. He then delicately placed a single length of linked bullets on top of the vegetation. J.W. also drew cans of machine gun ammo, but promptly tossed the bandoleers back into the brush and carried only the empty cases, panting and stooping under the burden each time a lane grader shot a glance at him.

* * *

The contingent marched toward a crest high in the Smokys, J.W. still in command. He headed for the ridge, despite the fact that it was several miles out of the way, mumbling that if his men had to walk along the side of a mountain, below the ridge but parallel to it, they would trek for miles and hours with one foot higher than the other, their ankles burning so painfully, they would soon be grousing that they couldn't go on. He had learned to beat the troops straight up the hills and get the pain over with in a single spasm, then to travel the ridge, where the walking was easier, and the aggressors too lazy to climb.

Rocky Mount, jewel of the range, loomed directly overhead as dawn broke. With the light, command of the detail passed to another Ranger, instantly leaving J.W. devoid of the adrenaline that had driven him through the night. For the first time since taking over as commander, the hunger and fatigue burned inside of him more intensely than anything he had imagined at Harmony Church. Even the mountain's magnificence could not blunt the agony, and he quit moving, dropping onto the frozen earth, faltering, talking to himself, grumbling about giving up until Branch slogged by breathing like a horse. He grabbed J.W.'s fatigue jacket and screamed, "Move your honkey ass."

J.W. crawled a few feet, then rose and finished the climb. At the peak, he looked out at the ancient forests and the towering granite. In one of the valleys was the highway that had deposited them in Dahlonega. J.W. followed it with his eyes to the bend in the road where his troop truck had

WILLIAM STUART GOULD, M.D.

hit the bear, and he remembered looking up at the peak on which he now stood. How far away it had seemed at the time, and how sure J.W. had been he would never be forced to climb that high.

* * *

The Ranger leader read his orders aloud. They were to reestablish contact with the partisans, and this time there would be food: it said so right there in the orders. They pushed on for hours, drawn forward by hope. Nearing the rendezvous point, the lead scout discovered evidence of an ambush. He doubled back, empty ammo cans clanking like so many cowbells, and recommended to the Ranger platoon leader a roundabout route to join the partisans from the north and avoid the trap. That stratagem, though superficially sound, neglected the snag that there was no way to signal the "friendlies," the partisans, that the patrol of Rangers had altered their route and would approach from the rear.

Bearchild and J.W. were assigned the point and crawled an inch at a time until they stumbled upon a partisan lying on his back in the dull shadows of dawn, snoring as though a logger cleaving the forest primeval with a chain saw. The partisans were dressed in the peasant garb of the French underground, a throwback to the glory days of the Second World War. J.W. laughed to himself, imagining the third sub-basement of the Pentagon where an anonymous brigadier general sat as Director of the Ranger School Planning Committee, reliving his youth as a shavetail lieutenant, making up scenarios to aggrandize the French underground of The War, recalling the most alluring night of his life and the magnificent young woman with whom he had made love and cried. And though they could barely understand the other's tongue, they held each other that entire night as they slept in the forest of Provence, the rockets and tracers sailing miles, they believed, above their passion. He surely remembered that dawn, her warm, soft, nude body draped over his, now her turn to cry as they rose and dressed to leave each other, soon gone their separate ways, never to feel the intensity of that night again in their lives.

The tribute seemed very silly to J.W., and the allure of sex even more absurd than the garb of the "partisans." But if those troops were the

170

bearers of food, it mattered not if they were dressed as Barbie Dolls or flower children. J.W. prepared himself to treat them with respect and to grovel at their feet, to beg, to crawl for hundreds of meters along rock-hard crooked roots, if that is what it took to establish contact and make them sufficiently happy to give him something to eat.

As he approached the snoozing partisan, one of J.W.'s ammo cans caught in a piece of twine stretched between two trees. He had, in fact, seen the twine before crawling under it, and even thought about it for a split second, but in his state of conscious stupor, he had ignored it as simply a piece of string in the forest tied neatly between two trees. To puzzle out how that fiber had found its way out into the Smoky Mountains apparently would have cost too many individual calories for J.W. to expend, and he went on his merry way crawling toward the fantasy of a bite to eat. On the other hand, perhaps the two calories spent in processing a thought would have prevented the ignition of the flare that was attached to the end of the string, and the subsequent explosion of light that blinded him and shocked the partisans awake.

The partisans took up battle positions, one screaming, "Blow the Claymores." The man sleeping on rear guard jumped behind a tree, and Bearchild lost sight of him.

Bearchild, not sure if the Claymores were real or blanks, crawled to J.W. and grabbed him by the fatigue shirt and pulled him back. J.W. rose to run, but as he took the first step, he felt a body pounce on his back, dashing him into the ground. An instant later, his arm was being twisted into a crushing, numbing hammerlock.

"What the hell are you two doing here?"

"Sir, we're Rangers. We were supposed to make contact with you for food. We need to eat real bad," J.W. begged.

J.W. twisted his head to the side. He could see his captor's uniform. It was, indeed, a partisan, thank God, but when he stretched his neck to get a better look, he noted the most salient feature of the man's persona—one eye of green, one of brown.

"If you were really Rangers," the man hissed, not yet aware of just whom he had captured, "you would have entered from the south. You're lying. You two don't know the password, do you?" J.W. was silent. "You don't even look like Rangers. Look at you. Your uniforms, if you can call them that, are ragged. And you got bad attitudes."

"Bad attitude, sir?" J.W. whined as the hammerlock tightened.

"Yeah, all you want is food. You don't give a damn about us, do you? You just want to feed your fat gut, that's all. Did you bring the ammo for us? No ammo, no food."

J.W. looked toward Bearchild, who twitched in a subtle nod. "Yes, sir, we have the ammo, sir," Bearchild offered confidently. "May we show you, sir?"

Bearchild sat up and untied two cans of .30 caliber, belted, machine gun ammo from his rucksack. He snapped open the tops and displayed the contents to the partisan, though for less than one second did Bearchild allow the single layer of brass shells to reflect in the early rays of the sun, just long enough for the glint of metal to entice the partisan. He then closed the cases quickly, as if hawking fake Seiko watches on the streets of Saigon, not allowing the man to see the strands of grass poking up along the sides. With the show and tell complete, the partisan loosened his grip on J.W.'s arm, ordering the two Rangers to their feet.

J.W. pulled his cap over his brow as far as he could, and looked down, staring at mother earth, hiding his face. Another man came out of the perimeter carrying blindfolds. As he started to tie one over J.W.'s face, the guy with the funny eyes burped in laughter. "No shit. Lookey who we got here. This is going to be a fun week. I think I'll have this asshole carry my pack for the next few days."

The two captives were led into the partisan camp. A marvelous aroma floated through the clearing, and J.W. peeked under his blindfold to witness four men preparing Cs. He waited to be fed as a condition of the Geneva Accords, but not one of them offered so much as an empty can of Ham and Limas to lick out.

J.W. and Bearchild were tied to a tree. The blindfold was pulled from J.W., and the sergeant with the strange eyes began an interrogation. "So, fuck face, how many men in your patrol?"

"None, sir."

"Cut the shit. I'm going to kill you and dump your body off a ledge. Is that what you want?"

"No, sir."

"I'm just gonna kill you right now and tell 'em your pal here did it."
The sergeant took an antipersonnel grenade off his web belt and very
carefully pulled the pin, but kept his hand tight on the spoon. "How many
men do you have with you?" he threatened placing the grenade into J.W.'s
crotch, but J.W. remained silent. "I'll ask you one last time, numb nuts,
how many men?"

As J.W. was about to blurt, "Twelve, sir," Bearchild's hands came free,
and he grabbed the multi-color-eyed sergeant by the neck, throttling
violently. The grenade fell from his hands and Bearchild dropped to his
knees, though as he did, he realized there was not time to crawl onto it. He
spun around and tackled J.W. and the sergeant, knocking them both to
the earth, throwing his own body over theirs.

Other than the din of crashing branches and cursing Rangers, there
were no other sounds, no explosions, no carnage. The sergeant snapped,
"Get the hell off me. The grenade's a dud, like your friend here."

* * *

The main party of Rangers swept across the tiny camp, subduing the
partisans, pilfering their Cs and cigarettes. A lane grader caught up with
them, however, and warned, "If one Camel is missing, the whole
company will pay with three extra weeks in the Mountain Phase. Don't
believe I can do it? Watch me now." With that counsel, booty dropped
from armpits and the insides of the shorts of those Rangers who still wore
them.

A shaky truce was struck when the five partisans were released, and the
Ranger leader was brought to a small clearing where a tarp covered a
dozen burlap bags of potatoes and carrots. The partisans agreed to trade
their food for ammo, but only after the leader demanded, "American
soldiers, show us the bullets you bring."

Bearchild, by now an old hand at exhibiting his wares, was the first to
step forward and place his two cans on the ground. He opened them
nonchalantly, though quickly, then snapped them closed. He hit them
with his palms and both toppled over. He bowed respectfully, then lifted

173

his ammo cans, and quietly walked to the back of the congregation to stand innocuously, gazing at the trees, humming a dissident Native American chant. One of the partisans looked curiously at Bearchild, then strolled toward him suspiciously, stood there for a second and screamed, "Hey, Ranger, what's your problem?"

Gillette rushed to the partisan's side. "Sir, Ranger Bearchild's presenting his gift in the traditional Native American fashion. He feels true pride in having helped his friends, and you see, now he's stepping out of the limelight in humility. He will not answer you. He can't. If he did, he would lose face. We need to respect his cultural imperative."

The partisan leader shook his head, muttered, "What the...?" then nodded politely and went back to his companions. J.W. was ordered to open his own cans. They were as empty as they were the moment he'd tossed away the ammo nearly a day before. He was ordered to stand by a tree. One by one, the others opened their cans to the angry stares of the partisans until a new final tally of the air drop episode was reckoned: twelve foodless men; one man allowed to continue without ammo; eleven other Rangers now ordered to carry ammo cans filled with wet dirt. Added to their burden were several burlap bags of rotting carrots and smelly potatoes. The *piece de resistance*, however, was presented to J.W. Weathersby by the sergeant with multi-colored eyes. J.W. was ordered to heft a bamboo cage stuffed-full with live, cackling chickens back across the mountains to his platoon.

Morelotto, still holding his hand and middle finger in a defensive posture from the trauma at the drop zone, demanded to know where the real food was hidden. That apparently disturbed the partisans, who suddenly spoke with harsh, idiotic accents, claiming that what the Rangers had been given was better than their own families were eating, that their children were starving because they had gathered these supplies for their liberators. Morelotto apologized. "Hey, I'm sorry, I didn't know. O.K.?"

Liberators? J.W. was already borderline psychotic, and that word triggered another hallucination. He was back in World War II France again; it was early 1945, and he was suffering from battle fatigue. In his dream, he walked along the cobblestone roads of Provence, searching for the gorgeous, Gaelic women whom he had heard poured from their bunkers to welcome the liberators. He dreamed of sweeping one of them up in his arms, perhaps like the general at the Pentagon who had conceived of this mad simulation, and taking her home to love for all his life. His wife would cook food every day: French food, German food, even English food. They would eat and eat and eat and stop only to sleep, the notion of making love never entering his fantasy. He pictured the marriage ceremony and the reception and then the unending feasts, but just as he sat down to partake of pheasant under glass, and *de cheval* and *pommes frites*, a huge explosion made mincemeat of the dream.

J.W.'s eyes opened, but not to lace tablecloths and a cornucopia of victuals; it was to muddy trails again, ferns, moss, and the same Rangers with whom he had tracked the hills of Georgia for weeks. There were no aquiline-featured women, no Paris, just a bang on the top of his head as one of the partisans brought him back to Dahlonega with a rock. The stone cracked his head so hard, he was thrown into yet another fantasy. This time, he found himself on a pockmarked, Vietnamese road, dodging the ancient French mines that laced the countryside. But just as he focused on the tortured face of a Vietnamese father carrying a dead son, more trauma befell him, this time a volley of fists pounding his head, and J.W. snapped back to life.

"Put that cage of chickens on your back and bring it to the main body of your unit, asshole."

J.W. looked up into a green eye and then, as he averted his gaze, to a brown one. Realizing the partisan had beat him in his sleep, J.W. was suddenly enraged. He jumped unsteadily to his feet, quickly shoving the partisan, taunting, "Come on you funny-eyed fuck. Hit me when I'm on my feet if you have the balls." J.W.'s body tightened, falling into a rage he had seldom known in his twenty-three years. He would fight back this time; nothing would stop him. But as he raised his fists, the other partisans came to their colleague's side. J.W. looked anxiously about for his own brothers, praying for their support, but the other Rangers had seized the rare opportunity of preoccupied partisans to busy themselves scouring the camp for wayward Cs and smokes. With the absence of friendly backing, J.W.'s bravado cooled a degree or two, and he took a nervous step back uttering, "Just let me catch your ass out there in the woods, pal." In truth, though, J.W. was actually praying he would never again lay eyes on that sergeant, yet that supplication, as with all others in Ranger School, was unlikely to bear fruit.

* * *

The bamboo rungs of the chicken coop assigned to J.W. had sharp ends which tormented the open sores on his neck, leading him to stuff his shirt with a wreath of frozen moss; but that hoarfrost melted and dripped in unending freezing rivulets down the inside of his fatigues. After several hours, J.W. gave up, finally ignoring the problem of his bleeding neck, forcing himself to trudge the hills numbly, toting his cackling, miserable, feathered companions.

Somewhere in the forest, Cowsen appeared, pulling up alongside Fricker, asking, "Ranger, you know how to peel carrots?"

"Yes, First Sergeant."

"Good."

"Ranger Branch, Y'all went to basic training, didn't you?"

"Yes, First Sergeant."

"You learn how to peel potatoes on K.P., there?"

"Yes, First Sergeant."

"Good. Every man peels what he carries."

When it dawned on J.W. that even Cowsen would not eat a live chicken, and that someone was to be tapped to peel J.W.'s passengers, he went to Cowsen on a break. "You know, First Sergeant Cowsen, I don't kill things. I didn't grow up like that."

"Just take it easy. No one's gonna make you eat those chickens, Ranger," Cowsen assured.

J.W. felt better, for all he could think about were his neighbors in New York, returning from up-state each autumn with another buck strapped across the right front fender of the father's '56, Borough of the Bronx, Department of Inspections (For Official Use Only), Ford. Every year, they roped their upside down, tongue-dangling trophy to a branch of the backyard oak tree, "To let it bleed," they explained. And the carcass hung there for what seemed weeks, swinging from the same branch that held the family swing during July and August, the one on which their eleven children had courted mates during the balmy New York summer nights. It wasn't until that moment that J.W. realized the beast had been strung up for display, not to render it kosher. The thought left him ill.

Cowsen stopped them late in the afternoon. "Rangers, I'm gittin' a mite hungry, aren't you? I am going to instruct you in the military method of making chicken stew."

The contingent of malnourished would-be Rangers gathered at lightning speed, all ears and drool. "Ranger," Cowsen called to J.W., "y'all hand me one of your ammo cans. Transfer the mud from the ammo cans into your rucksack. You know, I'm still very upset that you destroyed military equipment. It hurts me inside. Knock off fifty and one for your trouble. Maybe I'll feel better after that."

As J.W. dropped slowly into "the position," the other eleven men fell to the earth creakily joining him, and J.W. smiled that this time the watershed had undeniably been crossed; the true core of men had coalesced, and that with a unit working together as smoothly as his contingent from Second Platoon, no one would be lost from that moment forward. J.W. vowed at that moment to carry every straggler on his back, to claw the earth to save a single Ranger from the ignominy of defeat by the enemy. The aggressors may have been Green Berets and troops from the 197th Light Infantry Brigade, but the *enemy* was the corps of cadres. Sides had been chosen. There would be no more solicitous obedience; the game would be played by Ranger rules from that point forward—glory halleluiah.

The fifty-first push up behind them, Cowsen scraped the dirt out of J.W.'s ammo can with a stick, though spoonfuls of mud still clung tenaciously to the inner walls. Cowsen commented, "There's gonna be a tad extra pepper in yo stew tonight, Rangers." Cowsen then stripped the black rubber gasket out of the shoe box-sized, olive drab, metal ammo can and added, "Gentlemen, you will be poisoned if you cook in an ammo can with the gasket in place. May blow up. Be pieces of chicken stew and pieces of Ranger splattered all over the Smokys."

He stared directly at J.W. "Ranger, bring me a chicken."

The command set J.W.'s exhausted brain into another of the surrealistic Ranger trances in which his past roiled up, memories of long forgotten incidents sent back to guide him in making sense of the present. This time the convoluted string of ideas began with the chickens. Though J.W. had carried the caged poultry on his shoulders for hours, he had not fostered a profound relationship with his feathered cargo. And it hadn't been an unsoiled journey by any stretch of the imagination. Early in the march, J.W. squandered dozens of precious calories brushing the still-slimy pistachio-green chicken droppings from his fatigues, but after a while, he found it easier to let the guano freeze on his uniform, for it peeled off far more readily while in the frozen state. If he let the chicken turds really freeze hard into a rigid lump, he could flick away the solid little crescent with a snap of his finger, leaving only the slightest trace of the silvery-gray ellipse on the cloth of his fatigue shirt. If, however, he became impatient and failed to wait for the guano to freeze, and tried to detach it from his fatigues while it was still wet, he was left with the soggy, tapering, green, mucoid smudge of premature removal, which froze anyway, more quickly, and spread the cold over a greater surface area of his fatigues.

For hours J.W. had trudged along, passing the time attempting to remember a formula or a theory relating to the transfer of heat from a lump of chicken crap to cotton fatigues. It was probably taught on one of those Saturdays he missed ME 153, his mechanical engineering course in thermodynamics at Penn State. For reasons unclear to an eighteen-year-old sophomore, his college guidance counselor suggested J.W. take thermo in the fall semester, during football season, when J.W. was fighting to gain the attention of the varsity coaches. The course instructor, a young graduate student not quite five-foot-four, and who had scarcely begun to shave, but who haughtily packed two K&E slide rules slung in hip holsters, made it clear from the onset that he had no sympathy for those with interests other than the natural sciences. As Captain Vock despised married men, the thermo instructor especially detested crew cut football players.

The mechanical engineering class was subjected to a quiz every Saturday morning at 8:00 A.M. J.W. was usually with the football team at that time, a thousand miles from both campus and thermodynamics. The instructor, while allowing no excuses, was kind enough to drop the highest and lowest quiz grades at the end of the semester, averaging the remaining grades. The rub was that J.W.'s maximum score for the exams he managed to attend was a fourteen, and that was out of one-hundred points, and he had to drop that one. That was why a "B" in the course, one of the highest grades he received in college, surprised him so.

He subsequently learned through the grapevine that while his average had been a nine, more meaningfully, his pal the instructor had been caught as a member of a ring of erstwhile scientists dropping pennies into hydrochloric acid, reducing them to the size of dimes to fit into the pay phone on the dormitory floor. This was a transgression for which the misdirected numismatist and his cronies had been summarily expelled from graduate school, and everyone in ME 153 was awarded a "B" to keep them quiet. But J.W. asked himself as he sat there deep in the Smokys, picking chicken droppings from his military uniform, "Yeah, but how much thermo did I really learn?"

Cowsen hollered, bringing J.W. back to life, "What the heck you babbling 'bout, young Ranger? I said, carry me a chicken over here."

The bamboo cage was lashed shut with wet twine, the knots locked so tightly, the only way to open the cage was to cut the hemp. J.W. drew his bayonet across the rope a bit too eagerly, the tip cutting through several of the bamboo rungs. Two chickens scampered out of the rent in the cage to freedom, and J.W. leapt forward onto one, but as he grabbed it by the neck, it raked J.W.'s hands with its feces-covered talons.

Fricker pounced on the other bird and shoved it back in the cage, but J.W. lost his prey, and Bearchild sprinted into the forest after it until the bird came to rest perched at the edge of a deep valley. Unconcerned with heights, Bearchild snuck up on it, but the animal tumbled over the side, fluttering and cackling, trying unsuccessfully to fly, for its wings had been clipped to avoid just such an event. Soon it was but a speck of white splattered on the valley floor a quarter of a mile below. It took over a second for the report of a dull thud and a weak cluck to reach them.

After the push-ups, Cowsen asked if J.W. would be kind enough to bring him one of the remaining pullets, and waited until J.W. was standing over him with a bird in hand. Without looking up, the first sergeant ordered, "Ring its neck, Ranger."

"Can't do that, Sergeant," J.W. protested quietly. "Remember, I don't kill things."

"Ring its neck, or I'll ring yours!" It wasn't that J.W. didn't eat meat. J.W. loved chicken. But this was *a* chicken, and J.W. had never touched a live one, or for that matter, given a single thought as to where chicken came from. But, since there seemed little value in protesting, J.W. tightened his hands around the bird's neck and squeezed, ignoring the thrashing and clawing.

Cowsen tolerated the bungled execution for a few seconds, then ordered, "No, no, Ranger, gimme the doggone thing." He grasped J.W.'s chicken by the head and twirled until the neck snapped. Cowsen then cut through the neck with a pocketknife, and the body dropped to the ground, its scrawny legs still running the headless carcass in circles. Everybody laughed, and soon there was a chicken, or at least a piece of one, in every ammo can. Cowsen added unpeeled carrots and the mushy, blackened potatoes Morelotto had lugged to the brew, poured in putrid water, latched the top back onto the can, and threw the whole thing into the fire. It wasn't until years later that J.W. learned they were supposed to have lined the can with tin foil so the toxic paint that blistered the inside did not mix with the stew.

The meal was undercooked and mushy, with rare, semi-defeathered, lukewarm, chicken parts, a bloody ooze running from between the layers of the pink meat, and flakes of crunchy olive drab paint and lumps of crunchy mountain mud suspended in the broth. Nonetheless, J.W. sat back against a huge fir and enjoyed the most delicious of meals. He savored each drop of stock and used his lips to make mush of the unwashed potato skin and sour carrots.

Though he snuck off after dinner and wrote the recipe on a piece of burlap, when he tried several times over the years to reproduce that stew, it was never again that delicious. Maybe it was the green paint, perhaps the earth of the Smokys. It certainly was not the nutritional value, for the calorie count—paint, feathers, and dirt—came to only a fraction of the double rations they had been promised. In two days all the food was gone, the final tally amounting to a couple of carrots, a half a potato, and a shred of chicken per man per day; that is, for those who didn't scarf the lot on the first sitting. Five men saved a portion until the next sunrise.

By week's end, J.W. was able to open his mouth half-an-inch, but if he tried to drop his lower teeth just a bit farther, an electric shock raced through the left side of his face. He limited his intake to water, but that's all they were able to find anyway.

* * *

Over the next weeks, Class 68-B crawled the entire range of mountains, often coming upon the long-abandoned CCC camps J.W. had seen from the mountainside on the first day in Dahlonega. Although he searched the ruins for scraps of food left behind by aggressors or hunters, he never found a particle. He sought, on one of the longer marches, to estimate the number of calories Rangers had frittered away over the millennium in the absurd pursuit of "free" food, and wondered why the uncounted units of wasted heat had failed to warm the earth.

Survival in the mountains soon became a full time endeavor, a total commitment to foraging. But one had to know, *de novo*, what was edible, for alpine gastronomy was not one of the courses in the Ranger curriculum. Fricker learned that lesson when he ate berries from the last autumn's crop, shriveled little black specks that had managed to stay on the vine through the winter winds and snows. The taste in his mouth after he spit them out lasted for days, and he asked a lane grader, "Hey, Sir, how long before all I can taste is my usual didn't-brush-my-teeth odor?"

The lieutenant answered, "Hey, hunter-gatherer, how would I know? I brush my teeth."

* * *

On a deep, gray afternoon, a light snow began to powder out of the dull sky. J.W. worried about the coming night, but, despite being clothed in only the shreds of what was left of his fatigue pants, and despite the numbness in his fingers, he again became enthralled by the majesty of the

181

Smoky Mountains. As dusk fell, with snow now blanketing the earth, he experienced a sense of elation that surprised him, and which made thoughts of the frigid hours ahead tolerable. While J.W. could already taste the bitter cold, and though he was aware of how much worse it would become before Sylvester reappeared to bring the temperature back into the low thirties, for the first time in weeks, it seemed not to matter. Another dawn would arrive when it did, regardless of how hard he cried. He sat against a tree and realized for the first time in his life that only patience would serve him.

And the temperature did creep steadily downward, slowly at first, then precipitously. Hours passed, and the patrol neared the ridge of a particularly high range. There, the cold he had feared met them, and at the first break, he entered a thicket of trees, found a tiny spot in which to crouch, and prepared to sleep for a minute bathed in the warmth of the timber. As he leaned back, his hand brushed a soft lump in the dry snow, and J.W. hesitated, remaining perfectly still, calculating if it was worth the labor of reaching forward six inches to discover what he had unearthed this time. Back and forth his mind raced, a struggle between conserving his strength on the one hand, and the possibility of hitting upon treasure on the other. Then, realizing the chances of stumbling upon riches twice in one Ranger School were diminishingly small, he set upon castigating himself for frittering away the mental energy, the abject waste of treasured calories, thinking about whether he should be thinking about it or not.

But J.W. Weathersby was far beyond controlling himself at this juncture in his short life, and, though thoroughly exhausted, he contemplated his options carefully, considering the mathematical odds of striking the mother vein of happiness in the barren wilderness of the frozen Smokys. When he considered again that the process of deliberation was costing calories, he sought to put the matter of the lump in the snow out of his mind forever. But it clung there, an uncomfortable, constant, gnawing notion, as if an ulcer, or Cowsen's presence. Awash in his disquiet, J.W. managed to hear the lead elements of the platoon begin moving along the crusted puddles ahead, and he moaned that if he didn't grasp the moment, that lapse would tarry on his mind, like a song that wouldn't go away, and maybe for the rest of his life.

The pressure in his brain built further, and J.W. finally summoned the intestinal fortitude to let his fingers open from their clenched curl and reach forward, believing that if he did so slowly, he would consume fewer units of energy. His nearly numbed hand traveled through the snowy powder, inching along, until his fingers brushed against a foot-long mass. He sucked in a deep breath of glacial air, mumbling an entreaty to the Lord for a miracle, then examined the lump of God-bestowed hope by Braille. The object softened subtly in the meager warmth of his hand, and J.W. soon appreciated a fur-fringed tube with smaller tubes protruding from one end, as if an animal had died and turned inside out. J.W. slid his frozen hand an inch further into the bushy part. It fit like a glove.

He pulled the gift out of the snow and played his flashlight on it. It was a glove, a thick, leather, fur-lined, arctic glove, just one, left behind by a pitiful aggressor, or a cadre, and not that long before; the leather was still dry.

J.W. considered screaming for joy to let the world know of his good fortune, for he was in sole possession of what had been, seconds before, only an angry emotion for the being who had lost it, destined to be a forgotten useless bump on the great expanse of the Smokys. Suddenly, however, it was a magnificent gift from the heavens, from a genie. J.W. reveled that perhaps he had served his penance, that life had taken a positive turn; and even if his discovery did not portend heavenly dispensation, at least his right hand would be beautifully cozy and warm for the rest of his life, and even better, for the rest of the night

"No," J.W. whispered aloud, "I'm not broadcasting my good fortune to the world. Not this time, no way. First thing you know, the less fortunate's gonna' demand to borrow it. Then they'll let it slip through their fingers, lose it, just like the dud who dropped it in the first place." And for the next several miles, J.W. switched the glove from hand to hand until the column came to rest in a large clearing. The delay approached thirty seconds, and J.W. made the decision to invest the energy in squatting to the earth and sleeping until the column moved forward again. If the respite lasted two more minutes, he would cherish it as an eternity, a poor man's equivalent of a full night's slumber, one embellished with the notion that one of his hands was not numb.

Anywhere else on earth, he thought, two minutes was an irritation at a red light, perhaps the wait for a MacDonald's hamburger, but in Ranger School, it was a major breakpoint, for any stop beyond that meant calamity for the platoon leader, generally a relief of command for having become irreparably lost, and then another fifteen minutes while the new platoon leader oriented himself. Yet J.W. felt no guilt in greedily savoring the momentary reprieve purchased at the price of the student leader's angst. If time was money in the real world, time was beautiful, warm, cozy sleep in his.

Absorbing what heat he could from the earth, J.W. ignored his other carnal concerns, and slept, unaware of the movement around him. The cold intensified, but he didn't care, and simply crawled into a tighter ball, his mind lifting itself out of the depths of hopelessness as he considered remaining there in the fetal position forever. J.W. had heard that dying in the frozen mountains was peaceful, pleasant, like drowning, once one let go of his fear.

He accepted that the only spark left in him was not the beauty of the Smokys, but the warmth of his right hand. Surprised that the heat began spreading throughout his body, his eyes closed tighter, but soon he understood that the warmth had only brought his brain to the point that he could recognize his life ebbing away. With that awareness, he could not force himself to his feet, nor did he wish to. He fell deeper into the semi-conscious sleep, unable to move and never intending to do so again. Slowly, his heart filled with a smile, as he believed his debt for the transgressions about which his mother had accused him had been paid. He drifted further and further from Dahlonega, though he did not know where he was destined, and nor did he care. The journey proceeded slowly, a sensation of great peace soon blanketing him. He believed he had reached nirvana, that despite all the threats he had endured, he was about to enter heaven.

Just as he felt himself ascending into the midlevels of paradise, his spirit suffered a sudden jolt. The quiet and the peace, the feeling of completion, all of it, jerked away violently as J.W. felt the thud of a combat boot on his head. He looked up to see First Sergeant Cowsen waving a snow-encrusted pine bough, readying to christen a new platoon leader.

"Are you out of your cotton pickin' mind? A Ranger doesn't sleep in the snow. Haven't we taught you anything?"

Cowsen walked on, snapped Bearchild on the butt, and handed him the feared manila envelope. Bearchild, who had been asleep as well, jumped to his feet and shouted, "Yes, Sergeant," and studied the orders for a moment.

"Do you know where you are, Ranger?"

Bearchild paused. He, too, had not consulted a map in days, perhaps weeks, but Cowsen's tone betrayed an air of the respect he held for none of the rest of the trainees. It was as if he fully expected Bearchild to be capable of taking command, for to Cowsen, Bearchild was his great dark hope. He would push Bearchild and Branch harder than the others to prove themselves, to confirm Cowsen's belief in himself. Despite the humiliation Cowsen had swallowed as a child-sharecropper, and what he had faced as a black man in the white man's army, his quality had entwined him with the best of the best, the Bearchilds and the Branches.

* * *

Bearchild was instantly awake, pulling a map from his rucksack, placing a dirt-blackened, lacerated index finger on the symbol of a high ridge deep in the mountains. Cowsen's expression did not change. Bearchild declared they would descend from their ridge and plow through the thick underbrush to hit the enemy from behind. The aggressors would expect them to follow the ridge and funnel into an ambush, for the Rangers were buried in hunger and sleeplessness, devoid of the stamina to pick through the thick stands of rhododendron encircling the mountain slopes.

Cowsen asked Bearchild, "Ranger, you sure you want to forsake the comfort of this ridge for that tangled forest?"

Bearchild did not answer. He summoned Branch and then J.W., informing them of his plan. J.W. argued there was no way to move quickly through the dense underbrush if the men remained attached to rucksacks and pistol belts. He offered a dozen reasons why they would fail taking the harder route.

Patiently, Bearchild asked, "What do you think we can do to move faster?"

Branch suggested they leave their gear behind, but J.W. warned that if they did, Cowsen would inform the aggressors, and the Rangers would never see their equipment again. "They let us get away with it once, but they won't again," J.W. warned.

Bearchild thought for a second longer, then proposed, "You and Branch stay behind. Guard the stuff."

It was a stroke of luck beyond which J.W. had never dreamed, the Irish Sweepstakes won. A feeling of serenity and security washed over both Branch and J.W. for the reprieve they had been granted. Their hands and faces would be spared the violent ripping and tearing of those forced to navigate the rhododendron thickets on the run, and then chase the enemy into the forest to mop up. Though they wouldn't have the opportunity to pilfer Cs from the vanquished, both he and Branch agreed that their lot was better than that of the peons, and they swore to Bearchild that they would take their guardianship seriously.

After Bearchild briefed the platoon, Cowsen announced that two Rangers from the previous class had been lost at the base of that very mountain. He suggested they keep an eye out for the bodies. An extra meal would be granted the first Ranger to uncover the remains. J.W. suddenly reconsidered and advised Bearchild that perhaps he was needed on the attack, but Bearchild ignored him.

As the other Rangers dropped their gear by squads and loaded their M-14's with blanks, Branch and J.W. pretended to study the trigonometry of the three neat rows of rucksacks. They prepared fields of fire, and finally blackened their faces with camouflage sticks. It was a ruse, for their only responsibility was to be awake in three hours, and everybody in that clearing knew it. Cowsen would never allow the aggressors into direct, unchaperoned confrontation with two crazed Rangers; the last thing he needed was another death on his hands.

Branch and J.W. remained behind with a radio transmitter and an extra battery so they could direct the platoon back to the clearing after the attack. Though the two would spend the hours sitting, and were thus destined to be colder than their compatriots, the gift of rest was, they agreed, worth the exchange.

"Yeah, but what about finding those bodies? An extra meal," J.W. groused.

"That's bullshit," Branch muttered. "Cowsen's bluffing. Even if somebody finds the bodies, there isn't gonna be a meal. You nuts or something, man?"

Branch and J.W. planned to sleep until the fury of the battle sounds woke them, and then they would, through the judicious use of their radios and the Ranger bird, guide the platoon back to its gear. If they did well, they would be forever trusted custodians of their compatriots' holdings, and this would be only the first of many rear guard nights. It was a challenge to be savored, though as the attack party left the staging area, Bearchild came to Branch and J.W. whispering, "Don't let me down." Both Branch and J.W. nodded solemnly to him and then to each other.

* * *

Within thirty seconds of the departure, however, Branch and J.W. had snapped their ponchos together into a makeshift shelter and found a comfortable, moss-encrusted hemlock against which to lean.

Branch asked "What are we smoking?"

J.W. suggested, "Your Chesterfields."

They lit up but didn't inhale, using the glowing embers to warm the inside of their primitive mansion. When Branch finally complained that his eyes couldn't take the smoke, J.W. took the cigar box-sized spare radio battery out of his rucksack and cut the cardboard cover away. With his teeth, he stripped plastic insulation from the wires of the six cells, and twisted the bare copper together, creating a dead short-circuit in the battery which gave off a malodorous, but mellow, warmth.

When the metal casing started to melt, however, a drop of the molten lead fell onto J.W.'s bare crotch, and the fumes of sulfuric or some such acid hissing from the boiling battery became more than even J.W. was willing to trade for the warmth. Branch had long since fallen backwards against the tree, either dead from the poisonous vapors, or asleep, so J.W. lifted the edge of the poncho.

But Branch was alive, and in his stupor mumbled, "Man, why does it take so long for white men to go to bed with their women?" He rose further from the dead, leaned an inch closer to J.W., opened his eyes, and asked, "Is it true?"

"Is what true?"

"Do white girls really make you wait 'till the third date before screwing?"

J.W. had to admit he had no firsthand information to the contrary. "See, I gotta admit, if you won't say anything…" he paused.

"No, man, of course not," Branch reassured.

"See, I haven't been all that lucky. I mean, well…"

There was silence, for so lofty a conversation was calorically quite expensive, and there wasn't a lot left inside either of the deliberators to argue a subject so impossibly remote. Branch faded for nearly five minutes, but he gathered incredible strength and came back. "That's the way the white man lives. Why y'all so 'fraid of everything? What the hell they gonna do to you, Ranger? Yell? Who gives a shit? I been yelled at all my life, 'cause I'm black.

"Teachers, cops, you name it, man. And I'm here same as you, cold and pissed off. Yes or no?"

The last volley sapped a good portion of the steam left in Branch, and he fell back against the tree before continuing. "They told me I wouldn't get an M.A. in psychology 'cause I was gonna do my thesis on black officers in the army. Touchy shit. I wrote that black troops don't respect black officers. They don't believe a nigger can lead 'em. I can't take that shit, Ranger. I can't live with it."

Branch sat forward again. He crushed out a cigarette angrily. "Man, I'm sad. No, I'm pissed," he slurred his words, burning with indignation. "Do you know the shit heaped on me since I was kid comin' up in Bed—Sty? Guns, and fightin', and hatred. Then my mother looked around one day, and said the place was a pit, enough was enough, so she moved us uptown to Harlem where there was supposed to be community, people who saw a brighter future for the black man. There was a renaissance of the spirit she said. Blacks were moving up in the white man's world. Blacks from Harlem on TV; shuckin' and jivin' maybe, but they were right there on the screen working alongside the white man. No more segregation in the military. Black athletes bein' respected. Jackie Robinson got a college degree from UCLA. Scholar athlete. He comes to visit Harlem, but don't go near Bed-Sty which is right in Brooklyn where the Dodgers live.

"So off we go to Harlem. Wasn't no different. Maybe less death by guns, but the same death by despair. Schools falling apart. Teachers angry and scared. We laughed at them. Those teachers were pussies...do-gooders. Wanted to be part of the 'black experience,'" Branch waved his head like Stevie Wonder, with a sickly smile. "Black culture. What culture? Bullshit. Just fightin' and drinking, and knowin' that's all there's ever gonna be. And these white liberal asshole teachers from the burbs. So brave doin' it in the ghetto. Arrogant bastards. Thought they were so gotdamn smart. Bring the white man's ways to people who ain't never gonna have the dough to live those dreams. Who wants to anyway? And I'm just as gotdamn smart as they are. I told 'em that, too."

Branch took a long breath to go on, and J.W. interjected, "Bet you did."

He was silent again, but for a moment only. "You know what's worst of all? No matter how many degrees or how much rank I ever get, man, the best I'm ever gonna be is the token nigger. That's if I don't get uppity. If I open my mouth, the honkey'll be on my ass like stink on shit.

"I've been there before. Lot of 'em yelled at me," he snapped forward and spit onto the earth. "Lots of pissed off officers when I was doing my research. No sweat. I worked my butt off for it, and got my gotdamn M.A. last year from Penn, man, Ivy League nigger. Published that sucker, too. Don't matter who yells at ya, Ranger. They can't do a damn thing to you unless you let 'em."

J.W. reflected on his own life. "I guess I wasn't raised so brave as you; wish I had been. I know you're right, man. I just don't have the balls to do it your way. I spent my whole life trying to please somebody else, not because it makes me feel good, but because if I don't, they'll get angry."

"Who's *they*?" Branch snapped.

"I don't even know."

"That's the whole point. I'll tell you who 'they' are, Ranger," he shot back, now fully awake, and as angry as J.W. had ever seen him. "It's a creation of your own frontal lobe, man, reinforced by coaches and teachers and parents, and friends' parents, and all the rest of 'them.' Everybody who's protecting their own little piece of the pie. Got nothin' to do with who you are; it's about upsetting their little social apple cart. I'm right and I know it, and everyone else's nuts, man. You been living by the mirror image of that. I'm tellin' you a fact.

"You ever hurt anybody, Ranger?"

J.W. thought for a minute. "Nope, not really."

"Well, then why haven't you done it your own way? If'n you ain't hurtin' nobody, what do you care if you do it a different way? Tell me that."

J.W. contemplated those words, wondering if it was too late to change. Branch shook his head sadly. "Mirror image, I'm tellin' ya." He lit another cigarette, leaned back against the tree, and fell asleep. Warmth and peace filled the poncho, and J.W., too, dreamed.

* * *

The next thing J.W. remembered was a snippet of light under the edge of the poncho, the burning ember of the cigarette that had just rolled out of Branch's hand, he assumed, but the radiance was silver, not red, and J.W. shook Branch. "Get up, man. Platoon's comin' back."

J.W. lifted the poncho. A blast of light hit him, and it wasn't the flashlights of the Rangers. It was Sylvester, and it was well past dawn. Branch jumped up and surveyed the clearing. The equipment was gone, every stick of it. They listened for the rustle of the platoon, a sneeze, the Ranger bird, but there was only a light breeze rattling the icy twigs of oak and white birch.

Sliding and slipping along the thickly wooded mountainside, they were drawn to human voices coming from the base of the hill, and Branch motioned with his hand to slow down, but J.W. trotted even more quickly, anxious to make contact with the platoon and gobble his share of breakfast.

Branch whispered, "Slow down, damnit. I smell trouble," but J.W. plowed ahead even more intrepidly.

"You smell trouble. What are you, Bearchild all of a sudden? Well, I smell breakfast, pal, and from now on, I'm goin' after whatever the hell I want." J.W. laughed, now rested and totally consumed with the dream of filling his belly.

He was suddenly driven forward, stumbling toward the scent of cooking C-rations floating from a clearing at the base of the hill. At the far corner of the camp, a dozen troops huddled around a gigantic bonfire. Their field jacket hoods were pulled over their heads, and empty C cans were scattered carelessly about their feet. J.W. moved closer. Though Branch frantically motioned for J.W. to get out of the clearing, Weathersby envisaged only the food, ignoring the image of the colorful unit patches on the shoulders of those warming themselves, seeing only what he wanted to see. He took a step closer, then felt a mighty tug on his fatigue blouse. Branch dragged him back into the brush.

"Asshole, what the hell you doing?" Branch spit in a whisper. "Man, that's the gotdamn enemy." J.W. looked back toward the fire. The uniforms were pristine, bedecked with unit insignia and rank. As an aggressor turned, sensing their presence, Branch threw J.W. to the ground and the two lay perfectly still. The Green Beret walked toward them, studied the crushed snow, and followed the fresh tracks. Branch tensed to jump him, but the soldier paced toward the fire for call for backup.

Branch sprang to his feet, smacked J.W. in the head, and crashed through the rhododendron and Douglas fir. For an hour they traveled the thickets until the din of the Ranger platoon drew them through the gray dawn. They crawled into the bivouac area, flabbergasted that while the Rangers sat with heads hung between drawn-up legs, each man had his equipment. Branch and J. W took seats at the fringes of the clearing, chattering as if they had been there the whole time.

Bearchild had made it through the night without being relieved of command. He approached Branch and J.W. and thanked them for their good work, and Cowsen stopped by as well, congratulating them on the security they had provided the main body. He then appointed Bearchild, Branch, and J.W. as rear patrol, their mission from that point forward to hang a mile behind the balance of the unit and guard against enemy infiltration from the rear. J.W. thought he might have heard Cowsen mumble, "You're the only ones I can trust."

Branch could not hide his smile and whispered, "Another gift, man. Can you believe it? O.K., here's what we're gonna do. Listen to me. We rest when the platoon leaves. Stay right here. We don't move. They travel so slow, we can catch up with 'em in a minute. Then we make a racket so they think we've been there the whole time. We play easy catch up, and then we do it again; rest whenever we want. Lord be lookin' out for us."

Bearchild stared questioningly at Branch. "You sound pretty chipper for having been up for the past month."

Branch became more serious. "Look, my man, I'm in control of my life from now on. No more torment. I got this thing figured out. Just watch me."

Eight minutes later, Second Platoon departed to the north on their next mission, and the three musketeers swaggered out of the clearing to the south, as if assuming their position for rear security. But when the platoon was safely gone, Bearchild and Branch dropped down against a tree and slept. J.W. took five minutes to search the clearing for cans of Cs not licked clean, then joined his brothers in a nap.

Fifteen minutes later, Bearchild banged on their legs while the din of the main contingent could still be heard thrashing the woods less than a quarter of a mile away. The three followed the cacophony for a while, then took a break at the edge of a paved, two-lane highway that snaked through the hills. They lit up and talked for a while, Branch inquiring if Indian women were prudes on the first date. Bearchild grumbled, "Ask Weathersby," but Branch didn't bother.

As they rested by the side of the highway, an ancient, hand-painted, milk truck came around a bend. J.W. began to stand to flag the vehicle down, laughing, "Gents, anyone for chocolate milk?"

Branch grabbed him and pulled him down away from the road into a ditch. "Fool, they're aggressors. Look at 'em, clean, drinking coffee. It's a captured vehicle. They're trolling for stray Rangers to capture and torture. Just stay down, and Black people don't drink chocolate milk. Now you're goin' to tell me you do."

The three peered out from the snow-covered swale to see two men with scraggly beards, a driver sitting on a soft, high seat, and a passenger, both in civvies, their hands laced around steaming cups of coffee. J.W. observed, "They're aggressors and I'm Napoleon. Look at 'em. The driver doesn't even have teeth."

As J.W. started to crawl forward, Branch grabbed one of his arms and Bearchild the other. Branch whispered angrily, "You won't have teeth either if you move one more inch, Ranger. I'm not in the mood to screw around with you. Just sit here and don't budge. Can't you get it through your thick head that there's only two kinds of people on the earth: bald and dressed in OD rags like us, and all the others, and all of the others are your enemy."

J.W. yanked his arm away, and yelled in a whisper, "Man, what is it with you that when a man looks different than you, it's so frightening? That's the whole problem with society today. Segregation and all that. I say we take a chance and flag 'em down and beg for coffee and milk. Maybe they got some breakfast rolls on board."

The notion of coffee and donuts gave Branch pause, and he looked questioningly at Bearchild who nodded no.

Branch spoke for his silent partner. "Be smart, man. You got enough paradise here, just bein' away from the main body. No one's botherin' us. Be cool. Don't blow it."

J.W. cooled down a bit and allowed, "Yeah, I suppose you're right, but think about it for a minute. They got freedom, those milkmen. Man, can you imagine buying a cup of coffee whenever you choose, and ridin' in some old broken down truck instead of slogging through the snow? That is satisfaction, my man. Those are some lucky sons a bitches." J.W.'s brothers thought silently about the proposition and nodded in unison.

After the rusting truck ground by, the three Rangers crawled out of their ditch and crossed the highway. J.W. whined as he trailed behind, "When I'm living in the real world again, no matter what the hell is going on in my life, when I open my eyes everyday, I get a cup of coffee. I don't care what you two do. Nobody stops me. Never again, not in my life. You got that? And if I want to drink chocolate milk, I will—a quart if I want, every morning."

Branch asked, "Bearchild, what the hell's up his ass?"

* * *

At the far side of the highway, they followed a dirt road parallel to the forest path taken by the bulk of the platoon. They halted at a ramshackle farmhouse surrounded by a host of dilapidated, widely separated outbuildings, each more rotted than the last. They chose the least eerie of the huts in which to search for food, and when that failed, they traversed a field stubbled with the remnants of last year's corn. Bearchild kicked snow away from the stalks, searching for an errant cob, something to boil in melted snow and drink, to warm them and sweeten their mouths.

J.W. asked how he knew about such things, and Bearchild spoke for the first time in a day. "When I lived on the res in South Dakota, my mother could make a meal out of nothing." He squatted and pulled hollow stalks from the earth, then tossed them disgustedly into the wind. "This field's bare, picked clean. The poverty's already arrived in the Smokys. Got here long before the Rangers did. Just like home."

"Bein' honest, Bearchild, I can't imagine not havin' food. Not in America."

Bearchild went on. "The fields at home were bare by late winter. Nothing in the house, hardly even firewood. The only thing makin' us warm when we went to bed was a cup of corn tea, old corncob boiled in water. Heat drew the sugar out of the cob. My mother served it to us children in chipped porcelain mugs. It was the best. I always saved a swallow or two by my bedside to give to my little brother, Steven War Bonnet. First thing in the morning, Steven'd get up and smile at me. But that's..." Bearchild's voice trailed off, and Branch saw the anger in his friend's eyes.

An uneasy silence settled over them, and J.W. walked toward the main house, drawn by the wisps of dark, chimney smoke rising into the still, frigid air. "I'm goin' to the house to beg," he mumbled.

Branch and Bearchild followed several meters behind, searching left and right with their eyes, true commandos, until a few orange embers drifted from the chimney toward them. One landed on Branch's bare forearm, and he let out a yelp, brushing the glowing fragment from his skin. The burn blistered instantly, and Branch, cursing vituperatively, piled the lesion with snow.

The disquiet brought a face to the window of the decaying farmhouse. A moment later, the thick, rough-hewn wooden door creaked open, and a cachectic, sallow-complexioned man stepped over the threshold. He left the butt of his antique shotgun on the porch, but gripped the barrel, allowing it to lean subtly forward.

Branch turned to walk away, still holding a snowball on his arm, but kept his other hand tightened on the business end of his M-14. J.W. turned and stopped him with his hand, whispering, "Let me handle this, man. I'm hungry. I'm gonna appeal to the man's sense of patriotism."

Branch hesitated, turned again, and riveted his eyes on the silent figure in the doorway, then whispered back, "You mean you're gonna appeal to his sense of Bronx bull crap. Let's get back to the unit. I don't like this shit."

J.W. walked fawningly toward the rickety porch. He smiled. The old man's grip tightened on the barrel of the shotgun, and the stock lifted off the porch a fraction of an inch. J.W. looked into the dull eyes, then began tentatively.

"Sir, we are three cadets from the United States Army Ranger School. I understand that some of the summer Rangers have been inconsiderate of your crops in the past, and we have been dispatched by the high command to come here and assure you that will not happen again, sir."

The farmer stared at J.W. as if faced with a lunatic, as did Branch and Bearchild when J.W. turned back to see if they were still there. Nonetheless, the farmer's hand relaxed on the barrel, and J.W. continued. "Sir, I do have to tell you that we are very, very hungry. We haven't eaten in the week it took us to get here. We're very shaky, sir. I'll be honest, sir. We need some food, anything you got. We'll pay for it, of course. I mean we are not here to beg, no sir, we're gonna pay."

The aboriginal face stared a while longer, then lifted the butt of the gun over the threshold and took a step backwards, to gun them down with one blast and not waste additional shells, J.W. feared, but the man leaned the barrel against the door sill and stepped back out. He spoke without having taken a breath, blinked his dull gray eyes, or moved his pale lips.

"Lemme' see de culluh o' y'alls' money."

The man's words introduced a complication to the convention of the deprived. While J.W. paused to decipher the quasi-English, he suddenly understood that it was now four worlds that had collided on a patch of frozen corn waste in the mountains of nowhere. In common, however, was need, and the one with the least was the one who by all rights was the neediest.

The meeting was beginning to consolidate into a very simple formula: on one side of the equation were the four or five dollars the Rangers were promising, and on the other side of the equal sign was a bowl of corn grits or stale bread. Yet they could see in the man's face that while money in those mountains was a windfall, he had survived for a very long time without it. The food, however, was a potential miracle. They needed him more than he needed them, far more.

Branch and Bearchild watched to see how their Bronx-born compatriot was going to extract himself from this one. When J.W. saw they weren't going to be of any assistance, he concocted in his mind several ridiculous fairy-tales in record time, but the man's eye's hardened, and Weathersby made a command decision, against his better judgment, to just tell the truth.

"Well, sir, as I'm sure you know, they don't let us carry any money. But, sir, I swear on my father's grave we're going to pay for any food you would be kind enough to share with us. We need the food, sir. We will send you the money, I swear."

The farmer paused, looked out mistrustfully at the pleading, desperate faces, then stepped inside backwards, keeping his eyes pasted to his guests, leaving the shotgun on the threshold of the open door. The Rangers shrugged, moved slowly forward, and craned their necks to scrutinize the innards of the house. "It's mountain modern," J.W. mumbled, as they peeked in on the bare walls, raw furniture, and an old TV with more snow blanketing the screen than on the ground.

Suddenly, the man reappeared, catching the Rangers many steps closer to his home. He paused and looked down at his shotgun, a gesture not lost on Branch, who slowly loosened the grip on his ammo-less M-14. Bearchild rolled his eyes at Branch, and grabbed the muzzle away from him. The old man stared at Bearchild for a moment, and then turned away, shuffling into the house. The Rangers followed suit stepping backwards into their original footprints in the snow.

After a few minutes of no movement within the shelter, Branch whispered, "Hey, man, I wanna leave while I still got all my parts," but there was suddenly a clanking of cooking pots, and in Pavlovian fashion the three were again drawn closer to the shack.

The old man reappeared in the doorway holding several packages wrapped in grease-stained brown paper. He walked onto the bowed steps and cautiously handed the parcels to J.W., started back, then turned to them and mumbled, "Y'all teh dem ta leave my crops 'lone, ya'all hear? We ain't dun nuttin' to harm y'all."

J.W. was not sure if he saw a tiny smile as the old man turned back before entering his home.

* * *

The three rushed off with their haul, Bearchild stopping at the edge of the property to copy the name "Sullens" from the long-neglected mailbox. At the tree line, they halted, ripping open the paper sacks, discovering six guano-coated raw chicken eggs, half a loaf of fresh bread, and, most revered, a pound of fatback bacon. They even had paper to start a fire.

J.W.'s suggestion was that the banquet commence right there and then, but Branch demanded, "Are you crazy? Take one bite, and then let's get into the woods and cook a proper meal, like the civilized human beings we are."

Bearchild nodded in agreement, took one of the eggs, cleaned off as much of the chicken droppings as he felt was adequate to insure his bacterial health, then pulled the shell apart with his grit-blackened, crud-encrusted fingernails. Before a single strand of the slime was spilled on the ground, he extended his neck, put the shell to his lips and allowed a continuous string of yellow mucous to slide into his throat, his eyes rolling at the deliciousness of it all.

J.W. could not decide between the raw egg or the raw bacon until Branch ripped a piece of the salt-covered pork off with his teeth, chewed a few times, gagged, and spit the lump of lard onto the ground. J.W. gagged in parasympathetic sympathy, and settled for a bite of bread.

A gentle breeze was blowing toward the platoon, and the three sought a deeper corner of the forest, finding a secluded thicket where they dug a pit, then constructed an oven for the latest of their culinary adventures. Bearchild started the fire with a single match, igniting the greasy paper that had covered the bacon. He was soon placing thin twigs directly on the oily, yellow flames, barking orders with his hands for special-sized twigs, sticks, and finally logs.

In minutes they drooled beside a respectable wet-wood fire, with Branch and J.W. nodding in concert that it was time to start cooking. Bearchild, however, would not hear of such disrespect until the deadfall tree trunks he had ripped from the earth had ignited, climaxing one of his crowning efforts. J.W. voiced his concern about the smoke, but Bearchild assured him the fire was so hot it endowed the smoke with sufficient energy to rise high above the platoon; the cadres would never notice. Branch stuck his head between them and asked J.W., "Didn't you ever take thermodynamics, man?"

Branch sliced the bacon into bite-sized, one-inch cubes, then cracked the eggs and dumped them into his pristine mess kit, which was about to double as a frying pan. Bits of shell sprayed in as well. And into the midst of the spectacular conflagration was thrust the loaded frying pan. Branch then gathered flattened stones, placed them near the fire, cut the bread into ragged slices with his dull bayonet, and made toast against the steaming rocks.

With the drudgery of cooking accomplished, the three sat back, contemplating the imminent feast, cozy and warm beneath the forest behemoths, enjoying a fire given them by the Stradivarius of flame. It was hard to imagine why their lives had taken such a pleasant turn, and the comfort made the alternative hard to imagine. The pain they had endured seemed distant, as if it had never really happened, and if it had really happened, the three of them were convinced by the splendor bubbling before them that it never would again.

The cracking of the fire was almost deafening, and the spattering of their food added to the charivari. Preoccupied as they were licking the spraying grease off their arms, and laughing like loons at the state to which they had been reduced, they did not hear the snapping of twigs becoming swiftly louder. *Le Chef* Branch leaned forward, still smiling, to stir the pan with a twig and pick out as much shell as he could, but he managed only two loving revolutions around the pot before his eyes were drawn toward the tree line. The excited but gentle expression J.W. had never before seen in Branch then melted with warp speed, compelling Bearchild and J.W. to turn and look up as well.

J.W.'s heart crawled into his throat, and his first thought was to blurt that Branch and Bearchild had forced him to do it. His second thought was to run, but Cowsen, with folded arms, stood before the only egress from the clearing.

The first sergeant rubbed his chin quietly in deep consideration, then began a gentle diatribe. "Rangers, I am truly hurt that I was not invited to your party. Do you think I enjoy partaking of fresh egg salad sandwiches, tuna sandwiches and hoagies with an assortment of smoked meats, while you feast on such a sumptuous repast?" His voice raised several decibels. "On your feet, gentlemen. Dig!"

At first, J.W. thought First Sergeant Cowsen was asking if they understood his command to stand up, but Bearchild slipped his entrenching tool, the army's spindly excuse for a shovel, off his web belt and began to pick at the hardscrabble. Cowsen marked a six-foot-by-six-foot outline in the snow, then added, "As deep as Bearchild is tall, Rangers. I want a two-hundred-and-sixteen-cubic-foot hole where there is merely forest floor now."

J.W. and Branch then stood and pecked with their entrenching tools at the icy earth, netting half a coffee can of frozen dirt with each bladeful, appealing to Cowsen with doleful eyes, beseeching the first sergeant to allow the excavation to end there. Cowsen's eyes, however, did not flicker, and they dug and dug until they arrived a foot-and-a-half below the surface, and J.W. smiled, "Hey, this is where the earth's not frozen anymore."

But Branch spit, "Yeah, well this is where the granite begins, fool."

For the next two hours, as the pit assumed the shape of a mass burial pit, J.W. wondered if Cowsen had become creepy from the scent of the food, and was going to act out what he had witnessed in World War II, prisoners digging their own graves in the POW camps. But at the end of the excavation exercise, Cowsen didn't order them to stand before the pit and wait to be executed. He only laughed sardonically and glared at J.W. "Ranger Weathersby here is going to bury dinner."

J.W. heard himself begging through the haze of fatigue and hunger, "Sergeant Cowsen, sir, do you know what we went through to get this stuff?"

The sergeant bellowed, "Don't call me sir. Serve dinner, Ranger!"

J.W. lifted the mess kit in which the contents had congealed into a frozen brick of white lard marbled with yellow streaks of free-range chicken yolk. He stood, turned the frying pan upside-down and let their salvation pull slowly away from the pot, the whole mass plopping slowly into its grave. Branch mumbled, "Don't he know nothin' 'bout the starvin' children in Africa?"

Cowsen turned to Branch. "Into the hole, Doctor Schweitzer."

Branch lowered himself into the pit, standing there mindlessly, staring at the muddy walls.

"DO IT!" Cowsen exploded.

Branch stepped into dinner with both boots and ground the dream into humus. As he kicked angrily at the mash, the walls of the pit began to crumble in, and Branch was pushed down onto his knees into the coagulated banquet. Now the dirt flowed from the walls in torrents, covering the little man to his waist.

Bearchild and Weathersby jumped toward the hole to save Branch before the dirt covered his head, but Cowsen snapped, "You two stop right there. Get out of that hole this minute, Ranger."

Branch, in his fury, exploded out of the mire on his own, dusted himself off, aside from the dirt stuck to his greasy knees, glared at Cowsen, whispered something to himself, and, as if counting to ten, suddenly relaxed. He turned back to the pit, and being the most pious of the cabal, stood over the crater and intoned a prayer. "From dust to dust and from chicken and porker to dirt."

Cowsen smiled. Branch and J.W. laughed out loud for several seconds, right up to the time Cowsen ordered them, "Fill the hole. We don't want no tired Rangers fallin' in there and eatin' that stuff. That stuff's poison, Ranger."

When the grave was topped off, Cowsen invited them back to the main platoon to assist those who were digging in for the evening, pairs of men preparing "six-by's," in case they were attacked. Since Morelotto had lost his buddy, J.W. was assigned to dig with him.

Fricker was next door digging alone, his latest Ranger buddy a casualty who had gone berserk during the march and fallen from a tree. "What the hell was he doing in a tree?" J.W. asked, shoveling earth, not looking up.

"I don't know. He just kept saying he was seeking political asylum in the embassy."

"In a tree?"

"I don't know, man. He was nuts, I told ya. Then he started to climb up farther, you know, into the thin branches. Said he demanded to see the ambassador. That's when he fell. Broke his arm, I think. Maybe he ate one of those funny mushrooms or somethin'."

* * *

With the hours of digging nearly concluded, and a platoon of foxholes neatly drilled into the mountain earth, and not a moment sooner, a new platoon leader was appointed, given a fresh mission, and a new enemy. Second Platoon was ordered to abandon camp immediately, but not so urgently that there wasn't time to fill the holes and cover them carefully with leaves and deadfall to make it appear as though thirty men had not squandered nearly a day of their lives in a patch of remote earth no one wanted. With the forest restored to its primeval state, Second Platoon moved out in yet another forced march to capture an objective far above the timberline.

* * *

Halfway through the night, the airborne-qualified Rangers were collected together in a clearing and given orders to parachute into the next area of operations, a twenty-mile hike from their present position. The jump-qualified troops were ecstatic, smiling, shaking hands, until word circulated that it was to be a night jump. Seven men went to Cowsen and swore the airborne list was inaccurate, that they had never been to jump school. Since there was no way to check the list, and no way on earth to force a man to jump who said he didn't know how, those men rejoined the walkers, or "leg Rangers," as the cadres sniggered.

The Rangers who fell into the airborne detachment left their platoons with mixed emotions; while relishing an excuse from another nature walk, a night jump was fraught with danger. Some of them might not make it, and at the last minute, several more besieged Cowsen with declarations that they had washed out of airborne school before getting their wings. But the first sergeant ignored them, and the airborne detachment marched to a helicopter landing zone.

From there, they would be airlifted by a HUEY to a larger LZ, where they would board twin-rotor Chinooks for the actual drop. Double-timing through the forest, they were forewarned that if they were late for the pick up, the pilots would presume them dead or captured, and leave immediately. Then they would have to walk into the tactical problem, just like the non-airborne troops, but twice as far, for the airborne pick-up zone was several miles in the opposite direction of the final objective.

They arrived fifteen minutes early and set up into sticks for boarding, then waited two hours until a pair of tired "B" model HUEY helicopters retired from combat duty in Viet Nam because of age, combat damage, and or unfixable mechanical problems, skidded in. J.W. jumped aboard the lead ship, but it was so heavily loaded, the ancient tub groaned as the pilot pulled more and more collective seeking to lift into a hover. He tried to rock the ship into a skidding takeoff, yanking back and forth on the cyclic as if in a car stuck in snow, jamming the gears from drive to reverse and back again, over and over and over. Though everyone aboard was nauseous and preparing to urp up food that wasn't in their bellies, the ship didn't budge.

The pilot dropped the collective and ordered J.W. off the aircraft, but J.W. made a fist around the base of the pilot's seat and refused to let go. The pilot yelled over the engine howl that they would be back in ten minutes, then leaned over and uncurled J.W.'s fingers from the seat rail, pulled the collective harshly, and left J.W. lying in the snow.

"You *better* be back here in ten minutes!" J.W. screamed.

The ships returned, but they were over an hour late. When the pilot looked forward after the Rangers boarded, J.W. gave him the finger. The pilot turned quickly and stared at J.W., then laughed mockingly. J.W. saw the pilot's hand on the intercom switch, and the cabin lights suddenly flicked on, allowing the co-pilot to look back and laugh as well. J.W. glanced down to see what was so funny; but all he observed was the completely torn away inseam of his fatigue pants. Maybe they were laughing because J.W. wasn't wearing underwear.

The lights switched off as they gained a bit of altitude, skids slapping the treetops. The whack of the rotor and whine of the turbine invoked familiar sensations in J.W., sounds that had been ground into his subconscious over the hours and days and months of ass chewings as a student pilot in flight school. Nonetheless, at that moment, J.W. felt aloof, in control, for the first time in months. He knew more about this machine than any Ranger or instructor in Dahlonega. He crawled up to the officer in the right seat and told him, "I'm a chopper pilot, too."

The aircraft commander nodded knowingly and smirked down at J.W. "Yeah? Most of the pilots I know wear clothes. Don't see no wings on your fatigues."

On final approach, one of the pilots turned and flipped a brown paper bag at the Rangers' feet, but they were so gun-shy, no one dared touch it. The co-pilot had to yell at the top of his lungs over the engine howl, "That's for you clowns. Hurry up before I take it back."

Fricker was the first to pounce on the bag, opening it by slamming his fist inside like a drowning man grabbing for a bobbing log. Whatever was inside that sack, it turned Fricker's expression into a mad glare, which caught J.W.'s attention, as did the Mars Bar Fricker extracted from the sack. Seeing food, J.W. involuntarily leapt forward, snatching the bag. He retrieved a Three Musketeers, then greedily fished out a Snickers and a Hershey Bar with Almonds as well. He shoved them into what was left of his fatigue pocket as the flight drew to a close.

* * *

J.W. remembered neither the jump nor the landing. He was asleep. Branch stood over him and shook his head. "Man, you landed as hard as a fat lady jumping off a footlocker. You O.K.?"

J.W. was about to answer when he and Branch were startled by terrified screams from one of the trees ringing the drop zone. Those who had landed safely stowed their chutes in their packs and ran toward the cries. It was Morelotto, snagged in one of the hemlocks, dangling forty feet above the forest floor.

J.W. wasn't surprised Morelotto was the only airborne troop to land south of the DZ. They had been briefed before the jump that the winds were northerly at nearly ten knots, almost high enough to cancel the exercise, and certainly brisk enough to mandate steering hard north to compensate. All of them did so easily, except Morelotto, who, rumor had it, had also landed far from his unit on his cherry jump in Airborne School.

One of the cadres walked under the tree from which Morelotto was swaying and hollered, "How the hell did you miss the DZ, Ranger? What the hell's wrong with you?"

Morelotto had become too anxious to answer as he swung from the high limbs, and one of the Rangers told him to climb the parachute risers into the tree, but Morelotto became tangled in the spaghetti-like nylon cords and disturbed the precarious balance that supported the canopy. After a few snaps of thin twigs, branches began breaking and the troops ran from underneath Morelotto. As he fell, a subtle whoosh accompanied the body, though it was nothing like the beautiful, crisp snap of a canopy deploying at altitude.

Toward the lower branches, Morelotto tumbled a couple of times, and J.W.'s mind flashed to Smith, but there was no thud this time. Morelotto hung for a second, undid his harness, then, ignoring the danger of a fall, collapsed to the earth, weeping that his legs had snapped. He moaned then screeched that he was losing consciousness, unable to breathe, that his neck had been broken. "Medic! Medic! Medic!" he screamed, but there were no health professionals out in the woods at that hour, only cadres.

Unwilling to touch a man whose spinal cord had obviously been snapped, the Rangers stood in frozen horror until Sergeant Poliak pushed his way to the center of the crowd, measured the height of the chute and harness, spit on the ground, just missing Morelotto, and stepped over the writhing Ranger's hulk.

"What the fuck is your problem, Ranger? Get your ass into formation."

J.W. studied the chute hanging from a branch near the end of the final fall. Morelotto's feet were less than two feet from the ground when he opened his harness and jumped toward mother earth. "You just completed the gentlest landing you'll ever have as a paratrooper, Ranger," Poliak grunted. Get your chute out of that tree and stowed, or I'll make sure you pay for it."

Morelotto sheepishly folded his canopy and tied it to his pack, as had the rest of the Rangers, though soon a freezing rain soaked their parachutes and iced the silk. Fricker raised his hand and asked Cowsen where the drop-off point was for the airborne gear, but Cowsen did not respond, and Second Platoon carried the soaked chutes for another week, until the end of Mountain Phase.

* * *

After the last field problem in Dahlonega, they were marched to the huts and given fifteen minutes to pack the gear they had never unpacked. Then they boarded the same open canopy troop trucks that had brought them to Dahlonega, for the six-hour downhill journey back to Harmony Church.

Still desperately cold and saturated with slush from the torrent that had accompanied them down the mountains, they were, nonetheless, held in formation at Harmony Church in front of the barracks and abused by

Captain Vock for being in filthy uniforms. Then he turned suddenly and ordered First Sergeant Cowsen to instruct the men in the proper behavior with which elite soldiers comported themselves during passes in Columbus, Georgia.

Cowsen barked, "When you return here in four hours Gentlemen, you will pack for the final stage of Ranger school. I would suggest you all order dessert tonight. You may have heard that a good meal is best finished with something sweet. Rangers, do not be fooled. That is how life ends in the restaurant world. That is *not* how living in Ranger School ends."

* * *

J.W. called Krista from a pay phone on main post. She wasn't home, and he accompanied his platoon, shy Bearchild, to a restaurant in Columbus several miles from the gates of Fort Benning. He dialed again before they left town, but the line was busy, so he gobbled his near-raw steak and tried to ignore missing her.

At midnight, they were rousted off their bunks to fall into formation for the final spasm, the Jungle Phase in Florida. This time the cattle trucks were covered with thick, hot tarpaulins for the trip into the tropics.

CHAPTER III

Swamp Fox

The long, sweltering journey to Eglin Air Force Base in Florida's panhandle, home of the jungle-training phase of Ranger School, concluded with an explosion that sent a cubic yard of wet sand heaving through rips in the hot tarp that had covered their truck. Sharp palm fronds shot through the open tailgate. Second Platoon had been asleep, and they sprang from their hard benches, startled by the violent welcome to their new home. From outside the cattle trucks, an unfamiliar voice shouted, "MINE!"

A second's hesitation intervened as the men of 68-B sought to decipher where they were waking. Fricker grumbled, "Why does the act of finishing a few minutes of sleep always have to hurt so bad?"

"MINE!" was screamed again. It did not work that time either, so the new voice shouted, "FALL IN!" That brought the Rangers tumbling out of the trucks, clawing their way over each other, landing in their usual, preordained positions. Gillette postulated that platoon formation was not a natural phenomenon at all, but an aberration, which he characterized as "The Entropic Theory in Reverse." Bearchild nodded and smiled in agreement.

The company stood dripping with the earth of their new home. In command of this motley remnant of America's military elite was an Hispanic staff sergeant with a deep-colored, crescent scar that ran the length of his left cheek. J.W. closed his eyes, assuring himself this was just another in the string of recurring nightmares, and that he was actually at home in bed, warm and secure, the taste in his mouth a product of a dozen nights of drunken partying, not from rotting in a prison.

Then, as he had for the past month-and-a-half, he opened his eyes to become slowly aware that it wasn't a dream. It was reality re-entrenching itself, and he was again blanketed in the despair of knowing that, as sure as time flowed, another minute would go by, and that minute could only engender a deepening of the nightmare. His ears buzzed with a hum of psychotic proportions, and the skin of his cheek felt very tight. J.W. supposed he had been wounded in the explosion and slipped a shard of what was left of his shaving mirror out of his rucksack, fearful of actually facing the damage that had been wreaked upon his features. But when his eyes were able to focus after the blast of tropical sun, he saw it was simply dried spit caked on his cheek from the few hours of deep sleep in the trucks.

The company was in formation, facing the tropical sun, and though it was early morning, the glare was overwhelming. Fricker winced in the bright light, then turned his head toward the shadows. In an instant, one of the new cadres had him on the ground, arms extended for five minutes. "Ranger, if you're looking over there, you're not paying attention, are you? This here's the Jungle Phase. It's for real from now on."

The entire company joined Fricker, furnishing J.W. time to observe his new surroundings. He was struck by the Spanish moss clinging to the budding, deciduous trees, the thick, palmetto brush, and the broad-leafed tropical growth he had seen only in movies. He glanced surreptitiously at the new cadres strutting in front of the formation: a swarthy lot, darker and smaller than their brothers in the Mountain Phase. Several Hispanic instructors stood off by themselves. J.W. heard one grunt disdainfully, "Da reech bastards. We teach dem something."

The cadre in command, Sergeant Esposito, the one with the scar, wore his uniform so tightly tailored every thin streak of his musculature rolled on the surface of his camouflage fatigues. He spit disgustedly on the sand as he purveyed his new crop of psychological fodder.

"Welcome to Florida, Rangers. This ain't college no more." He continued in a thick Spanish accent, "You may think you are almost done, but we have you for enough time to teach you something. In the Jungle Phase, you will learn to drive on."

J.W. yawned at the customary welcoming fare, but the man's face betrayed more than the usual disdain for trainees. J.W. noticed Esposito's Combat Infantryman's Badge, the C.I.B., a Revolutionary War musket surrounded by a wreath, and he remembered that to wear the decoration, one had to have been part of an infantry unit that had survived a lot of real combat. J.W. wondered what Sergeant Esposito had been doing the past four years, during the semesters J.W. had passed guzzling beer at loud fraternity parties, sleeping through eight o'clock classes, and fighting mock battles on the prim fields of Penn State's R.O.T.C. quadrangle.

While most of the men on J.W.'s side of the formation would be moving into the professions, the only moving the Sergeant Espositos would be doing was of grunts, and for the rest of their twenty years. There were few occasions in the military, or elsewhere for that matter, where such a concentration of the educated and lucrative-futured found itself under the absolute control of those whom they would eventually dominate. It was only for a thin a slice of the present, but it was a sobering thought.

* * *

J.W. heard a bellowed, "Move out," and Second Platoon covered the unfamiliar terrain without a unit leader, until one of the sergeants tapped Bearchild on the shoulder with a stick, then handed him a sheaf of papers and a map. Bearchild looked toward Branch and J.W., lifted his hand, and motioned with his index finger toward the back of the platoon. The two moved to the rear of the column and, with a nod, Fricker took point. Though not a word was uttered, squads broke into fire teams, protecting their machine gunners and grenade launchers by placing them in the center of the flow.

When Bearchild raised his open palm, the team moved smoothly forward into the jungle. The torment of Harmony Church and Dahlonega had softened their boots, and they had to listen harder for the crunch of the Ranger in front to keep from falling behind. In a mile, they crossed out of the thick tropical vegetation onto golden brown sands from which grew emerald vines that had to be hacked away. In open areas, the savanna grass was higher than the tallest man, and it took several hours to traverse a few hundred meters.

But it wasn't just the terrain that drew their movement to a near standstill, there were myriad booby traps that had been set at crossroads, and violent explosions tore at the platoon every hundred meters as they ventured onto worn paths. The cadres had deposited hunks of dynamite in crevices of tree trunks and from branches throughout the Jungle School, allowing aggressors hidden in the lush undergrowth to detonate the extraordinarily loud devices over the Rangers' heads at will. Occasionally, J.W. spotted the TNT-filled devices hanging from the limbs of the jacaranda and tung oil trees under which the platoon stopped to rest; but it was always too late, and the fake bombs showered them with atomized cordite, burned gunpowder, which stung like burning grains of pepper.

* * *

Fricker forged ahead on point, detonating the majority of the mines and booby traps, trucking across the deadfall until he came to a narrow stream. He had the sound tactical judgment to parallel it, avoiding the munitions, and chose a shallow section to ford. But his fatigue got the best of him, and he suddenly broke another rule of the jungle, to which they had not yet been privy, crossing a body of water alone. When he crawled onto the far bank, he became mired in mud that pulled and tugged at his legs relentlessly, scaring him into a breech of tactical etiquette. He broke silence, screaming madly for help. Even Branch and J.W. heard him, but they agreed in a whisper to maintain their vigil and protect the platoon's rear.

Bearchild cautiously led his men through the thick, tropical, streamside vegetation, hacking at the brush, skirting the cleared trails, fearing more land mines or perhaps a live ambush. Though his immediate concern was to find Fricker, he refused to rush headlong toward the screeching, for the enemy might have captured Fricker, tortured him, and forced him to lure the platoon into a trap.

Slowly they inched forward, Bearchild guiding them in a half-loop to approach the yowling Fricker from behind. The new point man, Gillette, stealthily returned and whispered to Bearchild, "I can see him. Just his head and shoulders. He's stuck in the mud, probably quicksand."

At the streambed, Sergeant Poliak appeared and hissed disgustedly, "Stop moving. Just lay there, ya dumb shit. Why the hell did you get into that crap?"

Fricker tried to answer, though he was too exhausted to speak. He gathered his strength and scissor-kicked, but that only drew him more deeply into the sinkhole. Gillette called to him, "Hey, Fricker, the density of your body is less than that of the sand. Less dense comes to the surface, yes? Like oil floats on water. You can float if you stop moving, and just lean backward and let your legs float up."

Fricker, numb with fatigue, hunger, helplessness, and hopelessness, whacked feebly at the mire until he was devoid of all energy. The moment he stopped thrashing, letting his body fall back, he began to bob upward toward the surface. When his arms emerged, he stretched them to the sides, as if crucified. An inquisitive scorpion jumped from an overhanging puff of Spanish moss onto Fricker's hand. Though it was only a small green spider, just a baby, Fricker found the strength to scream for help.

"Leave it the hell alone," Poliak offered nonchalantly, but Fricker's arms wound like windmills. The sergeant raised his voice. "Sit still! It'll crawl off if you don't screw with it. And if it bites ya, you'll probably just get sick to your stomach. Just leave it alone. And while you're at it, get the hell out of that quicksand pronto like."

Fricker, deaf to the advice, took a swat at the spider and scared the creature, who lifted its petite green tail and brought it down onto a bulging vein on the back of Fricker's hand. Fricker screamed again and slapped his arms against the sand so violently, his body lifted out of the muck like a Titan rocket leaving the launch pad. Free of the ooze, he sprinted onto the bank, ran in circles for a few revolutions like the headless chicken in the mountains, then stopped, vomited on his boots, and fell to the ground, lying on his back like a dead bug.

Several Rangers dashed across the water and lifted Fricker from the ground. His right hand had already swollen to the size of a grapefruit, and he held it up to the sergeant, who forded the rivulet and stepped over Fricker, ignoring him, not even looking down.

The platoon moved across more savanna into swamp, sloshing through stands of cypress. Fricker tried to go on, but he collapsed into the muck repeatedly. On one fall, he aspirated the scummy backwater and threw up again.

Morelotto mumbled indifferently, "What the hell's he got left to urp up? Shit, the last time we ate was in Columbus."

Fricker's jaw tensed. He growled, "Drive on, Ranger," and lifted himself off the ground. But he took only two steps and dropped to the earth again, sweat streaming off his face in torrents. His breathing shallowed, but the rate went up precipitously as he crawled into a fetal ball. His limbs began to shake until the marsh water vibrated in resonance with the tremor for half-a-minute. J.W. was sure Fricker was dead, but his pal again opened his eyes and hissed, "Drive on," and crawled out of the slime. That ponderous grovel was to be his final volitional act of Ranger School.

J.W. lifted Fricker out of the slough and lugged him for hundreds of meters, screaming at him the whole time to move his ass, but whenever J.W. let go of Fricker's fatigue jacket, the wounded compatriot lay back in the swamp water, barely able to keep his head out of the muck. Eventually, Fricker's eyes rolled back into his head, obliging J.W. to fling him over his shoulder in a fireman's carry. After an hour of hauling his moaning cargo through the swamp, J.W. dropped Fricker on a dry patch. Cursing and screaming, J.W. played his last card to save Fricker.

"Drive on, Goddamn Ranger! Move your ass. You can do it if you want to," but Fricker, unable to speak, begged with his eyes not to be left behind.

Branch and Bearchild lent a hand carrying, until they saw in the distance a clearing in the triple canopy jungle, the Eglin Air Force Base Ranger Camp at Field Seven. Fricker focused on the barracks and smiled weakly, but as they crossed the last patch of savanna, he passed into a nether world of babbling incoherence.

Second Platoon broke out of the swamp half-a-kilometer from the billets, white, two-story buildings that made J.W. recall the first night at Harmony Church when it required fully eight large barracks buildings to house the company. Forty-three days later, Ranger Class 68-B fit comfortably into two.

Dropping rucksacks and Fricker at the barracks, the platoon marched to the mess hall for a quasi-lunch of undercooked chicken and potatoes. J.W. had promised to bring something for Fricker, but when he walked back to the barracks ten minutes later with greasy, pink chicken parts wrapped in a thin paper napkin, Fricker, his gear, and the stenciled name on his bunk had vaporized.

"He worked so hard," J.W. argued. "Man, he was a good Ranger. There has to be some justice, some damn reward for the sweat he paid."

Branch offered his own theory. "Man, he's just at sick call. Calm down. He's too funny to die."

J.W., however, did not buy Branch's account, and he burst from the barracks and charged back to the mess hall. He ran to the first table of cadres, the Hispanic cabal. Sergeant Esposito looked up and, seeing a Ranger, returned his eyes to his plate.

"Sergeant, I want to know where Fricker is." J.W. asked a bit louder than he had intended.

Esposito looked up again, staring maniacally into J.W.'s eyes, expecting the violent expression to cause J.W. to turn and flee, but J.W. held his ground. Esposito pursed his lips and spat with a heavy accent, "You want to join him?"

This brought fits of laughter from the table, until J.W. muttered, "Assholes," but so quietly, no one was sure they had heard him.

"I want to know what happened to Ranger Fricker," J.W. persisted. "I carried the son of a bitch for six miles. Where is he?"

Esposito rose, fist cocked by his side. J.W. dropped back a step, and at that, Esposito and his *amigos* guffawed, and slapped their hands against each other. One of them pulled Esposito back into his chair, and the conversation resumed in Spanish.

J.W. pointed a finger at Esposito, who jumped back to his feet and slapped J.W.'s hand away. J.W. shook his head angrily, forming plans to return to Florida after the end of Ranger School and ambush the cabal, this time with real ordinance. It gave him the hope and strength he needed to turn and speed off to the command shack to search for Cowsen, but the duty officer had never heard of a first sergeant by that name.

At the barracks, Bearchild opined, "Fricker'll only have to repeat the Jungle Phase to get his tab. No one would make a body go through the whole thing again."

Branch was more confident. "Man, I'm tellin ya, he's just at sick call. Let him rest a few hours, get a shot of antivenom, or whatever the hell it is they give you for bug bites. He'll be back tonight. They're not gonna leave his gear around; they took it to the hospital with him."

"It's antive*nin*," Gillette corrected.

* * *

In formation, Gillette mumbled, "We always face the sun. Working at the Ranger School in the corps of cadres must require a damn degree in meteorology."

But no matter into which compass direction they turned during the first run of the Jungle Phase, it was, without fail, into the sun. That first dash in Florida brought them to a set of bleachers anchored in two feet of tepid swamp. In Florida, the balcony was reserved for the alert; only the reputed sleepers were assigned front row center seats. J.W. and Branch, the first to be assigned to the front row seats, found it a challenge to hold themselves down and keep from floating away.

Several small burlap sacks were piled on a table in front of the bleachers; "Great, another fuckin' show and tell," came from deep within the peanut gallery.

A spit shined instructor, standing and lecturing in a foot of water, welcomed them to the Jungle Phase, then demanded to know which of the Rangers had made the introductory comment. After several sets of waterborne push-ups, Morelotto finally admitted his gaff, and the instructor had him stand next to the podium.

The company was offered the standard threat about having lost men already, before the training for that most important of phases had even begun, and there were the ubiquitous promises that there would be more. Second Platoon stared at the spot in which Fricker should have been floating.

Another cadre took a position at the lectern. He surveyed the undulating burlap bags, selecting one that wiggled particularly vigorously. J.W.'s eyes enlarged, but Branch reassured in a whisper, "Just a sleight of hand trick, man. Whutch you worried 'bout?"

"Rangers, you will be meeting all sorts of creatures in the swamps. Be careful. Some of these fellas can clean your clock." The instructor opened the sack and brought forth an ugly, green serpent. The reptile flexed and extended furiously, seeking to turn its fanged, unhooked jaws toward its tormentor. The sergeant laughed. "This is a bad actor, Rangers."

He handed it to Morelotto by its triangular head. "Don't hurt it. Be gentle, Goddamnit." The monster opened and closed its jaws rhythmically, as if it were playing Ravel's *Bolero* on a self-contained Sony Slitherman, glistening drops of venom dripping from its fangs as it oscillated hypnotically. Morelotto relaxed, and at that moment, a furious hiss ushered from the snake's mouth. Reflexively, Morelotto squeezed the serpent's head, and droplets of caustic venom sprayed onto his face. He threw the snake to the ground, which was actually water, and the creature swam in a fury under the bleachers and then further into the swamp.

Sergeant Esposito, who had been standing on the other side of the podium, dove after the snake as it struggled to escape. He went one way, the snake the other. Esposito slipped in the slimy drink, falling face first into the murk. The snake reversed course and swam within inches of Esposito's face, as if to bid his captor farewell, then vanished at a miraculous velocity into the reeds and the cypress.

The instructor started after Morelotto, who had retreated into the bleachers, moving toward the top tier by bounds, apparently not having given a thought as to what in the hell he would do when he got there.

Esposito also leapt after Morelotto, and the three collided halfway up the seats. Esposito's foot skidded on the algae-coated wood, and his leg dropped between the seat and the floorboard, though the momentum of his furious body was still headed toward Morelotto.

A crack as loud as Smith's snapping rifle butt back at Harmony Church eons before echoed off the swamp, and Esposito gasped as he looked down to behold his bleeding tibia poking through his skintight fatigues. It was the last sound from Esposito, and J.W. thought the sergeant was dead. The cadreman was, however, silently bargaining with his torment, waiting for the medics, unwilling to squander energy on useless reproach.

J.W., ecstatic with the thought of a corps of cadres depleted by one, whispered in a Spanish accent as the sergeant was loaded on the litter, "Say hello to Fricker. Guess you gonna join him!"

Esposito spit in reply.

The instructor at the podium took up where he had left off, adding not a word to his prepared lecture. He opened another burlap sack, extracting from it a beautifully-colored, orange-and-black banded snake. Though this creature was small, thin, and docile, the instructor handled it more carefully than the pit viper, warning, "This is the most poisonous reptile in the Americas.

"Now Rangers, the coral doesn't have fangs. It has to gnaw its victim to death, and it has to be soft skin like in the web of the toes or hands." The instructor must have suddenly remembered the green snake, because he held the short, vividly colored serpent aloft and screamed, "You will not be allowed to handle this animal! Except maybe for you, Ranger." The sergeant climbed into the bleachers and waved the coral snake in Morelotto's face.

The next exhibit was a repulsive, tawny viper, passed around for every Ranger to fondle. Bearchild handed it directly to J.W., skipping Branch, who refused to touch it, and then passing over Morelotto, who couldn't be trusted to touch it. J.W. grasped it with his eyes closed, pinching the serpent's head between his thumb and index finger, acting as gently as could have been expected, considering the handful of slimy, deadly poison he anticipated. But the snake was cool and dry, like fine leather, and curled itself around the warmth of his hand. J.W. liked the feel, and relaxed his grasp. The snake liked that, too, though only briefly, for it lunged toward J.W.'s eyes, and he pinched so hard the snake writhed in pain. Grabbing the head with his other hand, J.W. cocked his arms to heave the snake into the swamp, but the sergeant dashed forward through the water and swiped the creature out of J.W.'s hands, dropping it angrily back in the sack.

The rest of the session was all tell, no more show. At the end of class, J.W. raised his hand. "Sergeant, do reptiles sleep at night like people are supposed to?"

"Gentlemen, night operations are the commonest time to suffer pit viper envenomation. If you encounter one of these creatures, you are to give it a wide berth."

* * *

The company split into platoons and departed on the first tactical problem of the Jungle Phase. Branch, tapped as the initial cadet platoon leader, took the manila envelope, reached into his rucksack, and pulled out rimless glasses. A black sergeant watched Branch and laughed, "You look like you know something there, Ranger."

Branch snapped back, "What do you mean? You didn't think a nigger officer could know something?"

Branch turned away seething, but soon took a deep breath and studied the orders, then raised his hand with an open palm; Bearchild and J.W. took the rear. Branch closed his hand until only the index finger stuck skyward, then looked toward Flanagan, one of the three sailors who had just joined the class.

Unbeknownst to the Rangers, the navy had struck a deal with the army, sending some of their navy SEALs in training to Ranger School for part of their instruction. The Rangers, irritated that the SEALs had not gone through the first two phases, and were there only for jungle training, took every opportunity to embarrass them. What the Rangers didn't know, however, was that the SEALs had already been through a year's worth of the first and second phases, and only one out of ten of their starting class had made it this far. When Branch's finger went up in the air, he expected Flanagan to ask why he was looking at him, but the new man nodded and slipped out of the clearing onto point.

The triple canopy jungle covered a stinking marsh dotted with the rounded stumps of young cypress trees. Further into the mire stood the tall thin trunks of mature cypress, their dark, feathery leaves forming a gloomy canopy over the swamp. What meager light filtered through the trees was absorbed by the Spanish moss that hung so thickly, there were times, even at noon, that the troop to the front was only an eerie shadow. The green, velvety web of moss, though beautiful from a distance, entangled easily in clothes and weapons, and a Ranger's open mouth activated a cosmic attraction between the intensely bitter moss and his tongue. Once in a Ranger's mouth, the next hour was given to picking the fine tendrils from his mucous membranes.

The swamp water was a different matter. Though the cadres warned that if even a drop of the slough liquid was swallowed, the ensuing illness would be one Rangers rarely survived, a mouth rinse of swamp water was the only way to clear the mouth of the tenacious, caustic Spanish moss. But the bog water also left an unsavory, lingering aftertaste that made not brushing one's teeth for a week seem relatively pleasant.

In the swamps, one had to follow the splash and gurgle of the footsteps to the front, for the territory was devoid of snapping twigs. Rangers who fell asleep on the move soon tripped over cypress stumps, falling headlong into the drink, waking to gulps of swamp water sliming down their throats, followed immediately by fits of coughing so intense, that level of hacking was generally encountered only in TB wards.

After their submerged skin had become sufficiently wrinkled and white, Sergeant Perez, Esposito's replacement, stopped Branch and suggested they leave the swamp and cross back into the savanna. He tempted Branch, pointing to the thick plains covered with endless thirteen-foot stalks of beefy elephant grass. "Dry up there, Ranger. And see those trees in the fields, the tall thin ones? You can send a man up one of 'em and look out *mucho* 'sees'."

Branch listened politely, then gathered the platoon into a huddle and drew on his hand with a pen. His plan to overwhelm the aggressors, reportedly occupying a swamp-bound compound, was simple: launch an attack two hours earlier than expected by keeping his men moving through the fetid swamp, instead of through the slower, but seemingly more pleasant, savanna. Branch solidified his final battle plans, raised his fist and was about to call out, "On me," but he was stopped in his tracks by a miffed Sergeant Perez, who took a palm frond, slapped him in the head, and declared Ranger Branch killed in action.

In nearly the same motion, the broad leaf fell upon Morelotto's shoulder. Plans changed dramatically. Morelotto ordered the platoon to move across the dry plains and avoid the swamp at all costs. He explored the land with his eyes. From a distance, the savanna appeared to be ordinary grass, an arid, unmowed lawn. Though the troops were initially delirious with the absence of water when they lifted themselves out of the swamp, the broad, sharp blades of elephant grass soon sliced their skin with knife-like precision.

After an hour tramping the untamed monster grass of Florida's panhandle, Second Platoon was forced to draw their hands up into the sleeves of their fatigue jackets; fingers scrunched so tightly into fists, the tips became numb. Though weapons were tethered to their belts with bootlaces, the leather of those ties had long since rotted, and several of the commandos went on sleep walking, their fingers so insensate, they were unaware they had dropped their rifles along the way.

J.W.'s fingers were as numb as if he had slept on them for weeks, and he, too, dropped his M-14, but in his case, the metal barrel struck a rock and bounced up against his right shin. That he felt, and the blood, which seeped through the remnants of his fatigues, coagulated the wound to his pant leg, hardening until every step pulled painfully on the crusted laceration. When he could no longer stand it, he took a deep breath, closed his eyes, and yanked the pants free. But this only restarted the bleeding, and his pants stuck to the laceration again. On the third cycle of pain and pants pulling, he cut a rectangular piece of plant flesh from the eight-inch wide blades of savanna grass and wrapped it around his leg. The humble dressing kept his pants away from the wound, and also allowed the blood to run freely down his leg, engendering an even more squishy boot. All in all, he was satisfied with the deal that left him, on balance, in a lesser state of torment.

Those lads who emerged from the jungle without their rifles were sent to appear before a panel of cadres, Sergeant Perez at the center. He challenged each man: "Ranger, you been carrying that piece for two months. What the hell do you mean you don't know when you lost it? Now you and your platoon get your asses back into that terrain and find it ASAP. I don't give a shit if it takes a week. I got no hurry. You don't finish the course on time, we'll keep you here until you do."

By 2300 hours, with all weapons retrieved from the savanna, Morelotto steered his charges back into the swamp. J.W. thought incessantly of the ugly green snake and its viper siblings, more concerned with the venomous fauna than his fatigue. He was not alone in his fear. Each time the platoon stopped, those not involved in planning the tactical problem climbed into trees to escape the water. In the moonlight, J.W. saw Rangers propped high in the cypress, resting like night jungle creatures, ready to strike. Alas, however, even the fear of death by serpent was not sufficient to keep them awake, and one by one, the Rangers, in their deep stupors, dropped into the swamp, gurgling angrily, "Fuck me, fuck this shit. I hate this fuckin' place."

Deeper into the muck, Branch, Bearchild, and J.W. were assigned rear patrol, where they moved as lone foxes. At 0200 they passed a black figure, a bear, J.W. was sure, and whispered to Bearchild, "I think it's your father, man."

Actually, it was Morelotto crouched in the slime, babbling to no one in particular. Somehow, he had managed to stay plump, a Pillsbury Dough Boy with a greasy stubble of black hair. Branch shook the poor man, who jumped up and kicked one of the cypress stumps, then cursed, "Goddamn machine!" He turned heatedly to Branch. "Hey, man, gimme a nickel. You owe me the money. You're the one who broke into my footlocker last night."

"We were on the cattle trucks last night, dick head," Branch retorted, semi-amused.

"You black mothers broke into my footlocker."

Branch's fist cocked, but Bearchild grabbed it. "Give 'em the money," Bearchild suggested, staring intently at Morelotto.

"Fuck, no," Branch spat.

"Then I'll give it to him," Bearchild groaned as he picked a pebble out of the water and handed it to Morelotto, who tried to put the stone into the stump he had been kicking. When the tree remained inanimate, Morelotto punched the wood with both fists, tried the pebble again, then turned back and yelled at Branch, "I asked for a nickel. You gave me a Goddamn quarter."

"Don't blame me, man. Bearchild gave you the money."

Morelotto now targeted Bearchild. "The Goddamn Coke machine don't give change. And you know it, Chief."

Branch corrected him. "Don't be an asshole, man. The machine's stuck. That's the problem. You need to kick it a few times as hard as you can. Hit it with your hands. Punch the shit outta the son of a bitch. And don't call Ranger Bearchild Chief."

Morelotto, not satisfied with that explanation either, swung his rifle at Branch's head; but Bearchild restrained Morelotto, and J.W. pulled Branch away.

"So, Morelotto, who's minding the store? You're the spittoon leader, right? You gotta get back up there and lead us into battle. We need you, man," Bearchild suggested as he tugged him gently toward the main contingent. Morelotto emerged momentarily from his psychosis, and walked peacefully forward to his post and retook command.

For an hour, Morelotto marched at the head of his unit, but then dropped back again, puffing, though working sufficiently hard to stay a few meters ahead of the three men on rear guard. He was, however, still close enough for Branch to take his considered revenge. "Think of it, Morelotto," Branch whispered seductively, "a large pizza, man: black olives, Italian sausage, pepperoni." Branch then popped his trump card. "Cold beer, Morelotto—five, six, no, seven glasses of cold Shaefer beer to go with the pizza. Much as you want, man."

Branch elaborated, remaining only feet behind his prey, frequently adding another topping to the pie, "onions, mushrooms, anchovies," smacking his lips, groaning in gustatory pleasure until Morelotto started to weep. It was at that point J.W. believed the last molecule of Morelotto's biological energy had been tapped, and that it was finally time for the Dough Boy to unite with the ranks of the disappeared. Morelotto dropped to a knee, and the three passed him. J.W. wanted to stop and drag him, but Branch whispered, "Let him be. Let the cards fall where they will."

* * *

The three men on rear point stopped frequently to rest, speaking of Morelotto, and how racism had finally taken its tariff. They also bragged that they had evolved into nomads of the swamp, men capable of going without, toughs who existed on a plane far above that of the fodder in the ranks. J.W. set his jaw, proud of what he had become. He acknowledged, for the first time in his life, that maybe he was better than at least one person he knew, and as the three moved on, he walked with a swagger that made him feel even more splendid, so wrapped up in his new persona that he did not hear the slow, deliberate, silent steps that should have forced him to take notice of the intruders closing in from behind.

When the thick rustling of a full patrol behind them became loud enough to hear over J.W.'s gloating saunter, Branch cursed, "Shit, I knew it. We should'a hooked south."

J.W. nodded in agreement as did Bearchild, the three accepting that in their laziness and enjoyment over belittling Morelotto, they had failed to swing back around through the savanna to ensure no one was tailing them. When the cacophony of blades of elephant grass smacking together came close, the three dropped to their knees, preparing to jump the intruders.

Measuring the level of clatter, Bearchild whispered, "Too many of 'em. A squad. Don't move. We'll hit 'em from behind after they pass."

But it was only a single body that crashed through the vegetation to pass in front of them. Branch laughed derisively as he called out, "Green olives, Genoa salami."

Morelotto barely turned to flip them the finger as he jolted through the weeds. He jogged back to his position at the head of the platoon, reporting to Sergeant Perez, "No enemy troops back there."

"How do you know, Ranger?"

"I checked back there myself, Sergeant." He started to add,

"Sometimes you can't…" but slapped his lips shut before he uttered the words "trust those assholes."

"Good. You're off the hook, Ranger. Tell your men to take a load off while I go back and bring in the rear point."

As Perez moved toward the patrol's rump, he found the three tail gunners sitting against a tree smoking, laughing about how close they believed they were to riding themselves of Morelotto. That was precisely when Sergeant Perez snuck up behind them. He had them drop into the swamp and commence fifty plus one, with a jungle twist in which the long stroke of the push-up was not the painful arm-extended position, but the phase with one's face next to the ground, i.e., in the putrid water.

Perez explained, "That's for not paying attention to someone sneaking up on you. And Rangers that will also help you learn how to hold your breath for long periods. A Ranger never knows when that'll come in handy."

With the patrol back together, Branch went looking for Morelotto, and greeted him with a, "Double thick crust, extra cheese."

Perez overheard Branch's taunt, but he did not react to the misdemeanor of one Ranger seeking to harm another, only to the felony of ranting about food. That cost Ranger Branch and his fellows, including Morelotto, a march back a few hundred meters into the drink for a sloshing fifty and one.

* * *

With a new platoon leader chosen, their next objective was a guerrilla command and control center guarded by an elite enemy force. Intelligence reports indicated thirty to fifty well dug-in, heavily armed troops with automatic weapons. That, however, was the extent of J.W.'s recollection of the briefing. The rest was lost in the steaming scent of the hot can of Beef Stew being consumed greedily by Staff Sergeant Perez.

Earlier in his army experience, J.W. had found the stew to be a particularly nauseating C-ration selection, on a par with his Aunt Fanny's Hungarian goulash, or Branch's fantasy, the Ham and Limas, but just the aroma of Beef Stew precipitated one of his more and more frequently occurring schizophrenic breaks. Searching the clearing with his eyes, J.W. was sure every one of his Ranger compatriots, not just Perez, was enjoying olive drab tins of food, and he walked in circles begging for his share. As he approached each sleeping soldier, however, the meals vanished, leaving only a lingering scent of Franks and Beans, Ham and Eggs, or Spaghetti and Meatballs. Some of the men looked up at him and asked, "What's your problem, man?

When he tried to answer, all he could whimper was, "I just want my share of the chow. Is that so bad?"

Yet, as his hunger deepened, J.W. became increasingly and profoundly despondent, convinced he had reached a permanent state of painful starvation from which he would never escape. He began to surrender to the biting emptiness in his gut and his heart, and the old thoughts of quitting roiled back into his consciousness. He announced to Branch and Bearchild at the next checkpoint, "I'm gonna sit this one out. You go on. I'll catch up."

Branch shook his head irately. "Sit this one out, my ass. Drive on dud. Plenty time to rest when you're dead." Though the words did not motivate J.W., when Branch kicked him in the butt, J.W. rose to his feet and marched weavingly behind his partners. In a few minutes, though, J.W. drifted back into semi-consciousness, falling victim to a profound food hallucination. The only difference between Morelotto and J.W. was ethnic memory. In front of J.W.'s eyes was not pizza and beer, but a plate of hot, buttered, egg noodles dusted with crystals of sea salt and a few nuggets of freshly-ground pepper. In the center were two plump, kosher hot dogs straight from the grill at Nathan's Deli on Coney Island.

J.W. drifted alongside Branch and asked if he knew where he could find Goulden's mustard to complete the feast, but Branch was busy chattering to himself, and in the haze of his nightmare, J.W. thought he heard Branch praying for ribs and cornbread. Bearchild also maundered to himself, but naming foodstuffs about which J.W. had never heard.

J.W. chased his apparition for hours, the steaming pasta and glistening franks emanating a luscious fragrance that drew him incessantly forward. Several times his arms reached out for the meal, but his fingers were always several inches from seizing it. The vision, so close yet so far, had become painful, and J.W. thought only of quitting Ranger School and calling his Aunt Fanny to beg for a bowl of her goulash.

Eventually the visage of Fanny faded, and J.W. chased his frankfurters and noodles again until he tripped and landed on his back in a yucca patch. One of the toothpick-sized, spear-tipped prickers broke off in his butt, shattering the prospect of ever overtaking the mirage. As Branch pulled him to his feet, J.W. begged, "You gotta help me, man. Something's stuck in my ass."

"Man, what is it with you? Shit, pull down your pants."

Puzzled as to where his rear guard had gone, Sergeant Perez popped into their clearing just as Branch was completing the extraction of the remaining fragment from J.W.'s butt. Branch's vivisectional efforts were summarily recorded in Perez' notebook, who ordered disgustedly, "Pull up your pants, sick Ranger."

Back at the main contingent, J.W. watched, mouth watering, as Morelotto, now the forward scout, reported a small group of aggressors sitting around a campfire two hundred meters ahead. "They're surrounded by boxes of C-rations, cans of Coke, Mr. Pibb, Orange Crush, 7-Up, and a small carton of Hershey Bars, some with and some without almonds. The box appears to be half-full of candy, and the cartons of Cs have hardly been touched."

The platoon leader wrote notes and nodded his head in thanks for the valuable intelligence, but Sergeant Perez interrupted. "What about their weapons, Rangers? What about security?" he demanded.

Morelotto thought for a moment, then apologized. "Sorry, Sergeant, I guess I forgot to check on that."

* * *

The enemy pretended not to hear Second Platoon approach, the Ranger lead elements sliding relatively silently through the water, drawn to their objective by an enormous bon fire. "Man, these guys are stupid," Morelotto shook his head. "A fire like that? Shit, you can't miss 'em."

"Man, it's you who's stupid." Branch muttered. "Bigger the fire, even you could find 'em. Sooner we find 'em, sooner the attack's over, sooner they get to sleep, sooner we got another damn mission. They win, we lose. SOP."

The aggressors were silhouetted by the fire, lounging comfortably on the wicker porch of a tropical house suspended two feet above the swamp on stilts. The Ranger platoon leader raised his hand. Safeties clicked off, and when his arm dropped, Second Platoon commenced firing. The aggressors vaulted out of their hammocks, startled, confused, and disoriented. The attack was so fierce, there was no escape for the enemy. Each of them died in place. As the last enemy fell theatrically onto the dry porch, their lieutenant appeared, had the deceased aggressors stand, counted their noses, and told them to retreat to their rallying point in the swamp.

Most of the Rangers, believing they had crushed their adversary, dropped onto the abandoned hammocks to rest and savor triumph. The cadres, however, appeared out of the night, cajoling, "Rangers, pretend these are North Vietnamese regulars and Viet Cong guerrillas. You need to hunt them down. They're dead tired and hungry. They don't even have helmets. They're running bareheaded, Rangers. That tells you they're running for their lives. Their discipline is gone. All that training, the months and years. All of it gone. Don't let up on 'em, Rangers, pursue and destroy!"

Those Rangers in the purview of the cadres reentered the swamp, slogging through the putrid water until a lane grader called them together half-a-mile beyond the objective. "O.K., that's it men. You did a good job, Rangers. In Viet Nam, after an attack like that, you will come to cowering enemy troops. Begging to live. Some will run from you and trip over their dying compatriots. You'll come upon others weeping like babies, wondering if they're going to live to see the sun.

"Your job as soldiers is to fight, not murder. You are still human beings, actually superior human beings, and you will act as such. The enemy, once beaten, is not to be tortured or spit upon. To kill a captured soldier is murder, murder, not combat. And you are not murderers. That is not what you are. When the battle is over, you will treat them with respect, for they are soldiers, no happier to be there than you are. Don't any of you ever forget that."

* * *

Those Rangers who had escaped notice by the cadres at the original objective forced their way into the jungle house, shrieking with delight upon entering. The shouts reverberated through the swamps, drawing most of the Rangers away from the sermon being delivered by the lane grader. The troops ran through the swamp back to the building where the Ranger platoon leader watched helplessly, then climbed a cypress, imploring his men to abandon the house and form a perimeter. The more vehemently he extolled his men to act like soldiers, the faster the returning Rangers galloped toward the house to see what had happened inside.

J.W. arrived at the doorway as a collection of Rangers in a circle pulled and tugged, screaming at an object to their center. He gasped, realizing they had captured an aggressor and were gutting him. A sense of repulsion consumed him, and despite his hunger and fatigue, he dove forward into the fracas to stop the outrage. When he clawed his way into the middle of the melee, he found his fellows pulling, not at an enemy troop, but tearing cardboard boxes of C-rations apart with their teeth, handing the spoils of war to their buddies.

J.W. reached for his share, seizing an ugly little can of bad tasting, under and over cooked, incorrectly spiced, not spiced, unpopular selection of military "food." The more reasonable troops satisfied themselves with one can, and then escaped, sprinting pell mell into the swamp to feast quietly. A few pawed for an extra tin, their egress delayed just long enough to allow the return of the deceased aggressors, who squeezed into the hut and pulled the Rangers violently off the cache. Most of the avaricious Rangers wound up with nothing, though a few held desperately to a can as they were hurled through the door by the enraged aggressors, Ranger bodies landing face first in the swamp.

J.W. escaped with his precious tin, diving over the railing into the slough. With feet firmly mired in the mud, he squatted and placed his P-38 can opener on the lid, greedily anticipating the first wisp of the aroma of cold Ham and Eggs. As the metal was pierced, however, the vacuum was so strong, it blew the little can opener out of his swollen fingers into the water. He pried open the rest of the top with his teeth and bayonette, and slurped down the congealed concoction, commenting to himself that the meal was excellent, though the facilities were, albeit, a bit wanting. J.W. lay back against a cypress stump and burped for the first time in weeks, then relived in his mind, over and over, the fine dining experience.

Some of the Rangers tried to hide by squatting under the water holding their cans above their heads. The cadres sloshed through the swamp, slapping and kicking C-rations out of Rangers' hands. Then they ordered the company into formation, where the troops braced in three feet of water. The command was given for mouths to be opened for inspection, and the names of those found with telltale fragments of food on their scummy teeth were recorded.

J.W. beat the cadres. He had rinsed his mouth with swamp water, gargling out rancid rodent and bird parts along with bits of illicit C-ration, laughing that it was not necessary to inspect mouths to determine who had eaten. The fortunate stood less slumped, their muscles not shuddering in a vicious tremor. As J.W.'s body absorbed the calories, he felt wonderful, more alert than he had in weeks, though within five minutes, his nervous system started to function again, and he became more attuned to the pain in his legs, the burning lacerations on his arms and, mostly, to his biting hunger. In ten minutes, J.W. Weathersby was again ravenous, and this time he was alert enough to realize it.

* * *

The new platoon leader, Wardally, an exchange lieutenant from the Grenadan army, dispatched Bearchild, Branch, and J.W. to forward point, asking them to scout ahead and rendezvous with him several hours later. The three ventured forth on their sortie, and J.W. imagined his strength renewed, his mind clear. He laughed aloud, considering his part in the dog and pony show featuring the three loose canons on auto pilot, amusing themselves, firmly entrenched in their specialty, board-certified point men, such respected legends in their own time, even the foreign students looked to them for leadership.

But J.W.'s reverie was short-lived, as Branch was soon growling. "Man, I gotta get outta this water, it's burning my thing."

J.W. offered back, "What the hell you talkin' about? The water's only a foot deep."

"Well, *my* thing's draggin' in it. Mine's more than a quarter of an inch, white boy. No wonder you had so much damn trouble with the ladies."

Branch let out a howl of laughter, and even the corners of Bearchild's lips curled, though almost imperceptibly. "Yeah Bearchild," Branch cackled, "you tell 'im. You know what I'm sayin'. Looks like one of your braves scalped him in the wrong place. Must'a took it home to his squaw. Man, I can hear her laughing now. Put that thing on her necklace along with the other peas and beans and corn kernels, man. Plant it in the spring. Who knows what the hell you gonna get? 'Husband, you see this little plant comin' up outta the ground? What the hell is it? A infant carrot or somem'?'" Branch went on and on, mumbling more idiocy until something happened in Ranger school Class 67-8 that had never happened before, and would likely never again—Bearchild chuckled.

But in truth, the water was aggravating, and everyone's feet were tender from the unending hours in the soup. The three consulted their maps and made for the only dry ground within ten square miles, a dirt road, an access causeway that had been crafted decades before through the middle of the slough by the workers of the Civilian Conservation Corps during the depression. Bearchild's map study suggested three hours to the objective if they walked the causeway, five if they slogged the swamp ahead of the platoon as they had been ordered.

But J.W. warned, "That road's marked CCC. May not still be there. Those guys didn't exactly build things to last."

Then Bearchild went back to the map. "If it's where it says it is, that's one hour away. That's all we lose. Still beat the platoon by better than one hour. Worst case scenario; one hour sleep, best three. Worth the effort. We win every way you slice it."

That computed, J.W. whispered excitedly, "Man, if you're right, and I'm sure you're right, that's comes to one hundred and eight minutes of shut eye, even taking into account that we have to double back at the end of the march for a debriefing. No contest, baby. Let's do it." J.W. laughed.

"My brother's an accountant. Now that's two of us in the family. He works for Columbia Pictures, and I'm a jungle bean counter. But he's wrong. All that shit he's been telling me for years, that life's just dollars and gettin' laid, and in that order. He's misdirected, I'm tellin' ya. It's minutes of sleep and calories consumed."

As advertised, they came to the dry, raised road in one hour, and sat there for a short vacation, letting their feet breathe in the night air, eventually changing into dry socks. Then they walked slowly, happily through the pitch blackness, chatting and smoking. A mile later, they happened upon several dark, truck-sized storage containers on the shoulder. "A curious find, to be sure," Branch nodded as he moved cautiously through the dark toward the metallic, oily-scented structures. Suddenly, Branch gasped and broke ranks, shooting ahead, disappearing into the night. Bearchild and J.W. stopped dead, standing motionlessly until Branch reappeared and whispered loudly, "They're trucks, man. Deuce-and-a-halves. They got camouflage on 'em. Come look."

Branch vaulted aboard the lead vehicle and checked to see if the drivers were asleep. "Empty!" he called out, waving his comrades closer. J.W. climbed up into the cab and rifled under the seats, and then in the engine compartment for food, hitting upon only three packs of Winstons. "Not my brand," he whispered to Branch, who shot his hand forward and snatched them.

"Well, they just became my brand, fool."

In the meager starlight emerging from behind storm clouds, J.W. watched Branch eyeing, then playing with the ignition switch, flipping it back and forth gently between his fingers. J.W. smelled the wheels of Branch's brain grinding, his black eyes shining brightly, oblivious to the concept of actions begetting consequences. Branch whispered out the window, "Bearchild, get your butt up here."

As his Ranger buddy hopped into the cargo bed, Branch brought the engine to life, then nursed the truck out of the camouflage. With lights off, they crawled along the swamp-lined causeway a mile or two per hour. When one of the tires slid into the swamp, Branch cursed and jammed the vehicle into four-wheel drive; but unable to distinguish the edge of the road from the swamp, floundered further into the muck. The truck tipped sideways, the front wheels sinking deeper into the mud.

J.W. and Bearchild were about to abandon ship, but Branch called out, "Screw it," flipped on the lights, caught sight of the edge of the road, jammed the truck into low low four-wheel drive, first into reverse, then into forward, gunned the noisy diesel engine tachometer up to red line, and jumped back onto the causeway. With a few grunts and pumps of his muscular arm, he managed to ram the transmission into cruising mode, and they soon sailed along the road at thirty miles an hour until Bearchild, still in the truck bed, turned and spotted head lamps behind them pulling closer. He leaned into the cab and warned Branch, who downshifted smoothly, then floored the rattling diesel, squeaking out another kilometer before slowing and dropping the front wheels back into the swamp. The truck came to rest sideways, blocking the road, preventing a tow vehicle from gaining purchase to pull it free. Branch killed the engine by flooding it, then left the brights, heater motor, and ignition on to sap the battery.

The three abandoned ship swiftly, diving into the muck as they set out across the swamp. Branch sucked air like a racehorse, but laughed in a howl, the first and only time J.W. ever saw him happy. Then Bearchild smiled, and J.W. waited for another guffaw from the solemn man, but causeway high jinx were apparently not as hilarious as J.W.'s challenged purported reproductive apparatus. Exhausted, they stopped in a patch of tamarind and hid amongst the delicate, lacy leaves. A few shriveled brown seedpods hung tenaciously from the branches, having survived the winter. J.W. wondered why those few had managed, and others had not.

The three smoked Winstons, watching from a distance as the second deuce-and-a-half arrived at the crime scene, the driver and a few others wading ten meters into the swamp, searching for the perpetrators, then sloshing angrily back to the trucks. Branch's eyes were wide with excitement as the truck they had commandeered refused to kick to life. He was even more amused when the aggressor crew attempted to stretch a jumper cable toward the first truck. As Branch had strategized, it did not reach. Then, struggling and cursing, they removed the battery from the second deuce-and-a-half. Branch rubbed his hands in ecstasy, mumbling to himself, "Dumb fucks. No way for them to know, man. No way. They'll never figure out it was Rangers who fucked 'em."

The three felons slogged across more swamp toward the objective, protesting the awful stench of the putrid, viscous water, cursing the miles left to suffer, and the aggressors who had curtailed their motorized junket. Branch moaned, "We should'a pushed on for another mile or two before ditching the truck."

J.W. was about to agree when Bearchild put his finger to his lips to quiet them, then cupped his hands behind his ears, listening to an eerie howling miles away. J.W. heard it too, and asked, "Bearchild, what is that, my man?"

"Voices."

Branch listened harder. "They's calling us by name. Tellin' us to rejoin the platoon." He thought for a moment. "No, man, I'm not doin' it. We don't go back. We'll just tell 'em we never heard a thing." Bearchild and J.W. nodded in agreement. They can't prove nothin'. Just drive on. Man, we were just doin' our job, looking for the bad guys."

* * *

Deeper in the swamp, they discovered a thatch of twisted cypress in which they hung for an hour's nap. When the rest of the platoon came into auditory contact, the three point men shinnied down and drifted toward the sound of men lapping through water. It was time to rejoin the main body of Rangers and check in, but it took another half hour to reach Second Platoon, now just twenty-eight troops circled in a wet perimeter. The three point men delivered a report that they had spotted the enemy in the swamp some time before, but the aggressors weren't anywhere near the platoon, and in fact were moving away from the Rangers, so they didn't think it necessary to come back and warn them.

But even in the dark, it was hard for the point men to ignore the angry stares of their compatriots. At first, J.W. believed it was because they had rested, that their faces appeared relaxed, though he soon learned that Platoon Leader Wardally had been relieved of command, and the platoon was blaming them.

Wardally had been ordered to do a roll call in the middle of the swamp, accounting for everyone except his three point men. He had then been directed by the cadres to dispatch a patrol to retrieve them, even if that meant using the road, flashlights, even screaming names for the rest of the night, if that is what it took. When his point crew was not to be found, Wardally was forced to acknowledge publicly he had lost three men, an admission that cost him his job, and probably his place in Ranger School, and his future in the Grenadan military.

J.W. argued with Branch, "Man, this is bad. What did Wardally ever do to you?"

"Nothin'." Branch shook his head in disgust. "That's not the point, man. They're not going to toss the guy just because of one failed patrol. It's not gonna do Wardally any good if we fess up. Think about it. If we admit to taking the truck, we're history, and so's Wardally for failure to control his men. They can't prove anything. Nothin'. Like I said, we'll just tell 'em we heard 'em callin' us. Yeah we heard 'em, but we thought it was the aggressors, and we were too disciplined to compromise our position. Be cool. You white dudes worry about everything. Just keep your mouth closed, 'Mister Talk Forever'."

J.W. asked, "Bearchild what do you think, man?" Bearchild looked at Branch and nodded in agreement.

A fresh lane grader appeared out of the savannah and pushed the reconstituted platoon toward the enemy position for the balance of the night. At dawn, he called a formation and welcomed them to the first full day of the Jungle Phase. J.W. stared at the fiery morning sun and dug into the labyrinthine interstices of his mind to imagine anything in life as woeful as starting a new phase.

* * *

J.W. walked the rest of the morning wrapped in a cloak of powerlessness, recognizing that he was locked into a closed universe in which every move he made to lessen his own pain rippled through the lives of twenty-some other men. He spent erg after erg of psychic energy atoning in his mind for the damage he and his two pals had wrought the night before, but after a few personal castigations, the guilt fizzled, and all he could concentrate on was his vacuous stomach.

The new platoon leader moved them through savanna, then, as the sun arched higher and hotter, back into the swamp. By mid-morning, they had beaten through only four kilometers, less than two miles. There were still twenty-one kilometers left to complete the mission. The major impediment to movement was no longer the putrid water, but the constant harassing fire from aggressors who sniped at the platoon from behind, slowing the Rangers to a snail's pace. Despite the hours of scorching, humid, fake combat they endured that morning, by noon, the petulant griping from the peanut gallery apparently had it right: they were no closer to breakfast than they had been the night before.

J.W., Branch, and Bearchild grumbled unceasingly at the manner in which the platoon moved by fits and starts. It was the first time in weeks the three were not on their own, having been ordered into the main body of the platoon by the Training Brigade's commanding officer, one Colonel Brow, who had flown out that morning from Harmony Church at Benning, some two-hundred miles in a helicopter, to investigate the theft and destruction of government equipment. Branch moaned, "Man, our days as God's chosen are over. Prepare to suffer."

At noon, with the pace of the attack slowed to less than a kilometer every two hours, a new platoon leader was baptized. His first act was to summon the three poker-faced, restrained former luminaries to the front of the column. He assigned them to rear patrol, though the lane grader looked askance and asked, "Do you really want to do that, Ranger? A leader is supposed to know who he can trust, and who he can't."

"Sir, they're the only ones who can stay awake. At least you can trust 'em not to get lost." Waiting until the platoon was well into the swamps, the three quickly resumed their accustomed modus operandi, and spread out to grub for food, searching for plants or berries, anything to swallow. J.W. followed a worn path to a lone tree whose drooping stalks held brown pods. The leaves were early-spring green, some long and thin, others heart-shaped. "Fresh produce" he called aloud, "I'm gonna make me some fruit compote," then climbed twenty feet to a branch near the top, harvesting as many of the three-inch pods as he could stuff into his shirt. Harboring visions of roasting them over a Bearchild special, he summoned his friends with the Ranger bird and proudly displayed his find. Bearchild, however, seeing the fruits of J.W.'s labor, smacked the harvest out of his hand and squashed them into the ground.

"Tung oil beans. Kill ya—fool."

* * *

J.W. found nothing else for hours, though most of his day was spent washing and rewashing his hands. At two in the afternoon, he spotted an ill-fed bullfrog sunning himself, legs splayed across a cypress stump. J.W. waved to Branch, who saw J.W.'s prey and tracked quietly through the swamp, coming up on the frog's flank. J.W. moved to the front as a diversion, and Branch, who came within four feet of the amphibian hors d'oeuvre, tripped on a hidden log, slipped, and fell into the swamp. The frog, airborne in a nanosecond, landed in the water, ducked under a scrap of deadfall, then disappeared beneath the algae. It surfaced twenty meters downstream, and Branch charged, splashing mightily through the slough, a most ferocious hunter, but the bullfrog leisurely plopped under a another log, popped up a dozen meters down-slough, croaked, and was gone forever.

Branch was devastated. He cursed the frog, and then his life, but he soon leaned back against a log next to Bearchild and fell into a trance, floating half-suspended in the putrid water. J.W. dropped next to them, placing his hand on Branch's upper arm, reassuring him, "Don't worry, man, we'll eat soon."

J.W. dropped into a deep sleep, dreaming of the time when he was eleven. His parents had taken the family to Canada, to the French city of Montreal, where at dinner in an up-market hotel, his brothers ordered *sandwich fromage grille*, melted cheese sandwiches, because the selection sounded exotic. J.W., who thus assumed that his parents adhered to the belief that kids should be allowed to expand their horizons, opted for the *cuisses de grenouilles*, simply because they cost four times what his brothers had ordered. The waiter, calculating the tip, smiled unctuously, but became quite serious when J.W.'s father asked just what "green wheels" were.

"It is ze foot of ze frog!" the waiter bowed, adding, "*Trés délicieux*, ze most delicious."

Despite the warnings and threats from his parents, that if he actually went ahead with the order, he would sit there until the creatures were consumed, skinny little femurs, tibiae, fibulae and all, he swore he knew what he was doing. Alas, notwithstanding the flourish when the hapless frog's lower extremities were served, J.W. gagged at the sight of the shiny, slithery bits and pieces. His brothers reacted in sympathy to their older sibling's dilemma by puking up melted cheese onto the table, fostering an invitation from the maitre d' hotel to cut their meal short. "What was wrong with me?" he asked himself in the dream.

Branch was the first to wake. He shook his two companions, whispering he had spied a bird sleeping beside a log. Both Bearchild and J.W. followed him to the reposing dove, but Bearchild turned away in disgust.

J.W. shrugged, "I don't know. Maybe it's against his religion. Maybe the bird's on his totem pole or somethin'. As far as I'm concerned, man, that's breakfast, and I'll be happy to wring its neck and build the fire to cook the sucker, too."

Branch followed J.W., employing the same hunting tactics that had nearly bagged the frog. Weathersby moved with perfect silence, tasting the roasted magnificence of waterfowl, though admitting to himself he would eat it raw if need be. He cut a palm frond with his bayonet, planning to smash the bird back to earth if it attempted to fly. At two meters from their quarry, both he and Branch froze, studying the creature as it tremored in fear, seeking to lie motionlessly and blend into the carrion of the slough. J.W. moved in from behind, Branch from the flank, cautiously avoiding the deadfall. J.W. slid the palm frond into the air, then violently whacked down on breakfast.

"Got it!" J.W. screamed, then lunged onto the ground. The animal mustered no fight, stunned by the primordial hunting power J.W. had demonstrated; but when Ranger Weathersby gathered the creature in his hands, it had a squishy feel, wet with slime on its underside. The organism continued to vibrate in his hand until J.W. turned it over, grimaced, and threw it back into the water. Branch ran to survey their capture, but screwed up his face in dismay at the animal's grub-infested belly.

* * *

The early afternoon's revelry concluded with a forced march across a new plain of savanna, and the rumored reward from the new platoon leader of a night in the barracks at the end of the trek if they slogged it in less than three hours. J.W. felt as though he had lived in the bush for years, simply heading home after a day's work. He had become comfortable with the life of a transient, a man who did not know where he would sleep that night, or where his next meal would come from, if it came at all. He had become secure anywhere he dropped his pack, only portable objects defining his existence, in love with heating water in a canteen cup, an appliance that always worked and never let him down. With a roll of C-ration toilet paper, whose purpose he'd forgotten, matches, a couple of damp smokes, and the promise of a hot meal, J.W. considered himself blessed as he trotted those last kilometers back to Field Seven. During a break, he turned to Branch and smiled, "I'm a rich man."

The meal in the mess hall that afternoon tasted as if it had been pickled in brine for several weeks; even the milk was salty. Then, curiously, Sergeant Perez stood on a chair and urged, "Rangers, add as much salt as possible." When several of the troops looked at him inquisitively, he added without smiling, "*Muy caliente* out there, Rangers. This is the Jungle Phase!"

After the meal, they were afforded twelve minutes to visit the post exchange for cigarettes and candy. As J.W. made his way toward the PX, Sergeant Perez stopped him and ordered, "Ranger, where the hell you going? Report to the camp commandant."

After the initial blast of fear, J.W. ran toward the command shack realizing he was to be awarded bonus points for having saved Fricker's life. Headquarters Building was surrounded by a plot of sand enclosed by a heavy chain link fence. Free to roam the compound was a one-eyed, twelve-foot guard-alligator, apparently the team mascot. The reptile sat motionlessly, jaws spread wide, his chipped, ragged rows of green and yellow teeth a mountain range that dwarfed the Smokys. A sign above the cage read:

> BIG JOHN, THE LONGEST-LIVING RESIDENT OF FIELD SEVEN, TRAGICALLY LOST HIS EYE IN A FIGHT WITH CLASS 61-4. SEVERAL OF THOSE RANGERS ARE MISSING MORE THAN THEIR VISION. IT IS UNFORTUNATE THAT THEY WILL NEVER SIRE SONS TO BECOME AIRBORNE RANGERS.

And, in fact, an ugly scar sealed the alligator's sunken, empty left eye socket. Swarms of flying bugs entered and exited the cavern of his mouth in endless procession, a zoological Grand Central Station.

Inside, the commanding officer was waiting for J.W. He had parked himself at a little olive drab field desk. A lopsided, a mildewed portrait of LBJ hung on the wall behind him, the stale air stirred by a lopsided ceiling fan. J.W. looked down at the major's nametag. The name was Schwartz-something, but it was so long he did not have time to finish reading it before the officer blurted, "Ranger, got a call from Captain Vock. Says you threatened him. That so?"

"No, sir."

"Why would he say that if it wasn't true? Are you calling him a liar?"

"No, sir. He hates me."

"That's correct."

"He calls ahead to every hole in the wall I get sent to. Honest to God. I don't know why, sir."

"I don't either. He's planning to let you go through the course to the end. Even the last problem. Then he's gonna stick it to you."

"Can he do that, sir?"

"He can try, Ranger. Better keep your nose clean. By the way, you know anything about that trouble out there last night?"

"No, sir. We just didn't believe it correct to obey unknown voices in the swamp, sir. We've learned something in this school, sir."

He studied J.W. intently for a few seconds, then snapped, "Dismissed."

As J.W. waited for his salute to be returned, the major added, "Sergeant Perez doesn't like to find Rangers with their pants down out on patrol. You're ridin' on the edge, Ranger. Outta here."

J.W., cursing Vock for having kept him from replenishing his supply of candy at the PX, stood on the porch watching the cadres gather. Morelotto had stopped by headquarters to humor himself by pelting Big John the alligator with rocks. He laughed that since he had his bad eye turned toward him, "He'll probably thinks it's hail, nature tormentin' him, not a Ranger. Stupid thing."

The whistle blew, and as J.W. ran toward formation, there was a terrible crash behind him. He turned back toward the animal pen. Big John had slammed his jaws together so hard the ground trembled. He raced toward Morelotto with lightning speed, hissing and spitting a foul discharge from his throat. Despite the fence limiting his range, Big John had gotten Morelotto's attention, sending him flying past formation, sprinting into the billets, where he swung the door shut and leaned against it with all his substantial weight.

* * *

Following an inspection in which their just-purchased candy was confiscated, the company departed Field Seven, heading away from the swamp, entering a vast, dry patch of sand that stretched for miles. The salty earth supported only parched, brown scrub, scrawny plants bejeweled with shiny, pointed thistles. J.W. consumed the last of his water at 1400 hours, and had sweat that away by 1430.

Outbound a few hours on that mission, J.W. began combing old Ranger garbage tips for food. He was, however, beginning to accept that if he were unsuccessful in capturing or finding food, he would, very simply, go hungry. It had become quite clear to him that the life of the hunter-gatherer was wrought with one failure after another, and that gleaning even the barest of necessities from the land was a twenty-four-hour-per-day pursuit. To survive by foraging, there could be no time wasted on distractions like cadres and tactical problems.

The less intrepid Rangers gave up searching, accepting that they would suffer hunger and deprivation as they put one foot in front of the other to drive on. While they faced the pain of starvation constantly, no Ranger, it was said, had ever perished for lack of food. J.W. looked at his fellows: most were still sufficiently alive to have learned how to ease their load by traveling with rucksacks devoid of even a single pair of extra fatigues, a sleeping bag, or underwear. Canteens were kept only quarter full; in Florida, there was warmth and a plethora of water. Ranger school *was* water.

When the need to replenish fluids came in normal times, a Ranger dipped his canteen into a pond, dropped in a tiny, off-white, water purification tablet, shook hard, and waited 20 minutes. J.W. laughed that both the little brown wax-covered bottles and pills themselves were indistinguishable from the nitroglycerin his Uncle Nat had used in fits of squeezing chest pain. Nat clutched his mini-bottle of heart-soothing medication in sweaty palms all day, unwilling to be away from the life-giving medication, even in the men's room. As far as J.W. was concerned, his bottle of water-cleansing tablets was as consequential as his uncle's heart-sparing pills. While the tiny bottle of water-purifying powder added a few grams of extra weight, he appreciated the minuscule tablets which, when dropped into a canteen of slough water, rendered a medicinal-tasting, but presumably microbe-free, brew. The beauty of bacteria-free swamp liquid was the added protein of whatever carrion floated in the streams and stagnant pools. It was wet, it had calories, and it did the job.

Their mission that afternoon was to attack aggressors in the dunes of Eglan, many miles north, yet still within the bounds of the air base. J.W. perused the map for the next river or tributary to fill his canteens, but there was nothing except barren, dry plains for forty miles. By 1800 hours, his face was so dry and cracked, he dismantled his M-14 rifle and scooped gun oil out of the mechanism to smear on his lips. Pangs of hunger slowly disappeared, replaced by an obsession to drink anything that flowed.

J.W. planned to dip his canteens into the first slough he passed, one that had missed the mapmaker's attention. But the land only became drier with each sandy kilometer. As the company marched north, away from the Gulf of Mexico, they came closer, it seemed, to the Sahara. The lone saving grace was that there were no mountains in the Jungle Phase, the terrain finally as flat as he had fantasized about in the mountains, and as dry as he had dreamed of in the torrential downpours of Harmony Church.

Worse, however, than the dust of each step settling on the thickened saliva coating his teeth was the torment of the grittiness of the sand that had infiltrated his clothing. He trudged along in silence for hours, for moving his bleeding lips to complain or pray was laced with pain. Eventually, the sand permeated J.W.'s boots, and each step seared the bottoms of his feet. An hour later, he limped so antalgically, his left knee ached as though that leg had shortened.

J.W. knew in his heart he was hallucinating once again, but he was convinced the pain was real, particularly in his left heel, which burned as if being stabbed by twenty tiny daggers. By late evening, despite the moonlit silhouettes of his compatriots wandering across the desert, he thought of the figures as moving trees, and he dropped to his knees and crawled, chasing one of the silhouettes like a dying man, hoping he would find a cadre to whom he would whisper, "I quit this shit."

Moving on his knees took the weight off his foot, but not the desiccation from his mouth. He stopped to wet his lips with the gun oil again, then removed the boot to put oil on his heel as well. His hand brushed needles protruding into the shoe at the heel, and in the flicker of what was left of his flashlight batteries, he inspected the bottom of his boot. There was no heel. It had fallen off hours before, and the twenty tiny nails that had held it in place now pushed into the boot and into the flesh of his heel. J.W. was relieved to discover the source of his agony, and that he wasn't as demented as he had feared, though that relief dissolved as he considered the obstacle with which he was now faced.

He limped, barefoot, across the wasteland in search of any human being who had the power to address his pain, even a lane grader or a cadre. Passing Branch, who was curled up on the sand in a fetal ball, J.W. looked down at his quasi Ranger buddy and waited until the small man acknowledged his presence. J.W. asked pleadingly, "You got an extra boot?"

Branch stared up. "Man, what the hell you talkin' bout? Yeah, I'll give you a boot, for a quart of fuckin' ice water."

J.W. trod on toward the only animated shape on the dark horizon, a sergeant who was brewing coffee. J.W. advised the instructor of his footwear dilemma, and the man duly recorded the calamity in an OD spiral notebook, promising to radio main camp and have J.W.'s other boots sent on the morning chopper.

"In the meantime, Sergeant, do you happen to have a pair of pliers so I can pull the nails out of my boot?"

The lane grader patted his pockets. "Sorry, fresh out."

"Well then, could I get a little water to hold me over until we meet up with the mess crew?"

"Ranger, I don't carry supplies for maggots. You had a chance to fill your canteens just like I did. But you didn't, and I did."

"Yeah, but Sergeant, you got four canteens."

"Ranger, get your sorry ass back to your platoon."

J.W. crawled back past Branch, who looked up with only one eye. "You got pliers?" J.W. asked, but when Branch closed that eye, J.W. accepted defeat and sought his own patch of sand, where he pulled the nails out with his teeth, chipping another incisor.

* * *

The platoon did not reach the enemy until 0300 hours, and by that point, thirst utterly controlled them. While the boot debacle had been an unpleasant interlude, J.W. wished the foot hurt more, to divert the misery from his throat. Though Branch and Bearchild were only fifty meters away, J.W. felt extraordinarily alone, convinced no one could be suffering as desperately as he. At the next stop, J.W. left the platoon, setting out to find water. He hadn't tripped across fifty meters of brush before he came to a blubbery mass lying atop one of the sand piles, a lump that barely groaned as J.W. stumbled and landed on top of it.

"Morelotto, what the hell are you doing out here? Hey, wait a minute. What's that in your hand?"

"It's mine. Leave me alone."

"Bullshit. We didn't get Cs yet. Where'd you get that, man? Steal it from a cadre?"

"What if I did?"

"Just tell me what it is, man." J.W. tugged the can out of Morelotto's hand. "Fruit Cocktail?! Hey, gimme a sip."

"Kiss my ass."

"I'll trade you my next B-3 unit for one sip. Come on."

Morelotto laughed arrogantly. J.W. fattened the offer. "O.K., main meal, your selection."

Morelotto laughed louder and licked the can.

"Shit, three smokes, a quarter pack of granulated sugar, and my toilet paper."

Morelotto sneered, "What the hell am I gonna do with toilet paper? He then nodded almost imperceptibly, guardedly allowing J.W. to wet his lips on the olive drab can. Instead of a proper opening in the top of the tin, Morelotto had been drinking through a microscopic hole. J.W. was impressed, and whispered through scorched lips, "Man, you got a lotta discipline. Good job."

With that declaration, however, there was a snap in J.W.'s brain and he thrust a hand forward, snatched the can, and sucked as if it were the fluid of life. He held drops of the thick, sugary liquid in his mouth, allowing the syrup to trickle slowly into his throat, lubricating the parched mucosa, but not relieving the thirst. As he struggled to pull a few final drops into his mouth, Morelotto wrested the can away.

In ninety seconds, the dryness returned as if in retaliation for J.W.'s violent theft of the extra two drops of liquid, and in another thirty seconds, the craving for water worsened. J.W. composed himself, repeating over and over that it would not last much longer, for surely one of the cadres possessed a modicum of decency and was aware of the suffering around him. In desperation, J.W. lit a smoke, hoping for a homeopathic cure, using a drying agent to elicit moisture. The experiment failed miserably, and J.W. considered his life once again, embarrassed at his weeping in the previous phases of Ranger School over the trivial matters of sleep deprivation and starvation.

* * *

The sun rose, yet Morelotto still hadn't brought them to their objective, a stronghold in the dunes. The lane grader, sitting atop a fifty-five gallon oil drum, yelled to Morelotto. "Ranger, what the hell are you doing at the back of your platoon? Leaders are supposed to lead. Come here. You got a new mission. Due to your delay of nearly twelve hours, a Jungle Phase record, I might add, the enemy has invaded and taken Miami. Their rear units have advanced to a point twenty-three kilometers east of here. Your orders are to attack them and save at least the panhandle of Florida. Do you think you can do that?"

Morelotto threw his rucksack to the ground, refusing to go on until he was given water, a brazen performance that instigated the convergence of several cadres. A circle formed and a new leader emerged, having been ordained by the touch of the sandy root of a thistle plant. J.W. was excited at the prospect of a chopper flying in to haul Morelotto back to Field Seven, for it would surely bring water and a new boot.

But nothing dropped from the sky except unabated rays of tropical sun. The dunes became higher, the sands looser, the brush drier and sharper. They were marching further from main camp, not toward it, and as the day grew hotter, J.W. fretted that a freight-laden helicopter would be unable to land in the thin air.

Time slowed, each step, it seemed, lasting minutes. J.W. tried to pool spit in his mouth and save it for one good swallow, but it was too thick and granular to scrape off his teeth. Then he attempted the Boy Scout maneuver of sucking pebbles, but the tiny rocks added additional grit to the pot no matter how hard J.W. buffed them against his fatigue pants. Assuming a larger pebble would be easier to hold while polishing with bleeding, infected fingers, J.W. burnished a chunk the size of a grape, then placed it carefully in his mouth. That worked nicely, until he tripped, fell, and swallowed it. For a few minutes, his stomach smiled at the offering, then cramped violently until he vomited up the rock, chipping another tooth as it came back through his mouth.

The silver lining in the storm was that thirst kept his mind off his missing boot heel. Eventually, however, the spasms in his calf hobbled

him, and again, J.W. selected a rudimentary solution, stuffing his boot
with yucca leaves. A thick, green fluid oozed from the cactus stems, and
J.W. smiled that he serendipitously discovered a way to beat the thirst. He
removed his foot from the boot and licked greedily at the astringent fluid,
but the bitterness made him wretch acidy mucus laced with particles of
dirt. He smiled, whispering under his breath that, on balance, the vomitus
tasted better than the yucca sap.

* * *

At noon, the platoon reached the jump-off point for its attack on the
enemy troops that had captured Miami. The brush had become heavier,
and J.W. crouched behind a shrub to avail himself of the toilet facilities,
wondering the whole time what could possibly be in there to be
evacuated. He squatted near the earth and promptly fell asleep, waking
minutes later to the specter of a flock of black-bereted aggressors
retreating into a wooded area a hundred meters off. J.W. watched with
singular interest as the soldiers dropped their packs into a hole, which
they camouflaged carefully with brush. Biding his time impatiently, he
waited until the enemy dispersed, then crawled across the barrens to the
cache.

Not wasting the time to strip the brush from the hidden reserve, J.W.
shot his arm inside the cavity, prospecting with his hand until he came to
a cool, metal cylinder. A flash in his addled consciousness told him God
wanted him to have that treasure, and as J.W. pulled it from the crater, he
pushed on a button at one end of the tube. It hissed like a green snake. "A
can of Cool Whip!" he shouted. But the scent that followed the hiss was
tart, and though distantly familiar, was certainly not edible. He pulled the
object free, still holding to the prayer that it was drinkable, but it was just
a can of Right Guard. He pitched it over his shoulder angrily and reached
back into the hole, stretching even further, groping madly.

J.W. remained oblivious to the world outside the pit until a not
unfamiliar sense of impending doom blanketed him. He shook it off at
first as a reflex for having taken too much time to complete his mission
of finding a drinkable commodity, but the sensation was far worse than

245

that. He took a slow deep breath before turning his head. Bloused fatigues tucked into spit shined boots greeted his eyes. J.W. saw a gaunt, sick face reflected in the mirror-like toe—his own.

Before J.W. looked up at the figure, he gathered his spirit and jested nervously, "We gotta stop meeting like this."

"Ranger," the figure sermonized in reply, "The good Lord put me on this earth to watch over you, and make you do right. I feel like a failure in the eyes of God, Ranger, and that ain't good."

J.W. explained. "First Sergeant Cowsen, you see First Sergeant, I saw one of them ugly green snakes shoot across the dunes into this hole. I was trying to catch it and return what a fellow Ranger had lost. I don't know if you heard about the incident, but it really is true."

"Ranger, how do you figure a snake came up with a can of Right Guard, carried it to its den, and covered it with brush? Anyway, the green snakes live in the swamp, and there ain't no water within twenty miles of where you're layin'.

"This may be the big one, Ranger. Be'in as you're A.W.O.L, I am placing you under house arrest, and this is your house. You will stand guard over this hole, at attention, for the rest of the afternoon while your platoon lounges and drinks water."

"Water? First Sergeant!" J.W. begged plaintively, but Cowsen marched off through the brush, soon cresting the horizon of dunes. J.W. had his orders, and in lieu of fluids, he placed his Ranger hat on the highest branch of a thorn shrub, then dropped to the earth for a nap. Though as hot as he had ever been, curiously, he did not sweat.

He dreamed again of Viet Nam and plodding through a steaming jungle, searching for an enemy that was out of ammo and throwing rocks instead of firing lead. In the nightmare, one of the stones hit his head, and J.W. awoke with a start, jumped up, bracing at attention until he realized he was alone, victim again of another painful fantasy. He lay back down, but before he could fall asleep again, he felt another missile strike his head. He looked up angrily, annoyed at his own hallucinations, though, in fact, there indeed was a cadre throwing rocks at him.

"On your feet. Sleeping on guard duty is punishable by death in the Uniform Code of Military Justice, Ranger. Prepare to meet your maker."

The sergeant removed his .45 from its holster and snapped the slide back. He pointed the weapon into the cloudless sky, slowly bringing it down into firing position. J.W. looked up at the barrel, and his eyes fixed on the perfect, cloudless sky. His only thought was surprise that a man could die in such peace and quiet.

"Good. I don't give a shit, Sergeant. Send me back for court-martial. Kill me, I don't care. I qui…"

As J.W. formed the last consonant in his mouth, he was distracted by the whap of a Huey main rotor roaring in on a breakneck approach, skimming so fast and so low, the cadreman had to drop to the ground to avoid being struck. The ship skidded to a sand-enveloped landing fifty feet away, and J.W. abandoned his own execution to sprint toward it, relinquishing the last of his energy on what he believed to be his final run in Ranger School.

Fresh cadres belched from the belly of the helicopter, and J.W. looked past them for jerry cans of water. The first officer off the aircraft, however, chewed J.W.'s ass and ordered him back to the platoon.

J.W. stood fast. "Sir, where are my boots?"

"They're on your feet, dumb Ranger. What the hell is your problem?"

J.W. looked down. Indeed, his boots were where they had been for the past months, on his feet. J.W. nodded in agreement. "But you see, sir,…"

Then J.W. caught site of the sergeant who had been readying himself to consummate J.W.'s punishment running toward the ship, and J.W. ran to the far side of the helicopter to hide. The sergeant was waving his .45 as he jumped laughingly aboard the aircraft, and waved his hand dismissing his victim back toward the platoon. The lieutenant in front of J.W. raised a thumb to the pilot, and the ship crept forward on its skids for takeoff. The lane grader then turned back to J.W. and ordered, "Get back to your unit, Ranger, before I tell 'em you're AWOL and have you executed."

As J.W. hobbled back to the main body. Morelotto ran to him. "You got any water left, Weathersby? You do, don't you? I want some. You owe me."

"What the hell water you talkin' 'bout? You got water, I didn't, fool." J.W. snarled.

"Cowsen said you stole water and were executed for it." Morelotto spat back, shoving J.W. The lane grader ran over and ordered the two to move apart fifty feet, then sent J.W. to the rear for security detail with Branch and Bearchild. As the platoon departed for the assault, J.W. thought it a sad commentary on the military elite that he, who had been so close to execution several times in the past fifteen minutes, was considered amongst the unit's most trustworthy.

The platoon stopped at sunset. A supply helicopter rumbled in, fostering in J.W. and his mates more relief and happiness than they had experienced in many a week, for they saw in the landing aircraft a salvation from the worst of the tortures the mad cadres had perpetrated on them. There in front of them was the water and food for which they had patiently waited, and despite the dust storm generated by the main rotors of the HUEY, the entire platoon drifted forward toward the bird, foot over foot, several columns of zombies, as if in the *Night of the Living Dead.* But all that belched from the belly of the dust-engulfed helicopter was a contingent of fresh cadres carrying full canteens.

On the other hand, J.W. took the godsend of new lane graders, and the twenty minutes it would take to get them oriented, to creep away in search of a puddle. He shuffled dolefully through the endless sand, cresting a particularly high dune to peer over the top into an abandoned garbage tip, rusted C-ration cans and rotted cardboard strewn over half-an-acre. The very sight of food containers sent J.W.'s salivary glands into painful contraction, and he prepared to wet his lips with the coming saliva, but there was no longer any spittle to be expressed. Nonetheless, he took heart at his find, mind grinding as he considered plans to fabricate commodities from the trash to barter for water. He inspected each discarded can carefully, finding them all bone-dry, save for the usual crust in the Ham and Limas. He piled those tins into his pockets to entice Branch into a future trade for water. Some of the Cs had been opened on the bottom end with small slits only, the food sucked out by the enemy, packed with sand, and then placed right side up to look and feel as if they were full.

It was a fruitless pursuit; his brain was sure of it, and the tallying of calories he had already squandered seeking food gnawed at him painfully.

Yet his heart would not let him stop, and he dutifully booted each can, including a squat B-3 Unit, which he knew in his heart to be packed with dirt to fool him. Something, however, about the way that tin arced piqued his interest. Its parabola was distinct, higher than the sand-filled sort, but lower than the path of an empty. When it landed, it was an inch or two short of the spot his subconscious had come to expect. Oh, if he had only paid more attention to the physics classes he'd slept through. J.W. kicked it again. When no sand sprinkled from either end, he took the next step in the food-search SOP: he bent over and invested sufficient energy to lift the possible treasure out of the dirt.

The label read Fruitcake. J.W.'s heart skipped a beat. Slowly, tediously, deliberately, cautiously, he checked the top—sealed. He turned the can upside-down—the bottom was unviolated as well. He examined the metal for pin holes, rust, and then for booby traps. Negative. His heart pounded in wild expectation. Was it really happening? Was he about to score? J.W. calmed himself and took a seat amid the garbage to savor the moment of his good fortune. Slowly, with reverence, he took the tiny P-38 can opener out of his pocket and brought the tip to the edge of the can. Now, the rub was that it took 38 revolutions of the tiny device to fully open a C-ration can, hence the name. All he had to invest was one turn, and as he applied pressure, a curious sensation blanketed him and interrupted the moment of truth. A vision of his Ranger brothers swept across his spirit, and a flush of religious ardor overcame him. He kicked jauntily back to the platoon, grinning for the first time in weeks, singing quietly but reverently, "Seek and thee shall find, brother. And the Lord has found this poor sheep."

Branch looked up and shook his head. "A drowning man in his final hour."

"No, no, it's not the end." J.W. sang. "It's the beginning. I've found grace and mercy, baby." He pulled the cans of dried Ham and Limas crust from his fatigue pockets and wiggled them in Branch's face. "For you, my brother."

Branch's eyes reddened, but his body was devoid of the fluid it would have taken to produce tears.

J.W. then wiggled the can of Fruit Cake in Morelotto's face.

Morelotto's pupils closed to pin points, and his hand shot forward toward salvation, but J.W. withdrew his prize and held it up and danced in victory. As J.W. hopped about the dunes, the P-38 slipped from his pocket. Morelotto saw the tiny silver blade glint in the sun as it fell. He crawled surreptitiously to the opener and dusted sand over it.

"Now", J.W. went on, "please watch as God's chosen person samples the fruit of life." He reached into his left fatigue pocket, then his right; into his breast pockets and then searched the ground around his boots. As the supercilious snicker faded from his lips, J.W. replaced it with a poker face. The others watched as he searched the sand in growing circles.

When J.W. was facing away, Morelotto slipped the device into his own pocket, stood and called out, "Hey, man, if I open the can for you, you gonna give me half?"

"Hell no!" J.W. spit. "I only got a sip of your peaches this morning, or have you forgotten?"

"A slice, then?" Morelotto offered.

"O.K., a slice and I choose how big."

"A third."

"No way."

Bearchild rose. "Everybody gets a small chunk." He snapped the can out of from J.W.'s hand and opened it, but handed it back to J.W. to slice the lump of antediluvian fruitcake into twenty-some portions. Soon, Second Platoon sat about sucking on tender morsels of fruit, allowing the cake to dissolve in saliva that barely came.

"Compliments to the chef," Branch toasted as he nibbled with the greatest of moderation on J.W.'s tissue-thin offering.

Gillette wondered if there was a retail outlet for the product, proposing, "I'm going to purchase cases of this confection when I get home. Send it as Christmas gifts to my dearest friends. Stuff's great."

It was not long, however, before the Rangers of Second Platoon were making faces, scraping their withered lips and tongues against gritty teeth. "Man that cake was dry," Morelotto complained. "Goddamn it, now I'm more thirsty." He eyed J.W. angrily, and J.W. gravitated toward the rear, where Branch and Bearchild had taken up residence.

Though Bearchild rarely smoked, he took a cigarette, holding it awkwardly, allowing the smoke to filter through the scrub pines into the mauve-painted, tropical sunset. He sat cross-legged, as if in prayer, the smoke and the sky creating an ethereal forum.

J.W. was first to speak. "I figured it out. I'm going to be a doctor someday. A doctor doesn't starve. I never heard of a starving doctor. He can trade a chicken for a penicillin shot. I'll never starve again. That, I swear."

Branch laughed weakly, "Man, you got three more years on active duty, a year or two in Viet Nam flyin' round in a HUEY death bucket. Pilots is a dyin' as fast as they sends 'em there. If'n you live, it's a year of premed when you get out, then four years in medical school and three more in residency, before you can practice. That's, let's see, that's eleven years to go before you start makin' a living. That's crazy. You'll be near death by that age, if you even live that long."

"I'll put the years of work in," J.W. said setting his jaw. "I got no problem with time. But I promise you, by thirty-five, I'm going to be in charge. No one's ever going to do this to me again. When I came here, I didn't know what in the hell I was going to do with my life. I do now. Thank you, cadres."

"Doctoring's easy living. That what you figure?" Bearchild asked sarcastically, "Deciding who lives and who dies?"

Bearchild's face hardened, and turned away. Though he was as quiet as usual, there was a sullenness in him neither Branch nor J.W. dared challenge. Turning to J.W. he conceded, "You're O.K., man. Just promise you won't turn the poor away."

Again he was still, and Branch and J.W., assuming Bearchild had finished his most protracted discourse in Ranger School, leaned back to sleep, but Bearchild monotoned, "When my brother was a baby, he got sick as hell. None of the doctors in town would see him. They told my mother to take him back to the res, to the DIA clinic."

"What's DIA?"

"Department of Indian Health. It was closed for the Fourth of July. So she drove back to town to try again, and the car broke down in the heat. I was holding him in my arms. He was hotter than the tar on the road. When he stopped moving, I thought he was dead. So did my mother.

Then she started to cry, and she said it was a curse to be born an Indian."
Bearchild stopped.

J.W. lit another smoke. "What happened?"

"Steven War Bonnet? He had meningitis. He lives in a home on the res now. He just moans and cries, twenty-four-hours-a-day. He has seizures every few hours. Mostly he lies on his back, screaming and whining, whining and screaming."

"Does your mother take care of him?"

"Nah, she died a few months after he got sick. My father cared for Steven for a while. I guess it was better Steven was taken away. My father blamed himself. Then I was the only thing he had left. Embarrassed the hell outta me when he started going around town tellin' anybody who'd listen that his son was gonna be the first Rose Bud Sioux in the world to graduate from Harvard, and then go to Congress and change the rules."

"Is that where you graduated from?" Branch asked.

"Yeah."

* * *

The new platoon leader, Gillette, who had fashioned himself a great Vietnamese general at Harmony Church, now considered himself an Erwin Rommel. He laid plans for Second Platoon to attack the next objective by trooping straight across the desert plains and fooling the aggressors, who would assume the Rangers would take the easiest course, the one paralleling the river.

Morelotto interrupted. "Hey, man, what plans have you made to resupply? Particularly water. You got a responsibility to care for your men, ya know."

Gillette ignored him, consumed with planning another of his impossibly complicated assaults. J.W. took the time to peruse his own map and detected a small finger of slough obtruding into the sand, not half-a-mile off the course chosen by the Desert Fox. J.W. suggested they divert to fill canteens, but Gillette snapped, "That's poison. And anyway, we're not pussies, we're Rangers."

Branch, Bearchild, and J.W. took positions on rear patrol, waited until the unit departed, then sprinted for the water. As the sun dwindled, it became an effort to see obstacles in the flat light. Nonetheless, they pushed on, driven by a worsening thirst that caused them to collapse every hundred yards or so and lie prostrate on the dunes moaning. On one of the more theatric disintegrations, J.W. tumbled into a bog, coming to rest with the slime just millimeters from his face. It was all he could do not to suck in quarts of the rancid fluid that was so close to his burned lips, but the stench provoked within him an instinct not to consume the poison. Instead, he filled his canteens, sieving with his fingers the larger wads of creature-parts, sugar-cube-sized remnants of animals that had migrated to the slough to die. When he was done, Branch shined a light into the swamp, and J.W. could see vestiges of rotting carcasses washing back and forth, carrion swaying gently in the ripples generated as he crawled out of the stinking liquid.

J.W. could not find his water purification tablets. He cursed that an aggressor had stolen them while he slept. Branch at first refused, but then, reminded of the crusts of Ham and Limas J.W. had brought him, relinquished two of his pills. J.W. dropped one pill into each canteen, shook the stew, and put the containers back on his web belt to wait the requisite twenty minutes for the medication to do its magic. With the sound of gurgling coming from his canteens though, he controlled himself for all of forty seconds before ripping the canteens out of their canvas holders to chug-a-lug both.

The water, lumpish as curdled buttermilk, manifested its toxicity in seconds, forcing J.W. to vomit up the water and creature fragments. "Shit," he cried, "that shit's worse coming back up than going down." Branch and Bearchild deferred filling their canteens.

The three rejoined the platoon, J.W. periodically pausing to expectorate gummy vomitus and particles of animal. Each time he hocked the waste, a squirt of the familiar green liquor burped into his mouth from his innards, continuing the never-ending, vicious cycle that had begun, it seemed years, but really, only forty-two days before.

At midnight, the platoon traversed a narrow, freshwater stream. The lane grader and several cadres chased behind, yelling into the ears of each Ranger, "You are not to drink this water. It has been poisoned by the

253

enemy. You will die within minutes if it touches your lips, Rangers." In the dark, however, it was easy to hear the splashing of Ranger boots and the gurgle of water entering parched, dry canteens.

* * *

By dawn, some claimed there had been an attack, and that they had beaten back the enemy, but J.W. recalled nothing of the night except the awful taste in his mouth. As the aggressors had withdrawn into the jungles, the Rangers' next mission would be to ferret out of the tangle the few of them who had survived the attack. The entire company convened deep in the swamp to finish the enemy by conducting one of General Darby's favorite rituals, the essence, the jewel of jungle school, an amphibious assault.

The exercise began with a dozen-mile trek south along Turtle Creek to its confluence with Live Oak Creek near the town of Mary Esther, Florida, on the Gulf of Mexico. Tactical orders directed the Rangers to man rubber rafts hidden for them by partisans. From there, they would patrol and attack along inland rivers, finally hitting an enemy stronghold on a tiny island in Choctawhatchee Bay.

The secret documents held by the enemy on that island were vital to the security and future of the United States, and the company was commissioned by the President, Lyndon Baines Johnson, himself, to save the nation. J.W. raised his hand at the end of the briefing and asked, "We gonna be awarded The Presidential Unit Citation if we win?"

"Yeah, that's right, Ranger. And I'll be there to pin it on your ass."

* * *

When J.W. spied the first partisan, he sensed a problem. The face was familiar. Even from a distance, J.W. was struck by the *colors* of his eyes. J.W. slunk to the end of the line, but the man invited that very fire team into his rubber boat, smiling broadly as he handed out paddles. Though he kept one for himself, the partisan did little of the work required to move a fire team upstream several miles. His efforts were limited to prodding his galley slaves to paddle more vigorously against the stiff current of the Yellow River. For the first minutes, J.W. enjoyed being off his feet, but his arms soon tired, then burned, until the partisan at the helm relented, offering, "Go ahead, take a break, but wait until none of the other cadres are looking."

Second Fire Team paddled slowly until the last of their platoon mates' rafts sailed beyond a thickly vegetated bend in the Yellow River, and within a millisecond, they stopped digging at the water. They swore to the partisan, "It'll only be for a minute, Sergeant."

They drifted gently for a few seconds, and J.W. fell into a heavenly sleep, awakening as the boat orbited in a beautiful, peaceful, whirlpool. He was quietly at peace with the world until the sergeant with the brown and green eyes pointed at J.W. and ordered, "Do a map check, boy."

"Ah, shit," J.W. cursed, "the current's pushed us downstream. We've floated past where we began at Mary Esther."

"Rangers" the instructor warned, "this will reinforce another Ranger commandment: circumvention, like crime, never pays. Now get paddlin' to make up the time you lost."

As they thrashed back upstream, they passed a string of rubber rafts floating by, lazily turning circles. The snoozing crews were overseen by lounging cadres who puffed contentedly on cigarettes. J.W. called out to wake them, but that good deed begot fifty-one push-ups on the raft's rubber gunnel, from which he slipped twice into the water.

The assault came to pass, as did all things in Ranger School. There were no stray Cs that time, the aggressors having hoisted their comestible-packed ponchos into trees. The cadres also warned, "Rangers, those sacks contain deadly serpents. Anybody caught messing with that stuff will be considered attempting suicide and will be executed. In the Uniform Code of Military Justice, it is a capital crime to commit suicide. You can not graduate from Ranger School if you are deceased, Rangers, but there's no rule that says you can't repeat the jungle phase if you are dead."

* * *

The enemy successfully joined, Second Platoon reboarded their boats, hungrily anticipating the reward, a float with the current downstream.

The new orders, however, mandated they accomplish the next mission, and be in the Gulf of Mexico, by 0900 hours. That translated, in thermodynamic terms, to paddling harder and faster downstream than they had up.

There was, however, a rider attached to the orders, a promise that they would be transported via motorized launch and then truck back to Field Seven for breakfast, but only if they destroyed the enemy on schedule. There were cheers of ecstasy, but Gillette interjected calmly, "An on-time attack? Gentlemen, that's an oxymoron."

The trip was uplifting, cadence sung for the next hour-and-a-half by the eighty or so remaining Rangers, Morelotto howling the lead:

I want to live the life of danger,
I want to be an Airborne Ranger.
Some day my son will be like me,
He'll run all day,
He'll jump for his pay,
Airborne, Ranger
Ranger,
Ranger,
Ranger,
Ranger!

No one noticed when 0900 came and went, a milestone that passed with the troops still pulling at the river with their paddles and singing. At the mouth of the Gulf, the company boarded motorized launches, as promised, and the next few moments were amongst the most peaceful of J.W.'s life; reclining, taking in the early morning, tropical sun on the calm ocean, translating across the face of the earth by dint of another's labor. The partisan at the helm peacefully smoked a cigarette and steered the Mercury outboard, a single bead of sweat hanging from the tip of his nose. J.W. felt pity for the man forced to keep his eyes open while the Rangers slept.

The silence of a failed engine, however, soon shook J.W. back to life.

"Rangers, you are ordered to disembark."

Morelotto jumped up in disbelief. "No breakfast?" He screeched at the helmsman. "I demand to know why. You people are fuckin' liars."

The partisan glanced conspicuously at his watch. "Gentlemen, you did not fulfill your part of the bargain. Leave your packs, web belts, and boots aboard this watercraft and swim the short mile to the beach. Your gear will be delivered to the few of you who make it, those not consumed by gators, puff adders, or jelly fish."

J.W. stripped off his fatigues, rolled them into a ball, and stashed them in his crotch, thus converting himself into a streamlined bullet. He arrived on the white sands of the Gulf of Mexico long before his platoon, and then stood laughing at the splashing Rangers still a half-a-mile out to sea. Turning back toward land to find a shady spot to drop and sleep, he accidentally stepped on a sideways-scampering crab, which expired in a jumble of guts and seaweed. J.W. took the remains into the bushes and ate it.

Beyond the beach was a thicket of yucca into which J.W. crawled for an after dinner siesta. He spread his wet fatigues over the top of the spiked leaves and fell asleep, lying in the nude and savoring the steaming shade of his freshly-laundered uniform. He felt as though he had slumbered for hours, the pounding surf conjuring dreams of a tropical paradise. When he woke, there was still only the beauty of the waves, and he smirked that the others remained out at sea struggling toward shore. He dressed in his bone-dry fatigues and returned to the beach, where he found Branch and Bearchild flanking his gear, cross-legged on the sand, staring out at the water. As J.W. approached, they looked up from their sad vigil, their eyes widening.

"Man," Branch declared with disbelief, "Where the hell you been? We thought you drowned at sea. They said you were the only Ranger ever to die on the long swim. Even Cowsen was here. He said, 'And of all Rangers, the one who could swim forever.'"

"No shit! Did he seem upset?" J.W. asked expectantly.

"Man, I don't know. He didn't cry, if that's what you mean. But Bearchild, my man here, he bawled like a little baby."

That brought a bare grin to Bearchild's face, and Branch lifted a Chesterfield toward J.W., and then a light; Bearchild took one as well, and the three sat quietly for a few minutes, watching a small launch circling, searching a mile out in the Gulf of Mexico.

When the platoon was called into formation, Sergeant Perez was singularly displeased to find J.W. alive. "Ranger, you will swim out to the search boat and tell them your body has been recovered. This time you will wear your uniform *and* your boots. Move it! And the rest of you mourners, no breakfast until that asshole gets back."

At the boat, J.W. sputtered, "Ranger Weathersby reporting."

The pilot, without looking down into the water, ordered, "Into the boat, jerk off." The cadreman was silent until they reached shore, but as J.W. disembarked, the sergeant commanded, "Ranger, you had no right to accept a ride back in this boat. Just for that, you're gonna dry shave, and your buddies are waitin' here until you do."

J.W. was frightened of the sores that would open on his face if did as ordered, but his beard was so soft from the extended swims that morning, it was one of the best shaves he ever had. J.W. must have sported a look of ecstasy during the trim, because he was awarded fifty-one push-ups for enjoying himself. Then there were an additional twenty-six granted for having disappeared during the swim, and twenty-six more when J.W. protested, "Sergeant Perez, you can't punish a man twice for the same crime. It's in the Constitution. Ask Gillette."

Gillette blanched at the mention of his name, but his color returned during the push-ups he was awarded for quoting the *Federalist Papers*.

* * *

At Field Seven that night, J.W. complained of feeling fat and soft as he lounged in the mess hall after the meal. Morelotto used the hiatus to visit his friend, Big John, whose jaws were in their customary position, spread wide, motionless, bugs flitting past ruby lips, in and out of his drooling mouth. He became bored after tossing a few rocks at her, and turned to leave. J.W. laughed at the crash of jaws, the hissing, and then the thud of Morelotto sprinting and the slamming of the barracks door.

* * *

With the happiness of the thought of four and a wake up remaining, the past fifty-two days became a painful blur. The Ranger remnants were afforded a thirty-minute respite at the barracks to prepare for the final tactical mission. J.W. looked over the survivors, the gaunt, tanned, and numb readying themselves for the last maneuver, an easy one, rumor had it. J.W. had heard that the final days were a walk in the park; that the cadres had extracted their pound of flesh, and now all the soldiers were back on the same team, and they would be rebuilt physically and mentally. Nonetheless, there was an uncomfortable nagging in J.W.'s brain, and he finally realized it was the local CO's counsel that Vock was going to let him finish the course, then stick it to him.

Eighty some Rangers, each one personally divested by hordes of cadres of the just purchased cartons of Mars Bars, Snickers, and Three Musketeers, were forced to stand at attention with their eyes open as the contraband was tossed into Big John's pen for his desert. With the ground still trembling from the monster's charge, the troops were issued half-pilfered boxes of C-rations, and then ordered to move into the swamp. A new student-commander was appointed to engineer a massive assault on the remaining aggressors, those alive after months of unrelenting attack by the Rangers of Class 68-B.

A dozen cadres-partisans gathered at the bleachers. Dressed as Mexican peasants with *sombreros* and turn of the century muskets, they provided intelligence in Spanish, noting the enemy was dug in, heavily fortified with automatic weapons and artillery, and prepared to fight to the death. Gillette translated. "Rangers, these communists are serious about taking over the country. None of us are going home until we stop them. Our partisans here are pretty serious about this war."

J.W. nudged Gillette, "Ask them if they can really do that?"

Gillette shook his head whispering, "It's just a euphemism."

J.W. turned to Branch and asked, "What does euphemism mean?"

"It means they're going to be screwing with you until the end, that's what."

The full company set out together on the final mission, tramping into the deep swamp, then crossing now-familiar cypress stands. J.W. had named some of the trees after former girlfriends, though he laughed that the trees had treated him better than had the women. He had also grown fonder of the trees than most of the females he'd dated.

The company drifted into the savanna along trails they had beaten a dozen times, past huge individual blades of grass that J.W. recognized, freaks of nature taller and tougher than the rest. He smiled nervously, realizing they would still be there long after he was a half-a-world away in a jungle even more unfriendly than the one in which he had spent the last three weeks.

Second Platoon encountered harassing small arms fire along the way, and Branch, Bearchild, and J.W. were soon sent to guard the rear. It wasn't five minutes before they captured two of the snipers. The prisoners were uncooperative, and J.W. argued vehemently for tying them to a tree and leaving them for all eternity. Branch, however, insisted on taking them as bargaining chips, and the three wound up putting ropes made of vines around the enemies' necks, then dragging the prisoners who refused to walk.

When the hostages began screaming, J.W. tried to gag them with their own socks, though one resisted by biting J.W.'s index finger. A flap of skin pulled loose, and J.W. shrieked he could see his bones and tendons. J.W. let go to tend to his wounds, and the prisoner sprinted into the swamp. The other prisoner's eyes brightened, and he laughed with a heavy Eastern European accent steeped in derision, "Now you die, Student Ranger pig!" He looked up in the sky and smiled.

"Fuck you, asshole," J.W. sneered, but a moment later, an alien vibration blanketed the swamp. The air surged over them in silent, staccato waves that filtered threateningly through the triple canopy of vegetation. For an instant, J.W. was petrified that he would look up and find Sergeant Cowsen in his face, but there followed a sudden, horrifying crash, and then a clap of screeching thunder that rolled brutally over their heads. J.W. thought at first it was one of Big John the Alligator's cousins on the loose, but the whirling jungle air became a tornado and knocked Branch to the ground, drawing a trickle of blood from his left ear.

A black shadow raced over them, and J.W. realized a flight of fighter jets had criss-crossed only feet above them, pulling out of their strafing dives so hard, a blast of air drove him into the mud. J.W. cupped his hands over his ears against the supersonic Phantoms' afterburners, but it was too late. He was already deaf, a disability from which he would never completely recover. In reaction, the three Rangers dove under water, but even there, the blare of the fighter-bombers next pass was unbearable. Branch lifted his head out of the water for a breath and spied his prisoner loping toward the edge of the swamp.

Despite the second sortie of Phantoms soon swooping in over them, Branch sprinted after the POW and tackled him, tying his bootlaces together. As Branch dragged the aggressor back to their position, the air resettled into a sultry stillness; as fast as the jets had come, they disappeared.

Branch thought aloud, "That first guy's back to his unit by now. He'll bring 'em here in a minute. We gotta move. What'a we gonna do with this one?"

J.W.'s eyes narrowed. "Kill his ass, and there's one less to keep me from goin' home. Let's try that stranglehold on 'im."

Bearchild looked up and grunted. "Let 'em go. You got enough trouble as it is."

Branch agreed quickly, and the three Rangers watched as the aggressor walked off haughtily, swaggering as he vanished beyond the web of Spanish moss. Then the three broke into a sprint, not stopping until they reached the banks of the Green River. Without dipping their canteens into the aptly named waterway, they waded across, then trudged out into the dunes, past old objectives they had fought so hard to take, patches of worthless land now devoid of the life, or the spirit, or the learning that had taken place there; a football stadium on Monday morning. He laughed sadly at the mounds of sand and empty C-ration cans, wondering what it had all meant. Had good men died there? Was it just one of his ambulatory dreams, or had it been real? And if it was extant, what had it meant, the pointless, hollow suffering?

* * *

The sun dropped beyond the Gulf, but that night, no moon took its place. The sky turned dark, with clouds as black as J.W.'s heart. The rains began that night, his first monsoon. He had never imagined water pouring from of the sky with such tyranny, or that the dunes could be drowned so abruptly. Their ponchos, what was left of them, were as thin as rice paper, and rain poured through the large rips generated the night their wet weather gear had been dropped as parachutes in the mountains, a century before. The precipitation was a scheme concocted by the cadres, J.W. suggested. "It ain't happenstance, I'm here to tell ya. You notice it didn't rain the nights we almost died of thirst, did it?"

Bearchild agreed. "Water can be culled from the heavens if the right person utters the appropriate invocation."

"You're nuts. Both of ya'. Listen to me," Branch demanded. "It was the Phantoms. What do you think they did when they left here? They seeded the clouds. This is experimental rain, man. You're poisoned for life. Army don't care. It's the same shit they pulled on those Black soldiers when they gave 'em a dose on purpose just to see what happens. Wasn't that long ago. Army's still the army."

J.W. asked, "A dose? What's that?"

Branch snarled, "A dose of syphilis, man, a dose. Don't you white boy know nothin'? It's the same stuff they used back at the Benning Phase."

J.W. shook his head. "You mean they gave the Black Rangers syphilis at Fort Benning? You're nuts"

"No, fool, I'm tellin' you the army don't care about the health of its soldiers. They gave Black troops the syph twenty years ago, and they used radioactivity on us at Harmony Church. You remember the blue and the green light around the wires when it rained? That's radioactive shit, I'm tellin' ya'. I'm not goin' any further."

J.W. hunkered next to Branch. "He's right. FTA—fuck the army. I'm not goin' on either."

Bearchild shook his head. "It's rain. Just rain. Now calm down and let's find the platoon."

J.W. thought for a moment, then answered, "O.K., you're the one who took physics, but if my hair falls out, I'm comin' after you."

Bearchild had started walking, but turned back and whispered, "You don't have any hair to fall out."

Branch folded his arms and refused to budge, but by the time Weathersby and Bearchild had walked a hundred meters, Branch cursed and caught up with them. The three lumbered toward the first objective, moving quietly through the darkest night of their lives. To their left was a barely visible black shadow, large and round, perhaps a hill. To the right was the quiet rushing of the Green River, and they caught up with the company just as the unit funneled into the narrow patch of land between the two obstacles.

First Platoon pushed through the bottleneck without incident, but as Second Platoon entered the conduit, a series of shattering explosions erupted, hurling them into the mud. Though the flood of light from bursting plastique explosive obliterated their night vision, their eyes were still sensitive to movement, and J.W. was able to make out, along with the star-burst pattern burned into his retina, the stir of black forms descending from the flanks. One rushed J.W., grabbed his fatigues, and threw him to the ground.

J.W.'s attacker grunted in a senseless, foreign babble, while another gibberish-hollering man jumped on J.W.'s back, threw a rough-woven nylon bag over his head, and tied it tightly around his neck. Next, J.W.'s hands were bound behind his back with fishing line cinched so tightly, his fingers became swollen, then numb.

J.W. kicked and screamed, but with each flail of his legs, he caught a rifle butt in the kidneys. When he decided to remain still, he was pulled to his feet, shoved along, and after a mile, thrown into a thicket, striking his head on a low-hanging branch that knocked him to the ground. He struggled to his feet, stepped into a hole, and went down again. The bag over his head muffled his screamed refusal to go on, and he employed the tactics used so successfully by his enemy a few hours before; he dragged his feet. His masters, however, had apparently failed to sign the Geneva Accords, and they let him drop to the sand, happily allowing him to lie there while they pummeled and booted him. J.W. felt the dark vision of

Kenyon being kicked to death, remembering how little impact that loss had had on the world. He got to his feet.

J.W.'s captors pushed on for an hour, dragging and pushing him, halting finally in an open area where J.W. sensed a cooler and drier earth. Cs cooked over a crackling fire releasing magnificent aromas, but the cues bidding warmth and comfort were subsumed far beneath the pain and fear of the cadres' final trick.

J.W. was shoved into a pit so narrow and short, he could not lie down. When a grilled bamboo cover was dropped over the hole, he was forced to stand doubled over, making his abdomen burn with the fatigue of a thousand sit-ups. When he turned his face sideways, he cut his cheek on the sharp wood. The best he could do was spit out the blood that trickled into his mouth.

The foot of water in the bottom of the pit soaked his roughly worn, mottled, leather boots, causing his feet to swell into soft clubs. He stood flexed at the waist as the pain in his abdomen deepened, and finally screamed aloud. His captor shoved a sock through the bamboo roof deep into J.W.'s mouth, causing J.W. to gag up what was left of a long-forgotten meal. He had no choice but to reswallow it and hope it didn't trickle into his lungs.

Despite his circumstances, J.W. nodded off; but as the first nightmare played in his head, he was dragged out of the hole and lifted by several men into a wooden barrel filled with freezing water. His hands were left tied behind him, and his feet bound, but the sock was pulled harshly from his mouth.

"What is your unit, prisoner?"

"My name is J.W. Weathersby. I have no rank. My serial number is OF116336, and you can kiss my fuckin' ass."

J.W. heard the slap before he felt it. "What do you mean you don't have any rank? Are you a soldier?"

"J.W. Weathersby. No rank. OF116336. I told you to kiss my mother fucking ass!"

J.W.'s head was immersed in the water and held there, then raised for a moment. He spit at them, then coughed, "Fuck you and fuck your mother!" the bravado numbing his pain and fear. His head was thrust back, and a wooden cover slammed down. He felt the shock waves as the top was hammered shut.

The water was putrid. Slowly, it leaked into his mouth and then trickled down his throat. They had taken it from the slough, but he had no idea as to how they had made it so cold. Nothing was beyond their cruelty. J.W. realized he was about to die in a flooded barrel at the hands of ignorant men. His life had been nothing, and already it was over. He became furious, wanting a record to be kept of the travesty that had taken place in a filthy swamp of the deep South. Another decent man had been lynched, and for nothing.

He fought like a mad man to push through the barrel as he had out of the gas chamber so long before. His next thought was of Vock, and J.W. realized this was part of the mad captain's plot to destroy him. He pushed harder, but the barrel did not give way, and he noticed that the anger in him began to ebb, and that soon there was no more pain, all sensation becoming distant and slow. His head was stretched straight back to suck what little air floated between the top of the barrel and the water. In the haze of what was left of his life, J.W. heard someone banging on the side of the barrel, and then the top being pried off.

J.W. told the interrogators everything, and then some. As he was being dragged back to his cell, his captor sneered, "You are one worthless pussy," and jammed him into the pit. Every time J.W. closed his eyes, he cursed himself for having given in. When he fell asleep, the enemy banged a metal garbage can lid against the bamboo roof of his prison cage; and when J.W. started to whine, his guard laughed, unbuttoned his fly, walked to the back of the pit, and poured water in a stream from a canteen on J.W.'s head, pretending to have urinated on him.

As he buttoned up, the guard spoke in a heavy accent. I have a letter from your woman. We have captured it as we have imprisoned all of your worthless, weak soldiers. Now I read your letter to you. Even your woman pisses on you.

"Dear Baldini," the enemy soldier laughed moronically, "I just wanted to tell you how much I missed you at first, and how hard I tried to stay good. Then the fellow downstairs, you remember Gordon, helped me get the Volvo started, and things just happened after that. Now you're due home in a few days, and I don't know what to do. I had needs too, you know. Now I can't stop. I need him so much. I'm really sorry, but I had to tell you.

Signed, warmly, Krista."

J.W.'s spirit sagged lower than the soles of his flooded boots. He had never tasted such despair, never dreamed a heart could weigh with such agony. Even the first mountain in Dahlonega was bliss compared to what had been done to him here. He knew the guard could not have made up such a letter. No one in Ranger School knew his wife called him Baldini, a reference to his thinning hair, no one except Branch. J.W. had never told anyone about the problem starting the Volvo, except Branch.

So that was it. Branch had cooperated. J.W. screamed in outrage, but then calmed, realizing that he had ratted on his buddies as well. So it was just a made up letter, and had J.W. not hurt so badly, he would have laughed at his frailty, but the pain in his chest and viscera consumed him so, he cried instead. The pain made him think again of the letter, and J.W. realized he had never told Branch the man's name downstairs was Gordon, or even that there was a downstairs.

J.W.'s head drooped further, and the sadness consumed him more profoundly than any emotion he had ever experienced. It only worsened as the groans of other Rangers being drowned in the barrel and spilling their guts filtered through the POW camp. One soldier cursed his captors, but J.W. knew that courage was foolhardy, and that the Ranger was only prolonging the agony, and for what? That voice, barely familiar, and however weak, wouldn't give in, as had the others, but the obstinacy he showed only bought the man another plunge into the barrel. After the hammering and an even longer wait, punctuated with deep fits of coughing and gagging and another stream of profanity, J.W. caught a final, frail, "Kiss my dick, honkey," and then silence.

The hammering started again, and anger welled within J.W.'s chest. Now that same rage that he had tasted on the mountain in Dahlonega filled his heart, pushing from it the self pity that had entrenched itself over the past months. The voices that had thrust him forward up that first hill of the Mountain Phase were back he thought, but after a moment he understood it was he who was roaring, "If I fuckin' die tonight, it will be at the moment of my choice, not yours, mother fucker."

He squatted deeply and exploded upward out of the pit, snapping the bamboo roof off the cage easily; it had been fastened down only by a single filament of fishing line. J.W. crawled from the hole toward the sounds at the interrogation tub. He pulled his bound hands around his legs to his front, then tore the blindfold away to see two Green Berets standing by the barrel laughing. J.W. swung his head back and forth searching for the company of troops it must have taken to capture and guard the Ranger prisoners. Aside from the pair of Green Berets at the barrel, however, the camp was empty.

J.W. picked a heavy stick from the earth and moved from tree to tree silently, coming up behind the closer of the two commandos. J.W. raised the stick and drove it into the back of the aggressor's head so hard the wood cracked. The beret flew off his victim, and blood spurted as the guard collapsed. J.W. raised his weapon to strike the second man, but a dark figure burst through the wooden barrel-top like a jack-in-the-box.

It was Branch. His arm shot out like the green snake in attack mode, and grabbed the standing guard's throat, seeking with all his might to crush the life out of the man. Enough water splashed out of the barrel onto the collapsed Green Beret's face to bring him back to consciousness, and onto his feet, swinging and cursing.

In the melee, the barrel tipped, projecting a current of fetid water toward J.W. and the two Green Berets, flushing the foursome to the ground. The first soldier dove toward J.W. thrusting an arm around his neck, then squeezed until Weathersby's face hued into a deep blue.

"Stop moving, Ranger, or I'll fuckin' strangle you all the fuckin' way. Got that asshole?"

Out of the corner of his eye, J.W. saw Branch bop his adversary in the back of the head, and start crawling toward J.W., who, with the last breath in him groaned, "Crush his mother fuckin' throat, man."

The Green Beret holding J.W. screamed, "At ease, both of you. Calm down, or your fuckin' Ranger buddy here dies."

With "fuck this and the fuck thats" echoing through the camp, a chorus of hooting and ranting rose from the holes and cages. "Now look what you assholes have done," the troop squeezing J.W.'s throat cried. "This is part of the last problem, to be captured. Every Ranger has to go through it, otherwise you're not a Ranger. Jesus, look what you've done."

The four soldiers lay breathing fiercely, though quietly, each slowly relinquishing his prey, checking with every infinitesimal move to insure the process of disengagement proceeded bilaterally. When all arms and legs were free, J.W.'s Green Beret lit a smoke and seethed, "Release the rest of your buddies and get the fuck outta here."

J.W. and Branch went from underground cage to cage. None of the bamboo tops had been secured to the cells by anything more than single filament of nylon. Morelotto was silent when J.W. snapped the roof off his hole. He held his right arm defensively, close to his body, but let J.W. push up the sleeve of his fatigue jacket, the thin, worn material more gauze by now than cotton. Morelotto's forearm was curved in an ellipse, like the crescent moon that peeked from behind thunderclouds. A tiny point of jagged bone poked through the skin.

Gillette examined it as well. "Compound fracture of the radius. Shit."

J.W. frowned, "That must hurt like hell. We need to get you back to Field Seven."

But Morelotto grunted, "After the attack." As J.W. turned to Gillette for counsel, Morelotto added, "Hey, Weathersby, thanks, man."

* * *

J.W. searched futilely for Bearchild as the imprisoned Rangers gravitated together and fell into formation. The Ranger who had been in command when the company was captured took control and grouped his men into a circle to plan the final attack. Devoid of even a whisper of dissension when a forced march was proposed to make up for the time lost in captivity, Ranger Class 68-B agreed unanimously not to allow the company commander to be blamed for leading them into an ambush.

As they gathered their gear to move out, a Green Beret handed J.W. an envelope. Wet and faded, it was a letter he had never been given. It began:

"Dear Baldini. Having trouble getting the G-D Volvo started, so Gordon, the little guy downstairs, you remember, the nervous airline pilot, he looked at it and found the wrong something or other. It's great now! I love you. Can't wait to see you in a few days! Will write again tomorrow. I hope you've gotten my letters. I've sent one every day. Harry Steel's wife told me you aren't able to write during Ranger School. I want to hear all the stories. Bet you got a few. Love, love, love, Krista."

J.W. reread it a few times to be sure it was true, and then saw it had been postmarked only days before.

The company moved quietly through the jungle, though almost at a jog. Branch and J.W. hung behind, taking turns carrying Morelotto's gear, dragging over deadfall and prickers, always keeping an eye and an ear out for Bearchild. In the savanna they traveled worn but dangerous paths. Even with Morelotto in tow, if that pace could be maintained, they would hit the final objective in four or five hours.

"Gentlemen," the platoon leader counseled during the final briefing, "we know the terrain, we know the enemy, and we know who we are. No more Rangers gonna be droppin' out now. We made it, Rangers."

Curiously, J.W. felt no hunger or fatigue during those final hours. There was no bitching. When they stopped for breaks, men stood as they studied their maps; and every troop knew his position for the entire march. No one lit up. There was silent movement; even the Ranger bird had gone south, perhaps extinct.

They waded into the attack jump-off point in three-and-a-half hours, a class record, and hid Morelotto in a safe cove, covering him with palm fronds. Branch had two cigarettes left. He gave them to Morelotto, who shook his head no. "Didn't earn 'em."

Bearchild was finally discovered high in a cypress, lounging on a limb like a serpent. A rumor circulated that he had escaped the pincer movement of the enemy by wading into the river and breathing through a hollow bamboo stalk, an old Sioux trick. At first, he had followed the bound Rangers, plotting to attack the aggressors and free his compatriots, but he postulated to himself that they would be freed soon to carry out the final mission. He knew he would be of more use if he scouted the enemy position before the arrival of the company.

Bearchild gathered intelligence by hiding in the bushes near the cadres' camp, watching while they sat and drank coffee. Bearchild whispered that Cowsen and all the officers were there, even Vock, then looking directly at J.W., continued, "I heard him say, 'I'm gonna get that son of a bitch at the final formation. Watch me now.' Then the rest of the cadres laughed."

But Bearchild had gathered more than gossip. One of the cadre sergeants had left a communication radio near the perimeter of the aggressor camp, which Bearchild spied and eventually liberated. Taped to the side of the PRC 25 transmitter was a list of the frequencies for all the aggressor units. Bearchild copied it, then used the radio to guide the Ranger company to his position. As his colleagues approached him, he left their frequency for a moment, and while beating his chest with a fist to the rhythm of a helicopter main rotor, called the enemy camp and told them he was the supply pilot and needed directions to their position. The enemy radio operator provided not only coordinates, but troop strength, ammo, and food requirements.

Bearchild stayed on the radio directing the Ranger company through the jungle to their final objective, an open savanna less than half a mile away. Though the cadres had placed listening posts, every time one of the aggressors tried to warn his compatriots that the Rangers were passing him, Bearchild would intercept the transmission and howl like a wolf into the microphone, stepping on the enemy's transmission.

As the Rangers neared the enemy perimeter, the aggressors lounged peacefully in hammocks, not a one with an inkling of the nearness of the cadets. The aggressors, facing north, hadn't posted rear security, assuming the Rangers, no matter how motivated and clever, lacked the strength to sweep wide in an arc and hit from behind. After all, there were certain inviolate truths on this earth—as water sought its own level, Rangers invariably trod the easiest path toward mock battle. Class 68-B, however, approached soundlessly from the south and swept in like the divine wind, silent until they looked intently into the whites, and greens and browns, of their enemy's eyes.

As they moved through the encampment in victory, the Rangers took prisoners and confiscated weapons, binding the hands and feet of the captured and placing them in a circle in the middle of the compound. The Rangers then set about unearthing and pilfering the Cs of the vanquished: some features of life are destined never to change.

J.W.'s attention was drawn to a tree with a patch of mismatched bark on the trunk. On the ground were telltale bits of fresh wood, and J.W., assuming from his lessons in elementary school at P.S. 86 in the Bronx that termites didn't eat live trees, touched the bark curiously. It fell away, revealing a small niche into which he shined his flashlight, illuminating an OD can. He pried at it greedily with his bayonet. The tin had mass. The top end was sealed, and J.W. turned it over slowly, shaking with anticipation. The bottom was pristine. A feeling of well-being washed over him.

He had captured an olive green, black-lettered tin of Ham and Limas. His mind rushed to the sight of a P-38 piercing the bottom, the sound of air rushing into the vacuum, and then the perfume of twelve-year-old wisps of pork and beans wafting into the atmosphere. This was ecstasy, a precious life-moment, he smiled to himself, but he dutifully waded over to Branch and handed him the meal.

The aggressors, bound in their circle of shame, laughed at the jubilant Rangers, assuring them they would soon die. That meant, Gillette suggested, there was additional hidden food, and several Rangers were dispatched to find it. A carton of C rations was unearthed in a punji pit, brought back intact, and divided quickly, though with decorum. The aggressors were infuriated and kicked dirt at the Rangers. Several black aggressors called Branch a "nigger traitor," and swore at Bearchild, "Hey you fuckin' Chinaman."

The Rangers, their bellies full, sat about smoking, talking, convinced they had fulfilled their part of the bargain. They ignored the ranting of their prisoners, for school was out; every man had earned the Tab. Branch and J.W. went back to the cove and guided Morelotto to the victory site. He sat by himself, silently holding his arm as he stared into the swamp, a subtle grimace distorting his face.

Bearchild watched him for a moment and offered, "Looks like a Ranger to me."

* * *

Thirty minutes after the attack, a file of embarrassed lane graders crashed through the jungle, Vock in the lead. He ordered, "On your feet, fall in."

The entire corps of cadres materialized, milling about and growling. Morelotto was ordered to stand to the side, but wasn't tormented. Cowsen paced, rubbing his chin while the cadres picked out individuals to castigate, punishing them for real and imagined transgressions. At one point, three Rangers were on their feet, the other six-dozen in the push-up position, working off gigs for six-dozen unrelated crimes. J.W. was awarded twenty-six for unshined boots; Gillette, twenty-six for a wrinkled uniform; Branch fifty-one for kinky hair, what was left of it; Wardally twenty-six for wearing the patch of the Grenadan army; and Bearchild, fifty-one for straight hair. Each man screamed cadence at a different rate, each stifling the need to laugh hysterically.

When it was over, Cowsen stood before them and shouted that the attack was the sorriest performance he had ever witnessed from a Ranger class, and that they would do it over, and then over again, until they got it right. "I don't give a hoot if that means stayin' an extra eight weeks, Rangers. And I'm not done with you for the way y'all look. Sorry company of Rangers."

Eventually, Cowsen left ranks and ordered, "Left, face. Y'all got a long march back to main cap to resupply and do the whole cotton pickin' problem over."

Wardally, at the head of the column, passed his machine gun to J. W at the rear; ammo went to the penultimate man, Branch, the radio to Gillette. Heavy gear would be rotated during the march back. They reached into their packs, removing all unnecessary weight: cans of pilfered Cs, water purification tablets, smokes, and sugar, flinging them into the culvert by the side of the dirt road. J.W. fished out the half-tin of Beef Stew he had forced himself to save, and offered it to Branch, who made an ugly face. It, too, flew off into the brush.

Vock walked into formation, placing his lips a quarter-of-an-inch from J.W.'s. "Did I see you destroying government property, soldier?"

"No, sir!"

"You're lying, soldier! Step out of formation. Sergeant Cowsen. Did you see this man throwing government property into that ditch?"

Cowsen hesitated. His lungs filled slowly to answer, wasting seconds. With no time left to delay his answer, Cowsen parted his lips, but as he did, an air force sedan rolled up to the decrepit formation. Flying from its front fender was a small red flag embroidered with three white stars. Vock turned and saluted the car, then, as ranking officer of the Ranger contingent, ran up and reported.

The base commandant emerged from the car, followed by a civilian dressed in a silk Brooks Brothers suit. "Captain, I want you to meet the Secretary of the Air Force."

Vock remained at stiff attention as he shook the civilian's hand. Morelotto, who had been quietly awaiting his fate, was waved over, and tried to salute the commandant, but his arm collapsed to his side. The civilian rolled up Morelotto's sleeve and gasped. So did Vock. There was muffled talking, and Morelotto pointed animatedly with his good arm toward Weathersby, Branch, and Bearchild. The corners of Vock's mouth turned down as the civilian summoned the three bedraggled Rangers.

Morelotto stood at attention next to his father and spoke quietly. "I wouldn't be standing here now if it wasn't for these Rangers. Actually, Dad, I probably would have died out there. They're real friends, and they're real Rangers."

Cowsen, his face as relieved and calm as J.W. had ever seen it, swaggered to the front of the company and sounded the order to march, then upped it to the double-time. Second Platoon, at the rear of the formation, ran a quarter of a mile and passed word to the front of the platoon that it was time to trade the machine gun and other heavy gear. But that was the very instant the lead platoon rounded a blind curve, screamed, and broke into a mad sprint. Assuming they had been hit with chemical weapons, obviously tear gas, J.W. readied his mask. As the next platoon rounded the curve and broke into a sprint, howling and screaming, J.W. bitched aloud, "They have to squeeze the last Goddamn ounce of blood outta us? I will quit this shit before I execute another fuckin' attack."

Branch muttered, "And you'll do it again a hundred times if they tell you to. Who do you think you're bullshittin'?"

"Yeah, but it's still a sack of shit."

"The indoctrination has worked, gentlemen." Gillette laughed. "America's cream is a company of sheep, *la crème de le mouton.*"

"No," J.W. grimaced, "a colony of worker ants." Then added, "Beats bein' a maggot."

Twenty paces later, it was Second Platoon's turn to round the dreaded blind curve, and J.W. removed his gas mask and lifted it toward his face. But there was no gas, or machine gun fire, or green snakes. What greeted them one hundred meters further along were three cattle trucks, the first two swarming with delirious Rangers. Second Platoon ran to the third vehicle, climbing aboard and dropped onto the comfy wooden benches.

Cowsen and the corps of cadres followed leisurely. There was complete silence as the first sergeant stood in the middle of the dirt road, all eyes glued to his figure. "Y'all still look like fried doggone chicken!" But Cowsen snapped to attention and saluted each truck in turn. The bedraggled Rangers came to attention and returned his salute, then screamed in delight as they tossed their hats into the air.

The trucks drove slowly through the mud and humidity. J.W. was quiet the endless miles back to Field Seven. As the trucks pulled up to the barracks, he spoke to Branch. "Something important just happened." Branch nodded; so did Bearchild.

* * *

The company was dismissed to prepare for graduation rehearsal. That meant brushing their teeth. They marched at leisure time to the runway on Field Seven, Rangers bitching that the ride had softened them, and allowing that they were embarrassed for the churlish behavior they had demonstrated over the past two months. Then Bearchild observed they were still complaining.

Wardally threw his arms up. "You guys are never satisfied. In the Islands, we don't suffer guilt when we've earned our rest."

* * *

Rehearsal for the final ceremony consisted of jogging the four-mile runway at Field Seven. It was done at a trot, with constant grousing. After the run, at the reviewing stand, they stood dripping in the noonday sun, trying to remember to salute with the right hand and accept the diploma with the left. J.W. asked why he, a southpaw, couldn't salute with the left and take the diploma with his right. The cadres didn't laugh, but J.W. had a year before, when his grandma had asked the same question at his commissioning ceremony from R.O.T.C. at Penn State.

At the barracks, the troops lined up at the dumpster to place their boots with great ceremony into the trash, offering their farewells and thanks. J.W. however, had worn his dress boots in the field for the past two weeks, having long since buried his original footwear in the dunes. Then they changed into the one clean pair of fatigues each had dragged through the three phases, the uniform they had been ordered to keep wrapped in plastic, dress right dress at the ready, as if graduation could have been declared at any moment.

There was no hot water for showers in the barracks because the fuse on the water heater had blown on the first day, and no one had reported it. After cold showers, they double-timed back to the "parade" ground, and ran the entire four miles again, down one side of the two-mile runway at Field Seven, across it at the end, then back up the other side, finishing, dripping with sweat, at the reviewing stand. This time the stands were packed with onlookers, men and women, most in civvies. All of the cadres were there with wives and girlfriends. Vock was alone.

J.W. reassured himself that in a few minutes the army could no longer hurt him. There were no punishment schools left with which to torture him; he'd be in Viet Nam by the end of the month no matter what he did. He grinned, planning his final act at Ranger School: accept his graduation certificate, glare at Vock for a moment, then laugh in his impotent face.

When the ritual began, a major general, the post commander from Fort Benning, took the podium. He told the gathering that he had flown all the way down just for this graduation, for it was that important. He spun several yarns, the most captivating, a vignette about a Ranger cadet he had met sometime in the distant past, a lost soul who hadn't yet learned the power of the phrase, "DRIVE ON!" He mused aloud about that man. "I wonder if he ever discovered what those words mean?"

As J.W. accepted his diploma, the general shook his hand and growled "Raaannngerrr" in a whisper. Had he done that to the others? J.W. hadn't noticed, but he did recognize the scent of the general's aftershave, and it dawned upon him that this was the farmer in the car who had picked him up from the middle of the highway, listened to his plans to quit Ranger school, but given him given him a ride back to Harmony Church on that first night of the compass course.

* * *

Next to Big John's pen sizzled a barbecue with more beer piled in ice-filled garbage cans than J.W. had ever seen in one place in his life. He wolfed down so many grilled hot dogs, it was hard to walk. At the billets, J.W. opened the screen door and collapsed on the first cot to the left, not moving until after sunrise the next morning.

Although still digesting yesterday's dinner, J.W. easily wolfed several breakfasts, saving bacon for Big John, who refused to go near it. By 7:00 A.M., the company was aboard cattle trucks bound for Harmony Church. Absent was the customary fear of the next path, and they slept away their last few hours together.

At Harmony Church, the company donned real uniforms, J.W.'s decorated with the silver wings of an army aviator. Branch and Bearchild were astonished that he really was a pilot. They left for main post together, to have Ranger Tabs sewn on their uniforms. It was not as exciting as J.W. had imagined—"The melancholia of things accomplished," Bearchild mumbled—not until they walked out of the tailor shop and passed an older sergeant wearing the Tab who saluted and growled "RANGER!"

At Harmony Church, they packed to leave, but J.W. had been ordered to complete his paperwork for Viet Nam before returning to Maryland. At main post headquarters, J.W. filled out the requisite forms, releasing the military from all responsibility for the flight to Viet Nam, though it wasn't the trip there that worried him.

His veins were punctured by novice phlebotomists to ensure the blood type engraved on his dog tags was correct. As with most things military, though, it wasn't. His tags said "O" Positive; the technician claimed J.W. was "O" Negative. J.W. didn't care though, and refusing to make a fuss over plus and minus symbols, asked the private to be a good chap and ignore the problem.

"No, sir. You need to be issued new tags, sir. I can't take responsibility if you get shot in Viet Nam, and they give you the wrong blood and you go into convulsions or something and drop dead, no sir."

"O.K., Private, just gimme new tags, and I won't bother anyone anymore."

The technician, noticing J.W.'s less than calm demeanor and clenched fist, ran to the back of the clinic to fetch his superior. A buck sergeant walked in, and J.W. snapped to attention. With a suppressed laugh, the sergeant provided J.W. with the papers for new tags and explained they would have to be signed by J.W.'s commanding officer.

"I don't have a commanding officer. I'm just trying to go home!"

"Who's the CO at the Ranger School, sir?" the buck sergeant asked, thumbing through the post directory. "Here it is, sir. It's a Captain Richard Vock. Better hurry, sir. It's already 1400 and the dog tag center closes at 1600. It's across post, sir. They ain't opening again till Tuesday."

"Tuesday?"

"Yes, sir. You must'a been away for a while, sir. Three-day weekend. Memorial Day, sir."

* * *

First Sergeant Cowsen sat behind a desk outside the captain's open door. He stood and saluted. "Yes, Lieutenant. How may I help you, sir?"

"Sergeant Cowsen, I'm trying to get home. Got the wrong blood type on my dog tags. Need the captain to sign these."

"Is that your cab waiting outside with the meter running, sir?"

"Look, First Sergeant, I don't have much time."

Cowsen disappeared into the office, and J.W. heard hushed

mumbling, the dial of a phone, and Cowsen's report. "Sixteen hundred, sir."

Vock appeared in the doorway, and J.W. snapped to attention and saluted.

"Come in, Lieutenant." Vock walked back to his desk, signed the form, ordered J.W. to be at ease, then turned to the window overlooking the pull-up bar outside the mess hall.

"Lieutenant, I have a responsibility to insure only the best survive. You came here on reassignment. That ain't the way it's supposed to be."

"What does that mean, sir?"

"It means that you were an also ran. This is not a reform school. Let me be direct. You should have washed out five, six times, but you dodged the bullet each time. You lead a charmed life."

"Yes, sir."

"Did you learn something here? Maybe something about making light of someone's life? Did you learn anything, Lieutenant?"

J.W. answered unemotionally, "I did, sir."

"Let me ask you one more question. What hurt the most here, your mind or your body?"

"My mind, sir."

"Remember that, Lieutenant. And, you might be interested to know, I have submitted a complaint against Sergeant Hartack for dereliction of duty in the matter of Ranger Smith, and the death of Ranger Kenyon. If we here at the Ranger School have anything to do with it, Hartack won't see the outside of Leavenworth until 1999."

* * *

J.W. promised the cabby an extra five dollars to deposit him at the Dog Tag Center before 1600 hours, but they were delayed by troops, tanks, and fire trucks crossing roads. The cabby, in no hurry, had already made enough off the difference between a plus and a minus on J.W.'s dog tags to still be vacationing in Mexico long after J.W. was slogging the rice paddies of Viet Nam.

* * *

Back on main post, J.W. banged angrily on the locked door of the Dog Tag Center. The PFC who unlocked it apologized, "Sorry, sir, we're closed until Tuesday morning, sir, until after the long weekend."

J.W. begged, pleading that he had but a few days to spend with his wife before shipping out to Viet Nam, but the master sergeant who came to the desk to investigate the shrill anger in J.W.'s voice advised, "If the army wanted you to have a wife, sir, they would have issued you one."

The cabby dropped J.W. back at Harmony Church, marooning him for the weekend in the barracks, three days, a third of the time he had left before shipping out for the war. His found his personal gear strewn on a chair outside the barracks, and charged inside to chew ass, but there were just shavetail lieutenants lying quietly on their beds. The stenciled name on his bunk had been replaced with "WILKERSON". The other names were gone as well.

J.W., realizing Class 68-E had commenced and that he would have to spend the days on Main Post, ran out and tried to wave the cabby down, but only the red dust of his trail was visible. J.W. called the cab company and asked them to send a car. Told it would be two hours, he waited in the parking area, mulling the winter that had just passed, and the long, tropical year that lay ahead. As the sun began to fade, a loud whistle pierced the quiet of the Ranger camp. A familiar voice screamed, "Fall in," and the next sound was of men knocking on the command shack door. "Harder! They can't hear you in there, Ranger!"

* * *

J.W. arrived home the next week, sleeping through the night Bobby Kennedy was shot, dreaming he was walking across an endless, icy swamp during a night so dark he believed the moon and stars had finally abandoned the earth. Waking with a start at 3:00 A.M., J.W. realized it was just Ranger School; that heaven had only abandoned him, not the rest of the world.

J.W. put one foot in front of the other and came not to a cypress, but a refrigerator. He ate an entire Pepperidge Farm Angel Food cake and guzzled half a case of Cragmont orange soda. It was good to know it had only been a dream.

CHAPTER IV

Picking Up the Pieces

Before leaving Fort Benning, Bearchild collected five dollars each from Branch and J.W., and sent fifteen dollars to Mr. Sullens, the farmer in the Smokys. In the parking lot on the last day, Bearchild hugged J.W., then grinned, "I never hugged a man before. Tell me Viet Nam can't be worse than this."

Captain Marlin Bearchild served in Viet Nam, asking the whole tour why he was shooting at people who looked so much like him. While he was there, an aunt wrote that his father was up to his old tricks again, marching around town telling anyone who would listen that his son was going to be the first United States Senator born and raised on an Indian Reservation.

In 1992, Senator Bearchild retired from politics and created the Steven War Bonnet Memorial Foundation, a watchdog organization that insures the quality of medical care offered to the indigent; its main tenet: no doctor may ever turn away a patient in need.

Leonard Fricker finished Ranger School with the next cohort, Class 68-C. He served with the First Infantry Division in Viet Nam, and remained in the army for twenty-five years. He retired as a brigadier general. His only child, a daughter, graduated from West Point and flew Black Hawk helicopters in Iraq.

Antonio Morelotto slogged the paddies in 1970 as a platoon leader with the Americal Division. Though shot in his bad arm, which he eventually lost, Lieutenant Morelotto carried one of his severely wounded men several miles under withering enemy fire. He was awarded the Distinguished Service Cross by Richard Nixon on August 8th, 1974, one hour before the President announced his resignation. Morelotto went on to law school at Columbia University, and later served as a Federal Judge in the 9th Circuit Court of Appeals in San Francisco.

Erskine Gillette was a combat officer in the Central Highlands of Viet Nam. He distinguished himself by leading his besieged platoon over a mountain pass the Viet Cong never dreamed an American unit would or could traverse. He returned to Harvard to earn a Ph.D. in philosophy, and earned tenure in the Department of History. He died of leukemia at age forty-two.

Big John the Alligator, passed away of natural causes in 2001. He was originally captured in 1954 in the Field Seven area. As lore has it, he lost his eye, not in a struggle with erstwhile Rangers, but when the grass was being cut in his pen with a weed eater. His remains were interred in a corner of a field near his old pen. A small headstone marks the spot.

J.W. saw Lawrence Ellsworth Branch once again after Ranger School, in Viet Nam. His year of combat over, J.W. was on line at the air base just outside Saigon preparing to board the Freedom Bird home; Branch was on line with the FNG's, Fuckin' New Guys, who had just arrived. It took a minute for them to recognize each other, for Branch had gained weight and J.W. had lost even more. J.W. shouted across the terminal, "Where the hell you been while I been fightin' the war, my man?"

Branch yelled from his barrier, "Graduate school," then waved wildly, smiling so warmly, J.W. had to wipe his eyes. The two lines were hustled toward their very anti-parallel destinations, J.W.'s last image of Branch the scar on his arm from the drifting ember at the little farmhouse near Dahlonega.

J.W. learned in 1995 from the black marble Viet Nam Memorial that Branch had perished in combat on May 17, 1970. Some years later, when J.W. used the computer to track down Branch's mother in New York, he asked how she was. She answered, "Old. I got the sugar and the congestion. I can't walk too good, specially the steps to Lawrence grave. I take the bus from Harlem to the cemetery, and I stand there. What else can I do? You doin' O.K.?"

"I'm doing well, ma'am. Thank you."

"You gotta' job?"

"Yes, ma'am. I'm a doctor." J.W.'s eyes reddened. "I'm sorry, Mrs. Branch, I gotta go. You did a great job raising him."

"Wait a minute! You say your name's Weathersby?" She whooped. "Ain't you the one who said he could swim forever?"

CHAPTER V

And So I Found a Way

In June, 2006, nearly two years after I began pestering the Pentagon to allow me, nearing my sixty-second birthday, to participate in the Ranger Course at Fort Benning, it became clear that they would not budge. It did not require a degree in logic to understood their concerns: a middle-aged man really could just drop dead on the spot for no reason other than he had been alive for six decades. I'd seen it happen in my medical practice more times than I cared to remember. More importantly, I had to accept that the army was fighting a real war, and my participation would be a distraction to the young men learning to do so. I decided not to push any farther.

The next night, however, while reading over the final draft of *At Harmony Church*, I came to the part in which we Rangers, back in 1968, believed the cadres were actually going to force us to *march on foot* from Fort Benning to the mountain camp at Dahlonega. The memory of that night made me laugh, for the thought of them punishing us that harshly, even for those cadres, was beyond the pale. But the thought piqued my interest, and I began to wonder if the answer to my craving to relive the challenge of Ranger School might be, indeed, to walk from Fort Benning to Dahlonega on foot. It was midnight, but I couldn't stop myself from Googling the route. Though over two hundred miles, it did not seem all that terrifying. Then, in a fit of absolute madness, I plugged in the entire trek from Dahlonega to Benning to Field Seven, the jungle facility near Pensacola, Florida. The whole course, on less direct, but far safer country roads, was just shy of 500 miles, a distance that would take a bit over three weeks if one ground out twenty or so miles per day. That, too, seemed doable; after all, many older people participate in the Breast Cancer Three-Day, Sixty-Mile March each summer. I was then struck with the notion of finding sponsors and creating a college scholarship fund for the children and grandchildren of Rangers and 11th Armored Cavalry Blackhorse Troopers, the unit with which I had served in Viet Nam.

And so, on 18 Oct 2006, I closed my medical practice and set out on foot, accompanied by an old friend from graduate school, starting at Camp Frank T. Merrill—Merrill's Marauders—the new name of the old mountain training facility near Dahlonega, Georgia. We lugged forty-five pound packs stuffed with much useless gear and chose not to enlist the support of a "chase car." We were on our own save for the lessons I had learned nearly forty years before, and, perhaps more importantly, the hospitality of the citizens of Georgia, Alabama, and northern Florida, the best people I have ever met.

* * *

Much had changed at Ranger School. Time had marched on leaving my foggy memories and dreams just that, fantasies. The little cabins at Dahlonega had long since been demolished, though one had been rebuilt to serve as a tiny museum. It was neatly painted, both inside and out; the floor was carpeted; the beds were neatly made with thick pristine woolen blankets over crisp white sheets. There were pillows. Good gravy, pillows. I worried for my sanity when I saw it. Could this have really been the musty, rough-hewn, crumbling structure in which I had taken refuge from the downpour on my first day in Dahlonega? It seemed impossible my memory could have failed so completely, and I felt that perhaps the

Pentagon had been correct in their assessment that I was a very old man. I gave thought to retiring from medicine.

A sergeant major gave up his morning to show us around the camp, explaining that Ranger cadets were now housed in huge cinder block barracks, with privacy partitions between the double-decker beds. He brought us inside to show us the thick mattresses that covered the solid beds, though he allowed that the mattresses had to replaced every six months, for "Rangers still don't smell too good."

He informed us the students were far better fed than in bygone days. Vanished were the C-rations that had fed millions and millions of GIs over so many decades, those quasi-meals replaced by MREs, "Meals Ready to Eat," which boast dozens of selections from Vegetarian Lasagna to Chicken Fajitas to Pot Roast. Included in each pouch is a heat pack that soldiers activate with a few drops of water and place next to the foil-wrapped meal. After a few minutes, out pop, as if from a mini-oven, very hot, tasty meals anywhere, anytime—even on the moon. No longer do troops pilfer C-4 plastique explosive from mines to turn Franks and Beans from a congealed cold goop into a mostly-congealed tepid goop.

More shocking, the sergeant major told us of the safety considerations that have been enacted. Dozens of Ranger students have died over the years, even of hypothermia at the Jungle Training Facility in Florida. Though behind the scenes, and probably not evident to the Ranger students, medical evacuation staff with ambulances and even helicopters are ready in minutes to rescue the injured. It was not what I remembered as a priority.

At first, to be honest, the wholesale transformation made me angry. After all, I had held my entire adult life that Ranger training was stark, painful, and smacking with genuine deprivation. It was the only way, I had believed, to teach men to drive on in combat when there was no alternative but mission failure and death. These were values that had been set deeply in my consciousness for nearly forty years, and they were the pillars to which I had clung for dear life through my tour in Viet Nam, the numbing years of graduate and medical school, the despondency of internship, a return to Viet Nam as a medical volunteer three times, and decades as a doctor.

The sergeant major, however, sensing my perplexity, set me straight, explaining that the young men who go through the course these days are sent off to Iraq or Afghanistan within thirty days of graduation. He asked rhetorically what sense it made to debilitate them immediately before hurling them into the most demanding and dangerous period of their lives.

I also learned that medical studies, done decades before, demonstrated that Rangers suffered significant degradations in health signaled by changes in blood chemistry by the end of the course, abnormalities which took years to drift back to normal. Coupled with the deprivations of combat into which many Rangers were sent just weeks out of the course, the results were serious, long-lasting negative health issues for the cream of our military, and I would argue, the cream of our youth.

Complicated blood irregularities aside, those more recently responsible for designing the course apparently felt that sending young men into combat after dropping forty pounds over nine weeks was so obviously counterproductive, it was tantamount to purposely weakening our troops and threatening our success in battle. The seriousness with which these changes were explained, and the solemn commitment of the cadres with whom I had the privilege to speak, convinced me that my initial scorn was misplaced.

The instructors were quick to point out, however, that though the course is now less likely to harm Rangers, it is still designed to push men to discover just what they are made of, and many of the initial cadets in each class still do not graduate to bear the Ranger Tab. In fact, as in decades past, approximately fifty percent of those who start the course do not make it to the end.

* * *

Leaving Dahlonega, we marched for twelve days, often ducking off the roads twenty or thirty yards as the sun faded to pass the night in the woods. I covered myself with a poncho and a thin nylon blanket, a poncho liner, a brilliant invention that ties into the corners of the poncho.

It was created forty years too late, but it saved my bacon, or more precisely, warmed my bacon more than once.

In preparation for the trek, I did my due diligence as a good Ranger, consulting weather charts for the march route, noting the average nightly temperature lows for October and November over the past fifty years. I felt armed with sufficient data to make the trip without dying of exposure, and eschewed the thought of toting a heavy sleeping bag. But with Murphy's Law an inescapable ingredient of all projects, particularly those of a fanatical caste, it should not have surprised us so that we were confronted with record lows over several nights, awaking encrusted with ice, temperatures on the other side of the meager poncho dipping to 27 degrees Fahrenheit. I remember grumbling to myself at one in the morning, "Hey, knucklehead, you wanted to taste suffering again? Great. Open wide. Prepare for a full meal for the next six hours."

* * *

On day twelve of our odyssey, despite mammoth blisters in places we didn't know we had places, we charged into Camp Darby, the old Harmony Church section of Fort Benning. The ruins of the church are long gone, and the cadres, though vaguely aware of the name, did not know the site of the old building. Most of the top leadership admitted they had not even been born in 1968.

At Camp Darby, named after Brigadier General William O. Darby, who created Darby's Rangers of World War II fame, we were given a tour of the new facilities. These were sturdy, rugged buildings that will last for many, many years. As in Dahlonega, the students were treated with far greater respect than in the not-so-good-old-days, the emphasis now on imbuing these young men with the hard-boiled skills they will be called upon to exploit to stay alive half-way around the world in just a few weeks.

The old obstacle course is long gone, replaced with a name, The Darby Queen, and a far more functional and safer set of hurdles. The Ranger course itself is so bursting with military knowledge to master these days, the Rangers only enjoy traversing the Queen one time.

The "gulch" over which we had to monkey climb in 1968, and where

WILLIAM STUART GOULD, M.D.

I lost my first Ranger Buddy, has been long since abandoned and overgrown with trees and brush. The friend with whom I did this march, and who had suffered through my Ranger tales for thirty-four years, laughed derisively at the pit, having believed all these years it was really as deep as I had sworn. He did not accept my explanation that it had become filled with nearly half-a-century of silt and flora. The bleachers had also vanished. The stanchions, which I uncovered by digging with my fingers at the brambles, were just rotted old 4x4s. They were not nearly as far apart as I had remembered the perimeter of the bleachers, and again, my friend was quick to smirk.

* * *

We set off from Harmony Church, marching through the back roads of southern Alabama and eventually into northern Florida, where the weather turned hot and buggy. We crossed paths with a herpeterium's-contingent of snakes, most road kill by the time we happened upon them. The copperhead along a desolate stretch of road was our favorite, though the creature has since gone to its final reward. There were countless dog incursions, though just waving our pepper spray canisters at them was usually sufficient to send them off at a scared trot. There were also innumerable deceased armadillos, creatures evidently endowed with a gene that drives them to pitch themselves under the tires of passing cars. All that was left of most of them were sections of their black and white checkered armor plates, scattered like miniature chessboards along the highway shoulders.

And there were passing cars, probably a quarter of a million of them, most whooshing just two or three feet from us. Why older drivers refuse to pull to the left of an otherwise totally empty road to grant us more than six inches clearance from their side view mirrors is beyond me. With all the time I have on my hands now without nine hours a day of walking to get through, I might apply for a grant from Triple A or Congress to study this phenomenon.

* * *

On 11 November 2006, Veterans' Day, after twenty-four days on the road, with nearly 500 miles and close to one million footsteps beaten into our feet, we marched, heads up, shoulders back, into Field Six at Eglin Air Force Base, arriving five minutes early. Here, too, we were greeted with the utmost respect by the Ranger cadres. This facility is now named Camp Rudder, after Major General James E. Rudder, who commanded Rangers in World War Two. The saga of those Rangers scaling the cliffs of Pointe Du-Hoc, Normandy, France, on D-Day in 1944 is beyond remarkable. It is a tale that should have been hammered into our heads the first week of the course. Perhaps we would have more easily understood why we simply had to learn to drive on no matter the cost, no matter the pain.

The training area has been moved a short distance from the site at which I survived three weeks of swamp immersion in 1968, the old Field Seven. The new barracks and mess hall are quite impressive in size and sturdiness. The alligator pen boasts many relatively small occupants, one with a gnawed off hind leg. And on the subject of anatomically incomplete reptiles, there, on the stage of the university-quality lecture hall sits the stuffed carcass of Big John, his missing left eye and growling countenance somehow preserved. His innards, however, have been interred in a corner of the field.

The commanding officer was at the gate to greet us. He presented me with a raft paddle inscribed with the Ranger Creed, the date, and the words, "Reliving the Dream." My beautiful wife and precious daughter were there to greet us. I made my daughter, the Marine captain, promise that after my wife and I are gone, she would insure that the paddle was passed down to her kids and then to theirs, and that it would never be abandoned.